THE BELIAL

ORIGINS

Book 6 of the Belial Series

R.D. Brady

Scottish Seoul Publishing, LLC

BOOKS BY R.D. BRADY

Hominid

The Belial Series (in order)
The Belial Stone
The Belial Library
The Belial Ring
Recruit: A Belial Series Novella
The Belial Children
The Belial Origins
The Belial Search
The Belial Guard
The Belial Warrior
The Belial Plan
The Belial Witches
The Belial War
The Belial Fall
The Belial Sacrifice

The Belial Rebirth Series
The Belial Rebirth
The Belial Spear

The Belial Restored
The Belial Blood
The Belial Angel
The Belial Templar

The A.L.I.V.E. Series
B.E.G.I.N.
A.L.I.V.E.
D.E.A.D.
R.I.S.E.
S.A.V.E.

The H.A.L.T. Series
Into the Cage
Into the Dark

The Steve Kane Series
Runs Deep
Runs Deeper

The Unwelcome Series
Protect
Seek
Proxy

The Nola James Series
Surrender the Fear
Escape the Fear
Tackle the Fear
Return the Fear

The Gates of Artemis Series
The Key of Apollo
The Curse of Hecate
The Return of the Gods

R.D. BRADY WRITING AS SADIE HOBBES

The Demon Cursed Series
Demon Cursed
Demon Revealed
Demon Heir

The Four Kingdoms
Order of the Goddess

Be sure to sign up for R.D.'s mailing list to be the first to hear when she has a new release!

So God created mankind in his own image,
in the image of God he created them;
male and female he created them.
(*Genesis* 1:27)

The Lord God fashioned into a woman the rib
which He had taken from the man,
and brought her to the man.
(*Genesis* 2:22)

PROLOGUE

SPRINGFIELD, ILLINOIS

THE IMAGES SWIRLED through her mind: violence, despair, and death. Twelve-year-old Emma Riley sat straight up in bed, grasping for something in the empty air.

"Em?" her sister Vicki, age fourteen, asked from the other bed. "You okay?"

Emma's eyes flew open, staring in shock at her room. Her favorite puppy picture was on the wall. Her side of the room was painted pink, her sister's in purple.

It's my room, she told herself. *I live here.* But her pounding heart was taking a while to convince, still feeling the effects of the latest nightmare.

"Em?" Vicki asked again.

"I'm okay." Emma sat up, leaning against the headboard as her breaths came out in pants. She glanced over at her sister. They shared the same bright red hair and blue eyes, although Emma's were so dark they were almost purple. And even though they were fourteen months apart, people often mistook them for twins.

Vicki hesitated for only a moment before climbing out of her bed and into Emma's. She put her arms around her sister. "They're only dreams," she said softly.

Emma nodded into her sister's shoulder, but the fear and horror of the dreams wouldn't let go. She was in a city that was burning. And she and a friend, a tall man who couldn't speak, were trapped by a group of men.

Vicki kept her arms wrapped around Emma's shoulders. "Hey. There's no unhappiness today. Today is party day!" She wiggled in bed, her movements forcing Emma to wiggle as well. Then she crossed her eyes and stuck out her tongue.

Emma laughed, her sister's antics pushing away the darkness in her chest. "Please tell me you're not going to do that in front of my friends."

"Oh, I am so going to do that." Vicki hopped off the bed. "I'm also going to do my signature moves."

Vicki thrust out a hip and kicked out the opposite leg while throwing her hands in the air. Her ringlet hair flew in every direction as she moved. She looked like she was having a seizure.

A laugh burst from Emma. "Please, please, I beg of you. Not the signature dance moves. They all know we're related. I'll never survive the embarrassment."

Vicki flopped back down on her bed. "Well, as my birthday gift to you, I will refrain from my incredible moves."

Emma grinned, not for the first time grateful that she had Vicki for a sister. All her friends who had sisters complained about them all the time. But not Emma' Vicki was her best friend. They were attached at the hip and had been since Emma was born.

Vicki stood up again, her blue eyes shining. Then she reached down and pulled on Emma's arm. "Come on. Let's get dressed and get this party on the road!"

• • •

That night, when Emma fell back into bed again, she was exhausted. Exhausted and happy. Her mom and sister had outdone themselves decorating the yard. Balloons and streamers had been everywhere. Her dad had even hired a band and set up a giant tent.

And Chris Rosen had asked her to dance—twice. She hugged her pillow to her and wiggled with excitement. This was without a doubt the best birthday of her life.

When she closed her eyes, happiness settled warmly in her chest, and she drifted off to sleep.

The sun was barely up when her eyes popped open. She stared at the ceiling. *No. No. It can't be true.*

But deep in her heart, she knew it was.

One bed over, Vicki murmured and rolled over in her sleep. Emma watched her sister, her heart aching. *I can't do this. I can't leave Vicki.*

But she remembered all the times she had avoided the call - and all the deaths that had followed.

Shaking, she climbed out of bed and quietly packed some clothes in her backpack. She pulled her stuffed bunny from the bed. She'd had him since she was two' she couldn't leave him behind. She stuffed him in the bag, but kept his face out as she zipped it up.

After placing her bag quietly in the hall, she walked over to her sister's bed and knelt down. "Thank you for being my sister. I will never forget you," she whispered, then placed a trembling kiss on Vicki's cheek.

She watched her sister sleep, memorizing her face, then fled from the room before the sobs burst from her chest. Grabbing her bag, she crept down the hall, pausing by her parents' door. They were both still sleeping.

She wanted to run in there, hop in between them, and tell them everything. They would tell her that these were just dreams. They would tell her that everything would be all right. They'd tell her she didn't have to do this—that it was their job to be the adults and hers to be the kid.

But she knew the truth. Her childhood was over.

Her legs shook as she made her way down the stairs.

Her golden retriever Rex sat at the bottom of the stairs wagging his tail. As Emma looked into his big brown eyes, she nearly lost it then and there. She sank down next to him and buried her head in his fur, throwing her arms around his neck.

"I'm going to miss you so much," she said, glad she could say the words out loud. Rex couldn't make it up the stairs anymore because of his hips. Emma usually slept downstairs a few nights a week to keep him company.

Finally pulling away, Emma stood, walked to the back door, and opened it.

Rex looked at her and sat instead of running outside.

"Come on, Rex. This is hard enough. Go."

He hesitated before nature overrode his concern.

She watched him make his way slowly down the steps. Then she walked to the counter and pulled over the phone message pad. She pulled off a sheet of paper and wrote:

I love you all. But it's time for me to leave. Don't look for me. You won't find me. I'm not hurt. No one is making me leave. I made this choice a long time ago.

She paused, knowing they wouldn't understand that last line. Then she added:

I love you so much. Believe that.
  Love, Emma

. . .

A whine sounded from behind her. Rex stared at her through the screen, his tail wagging. She opened the door and let him in. She wanted more than anything to take him with her, but at age fifteen, he was having trouble walking. He would slow her down, and she needed to move fast.

She sat down, and Rex immediately sat next to her, placing his paw on her thigh. She rubbed behind his ears. "They don't give you enough credit, do they? You know something's up."

Emma glanced at the clock. She was taking too long, and this was just making it harder. With a shuddering breath, she trailed one finger between Rex's eyes, "Sleep, my friend."

Rex's eyes immediately closed and his legs gave out. Emma caught him and gently lowered him to the ground. She rubbed his belly. "I'll miss you, too, Rex."

Then she stood, swiped at the tears that ran down her cheeks, and slung her backpack over her shoulders, pulling the straps tight. Without looking back, she strode to the front door, pulled it open, slipped outside, and quietly pulled it shut behind her.

Not giving herself time to think, she ran to the side of the garage and grabbed her bike. She pedaled furiously out of the drive and didn't slow down until she was eight blocks away, at the pay phone next to the fruit stand. Hopping from the bike, she picked up the receiver and rang the operator. "Collect call," she said when the operator answered.

She rattled off the number and then waited while the phone rang.

A man picked up, his voice gruff. It was two hours earlier in California.

"Collect call from Lazarus. Do you accept the charges?"

"Uh…" The man paused, obviously shocked. But he recovered quickly. "Yes. Yes. Of course."

"Thank you," the operator said before clicking off.

"Mr. Draper," Emma said.

"Um, yes. Miss Smith?"

Emma let out a breath. He remembered. She had chosen him

because she had been assured he would, even years later. But still, it was always a gamble. Of course, if he hadn't remembered, she had other numbers and other people who were paid well to remember her when she called. "Yes. I'll need transportation immediately, as well as IDs."

"Where are you?"

"Springfield, Illinois." She rattled off the address.

"Give me the number of the phone you're at."

She did.

"Give me five minutes." He hung up.

Emma paced by the phone. Time seemed to crawl by. She kept expecting her parents to roar into the parking lot and demand to know what was going on.

"Come on," she urged, staring at the phone. Finally it rang. She snatched it up. "Yes?"

"I have a car on the way to you. It'll be there in ten minutes. It'll take you to an airfield. I've chartered a plane, and it will be waiting for you."

Emma nodded. If he was surprised that a young girl was calling, he didn't let it show. He was as good as she had hoped. Of course, for the amount of money he was being paid, he should be.

"Good," she said. "I'll give the pilot directions when I'm on board. I'll also need some spending cash. About five thousand should be good for now, until I get to a bank. And I'll need credit cards."

"Yes, ma'am. And the name for the new IDs and cards?"

Emma hesitated, picturing her sister doing her goofy dance. An ache pierced through her, threatening to drop her to the ground.

"Victoria," she said softly. "My name is Victoria."

CHAPTER 1

ONE WEEK AGO

BEVERLY HILLS, CALIFORNIA

GERARD THOMPSON STOOD in front of Elisabeta Roccori's desk. They
were in the office of her Beverly Hills home. White baroque furni-
ture dominated the room, blending in nicely with the pale carpet
and pale walls. Gerard knew that the color of the walls and carpet
was not actually white, but a color called Falling Snow. Elisabeta
would never go for something as common as white.

French doors to the right provided a view of the pool that had
been inspired by Elisabeta's Venetian home. Gerard was careful to
stand to the side of the doors so as not to obstruct the view.

He had just finished reporting on the condition of the Fallen
who'd been injured by Jorgen Fuld. The man was healing, but at a
normal rate—a human rate.

The thought of it still chilled him. What could possibly do that?
They were Fallen: impossibly strong, agile, and able to heal
wounds that would kill a mortal man in mere minutes. And yet

somehow the wounds inflicted by Fuld were immune to their healing.

Gerard had never thought it possible. And he didn't like the lickings of fear that stirred in him. He was used to creating that fear in others. Feeling it himself was not something he planned on getting used to.

He watched Elisabeta leaf through the financial reports of one of her holdings. Her head was bent, dipped in shadows, making her olive-toned skin, a gift of her Greek heritage, even darker.

Elisabeta was the heir to the Hindland Corporation and was on the board of over a dozen Fortune 500 companies. But her long line of titles and business accomplishments paled in comparison to her most important and most unknown title: Samyaza, head of the Fallen angels.

She appeared to be the consummate businesswoman—confident and in control. She made notes in the margin of the paper, acting as if Gerard's report on their brother hadn't rattled her.

But Gerard had seen the fear slash across her face when they had confronted Fuld yesterday. Elisabeta had recognized him immediately, and had ordered all of them out—while keeping her distance from the man. She knew who he was—*what* he was. And she was scared.

Elisabeta glanced up, raising an eyebrow above her dark eyes. "Is there something else?"

Her dark hair was pulled back in a chignon, which only seemed to accentuate the smallness of her eyes. But those eyes held a world of knowledge—an eternity, really—and absolutely no softness.

Gerard hesitated. There was one other bit of information he had picked up, but he wondered if he should even mention it. It hadn't been completely vetted yet. He glanced at Elisabeta. Not for the first time her eyes reminded him of a crocodile's. No compassion, no feelings—just pure predator. He didn't like to think, though, what would happen if he kept the information to himself and later learned that it was important.

"There may be," he said.

Elisabeta waved impatiently for him to get on with it.

"In Egypt, in Saqqara, there were reports that Jake Rogan was shot."

Elisabeta turned her attention back to her reports, flipping to a new page. "Yes, yes. I remember. But it turned out those reports were inaccurate. Rogan was fine."

"Yes…" Gerard drew out the word. "But we've uncovered some emails from Chandler Group employees from around the time of the event. They report that Rogan was killed."

"A miscommunication."

Gerard hesitated. "I do not think so. Chandler is not known for making mistakes, and this was a large one. And there are reports that an older woman was with the triad in Egypt."

Elisabeta focused on Gerard, and her eyes narrowed. "An older woman?"

Gerard nodded. "She had white hair and was only seen from a distance. But she stayed behind with Rogan after Chandler and McPhearson left. Then she flew home with Rogan and Patrick Delaney, dropping them off in Tennessee."

"Where did she go after that?"

"It's not clear. She seems to have disappeared. And we have no other reports on her."

Elisabeta leaned back in her chair and watched Gerard for a long time. He began to grow uncomfortable under her gaze.

"Our people in Egypt reported that Niall did hit Rogan, correct?" she asked quietly.

Gerard nodded. "Yes. Niall took the shot, and he is an incredible marksman. According to him, he got Rogan in the middle of the forehead. It *was* a kill shot."

Elisabeta twirled the pen in her hands, her eyes staring off past Gerard. "But Rogan was alive and well a few days later."

Gerard nodded. "Even if Niall had been off, he still hit Rogan—and yet there was no sign of injury by the time he got back to the States. He should have had some injury."

Elisabeta looked away. "What do you make of this?"

"I don't know. Rogan is human—I am sure of that. But it *is* unusual, and I thought it should be brought to your attention." He paused. "Do you have any idea what it means?"

Elisabeta began to smile slowly. "It means, my dear Gerard, that an old friend has come out of hiding. And she will be the reason we fulfill our true potential. Our *original* potential."

CHAPTER 2

BALTIMORE, MARYLAND

PRESENT DAY

DELANEY MCPHEARSON PICKED up the stack of books and carried them over to the bookcase, where she shoved them onto the shelf with more force than was necessary. The renovations of the library at the Chandler School had been completed a few days ago. Laney had taken it upon herself to re-shelve the books.

Crossing the room, she impatiently swatted at a piece of red hair that had come loose from her ponytail. She picked up another stack of books from the box by the door and headed for the shelves again. A book teetered on top of her stack, then crashed to the floor. Laney leaped back just in time to avoid it dropping onto her foot.

Damn it. With a growl, she placed the books on the shelf and snatched the offending book from the floor, then slammed it down next to its friends.

"Have those poor books insulted you in some way?" Jake asked from the doorway.

Laney glared at him over her shoulder. Normally the sight of Jake leaning against a doorway had the ability to pick up her heart rate and bring a smile to her face. Standing over six feet tall, he was a gorgeous specimen of the male of the species. But today, even the little flip in her heart at the sight of him couldn't cut through her mood.

"No. I'm just cleaning up."

Jake stepped into the room. "Right."

Laney ignored him and grabbed another stack of books.

Jake placed a hand on her arm. "Laney."

She looked up into his deep brown eyes and read the concern there. She placed the books back on the table and leaned against it. "Sorry. I'm just—" She shrugged. "I don't know."

He stepped in front of her, trapping her legs between his. "You're just royally pissed off that Victoria pulled another disappearing trick."

Laney felt the annoyance boil up in her, taking its place right alongside the feeling of rejection. "She said she needed to speak with us. That it was urgent—fate of the world urgent. And then she calls to say we'll talk in a week? What the hell is that?"

Jake pulled Laney forward, wrapping his arms around her, but Laney stayed rigid. "That's Victoria. And you know she probably has a good reason for doing what—"

Laney pulled back, stepping out of Jake's embrace. "You know, I'm getting really sick of hearing that—even if I know it's true. If her reasons are so good, why can't she share them every once in a while?"

Jake looked like he was about to answer her question, but then seemed to change his mind. "Well, she'll be back tomorrow—if she keeps to her word. So what should we do in the meantime?"

Laney shook her head. "Having stuff to do is never a problem." Which, sadly, was true: with the Chandler School to run and Fallen to track down, idle time was never really a concern.

And ever since they'd gotten back from rescuing the kids from Grayston in the Grand Canyon six weeks ago, they'd been even busier than usual, trying to figure out the best living situation for each child. Laney knew that all of the kids who were grabbed would eventually develop some abilities. Most were Fallen; some were nephilim. So how and where they were raised became a critical question.

Luckily, most went home; but some of the home situations were —in a word—problematic. So those kids were placed in foster homes—foster homes that Laney and Henry had personally vouched for and that were within driving distance of the school. When the kids were a little older, they would come here and go to school.

In fact, Laney had plans to offer *all* of the children places at the school when they were old enough. It just seemed like a good idea that when the kids came into their powers, they would be around other people who understood, and who could help them.

But the kids hadn't been Laney's only focus. She, along with Jake and the others, had also been trying to track down Samyaza. A week ago, Victoria had said that Samyaza was a female—that was right before she pulled her disappearing trick. Since then, Henry had managed to narrow the possibilities down to two: a German politician and an Italian heiress.

Laney's money was on the latter. She couldn't say why. There was just something about the woman's picture. And not just the entirety of the woman. To be honest, Laney was basing her assessment on a single attribute: the woman's eyes. There was not a trace of warmth in them.

But they couldn't get confirmation that this woman was Samyaza, because Victoria had disappeared. And Laney couldn't understand it. Whenever Victoria had stepped away in the past, it had always been to track down something. But this time was different. This time they had no idea what she was off doing.

Laney looked at Jake. "I just don't understand. What could be more important than the fate of the world?"

CHAPTER 3

SPRINGFIELD, ILLINOIS

VICTORIA STOOD with Ralph underneath the large maple a short distance from the rest of the mourners. There were at least three dozen men, women, and children braving the rain to pay their respects to Vicki.

A tremor ran through Victoria as she watched her niece place a rose on the coffin. Vicki had named the girl Emma. She had Vicki's hair and blue eyes. Her brother, Shawn, helped her back to her seat. Shawn looked more like Vicki's husband, but from reports, Victoria knew the boy had his mother's sense of humor.

The reverend stepped up next to the coffin. "Vicki Shelton lived a life filled with love. She had a heart that many benefited from, and she seemed to have an incredible amount of luck. Perhaps now she'll be a guardian angel for someone, in the same way that her guardian angel looked out for her." A few mourners nodded.

Victoria gave a small smile at the words. *She* had been that guardian angel. She had watched Vicki and her family grow up from afar, providing money and security for them when she could.

Two months ago, Vicki had been diagnosed with pancreatic cancer. It was a lucky fluke that they even discovered it. Vicki had fallen down a flight of stairs, and the doctor worried she might have fractured a rib. The x-ray revealed no fracture—but it did reveal the tumor.

When Victoria found out about it, she immediately wanted to rush to Vicki's side and heal her. But reality superseded sentiment —Vicki's cancer was advanced. A recovery at that late stage would have drawn media attention—which in turn would have drawn the Fallen. Vicki's whole family would have been placed in danger.

And Victoria knew in her heart that Vicki would not want that.

Vicki held on as long as she could, but Victoria's informant at the hospital told Victoria a week ago that the patient would not last much longer.

Victoria dropped everything.

And for the past week, Victoria had slipped into Vicki's hospital room late each night—just to hold her hand. Vicki never regained consciousness, but for Victoria those moments brought her unfathomable joy. She was with her sister again.

Under the maple tree, tears rolled down Victoria's cheeks. Ralph handed her a tissue without a word, and she nodded her thanks.

They stayed under the trees for the next thirty minutes as Vicki's family and friends paid their respects. Vicki had had a lot of people in her life. The line for the viewings at the funeral home had been out the door.

Ralph leaned down. "She was well loved, your sister."

Victoria nodded, but emotion wouldn't let her speak.

Finally, the last of the mourners departed. Victoria watched the final few cars pull away and drive out through the gates of the cemetery. She turned back to the grave as the cemetery workers, who had been waiting, moved forward to begin Vicki's final descent.

Ralph took Victoria's arm. "Come."

He led her over to the grave. He handed her the umbrella as she paused next to the coffin.

Ralph walked over to the workers. "Could you give us a minute?"

The two men glanced at Victoria and nodded. They walked back to their truck.

Ralph turned to Victoria. "Take your time."

Ralph walked off through the tombstones, giving Victoria a private moment with her sister. But she knew he wasn't far away. He never was.

Victoria looked at the dark mahogany coffin covered in red roses; this wooden box that held her sister's body. The memories of their time together swam through her mind—swimming at the lake, talking under the blankets with flashlights long after they should have been asleep, popcorn fights in the kitchen. She smiled even as the tears flowed.

Vicki, and the memories of their time together, had been a balm for Victoria through the cold lonely years. Even just knowing Vicki was somewhere out there made Victoria feel less alone. But now Vicki was gone, and the world was a colder place.

She stepped forward with a trembling breath. "I love you, Vicki."

"Hello?" a voice called from behind her.

Victoria wiped at her tears and turned as her niece Emma walked slowly up the aisle between the assembled folding chairs. Emma stopped to pick up a purse that Victoria hadn't noticed in the front row.

Victoria's heart pounded heavily. The girl looked so much like Vicki.

Emma stepped up to her, searching her face. "It's you, isn't it?"

Victoria stepped back from the grave. "I'm sorry. I just wanted to pay my respects to your mother."

Emma stepped in front of her, blocking her way. Victoria's breath caught as she stared into eyes that looked so much like Vicki's.

There was a tremor in Emma's voice when she spoke. "All my

life my mom has said that her sister, Emma, was her guardian angel. That she was the one looking out for her—and for us."

"That's a nice sentiment," Victoria said, trying to school her features.

"I grew up hearing all about her sister—all the crazy things they did."

Victoria looked away. "Yes. They loved each other a great deal."

Emma caught Victoria's gaze and would not let her look away. "My mom never believed her sister died—even when my grandparents did. She knew she was out there. She said she would feel it if she were gone. She also said there must have been a good reason why Emma left; she believed that one day, she would see her again."

Victoria put a hand to her mouth. Tears sprang to her eyes.

Emma continued. "When I got older, I began to look into all those 'guardian angel events,' as we called them—Shawn's and my acceptance to Harvard with full scholarships, the medical bills that magically went away, all that help that always seemed to arrive just when we needed it. Someone was looking out for us. It was you, wasn't it? Aunt Emma?"

Victoria couldn't say anything; shock held her in place.

Emma gently grasped Victoria's arms. "She never forgot you. Never stopped loving you. And I know you never stopped loving her." Emma wrapped her arms around Victoria. "Thank you for all you did for her. For us."

Victoria went stiff at first; then gradually she returned the hug, feeling grief wash over her again. Emma held her while she cried.

Finally, Victoria pulled back.

Emma reached up and wiped away her own tears. "Would you mind getting some coffee with me? I'd like to tell you about my mother."

Victoria grasped her niece's hand. "I would like that very much."

CHAPTER 4

BALTIMORE, MARYLAND

LANEY STOOD with her arms crossed as Danny Wartowski helped Max Simmons get the kite airborne. Danny was running across the field, and Max ran alongside, giggling.

Laney smiled. "Run, Danny, run!"

At last the kite caught the wind and took off. Danny unwound the string, letting the kite go higher and higher. Then he knelt down and handed the kite to Max.

Max's smile was huge as he waved his arms back and forth, making the kite dance.

Cleo, the giant Javan leopard Laney had saved from Amar Patel's estate, rubbed her head against Laney's chest. Laney ran her hand through the cat's coat. "I'm good, sweetheart. Go ahead."

Cleo glanced at Laney as if assessing her mood, then disappeared into the trees. Laney shook her head. The more time she spent with Cleo, the more apparent it was that the cat was so much more than just a leopard.

They were in the field behind the main house of the Chandler estate. The five-hundred-acre estate, dating back to the late nineteenth century, included the main house, Henry's own home which sat a few hundred yards behind the main house, and Sharecropper Lane—a mix of homes and offices for the employees.

The estate also came with a full-time security force—all former military. And even though Laney couldn't see them, she knew there were at least six members of that security force surrounding them.

Laney had shooed away Maddox Datson and Max's mom, Kati Simmons, about an hour ago. They hadn't left the estate in weeks. And Laney knew it would be a good thing for them to have a little time away. But she had promised Kati she would not let Max out of her sight.

Max let out a yell, and Laney glanced over as the kite crashed to the ground. Danny made his way over and picked it up again. Laney couldn't help but think of the last time she'd watched the boys fly a kite. At that time, they had known the Fallen were after one of the boys, but they weren't sure which one. It had turned out to be Max.

Max ran across the field behind Danny, his little legs struggling to keep up. The Fallen had succeeded in kidnapping Max. Laney and the others had gotten him back, but he was a little more serious now—not the innocent free spirit he once was.

And Laney still wasn't sure why they had grabbed him. The rest of the children who had been grabbed were potential nephilim or Fallen—every last one of them. But not Max. Laney rubbed the ring on her finger. She could feel when a child would evolve into a nephilim or Fallen. And there was no sign of that with Max.

But Max did have an ability that made him stand out from the other kids: he could speak with the dead. Laney shook her head, still having difficulty believing that. Which was saying something, with all the supernatural events swirling around these days.

Laney's phone rang. She glanced down at the screen before answering it. "Hey, Henry."

Henry's voice was tense. "Mom called."

Laney went still. "And?"

"She wants to see us."

"When?"

"First thing in the morning."

CHAPTER 5

ROCKLAND, MAINE

As Victoria sat next to Ralph in the Mercedes, she tried to think about the conversation ahead with Laney, Henry, and Jake. But her conversation with her niece kept intruding. Her sister Vicki had lived a happy life. And Emma—she was so much like her. *Laney and Henry would love her.*

But Victoria shooed the thought away with a sigh. She could never introduce them to each other. Laney and Henry had been pulled into this life—there had been no way to avoid that. But she couldn't expose Emma to it as well.

Up ahead, the gates to her property came into view. The tall wrought iron gates opened, then closed behind them as they passed through.

"I still think we should go to one of the safe houses and meet them there," Ralph said.

Victoria nodded, knowing that that was the smart call. But she needed the familiar around her right now. She felt raw from Vicki's death. And although the conversation with Emma had helped heal some of her hurt, it had also opened a door to a whole new level of hurt. Vicki had had a life full of love. And Victoria couldn't help but wish that she had been able to be a part of it.

Victoria didn't give in to self-pity very often. It wasn't practical —not in her life. Duty always came first. But she had decided that today she was going to let herself have her moment. And *then* she'd shove her feelings aside and do what she needed to do.

She reached over and took Ralph's hand. "I know. But I want to be home."

She looked up. The physical structure ahead of them dated to 1834. It was a large two-story white colonial with black shutters; fall flowers bloomed along the front. A tree swing lay still under a towering willow twenty feet from the house.

She had bought this property over two hundred years ago, but she had lived here on this land for even longer. Throughout all the change and turmoil in her life, this place had been her one constant.

And right now she needed that constant.

Ralph pulled to a stop and looked at her.

She could see the uncertainty on his face. She squeezed his hand. "We'll leave right after we speak with them. The world will keep for one more night."

CHAPTER 6

THE SUN WAS BARELY UP when Laney, Henry, and Jake began the trip to Maine. Like always, they flew to a field where a car was waiting for them. They clambered inside and settled in for the hour-long journey to Rockland.

Laney stared out the window at the now-familiar scenery. Neither Jake nor Henry spoke. Laney didn't want to talk either.

You need to know what you're up against. And every weapon and enemy you're up against—especially me.

Victoria's words drifted through Laney's mind yet again as she watched the scenery fly by. Those words had been on an unending loop ever since Henry had told her she'd called. Those were the words Victoria had said to Laney before she disappeared for a week.

Jake sat behind the wheel. His brown eyes were focused on the road, but Laney knew he was worried too. Victoria telling them everything was wrong was the equivalent of the beginning of Armageddon. Which usually would be hyperbole, but in this case…

Henry glanced back at her. They'd only learned they were siblings within the last year, but Laney knew she would do anything to keep him safe, and vice versa. "You okay?"

Laney looked into his violet eyes and nodded. "Yeah. Just a little nervous about what she's going to say."

Laney and Henry didn't look anything alike. Henry had dark hair like their father—the angel Metatron, also known as Enoch; Laney had their mother's once-red hair. But they had switched when it came to eye color. Laney had her father's—a deep green—and Henry had his mother's violet eyes.

And while Laney barely topped out at five foot four, Henry was an astounding seven foot two. His stature came from nephilim nature. It also provided him with incredible speed, strength, and healing ability.

Laney's nephilim nature came with a different skill set—she was the only one in the world who could wield the powers of the ring of Solomon. The ring's name wasn't entirely accurate—the ring actually pre-dated Solomon by thousands of years—but Solomon was the figure it had become most associated with.

With the ring, Laney could control the weather, animals, and angels. She hadn't, however, received any of the skills Henry had. She wasn't sure who had gotten the better deal. After all the gunshot wounds and other injuries she'd received over the last two years, she couldn't but think that Henry's gift of fast healing would have been a nice little bonus.

Laney glanced out the window. They were heading to Victoria's estate in Rockland, Maine. Laney had learned about her nature here, learned that the parents who had raised her until the age of eight had not been her biological parents. Months ago, when she had learned that Victoria was her biological mother, Laney had been wracked with questions. Why had her own mother given her up? Who was Victoria, really?

And how had she brought Jake back to life?

But Victoria had sidestepped every question. And now that Victoria was ready to talk, Laney couldn't help but worry about what she would find out.

Three black SUVs sped past them as they turned onto the short lane just before Victoria's road.

"What the hell?" Henry said.

A feeling of foreboding crawled over Laney. She twisted the ring on her finger, but she got no inclination that any of the individuals in the SUVs were Fallen. "Henry."

"I'm on it." Henry picked up his phone as they turned onto Victoria's Lane.

Victoria's home was located at the end of the block. There were only two other homes on the road, so it was possible the SUVs were from one of those.

Henry's eyes shifted to Laney and then back to his phone. "She's not answering. I'll try Ralph."

Laney pictured the massive garden Victoria had created in her back yard. She loved it out there. *She's probably just out in the garden and didn't hear the phone.*

Henry held the phone to his ear for a few beats before pulling it away with a frown.

A sinking sensation began to develop in Laney's stomach. "What's wrong?"

Henry slowly lowered the phone. "He's not answering either."

Jake pushed the gas pedal farther to the floor. Laney's anxiety grew worse, but she tried to shake it off. *It's nothing. They're both just away from their phones.*

Jake rounded the curve in the road, and Victoria's gate came into view.

It hung from its hinges, gaping open.

CHAPTER 7

DISBELIEF FLOODED Laney as she stared at the destroyed gate. Victoria was beyond security-conscious. There was no chance this was an oversight.

Jake slammed the car to a stop. "You sense anything, Laney?"

Laney shook her head. "No. No Fallen, no nephilim besides Henry."

"The SUVs or the house?" Jake asked.

Henry opened his door. "I'll take the house. You head back after the SUVs."

Henry sprinted away before Laney could reply. Laney watched him go with concern. She hated the idea of Henry going in alone. But splitting up made more sense.

Jake threw the car into a U-turn.

The motion jarred Laney into action. She grabbed the duffel bag from the back and retrieved her P90 and an extra drum. Her knife was already in the sheath at her waist. She pulled on a holster and placed a Beretta in it. Then she grabbed Jake's weapons and placed them on the console in between, along with Henry's weapons, which had been specially modified to fit his larger hands.

Jake was on the phone. "Jordan, I need any and all of the video feeds from around Victoria's and the airport. Call me back."

Laney nodded understanding; the airport was only a few miles away and it was the most likely destination if someone was trying to get away quickly.

Her gut clenched. *We're not going to make it*, she thought. Unless there was some miracle delay, the bad guys would be up in the air before she and Jake could do anything about it—or even find out who they were. *And that's if they're even headed there.*

"I need you to send a medical unit to Maine. One of ours." Jake rattled off Victoria's address into his phone. "And I need you there yesterday. Contact Clark at SIA and have him send agents as well."

Laney glanced over at Jake in shock. Victoria's home was a well-guarded secret. She wouldn't like—

Laney stopped short. They couldn't reach Victoria, and she'd warned them that danger was coming. The time for secrets was over.

A tingle ran through her and she glanced behind her as a blur raced for the car. *Henry?*

Henry leaped onto the roof. Laney opened the sunroof over the back seat, and Henry quickly climbed down, with more than a little difficulty. He sat down heavily on the seat next to her.

"What happened?" Laney asked.

Henry's face was tight. "She's not there."

Laney glanced down at Henry's hands. Blood was splashed across one of them. "Whose blood is this?"

Henry looked back at her, pain in his eyes. "Ralph's."

Laney gasped. Henry's tone told her all she needed to know. She closed her eyes and said a little prayer for his passing. And she worried even more for Victoria.

She wanted to ask more questions, but something in Henry's face held her back. So instead she reached over and grabbed the wipes she kept in her bag and silently cleaned the blood off his hand.

When she was done, he clutched her hand tightly. "Thank you."

She nodded. She reached down and handed Henry his weapons. He took them with a nod but wouldn't look at her.

Jake's cell rang and he snatched it up. "Jordan?"

Laney leaned forward to hear as Jordan's voice came over the car's speakers. "There's a plane waiting on the tarmac of the airfield. It's registered to Glacier Fields."

"Glacier Fields?" Laney asked, surprised.

Jordan's voice was grim. "Yeah. It looks like Jorgen Fuld has finally decided to stick his head out."

CHAPTER 8

LANEY SAT BACK. Jorgen Fuld—the Shepherd. He had been behind Grayston's abduction of the children. He had been the man Victoria had said would grab children just because he was bored. They had been looking for him and had found nothing. He had dropped out of sight.

Now he was here—and Victoria was missing.

"Jake," Laney said.

Jake managed to coax just a little more speed out of the car.

"We're heading for the airport now," Jake said into his phone.

"Jorgen's plane is at Hangar B." Jordan described how to get there.

"Warn the local authorities that the group we're going against is extremely dangerous and that they should stay back," Jake said.

"Will do." Jordan paused. "Be careful."

"We will." Jake disconnected the call.

His gaze caught Laney's in the rearview mirror. And she heard the unspoken rest of the statement—*If we can.*

Laney looked between Henry and Jake. "This doesn't make any sense. We've been looking for Jorgen for six weeks. And now he does this brazen strike on Victoria and uses a plane that's easily traced back to him? What the hell is going on?"

"Well, if he's alive after we're done with him, you can ask him," Jake said.

Laney sat back, not liking any part of this. Why had Jorgen shown up so suddenly? And leaving such an obvious trail? Something was definitely wrong.

Laney watched the trees blur by through the car window. She closed her eyes and said a little prayer for Ralph. He had been a nice man—and completely loyal to Victoria.

And that loyalty got him killed. Laney shoved the voice away. Here they were yet again rushing into danger equally as heedless of their own safety.

She glanced over at Henry and Jake and promised that she would do whatever was necessary to keep them safe.

They were a mile away from the airfield. Laney tensed as the distance flew by. A half a mile away she felt the first tingles. She gripped Henry's shoulder.

Henry glanced over at her. "What?"

"There are Fallen."

"How many?" Henry asked.

"At least seven," Laney replied. Could they be working with Fuld?

But there was another noise that was a greater surprise as they sped through the airport gates. "Is that gunfire?" Laney asked. The popping could be heard in the distance.

Jake gave a terse nod and slammed the car to a stop behind Hangar B. "Who the hell is shooting?"

"Maybe airport security?" Laney suggested.

Carefully, the three of them made their way to the edge of the hangar, Jake in front. Wooden pallets with tarps over them were set a few feet to the side; Henry stayed at the hangar while Laney and Jake ducked behind a pallet.

Laney peered out. "What the hell...?"

Two groups were exchanging gunfire in front of the running plane. Laney could see Victoria with one group, pushed down to the ground. And shooting at them were the Fallen.

"Jake." Laney nodded toward the two groups. "The group that has Victoria is human. The Fallen are shooting *at* them."

Jake paused, then shook his head. "Okay. Right now that doesn't matter. Let's just get Victoria back; we'll figure out what the hell is going on later."

"Jorgen," Henry called out.

A man walked across the tarmac. Dark hair brushed his shoulders, his trademark sunglasses in place. The daylight showed off his olive complexion. His bearing was straight and confident despite the gunfire that raged all around him.

Laney frowned. Something was off. *What is it?*

"No one's shooting at him," Jake murmured next to her.

Laney realized Jake was right. None of the shots were coming anywhere near Jorgen. Why the hell not?

The Fallen were almost all in position to easily tackle Jorgen as well. Yet no one moved forward. And no one shot at him. In fact, the gunfire as a whole diminished. *Almost as if they're afraid to shoot him.*

Well, I'm *not,* Laney thought, glaring up at the sky. She couldn't reach him from here with the weapons she'd brought, but there was another way she could stop him.

Clouds began to swirl and darken in the sky above.

"Laney?" Jake asked.

But Laney didn't respond. Her focus needed to be above her. She pictured the plane and stood. "Cover me," she said as she stepped out.

The first lightning strike blasted the ground two feet from the men who held Victoria. More strikes slammed into the ground around the Fallen. They quickly fell back.

"Holy shit," Jake murmured from behind her.

Jorgen stopped short and stared at Laney before yelling something to his men. They all turned and aimed at Laney. Jake grabbed her, pulling her back behind the pallet. Henry provided cover fire.

Laney slammed into the ground with a grunt, feeling a little lightheaded.

"Are you okay?" Jake asked, rolling off her.

She nodded. "I'm good." The lightheadedness passed.

Jake once again peered around the side of the pallet. He unloaded at the men.

Laney crawled to the other side of the pallet. She lined Jorgen up in her sights, but Victoria was right next to him—she couldn't get a clean shot. *Move, Victoria, move!*

Victoria stepped to her left just as if she'd heard Laney's mental urging. Laney smiled and lined Jorgen up.

But before she could pull the trigger, a bloom of red appeared on Jorgen's arm. A Fallen a few feet from him screamed and fell to the ground, writhing as blooms of red appeared on him as well.

Jorgen fell to his side. He reached out and grabbed Victoria. She fell with him, knocking off his sunglasses. Laney lined Jorgen up again—then stopped. Shock had rooted her in place.

Jorgen stared back at her.

The hair on Laney's arms stood straight up. *It can't be.*

Jorgen Fuld's eyes were pure black, without a single drop of white.

CHAPTER 9

LANEY SHOOK off her shock as Jorgen got to his feet, his hand wrapped around Victoria's arm.

A trick of the light. It has to be. Laney tried to find an angle that wouldn't also catch Victoria. But her window had closed. "Damn it."

Jorgen's black eyes remained etched in her mind's eye. She shoved the image away.

Jorgen's men flanked him, offering him and Victoria cover as they ascended the plane's steps. Laney, Jake, and Henry fired at Jorgen's men.

And they weren't the only ones. The Fallen aimed at Jorgen's men as well.

What the hell is going on? It was almost as if the Fallen were on their side, trying to rescue Victoria.

Jorgen's men flanked the plane as the door to the cockpit shut.

"No!" Henry yelled, taking off at a run.

"Henry!" Jake shouted. He ran forward, taking cover at a truck.

Laney stepped out, calling on the wind. She pushed a group of three Fallen across the tarmac. She threw another four of Jorgen's men up in the air. They crashed to the ground with a scream.

Henry blurred toward the plane, but it was already taxiing

away.

"Laney, stop him!" Jake yelled. "He's going to jump on the plane!"

With her heart in her throat, Laney realized Jake was right. Henry could survive a lot of things, but a fall from thousands or even hundreds of feet up was not one of them.

Laney concentrated all her energy on pulling Henry back. She threw a wall of wind up in front of him. The blur that was Henry slowly came into focus. He was pushing against the sudden gale.

The plane took flight. And finally Henry stopped his fighting, allowing the wind to push him back.

Laney lowered her hand, and the winds calmed.

Henry turned and ran back to her. "Why did you stop me? I could have gotten her." He towered over her.

Laney took a step back from his anger. "No. You would have gotten yourself killed."

"You don't know that." Henry clenched his fists.

Jake stepped in front of her, his tone hard. "You need to calm down."

Henry glared down at Jake, then walked away.

Laney watched him go, realizing she had actually been afraid of Henry for a moment. He walked to the edge of the tarmac. His shoulders drooped. His anger was gone now, and all that left was sadness. It pierced right through her. Was he right? Should she have let him try?

Sirens wailed in the distance, grabbing her attention. Jorgen's men lay sprawled across the tarmac, but Laney was pretty sure that most of them were still alive. Jake made his way through them, pushing their weapons out of their reach.

Laney looked around. The Fallen had disappeared. She hadn't even noticed. She'd been too busy trying to make sure Henry didn't kill himself.

She shook her head as she made her way to her brother. The Fallen had been fighting Jorgen's men. And Victoria had been the prize. What was going on?

CHAPTER 10

LANEY, Henry, and Jake used their SIA badges to keep their interaction with the police to a minimum, but it still took an hour for them to wrap things up at the airport. They all knew they needed to get back to Victoria's home. The cops would contain the scene at the airport until the SIA agents arrived.

Once they managed to detangle themselves from the police, Jake once again took the driver's seat. He kept his speed high the whole ride. With each mile they covered, Laney wondered why they were rushing. Victoria wasn't there, and Ralph was already dead. No matter how fast they got there, they couldn't help either of them.

When they reached Victoria's cottage, the SIA had already arrived. Agents swarmed the place. A tall brunette with a muscular build in a no-frills navy blue suit walked over to Laney as she got out of the car. "Dr. McPhearson?"

Laney nodded.

"Director Clark apologizes for not being here in person. He's stuck in Washington, DC. I'm Agent Aziz, and I'll be running the investigation."

Laney nodded. "Okay. Have you found anything useful?"

Aziz shook her head. "Not yet."

"What about the body in the kitchen?" Jake asked.

Aziz tilted her head. "Sorry?"

"The body? In the kitchen?" Jake asked.

Aziz frowned and spoke slowly. "There's no body in the kitchen."

Laney's shocked gaze met Henry's. They brushed past the agent and made their way to the kitchen.

Laney saw the bloody handprint next to the front door but didn't stop. She glanced down the hall to the left, but nothing looked disturbed. The living room on the right looked equally undamaged. But even from the front foyer, she could see the destruction in the kitchen.

Steeling herself, she followed Henry in. She gasped as she stepped into the room.

Bullet holes dotted the old wooden cabinets. More bullets had chipped away at the brick fireplace and blasted out the windows. And the blood—the blood was everywhere.

"Oh my God." Laney felt faint. How had Victoria survived this? She glanced around and swallowed hard.

Agents caught sight of them and stopped their inspection, respectfully retreating to the edge of the room.

Laney stared at the blood that dotted the room and the large pool that lay in the middle. No one could survive that much blood loss. She could even see where Ralph had lain. But that was the only sign that he had been there.

His body was gone.

CHAPTER 11

HENRY STARED at the spot on the floor where he had found Ralph earlier. He pictured Ralph's face, his mouth slightly open, his eyes staring at nothing. Someone must have taken the body. But who?

Agent Aziz stepped forward. "We've just begun. I can take you through—"

"How about you show me what you're doing?" Jake said, stepping in front of the agent and blocking Henry and Laney from her view.

Aziz shifted her eyes to Jake. "Of course, Mr. Rogan. If you'll follow me."

From the corner of his eye, Henry saw Jake squeeze Laney's hand. Laney looked just as shocked as Henry felt. She turned and laced her fingers through Henry's. "Where is he?"

Henry just stared at the spot where he had seen Ralph. He had been shot multiple times. Henry winced, remembering the bullet hole in Ralph's forehead. "This makes no sense. He was right here."

"I believe you. But where is he now?"

Henry looked around the kitchen, his eyes falling on the black and white checkered clock on top of the cabinets. *Of course.*

He turned to Laney. "Ralph installed security cameras in here."

Laney's eyes went wide. "He did? Victoria allowed that?"

Henry shook his head. "He never told her. He knew she wouldn't agree."

"Where's the recording?"

"I'll get it. You get Jake."

CHAPTER 12

LANEY GRABBED Jake from the agent, and they met Henry in Victoria's study. They closed the door, keeping anyone else out for now. They needed to see the recording before anyone else.

Laney looked around the room. Nothing had been disturbed in here either. Everything looked just as it had the last time she'd been here. The two couches flanked the fireplace on the right, Victoria's chaise lounge was positioned in front of the window, and her desk was on the left.

Laney shuddered as an image of the kitchen flashed through her mind. *All the violence was saved for in there.*

Laney stood in front of the desk. Jake stood next to her, his hand wrapped protectively around hers, and Henry stood on her other side. Henry linked the memory card to the monitor on Victoria's desk. His face was a mask, showing nothing, but Laney knew he must be terrified.

The recording started that morning when Victoria and Ralph got up. Ralph left his bedroom and headed to the kitchen to make breakfast. Victoria joined him a few minutes later and set the table. Then the two sat down and ate while reading the newspaper. The normalcy of the scene was jarring when compared with the now blood-soaked room. Laney wanted to yell a warning at them. *Run!*

"They didn't suspect a thing," Jake murmured.

A few minutes later, Ralph's head whipped up like it was on a string. Two canisters came flying through the back windows. They sparked.

"Flash bangs," Jake murmured. Victoria dropped to the ground, her hands over her ears.

Ralph paused only for a second; he seemed to barely be affected by the concussion weapons. He pulled Victoria to her feet as men poured into the room.

Laney put her hand to her mouth. "Oh my God."

Ralph and Victoria stood in the middle of the intruders.

And then all hell broke loose.

Ralph moved so fast Laney couldn't even see him. He blurred through the room, taking out man after man. It was a bloodbath.

Victoria moved back against the wall, keeping out of reach. But then one of the gunmen grabbed her and put a gun to her head. He yelled.

Ralph stopped moving.

Victoria shook her head, yelling at Ralph. The recording had no sound, but Laney could make out the words clearly: *No, Ralph. Run.*

On the screen, two men manhandled Ralph to the ground. One of the gunmen walked forward and shot Ralph point blank in the forehead. Ralph's head snapped back.

Laney gasped, and Jake tightened his grip on her hand.

Victoria slammed her fist into the groin of the man who held her; he dropped. She ran for Ralph, but another man grabbed her around the waist.

The gunman who'd shot Ralph in the head wasn't done. He pulled the trigger over and over again, emptying his magazine into Ralph's heart.

In the corner of the screen, Victoria struggled against the man who held her. Her arms reached for Ralph, her face contorted in pain and grief.

Laney stumbled back, her hand to her mouth. Jake slipped his arms around her, keeping her upright. Henry sat heavily on the desk. But none of them spoke.

Ralph's body jerked as each bullet landed. Then it stopped and went still. On screen, Victoria, too, stopped fighting, all but collapsing. The men picked her up and carried her out.

Another man walked into the kitchen then, and Laney felt a jolt of recognition. *Jorgen Fuld.* He walked over to Ralph and emptied his magazine into Ralph's heart.

"Son of a bitch," Jake growled.

Laney stared. Her body began to shake, and her mouth felt unable to form words. She looked over at Henry, whose face was frozen in anguish. All of Henry's childhood memories involved Ralph. Laney's heart broke for him.

Numbly, they continued to watch the video. The men gathered up their injured and dead. Finally, the men left, and there was only Ralph left on the floor.

The tape continued to roll.

And then a few minutes later, Henry entered. He went still at the doorway before running to Ralph and kneeling at his side.

Laney's heart broke again at the sight of the agony on Henry's face. Seconds later though, Henry sprinted for the door. Laney knew how hard it must have been for Henry to leave Ralph behind.

Laney felt empty as she stared at Ralph. She remembered him sharing with her the photo album Victoria had kept of Laney through the years.

All three of them stared at the tape, but nothing changed. Jake began to fast forward.

"Guys, look." Jake pointed at the monitor.

On screen, Ralph's hand twitched. Then it rolled into a fist. Ralph sat up—slowly, wincing. He got to his knees and stayed there for a moment before standing. Then he stumbled out of the room.

Jake switched to another camera view: the front hall. There was Ralph again, continuing doggedly onward, his posture straightening with each step. Before long, he sprinted out the door and out of the camera's view.

Laney stepped back and fell into the chaise lounge, stunned. She stared at the clock on the right hand side of one of the screens. "He was down for almost thirty minutes. How could he come back after thirty minutes?"

Henry's eyes were wide. "I don't know. It... it's not possible. It just isn't."

"Apparently it is," Jake said. "So now the bigger question is: How?"

Laney looked at the bloodstain where Ralph had lain. It was large. She knew nephilim and Fallen could regenerate, but not from wounds that serious. All that blood loss. And all those chest shots. Ralph's heart should have been destroyed.

Jake placed his hand on her shoulder. She looked up at him.

He nodded at the ring on the chain around Laney's neck. "Have you ever felt anything around Ralph?"

"No, nothing. I—" She stopped short. "Actually, I haven't worn the ring around him."

"But in Saqqara," Henry said.

Laney shook her head. "No. I've never worn it around him. He's been to the school with Victoria, but you guys know I don't wear it unless it might be necessary. And it's never been necessary when he's been around." She looked at Henry. "You haven't felt anything around him?"

"No, but if he's a Fallen, I wouldn't feel anything."

Laney looked from Jake to Henry. "But some of the kids at the school are Fallen. Lou is. She would have mentioned something."

Jake squeezed her arm. "I'm going to speak with the SIA. Tell them to put out an APB on Ralph."

Laney nodded numbly, still staring at the screen. Then she looked up into Henry's tortured face. And although neither of them said a word, the same question hung in the air between them.

What exactly *was* Ralph?

CHAPTER 13

THIRTY MINUTES LATER, Laney stepped out the back door of Victoria's home and took a deep breath. The house felt stifling even though she knew it was no warmer than usual, but at the same time a chill seemed to have settled over her. Jake had gone to speak with Jordan to see what he could find out about Ralph.

Laney glanced back toward the house. Henry had headed out the front door earlier. For a moment she thought about going to find him, but she quickly discarded the idea. He needed some time alone. And truth be told, so did she.

Through the window, she could see people walking around Victoria's kitchen. Victoria, a woman whose entire life had been a deeply held secret, was now having that life flayed wide open.

Turning back to the yard, Laney remembered Victoria's garden when she had first seen it. It had been a riot of color: roses, pom-poms, daisies, and dozens more. Now those colors had all been bleached as the cool weather had moved in.

Laney walked through the path that cut through the middle of the garden, her eyes flicking from side to side. Even with the cool weather, she saw signs of life. The mums had broken through the earth, signaling the advent of new, darker colors.

About a hundred yards from the house, she turned onto a path on her left. At the top of the rise she paused and looked at the white tombstone surrounded by its own little garden. A wrought iron bench sat nearby, under a rose of Sharon tree.

Laney walked to the grave. "Hey, sis." She knelt down and ran her hands over the engraving.

Sarah
She never had a chance to live,
but by her death helped save another.

Last year, when Laney learned that she was the biological daughter of Victoria, she also learned that her parents' own biological daughter had passed away at birth. Victoria had had the child buried and had tended to her gravesite all those years. Laney had struggled with what to think about Victoria and this other child. But then she'd realized that, at heart, she and Sarah were sisters.

Laney spoke to the tombstone. "I thought you should know: someone took Mom. But we'll get her back. I promise." She grabbed some leaves that had fallen onto the grave and tossed them to the side. She stood and turned.

Taking a seat on the bench, she watched a flock of geese fly overhead. She closed her eyes. She knew she should go inside and help. But she needed a moment to take in everything that had happened. Jorgen Fuld had Victoria. She pictured him at the airfield; the image of him with his glasses knocked off was in the front of her mind. His eyes had looked black—completely black.

But that wasn't possible. No one had completely black eyes. Even the Fallen looked human. *It had to have been a trick of the light, right?*

Why had he taken Victoria? To get to Laney and Henry? But why make it so obvious? He'd been off the radar. They'd had no signs of him. All his homes had been shuttered. So why stick his head out now?

Did *he* somehow know who Victoria was? His men had been prepared for Ralph. Even Laney and Henry hadn't had a clue as to Ralph's nature—and to be honest, they still didn't. So how did Jorgen's men know to take him down? And who—or rather *what*—was Ralph?

She clenched her fists, her annoyance at Victoria flaring up. If Victoria had told them who she was, maybe all of this could have been avoided. Maybe…

Laney cut herself off in mid-thought. That was a useless line of reasoning. What was done was done. She needed to focus on the here and now. Not what she wished had happened.

After all, there was already plenty to keep her thoughts occupied. She pictured the Fallen shooting at Fuld's men. What had that been all about?

They must have been under Samyaza's direction, but why were they fighting Jorgen? And why were they trying to rescue Victoria? Laney put her head in her hands. It didn't make any sense.

Unless Victoria is working with them, a voice whispered in the back of her mind. Laney didn't want to go there, but she wasn't sure she was going to be able to avoid that voice for long.

"Hey there."

Laney's head popped up as Jake walked over and took a seat next to her.

She wrapped her hand in his. "Hey."

"You doing okay?"

She shook her head before leaning it on Jake's shoulder. "I don't know."

He kissed her forehead. "We'll find her."

"I hope so."

They sat together in silence for a few minutes.

Laney finally lifted her head and looked at Jake. Frown lines had formed between his eyes. "What's wrong?"

"What? Oh, nothing—just worried about Victoria and Ralph," he said, trying to cover the frown.

Laney narrowed her eyes. "That's not it. What's going on?"

Jake looked at her for a moment. "Back at the airfield…" He paused.

"Yes?"

"When you called up that lightning. It was pretty powerful stuff."

"I guess."

"No. Not 'I guess.' Laney, you were practically glowing. Your hair was flying around. I could feel the power radiating off of you."

Laney sat back. She hadn't realized that. She paused, unsure whether she wanted to hear the answer to the question she needed to ask. "Do my powers… scare you?"

"Sometimes."

Laney jolted and pulled her hand away.

He reached out and grabbed her hand. "No, don't back away from me. It's not what you think. I trust you—with my very life. But you have weapons at your disposal that are new to you. It's like handing a loaded gun to someone who's never shot before. I'd feel better if they had a few lessons."

"Well, the only person I know who can control the weather is Storm from *X-Men*. Should I call Stan Lee, see if he has any pointers? Or maybe see if the Dog Whisperer has some free time?"

Jake laughed. "No. I don't think that will be necessary. But how about if we train a little bit with your powers? I'll set up some targets, and you'll take them down with different abilities."

Laney liked the idea. Anything that helped her get a better handle on her powers was more than okay with her. And the fact that Jake wanted to help her meant a lot. "Thank you."

He tilted her chin up. "You are the most important person in the world to me. Anything I can do to make this destiny of yours easier, I'll do."

"I love you, Jake."

"I love you, too."

Laney sat nestled in Jake's arms, letting herself take the comfort he offered. But her questions wouldn't stay still for long. Dozens of them whirled through her mind. And one question kept repeating over and over again.

Who is Victoria?

CHAPTER 14

BALTIMORE, MARYLAND

Sixteen-year-old Danny Wartowski stared at the screen, but his mind was focused on Henry's call about Victoria. He wiped a tear from the corner of his eye, hoping no one walked in.

He'd only met Victoria a few months ago, but they had taken to each other right away. It was nice having a grandma. She had called him every week, and she'd even stopped by for lunch, just the two of them every two weeks. He liked her. She took him seriously. And more importantly, she "got" him—the way grandmas are supposed to.

Cleo bumped Danny with her head, and he wrapped his arm around her neck. "I'm okay, Cleo."

Cleo kept her head pressed against Danny for another few seconds before she turned and walked over to the couch at the back of the office, where five-year-old Max Simmons was sprawled out, asleep. The boy had come to visit with Maddox. Maddox was on the phone with his sister just out in the hall.

Max sighed and turned in his sleep. Cleo lay down on the floor in front of the couch. Moxy, Danny's shepherd mix, padded over and curled up next to her. Danny smiled at the camaraderie between the two of them.

Laney had put Cleo on guard duty while she was away, and the giant Javan leopard was taking her duty seriously. She hadn't let Max out of her sight since Laney had left—except for when nature called.

Danny turned back to the screen, but he couldn't seem to focus on his latest project. Jorgen Fuld had grabbed Victoria, and the Fallen had been there too. There must be an explanation. He just had to find it.

He glanced behind him as Max murmured again and rolled onto his side. The boy looked so innocent with his floppy brown hair and his stuffed lamb clutched to his chest. In fact, Max looked like any other five-year-old—cute and harmless. And yet, Danny had the distinct impression that Max was much more important than any of them knew.

He turned back to the screen to the web page he'd pulled up. The words "Indigo Children" were written across the top of the page in white outlined in purple. Danny read quickly.

Indigo children are distinct from psychic children. Psychic children have always been reported, throughout human history. Indigo children, by contrast, have been identified as such only since 1978. And they have a range of psychic abilities.

In China, over a hundred thousand psychic children have been identified by the government. And the Chinese government is alleged to have spent millions researching them. Of course, the Chinese government doesn't call them indigo children or psychics. They explain the expenditures as studying extra human functions, or EHF.

But the children in the Chinese program don't just have the ability to predict the future or reach those who have passed. Some have truly unique gifts. One girl was reportedly able to make plants come to life with a wave of her hand.

Danny ran a hand through his hair. Was he really buying any of this? And was any of this related to Max? Was Max an indigo child?

Danny knew Max spoke with people who had passed. But the Fallen wanted Max, so there must be more to the story. After all, they could easily find someone else with psychic abilities—someone who was not nearly as well guarded as Max.

Danny clicked back to the search page and scrolled through the other websites that discussed the indigo children, unsure what he was looking for. Part of him couldn't believe he was actually considering this, but the other part of him acknowledged that science had its limits. And hundreds of years ago, planes, medicine, microscopes, robotic surgery—all these ordinary facets of modern life—would have seemed like impossibilities. Hundreds of years from now, would people look back and think the same about psychic abilities?

Danny shook his head, trying to look at the idea of psychic abilities rationally. There were two schools of thought on human evolution. One held that humans evolved incredibly slowly over a very long period of time. In fact, some research even suggested that human evolution was slowing down - —that fewer and fewer mutations in the genetic code were being transmitted from one generation to the next.

But there was also another school of thought—it argued that human evolution actually occurred in huge leaps.

But what if those leaps don't occur uniformly? What if they occur only with select people?

After all, the human family tree is a lot more complex than anyone ever realized, but somewhere we must all have had a common ancestor before new generations were born with all that variation. What if the indigo children weren't just humans with certain abilities? What if they were a new type of human altogether?

Danny's eyes strayed to Max, sleeping so peacefully on the couch. If the indigo children existed, were they the next leap in human evolution? Was Max?

Danny looked at the screen, a chill falling over him.

Am I?

After all, one of the alleged traits of indigo children was an increase in intelligence. And Danny himself was considered an immeasurable genius—someone whose IQ was so high it couldn't be quantified.

In fact, in recent years, more and more children were being discovered who met the criteria for genius. Danny had always thought that the increase in the number of genius children was actually due to an increase in the frequency of intelligence testing, not in the proportion of geniuses in the population. But was it possible that they were living in a time of humanity's next leap forward in evolution?

Danny's phone chimed, breaking into his thoughts. Normally, he turned his phone off to prevent just this problem. But with everything happening, he wanted Henry to be able to reach him.

He glanced at his phone and sighed. It was just an email, and it wasn't from Henry. It was from Professor Gleason at MIT. Danny had helped him create a computer model to predict fractal formation for his undergrads.

Danny shook his head. "I can't believe I have to explain this again. What's so hard about nonlinear mathematics?" he muttered.

"A lot of people don't understand that all systems are interconnected," Max said from behind him.

Danny went still. He turned, narrowing his eyes. "What did you say?

Max wiped his eyes. "Predicting the unpredictable. You know, the replicating patterns found in fractals. He probably needs to understand that better."

Danny felt his mouth gape open. "How did you know about that?"

Max shrugged and gave a big yawn. "I don't know."

Maddox walked in, dropping his phone in his pocket. At six foot six, with long dark hair, Maddox was an intimidating sight, and that was before anyone knew about his nephilim abilities. He walked over and scooped Max up, giving him a big grin.

And then you see him with Max and realize he's a giant yet deadly teddy bear, Danny thought.

"I thought you were going to sleep forever," Maddox said.

Max giggled. "Then I'd wake up an old man—like you."

"What? I'm not old." Maddox tossed Max in the air. Max squealed as Maddox caught him and hugged him.

Max seemed so carefree. Danny frowned. But how had he known that about chaos theory?

Maddox looked over at Danny. "We're going to grab some lunch downstairs. You hungry?"

Danny stared at him for a second before giving himself a mental shake. "Um, yeah. Uh, I'll just finish this up and then I'll be down."

"Okay. We'll get it started." Maddox and Max disappeared through the door; Cleo trailed silently after them.

Moxy came over and sat next to Danny. Danny reached down to pet her. Laney had given Moxy to Danny a year ago, and now he couldn't imagine his life without her.

Danny watched them go. "How did he know that, Mox?"

Moxy tilted her head as if listening.

Danny thought back to all the conversations he'd had about chaos theory. He couldn't remember Max ever being around for one of them. And even if he was, just remembering one of those conversations was a pretty amazing feat for a little kid.

Danny shook his head as he stood. "There's got to be a logical explanation."

He looked over at the couch and squinted. Something was peeking out from underneath the pillow Max had been sleeping on.

Danny walked over and picked up the pillow Max had been using. A book lay underneath it—*Chaos Theory: Making a New Science*, by James Gleick. It was the book Danny had used when writing the program for Professor Gleason.

Danny stared out the door and down the empty hallway for a moment before his eyes returned to the book. The ideas he'd read about the indigo children whirled through his mind. He shook his head. *No. That's not possible.*

Feeling a little shaky, he placed the book on the coffee table and walked to the door. He knew there was research that indicated that if you read before taking a nap it actually increased the likelihood of converting the information you just read from short-term to long-term memory, but he'd never read anything about absorbing knowledge through a *closed* book while sleeping.

I mean, Max can't even read yet.

Danny glanced down at Moxy. She gazed up at him with a look that was almost human.

Danny knelt down to look her in the eyes. "No one can learn the contents of a book simply by sleeping on it, right?"

CHAPTER 15

ROCKLAND, MAINE

LANEY, Henry, and Jake stayed at Victoria's home for another hour, but the reality was, there was nothing they could do there. The SIA agents were processing the scene, but they all knew the answers they needed were not going to be found in a crime lab.

Henry called the helicopter and had it pick them up right on Victoria's lawn—another reminder that the secrecy Victoria had nurtured was now gone.

When they reached the Chandler estate, Laney and Henry headed straight up to Henry's office, while Jake stopped by the analysts' room down the hall to get an update. Henry's office was huge, taking up two thirds of the third floor of the main house. The first time Laney had seen it, she'd been amazed by the floor-to-ceiling windows along one wall and the bookshelves, filled to bursting, that rimmed it. But now it was a second home.

Henry took his seat behind the giant-sized desk centered in front of the windows Laney sat down at the large conference table, set down her coffee, and pulled up a monitor. She rubbed her hands. "All right. Time to get to work."

For two hours, they both ran down different angles. And at the end of two hours, neither of them had anything to show for it.

Laney stretched. Her back was protesting having being hunched over the computer, unmoving, for so long.

Henry's phone rang. The change in his face told Laney it was Jen Witt. She gave a small smile. Jen was just what Henry needed right now.

Henry spoke quietly into the phone and walked out of the room. Watching him disappear into to an empty office down the hall. Laney hoped Jen could help lift his spirits.

Pushing away from the table, Laney stretched her back and then headed around to the other side of the conference table to check on Jake. After checking on the analysts, he had joined them, reviewing correspondence from different law enforcement agencies and verifying that they all had accurate descriptions of Victoria, Ralph, and Fuld.

Laney watched Jake for a moment, debating yet again whether or not she should mention Jorgen's eyes. But she just couldn't seem to convince herself that what she had seen was real. So instead she took a seat next to Jake and pulled over some of the papers he had brought from Victoria's office. Neither of them felt comfortable letting the SIA go through them.

A short scan of the documents convinced her she shouldn't have worried. Unsurprisingly, Victoria had left nothing incriminating behind.

Laney stretched again and felt Jake's eyes on her. She glanced up with a wan smile. "Well, I've got nothing. How about you?"

"Not really. The guys at Victoria's house were all trained. They even policed their brass. They also appear to have all been human, but I can't be entirely sure on that one."

"The Council?" Normally, when they ran into humans, it was the Council who had sent them. The Council was a clandestine group that dated back to the Inquisition. They used what they learned about Atlantean artifacts to fill their coffers and further their success.

Jake shrugged. "Could be. But it doesn't feel right, does it?"

Laney sighed. "No. But Jen was heading to speak with Phillip Northgram. Maybe Henry will know something."

Jake grinned. "Oh, I'm sure Northgram enjoyed that conversation."

Laney smiled in return. Phillip Northgram was the head of the Council, and last year, when the children went missing, Jen and Henry had had a little chat with him regarding Council activities. Jen had apparently made quite an impression on the arrogant CEO.

As if summoned, Henry stepped into the room. He looked so lost, so beaten down. Laney walked over and wrapped her arms around him, burying her head in his chest. "We'll get her back," she said softly.

Henry's arms closed around her. "I know."

Laney leaned back to look up at him. "*Do* you?"

Henry stared down at her, fear, confusion, and pain flashing through his eyes. "I don't know, Laney. Whoever Mom is, she doesn't have powers. We know that much. She can be hurt. She can be..." Henry's voice broke, and his arms tightened around her.

Laney rested her head back on his chest. "I know."

"Did Northgram have anything?" Jake asked.

Henry let Laney go and sank into a chair next to Jake. "No. Said he didn't know anything and that he had no business dealings with Jorgen."

Laney took a seat across from the two of them. "Does Jen believe him?"

Henry blew out a breath. "Yeah. And besides, we checked him for links to Jorgen even before all this. We came up with nothing."

"I know this is tough for you two," Jake said. "But we need to try and look at this objectively. Someone took Victoria. They could have killed her, and they didn't. Which means they want something from her."

Henry nodded. "If this were any other abduction, we'd learn everything we could about the victim."

Laney swallowed down a laugh—it wasn't a happy one. Learn about Victoria? As if they hadn't been trying to do that for the last few months! Laney shoved her doubts aside though. *Time to be positive.* "Okay. So where do we start?"

"Well, is there anything in the Flourent books?" Jake asked.

Laney pictured the books they had found in the ruin of Sebastian Flourent's home. Flourent's father had been a member of the Council. Each member of the Council kept journals of their activities, and Sebastian Flourent had come into possession of his father's journals after his death. The Chandler group had then rescued those same journals from the devastation of Flourent's home.

Laney and her uncle had been going through them, but other priorities kept getting in the way. Now, the books had to be the priority. "I'll hit them again. I still haven't been through about three quarters, although Uncle Patrick's made a pretty good dent. I'll see what he's got."

Jake nodded. "That's good. But normally in a missing case, I'd say we start with the victim's home. See if there's anything that would clue us in to what's going on."

"I'll do that," Henry said quickly. They had brought back boxes of Victoria's and Ralph's things and stored them in a conference room down the hall. "She wouldn't like other people going through her stuff."

Laney nodded, but she wondered if what Victoria wanted mattered anymore. She chased the thought aside. *Positive. I will be positive.*

A smaller part of her brain, though, mocked her. *Sure—stay positive no matter how impossible it seems.*

CHAPTER 16

BEVERLY HILLS, CALIFORNIA

GERARD CRINGED but tried to not move as a vase went sailing past his head.

"What do you mean you can't find her?" Elisabeta demanded. Hands on her hips, she stood behind her highly polished mahogany desk.

"We're running down all of Jorgen's known holdings. So far we have found nothing. But it's only a matter of time."

Elisabeta's chest heaved. Her dark eyes looked even darker, her complexion paler than it should be—except for her flushed cheeks.

And once again, Gerard was confused. Who was Jorgen? Why did he evoke this reaction in Elisabeta? Until Jorgen had appeared, Gerard had never seen Elisabeta lose her cool. But now, she was incensed.

Gerard spoke quietly. "Perhaps if you told me who Jorgen really is, it would help us locate him."

Elisabeta's head whipped around, and her eyes narrowed. "I have told you all you need to know to find him."

"Then perhaps you could tell me why Victoria Chandler is so important?"

Elisabeta looked at him for a moment and then away.

Gerard took a step forward. "Elisabeta, I can help you better if I know what the end goal is."

Elisabeta said nothing.

Gerard bit his tongue. Perhaps he had overstepped.

Her shoulders dropping, Elisabeta turned and resumed her seat. She gestured for Gerard to take a seat as well. Gerard held in his surprise as he sat down across from her.

Elisabeta stayed silent for a moment before she spoke. "What is our greatest power?"

Gerard thought for a moment. "Our ability to heal."

Elisabeta nodded. "Yes. We are difficult to kill. Now, imagine what you could do if you *couldn't* be killed."

Gerard reared back, then spoke slowly. "That's not possible."

"Oh, it's possible. Your memory is stunted. You've forgotten far more of your previous lives than you remember. But I remember more than any of you. I remember when we first arrived."

Gerard leaned forward. If Elisabeta had asked, he would have said that the second greatest drawback of their existence was their inability to remember from one life to the next. Every once in a while he would get snippets of memories from his past lives, but the whole picture was always out of reach. "You… remember?"

She nodded. "When the triads arise, the memories return."

Gerard wanted to ask about the other members of the triad, but he didn't. It wasn't often that Elisabeta took someone into her confidence, and he didn't want to ruin the spell.

"When we first arrived, it was glorious. We were gods among men. We still are. But it was even more so at first. Because at first, we were immortal."

"Immortal?"

Elisabeta's voice took on a wistful quality. "The earth was truly an Eden. Everything was available for the taking. The humans were fools. They had no concept of ownership or power. They shared and gave away all they had. It was like a candy store guarded by ants." She smiled.

Gerard had heard the rumors, but he had never truly believed them. "What happened?"

Elisabeta's face clouded. "That bitch. She took it all from us."

"She?" Gerard frowned.

Elisabeta spit out the words. "Victoria Chandler."

Gerard sat back, stunned. He had never felt any recognition around the woman. "How? She's a human."

Elisabeta's eyes narrowed, and venom dripped from her words. "A *favored* human."

"So we're looking for her in order to get revenge?"

Elisabeta shook her head. The smile that formed on her face chilled Gerard. "No. We're looking for her in order to get our immortality back."

CHAPTER 17

LITTLE ROCK, ARKANSAS

VICTORIA WOKE UP SLOWLY. Her head ached, but that wasn't what bothered her. It was the fog in her brain. She knew that feeling—she'd been drugged.

Open your eyes. Open them, she ordered herself. With a few false starts and more than a little effort, she managed it.

She was in a bedroom. It was Spartan: just a bed, window, and one chair. There were two doors. The one across from the window was likely the door to a hallway. The one next to the window hopefully led to a bathroom. Victoria sat up, and the room swayed for a moment.

An image of Ralph flashed through her mind. Grief rocked her, and she held on to the bedpost. She closed her eyes, willing away the waves of sorrow that crashed over her. *I'm so sorry, Ralph.*

She pictured his brown eyes, his calming presence. He had been her one true friend, the one person who'd stood by her through everything—in this lifetime and the others. A tear tracked its way down her cheek and a sob shuddered through her.

She shook her head and took some calming breaths. She couldn't give in to grief. Not now.

But Ralph's death on the heels of Vicki's was almost more than she could stand. The two of them had been her constants. And now they were both gone. She closed her eyes, gave herself one more moment, and then banished her sadness, locking it away for another time.

Opening her eyes, she got to her feet, holding onto the bedpost. On shaky legs, she crossed the room and opened the door by the window—a bathroom. She nearly wept with relief. She took care of her business quickly and took time to splash some water on her face.

The towel she used was fluffy and bright white—expensive. She placed it on the sink and headed back into the room. She stopped at the window, which overlooked a back yard in what appeared to be in a residential neighborhood. A man turned his head and looked up at her from the ground.

She met his glare without flinching. Finally, he turned away. Victoria stepped back from the window. *Okay, so someone is keeping an eye on me.*

The lock on the door rattled. Victoria turned, her hands behind her back. Jorgen Fuld walked in.

"Ah, you're awake. I was getting worried," he said with a smile.

"I doubt that," Victoria replied.

Jorgen took a seat on the only chair in the room, one leg crossed over at the knee. "Always so antagonistic. Why is that?"

Victoria crossed her arms. "Why am I here?"

"Maybe I missed you."

Victoria said nothing. She just waited.

Jorgen pulled his glasses off and wiped them with the edge of his jacket. He looked back at her. His eyes were pure black. He paused, then smiled. "You've never been taken aback by my eyes. Not even when you first saw them."

Victoria raised her chin a notch. "That's because I've seen your evil before."

He stared at her, and she could feel his annoyance. "You've never liked me. Not even when I was a child."

She stared into his black eyes without flinching. That wasn't entirely true. When he had first been born, she had marveled at what a beautiful child he was. His parents had doted on him.

But they had given him too much leniency. His cruelty went unchecked. At first, they were the cruelties all children engage in. But soon, they became more. His brother and sisters suffered under his hands. His parents were good people, but they were unable to remove the streak of unkindness in him, no matter how much they loved him.

Fuld tilted his head to the side. "You've never been afraid of me, have you?"

"No."

He sighed. "Well, that's a problem. Because you see, I need some of that knowledge in your head. And I don't suppose you'd be willing to help me—out of the goodness of your heart?"

Victoria said nothing.

He sighed again. "I didn't think so. Well, no matter. I still have a little time to convince you. There is one other piece of the puzzle I need before you are of use to me."

Victoria stiffened. No, he hadn't found him. He couldn't have.

Jorgen smiled. "You're wondering if I've found him, aren't you?"

She struggled to keep her face expressionless.

Jorgen laughed with genuine joy. "Do you realize that I know every expression on your face? I know you better than anyone else on the planet. After all, you are my mother."

Victoria lashed out. "I am *not* your mother."

He stood and brushed his hands on his pants. "You are my mother as surely as if you had birthed me from your own loins. You created me. You are responsible for who I am."

"*You* are responsible for the man you have become. Not me."

"Ah—that same old tune. I'm afraid we'll have to agree to disagree on that one." He walked over to her and raised an eyebrow. "But admit it, you *are* happy to see me. After all, we are the only people we can truly be ourselves with, aren't we?"

Victoria looked away, not wanting him to see the truth in her eyes.

He leaned down and kissed her cheek. "It *is* actually good to see you, Mother."

Victoria cringed but held her tongue. *It's good to see you too.* The thought appeared unbidden in her mind. But she couldn't argue the truth of it.

Jorgen turned and walked out of the room, locking the door behind him. Victoria sagged against the wall. She glanced out the window again, thinking of Henry and Laney and imagining them in a battle with Jorgen.

A battle they couldn't possibly win.

Please don't come looking for me.

CHAPTER 18

BALTIMORE, MARYLAND

LANEY WAS GOING over the books from Sebastian Flourent's home in the Red Canyon. She closed the journal in front of her and looked around Dom's office. It was modern, with all the technological touches. *Almost makes you forget that you're locked in a bomb shelter a hundred feet beneath the surface.*

They had decided to keep the books down here as a security precaution. There was simply no safer place on the estate. She'd been slowly making her way through them since yesterday.

It had been a full day since Victoria had gone missing, and they still had nothing. They knew that there were fourteen men who had infiltrated Victoria's home, but they had no IDs, no affiliations. Based on some of their tattoos, Jake thought some of them might be international mercenaries. But so far, Interpol hadn't had any luck identifying them.

"Hi, Laney."

Laney looked up; Max stood uncertainly in the doorway. She opened her arms, and he grinned and ran across the room.

Laney closed her arms around him. "This is what I needed."

She pulled Max up into her lap, keeping her arms around him. "So tell me, what have you been up to?"

"I was practicing my writing with Mom. I can do all my letters now." He grinned broadly.

Laney squeezed him tight. "I'm so proud of you."

Max glanced at the journals on the desk. "Are you reading those again?"

Laney nodded. "Yup. But these are different ones from the ones I was reading last time you were in here. They all look alike."

"Have you found what you're looking for?"

Laney glanced at the old books, her mind traveling over what she had found. She and her uncle had discussed what the references meant, but she wanted to go over them one more time before they shared that information with anyone else. To be honest, she was looking for an alternate explanation, because the one they had come up with seemed so impossible.

"I'm not sure. I think so."

Max nodded. "You'll figure it out."

"I hope so."

Max sat straight and looked at her, his expression serious. "You will. You're the ring bearer. You have to."

Laney searched his face for a moment. "Max," she began slowly, "what do you know about the ring bearer?"

"You're important, Laney. More important than anything." His face clouded for a moment. "Or anyone."

Laney narrowed her eyes. "What do you mean—"

"There you are," Kati Simmons said as she stepped through the doorway. Kati had the same brown hair as Max, the same small stature and high cheekbones. They were practically doubles of each other. The only difference was their eyes: Max's were a bright blue while Kati's were brown.

Max hopped off Laney's lap. "Hi, Mom."

"Lunch is ready." Kati looked at Laney. "There's extra if you want some. Meatloaf."

"Sounds good." Laney glanced back at the desk. "I'll be out in a little bit. I just need to finish up a little more."

"Okay." Kati held out her hand and Max clasped it. The two of them disappeared through the doorway.

Laney turned back to her desk with a sigh. She picked up the journal she'd been reading. *Okay. I finish this one and—*

The patter of little feet had her turning to the door. Max burst through the doorway and threw himself at Laney. He wrapped his arms around her and buried his head in her chest.

"Max, honey, what's wrong?"

"Nothing." But he didn't let go.

"Max?"

He looked up at her. "I love you, Laney."

Touched, she pulled him tight. "I love you too."

"Hey," Maddox said from the doorway. He glanced at Laney and raised his eyebrows. She shook her head, shrugging back at him.

"Max?" Maddox said, stepping in.

Max glanced up at Laney. She stared into his little face, remembering when she'd first met him—the day he was born. His little fingers had reached out and grabbed one of hers and that had been it. She was in love. And that love had only grown over the years.

"You need to remember you're important," Max said.

Laney stared at him, surprised by his intensity. "I will, Max. I promise."

He nodded, releasing her. "Goodbye, Laney."

Laney felt her heart clutch. "You mean see you later."

Max looked at her over his shoulder and then took Maddox's hand.

Laney stared at the empty space. Max hadn't corrected her. But his look had spoken volumes. And what it had said loudest of all was that she didn't understand.

Laney had a sinking feeling he was right.

CHAPTER 19

"Hey, Laney," Maddox said from the doorway.

Laney glanced up in surprise. "Hey. Tell Kati I'll be right out."

Maddox laughed. "Laney, we finished eating an hour ago."

"What?" Laney glanced at the clock above the desk. Almost two hours had passed since Kati had been in here. "Wow. Sorry. I totally lost track of time."

"Gripping reading?"

"Actually, yeah."

She had been going through more of the Council records from Flourent's home. And she'd found more references to a woman who looked incredibly like Victoria. But the journals didn't hint at an actual identification.

But that wasn't the biggest surprise in the books. Jorgen was in there—a lot. In most of the drawings, his eyes had been covered, but in some they weren't—and they were pitch black, just like she remembered.

"Well, Kati, Max, and I are heading back to the cottage. Max said he wants to take a nap," Maddox said.

"Really? He usually fights tooth and nail to *avoid* a nap. Is he getting sick?"

Maddox shrugged. "I'm not sure. He's been having some trouble sleeping at night."

"Why?"

"Nightmares."

Laney felt pressure in her chest. *Damn it.*

Pain crossed Maddox's face as well. Laney knew that Maddox would do whatever he could to protect Max. But he couldn't protect him from his own subconscious. And Max had been through more trauma than any little boy should ever have to bear.

Maddox shook off his concern. "But we'll put him down for a nap and see how he's doing when he gets up. See you later?"

"Yeah. See you later," Laney echoed as Maddox turned to leave.

Goodbye, Laney. Max's words floated through her mind, and a chill ran down her spine. She shrugged it off. Max was fine. He was with Kati and Maddox and on the estate. No one would be able to get to Max, because everyone on the estate would fight to the death to keep him safe.

Laney turned back to the books. *So why do I feel so worried?*

She lined up the journals on the desk. She had about four more to read, but she was pretty sure her uncle had already read those. She thought back on their conversation from this morning.

It wasn't possible, was it? Her mind twisted the information they had learned, pulling it this way and that, looking for an alternative. But nothing came.

Her stomach growled, and she shook her head, clearing it. *Okay. Food—then back to work.*

She stood up and stretched. She'd been at it since yesterday, only taking time off to sleep, and even that had been more just resting her eyelids than actually sleeping.

Guilt at her inability to find Victoria weighed her down. They had yet to find even a single lead. They had traced the SUVs that had been used in Maine, but they had all been stolen just before the abduction. There had been no ransom demands. No sign of either Ralph or Victoria. Jen had even paid the head of the Council another visit. But they all agreed he wasn't behind this; he was too scared of Henry and Jen to do anything this gutsy.

And of course they'd tried to find Jorgen Fuld—but he'd dropped off the grid again. They knew Jorgen had taken Victoria.

Laney frowned. *Which makes no sense.* Jorgen seemed to be very good at hiding himself. So why had he stuck his head out so blatantly to get Victoria? *It's almost like he wants us to find him. Or at least wants us to know he has her.*

Laney shook her head and picked up one of the journals, then headed to Dom's kitchen. She didn't feel hungry, but she knew she needed to keep her strength up. *Lord knows I'll probably be sprinting across a parking lot soon, avoiding gunfire in some town I've never heard of.*

Laney had just finished warming up some meatloaf when the bomb shelter blast door beeped. She pulled the hot plate out of the microwave and had just placed it on the counter when Henry and Jake appeared.

They made their way over to Laney and eyed her plate.

"Any chance there's more of that?" Henry asked.

Laney noted that a little color had returned to Henry's cheeks. She nodded. "I think I could rustle up a couple more plates."

Jake hugged her. "I've got a woman who cooks. I'm a lucky man."

She hugged him back. "You've got a woman who microwaves. Be content."

Henry and Jake got the drinks and silverware together, and Laney warmed up three more servings, just in case anyone else showed up. Sure enough, as soon as they sat down, Dom appeared. And for a few moments, everything was normal. Just a family having a meal together. By unwritten agreement, no one mentioned Victoria.

Finally, the dishes were cleared away and Dom disappeared back into his lab. "Anything new?" Laney asked.

Henry shook his head. "No, not really. Both the Fallen and

THE BELIAL ORIGINS 71

Jorgen have gone to ground. Of course, they both seem to have incredible resources, so I'm not all that surprised."

Jake clapped Henry on the shoulder. "We'll find her."

Henry nodded, looking around. "Where's Patrick?"

"Right here." Laney's uncle appeared from the hallway that led to the bedrooms. Patrick had been exhausting himself trying to find something on Victoria. It was only a few hours ago that Laney had finally forced him to go take a nap. And even with the short rest, his already pale complexion looked unusually colorless, and his blue eyes looked exhausted. Laney's uncle and Victoria had formed a bond over the last few months. And Laney knew that her disappearance was affecting him as much as it was the rest of them.

Henry stood up, offering Patrick his chair.

Patrick waved him back. "I've been sitting all morning. It feels good to stretch my legs."

Laney stood and gave him a hug. "Are you hungry?"

"No. I'm fine." He glanced at Henry and Jake, who were busy clearing the table. He spoke quietly, his eyes on Laney. "Did you find anything else?"

Laney shook her head, speaking just as quietly. "Nothing different."

Patrick nodded, his shoulders drooping. "I was hoping we were wrong."

"Me too."

Laney re-took her seat and looked up at her uncle. "Henry and Jake were just asking about our progress on the books."

Laney knew her uncle hated to give out incomplete information. He liked to find all the necessary information, synthesize it, and only then return a verdict. But right now, they needed to take some leaps if they were going to find Victoria.

Patrick nodded. "It's interesting."

Henry and Jake looked at him expectantly.

Laney bit back her smile, knowing her uncle was lost in his own thoughts. "Uncle Patrick?"

They'd spoken this morning in detail about their conclusions, but Laney had wanted more time. Now that time was up—and nothing new had come to light.

Patrick started. "Oh, sorry. Well, like I said, it's interesting. The books are from the Council, as you know. It's their record of their different searches throughout time for the relics and riches of Atlantis. And what we've found is that Victoria—or at least someone who *looks* like Victoria—is seen throughout the books. *All* the books."

Henry frowned. "How's that possible?"

Patrick shook his head. "I don't know. And they don't seem to either. She appears, and they note that she's involved with people associated with the relics. But all they seem to know about her is her name."

"And let me guess: different names?" Jake asked.

Laney nodded. "She appears in different times and even at different ages, but there's no denying it's her."

Jake frowned. "What do you mean different ages? Like different eras?"

"No, I mean her own age." Patrick gave Laney an encouraging nod. She took a breath. This was the part of the reveal she had been dreading. "The youngest we've seen her in the books is around the age of fourteen. The oldest, probably in her eighties."

Henry started beside her. "Her eighties?"

Laney's look showed that she shared Henry's confusion. "I know—I don't understand it either."

"Could it be someone who just looks like her?" Henry asked.

Patrick shrugged, but his tone conveyed his doubt. "I suppose, but the similarity is too striking. And again and again, throughout history, always involved with these relics? No. It's her."

"The earliest record in any of the books is from the year 1118," Laney said. "Victoria, or her doppelganger, is first mentioned in 1234. Then again in 1456 and 1619, and several dates after that."

"How many mentions of her have you found?" Henry asked.

Laney swallowed. "Since 1118, she's appeared in the book at least eight times."

Everyone was silent for moment while they digested that. Finally Jake spoke. "So what does that mean?"

Laney glanced over at Patrick again. He nodded. They'd debated this point time and time again, but had always circled back to the same conclusion. Laney took a deep breath. "It means she's lived at least eight lives. That we know of."

CHAPTER 20

Henry and Jake both looked shocked. And Laney couldn't blame them. She had probably looked the same way the first time she'd seen the double of Victoria in the books. But unlike Henry and Jake, she'd now had a little time to get used to the idea.

"So what are you saying? She's immortal?" Jake asked.

Patrick shook his head. "No. Like I said, in the journals she's different ages. But it does appear as if she's lived quite a few lives."

"From what we can tell," Laney said, "she lives a full life and then comes back in the next one looking exactly the same. Usually in a different country."

"How is that possible?" Henry asked.

Jake raised his eyebrows. "Really? You have a sister who's a half angel, who can control the Fallen, animals, and the weather. You're a half angel as well. Your father was one of the all-time most powerful angels. You, Laney, and I are part of some triad that appears when the Fallen are making a play for global domination, and yet the idea that your mother has lived a few times is stretching believability?"

A smile flashed briefly across Henry's face. "Okay, when you put it that way. My mother is some type of immortal being who has lived thousands of lifetimes. No problem."

Laney smiled too, but the smile disappeared just as quickly as it had from Henry's. They had wondered about Victoria for a long time, and the truth was, they were still just guessing. But this explanation made a certain amount of sense. Victoria knew too much about the Fallen. And when she spoke of the past, she always sounded like she had been an eyewitness.

But nowhere in the books did anyone say *what* she was—angel, human, alien. The journal writers appeared as stumped as they were.

"There's something else," Patrick said.

"What?" Jake asked.

"There was one other person who kept appearing in the books multiple times over the centuries," Laney said softly.

"You mean like Mom? Different ages, different time periods?" Henry asked.

Patrick shook his head. "No. This man—he's always the same age."

"Who is he?" Jake asked.

"We know him as Jorgen Fuld," Laney said.

Jake's and Henry's eyes grew wide.

"Wait, did you say the same age?" Jake asked.

"Yes." Laney glanced back at her uncle, who nodded at her. She turned to Henry and Jake. "Did you two notice when Jorgen had his glasses knocked off at the airfield?"

"I saw it happen. Why?" Henry asked.

"Did you notice his eyes?" Laney asked.

Jake shook his head. "Wasn't really a priority at the moment."

"I know. It's just—" Laney hesitated. "I saw them. And they were pitch black."

Henry frowned. "So he had dark eyes. I don't get the significance."

Laney pictured Fuld's eyes again. She was confident in what

she had seen. "No. Not dark. There was absolutely no white in them. None at all."

"It must have been a trick of the light," Jake said.

"That's what I thought at first."

Laney picked up the journal she had brought in with her and turned to the page she had marked. She turned it around so Henry and Jake could see. The man in the picture was undeniably Fuld. Everything was the same, right down to the haircut. The only difference was the style of clothes.

And in the drawing, his eyes were pure black.

Henry looked at Laney. "Are all the pictures like this?"

Patrick nodded slowly. "Usually his eyes are covered. But when they're not, this is how they're depicted. Without fail."

"Is there any medical condition that can account for that? Some genetic mutation?" Henry asked.

Laney shook her head. "Not that I could find. The only way to get completely black eyes, including the sclera, is through black contacts."

"And I'm guessing we don't think Jorgen was wearing contacts," Jake said.

"I can't see him going through the pageantry of black lenses, especially seeing as he wears those sunglasses all the time," Laney said. "I think his eyes are real."

"In the books, he's sometimes referred to as the Shepherd," Patrick said. "The Shepherd" was the name he went by when he instructed Nathaniel Grayston to kidnap potential nephilim and Fallen a few months ago.

"How far back do the references go?" Jake asked.

"Same as Victoria. Back to the first journal we have—twelfth century."

"So is he immortal?" Jake asked, disbelief lacing his words.

Laney shrugged. "Either he's immortal, or he has a really, *really* strong genetic line."

"Well, seeing as everyone at the airport was trying to avoid shooting him, I'm not surprised he's lived this long," Jake said.

Patrick went still. "What did you say?"

Jake looked at Patrick. "At the airport, no one shot at him. Bullets were flying all over the place, but it seemed like everyone was intentionally trying to avoid hitting him."

"Are you sure?" Patrick asked.

Henry and Jake exchanged a look before Henry spoke. "Actually, when Jake and I went back over the footage, we realized one shooter—one of Jorgen's own men—did get him, although apparently it was accidental. And then that shooter was shot."

"How many times was the shooter hit?" Patrick asked, his eyes intent.

"Seven times," Jake said slowly. "But actually he wasn't shot by bullets."

"What?" Three sets of eyes turned to Jake.

Jake put up his hands. "It was strange. I asked the M.E. to check again, which is why I didn't tell you guys. When the M.E. opened him up, there were no bullets—just wounds. And there was no path for the bullets to have followed. The M.E. said it was like the wounds just appeared. But the M.E. must have made a mistake."

During Jake's speech, Laney had kept her eyes on her uncle. With each word Jake spoke, Patrick had gotten paler and paler. "Uncle Patrick?"

"I'm sure I'm wrong," he began.

Everyone went still. Those words were always followed by some insight that the rest of them had missed. And Patrick was always right on target.

"Who is he, Uncle Patrick?" Laney asked quietly.

Patrick swallowed. "I can't be sure."

"Uncle Patrick," she said, a warning in her tone. She knew he would want to check and re-check before saying anything, but with Victoria in danger, they didn't have the time for that.

Patrick pulled out a chair and all but fell into it. He looked exhausted, but his eyes were bright. "The man that shot Jorgen was shot himself seven times—sevenfold the injury he created.

And his eyes are black as night, something that would stop anyone in their tracks."

Recognition tickled the back of Laney's mind. Sevenfold. She'd heard that before. She gasped as the reference hit her. Her gaze flew to her uncle.

He nodded at her. "I think Jorgen Fuld is Cain."

CHAPTER 21

LITTLE ROCK, ARKANSAS

VICTORIA PACED THE ROOM. What was going on? Jorgen hadn't been to visit her since that first time. Men had dropped off food, but none of them would speak to her. She had no TV, and it was made clear that she was not allowed out of her room.

Victoria stopped, her hands on her hips. The lack of information was driving her crazy. She looked at the door. *I wonder how far they're allowed to go to keep me here.*

She was pretty sure Jorgen had put a *do not kill* order out. And she still had a few tricks up her sleeve that might make this interesting.

Images of Laney and Henry flashed through her mind. There was no doubt they were trying to find her now. She shuddered, imagining them going up against Jorgen without knowing who he was. They'd be killed.

She couldn't let that happen.

I think it's time to find out exactly what orders Jorgen has given his men.

But just as Victoria strode across the room, the door opened. She came to an abrupt stop.

Jorgen stepped inside. "Let me guess. You've decided you'd rather chance physical injury to yourself rather than have anyone, particularly your two children, suffer harm in trying to rescue you."

Victoria glared but stayed silent.

Jorgen chuckled. "I keep telling you, Mother, I know you better than anyone."

"And I keep telling you, I am *not* your Mother."

Jorgen closed the door behind him. "We will still have to agree to disagree on that one. So, how are you enjoying your stay?"

"I'm not."

Jorgen glanced around. "Hmm. I'll have the men drop in some books. Give you something to do to pass the time. I know how you hate to be bored."

"Why are you here?"

Jorgen raised an eyebrow. "Maybe I just wanted to spend some time with you."

Victoria crossed her arms over her chest and stared at him.

Jorgen sighed. "Very well. I have to take a little trip."

"Where are you going?"

"Don't concern yourself. I'll be back soon." He laughed. "Of course, you're not really worried about my welfare, are you?"

"Not particularly."

Jorgen's face clouded. "You could show me a little respect."

"I could," she agreed with a shrug. "But I'm not going to."

He narrowed his eyes. "You truly think the punishment fits the crime? You really think it's fair that I've spent my long life paying for an action I committed eons ago?"

She looked him straight in the eye. "Why not? After all, I'm still paying for an action I committed eons ago as well."

"But your punishment was your own choice, wasn't it? And besides, it's not exactly the same as mine, now is it? In fact, I think a case could be made that *you* are responsible for many more deaths than I am. Why, some could say you're responsible for *all* deaths."

Victoria stared at the man she had known longer than any other. She shook her head. "We've had this debate more times than I can count. And we've never reached a resolution."

"And I suppose we never will," Jorgen said a little wistfully. "I know you think I'm joking or playing with words, but I'm not. You and I have known each other longer than anyone; you *are* my family."

Victoria looked at the man she had known as a boy; the man she had seen lifetime after lifetime. She thought of countering his statement, but in her heart, she knew what he meant. "I know."

Surprise flashed across Jorgen's face, and for just a moment, Victoria saw him vulnerable. But then his defenses slammed back into place. Jorgen took a step back. "Well, anyway, it's time for me to go."

"Where are you going?"

"To remedy a problem. You and I are similar, but we are not the same. I am unique, and I intend to stay that way."

CHAPTER 22

HE'S CAIN. The words reverberated around Laney's mind. *No. No way.*

"Cain, from Cain and Abel? That's not possible, right?" Jake looked around. No one answered him.

Henry sat down across from Patrick. "Maybe you could explain that?"

Patrick folded his hands in front of him. "In the Bible, Cain and Abel were the sons of Adam and Eve, as I'm sure you all know. Cain was the firstborn, but Abel was the favored son. And Cain was jealous. One day, they both brought sacrifices to God. For Abel, it was his prized cattle. For Cain, it was part of what he had grown from the ground. Apparently God was pleased with Abel's offering and not pleased with Cain's. A short time later, Cain killed Abel."

"Over jealousy?" Henry asked.

"Well, that's the Genesis and Quran accounts," Patrick said. "There are folklore stories that suggest the fight was actually over who each brother was to marry. Apparently, Cain wanted to marry his twin. But she was promised to Abel. Cain, however, thought his twin was the more beautiful of the two sisters. Their father, Adam, sent them to provide an offering to God to let God deter-mine how to resolve the issue. Abel brought his best offering and Cain brought his worst. God of course sided with Abel, and then Cain killed Abel."

"And then Cain was punished?" Jake asked.

"He was banished. Doomed to walk the world for eternity, but never to be within God's sight," Laney said.

"All for killing his brother?" Jake asked.

"Well, you have to understand, Cain was the first murderer. I suppose he was the one to make an example of," Patrick said.

"Jorgen calls himself the Shepherd," Henry said softly.

Laney nodded. "I suppose he's taking his brother's identity."

"You think he felt what? Remorse?" Jake asked.

Patrick shrugged. "It's possible. In one story, Cain was so distraught over what he had done, he walked around carrying his brother's body until he no longer could."

Laney shivered at the image Patrick's words conjured up.

"But that still doesn't explain why you think Jorgen is Cain," Henry said.

Laney pictured Jorgen's eyes. It hadn't been a trick of the light. She looked at her uncle. "His eyes."

Patrick nodded. "When God doled out Cain's punishment, Cain beseeched Him to reconsider. Cain said everyone who saw him would try to kill him. As a result, God placed a mark on him that would warn everyone to keep their distance. God also ensured that anyone who touched Cain would receive the same damage in return, sevenfold."

"You think his eyes are the mark," Henry said.

"The Bible never described what the mark looked like," Patrick said. "Scholars have struggled to figure out what it could be. But the problem with all the suggestions is that they tend to be culturally specific. A tattoo, for instance, could have one meaning in one culture and a completely different meaning in another. A scar or a disfigurement could warn people away in most cultures, but in some cultures it would actually encourage people to attack him."

Laney once again pictured those black eyes. There was no man who saw those eyes who would not at least hesitate. "The mark had to be something that would stop even the most hardened man in his tracks."

They all fell silent. Finally Jake broke the silence. "Okay. But why make him immortal? How is that a punishment?"

Patrick frowned. "I'm not sure. According to the Bible, Cain was 'banished from God's sight.' Perhaps that meant he could never leave this earth—he had to be trapped here forever."

Laney stared at her uncle and tried not to shudder. Perhaps she had become desensitized to violence because of how much she had seen, both personally and on the news, but having to pay for one's crime for *eternity*... it seemed awfully severe.

"So we can't hurt him?" Jake asked.

Patrick shook his head. "Not without receiving the same injury back sevenfold."

Laney shook her head. How were they going to combat an enemy they couldn't fight? That they couldn't even touch?

She looked over at Henry. His brow was furrowed, and he'd been awfully quiet for the last few minutes. "Henry?"

"You don't think..." Henry broke off, his face troubled.

"What?" Laney asked, her concern beginning to rise.

Henry met her gaze. "If Jorgen is Cain, do you think there's any chance that Mom is... Eve?"

CHAPTER 23

LANEY'S HEAD felt like it was going to spin off her shoulders. Eve? Jorgen as Cain she could almost buy—even if the idea was insane. But this...

Jake turned to Patrick. "Was Eve immortal?"

Patrick shook his head. "No, not according to the Bible. But I'll check some other sources." He frowned.

"What is it?"

"Nothing. I—" Patrick shook his head. "Nothing. I'll see if maybe I've—"

Dom ran in, his words coming out in pants. "You have to see this." He turned on the TV in the corner. A breaking news story was splashed across the screen.

"...dible situation in the suburbs of Little Rock. A neighbor caught most of the shootout on their cell phone. We're about to play the uninterrupted video. But be warned, the tape is very graphic."

Everyone at the table went silent, their attention focused on the screen. A feeling of dread settled over Laney. Her uncle stepped next to her and took her hand.

On screen, a teenager walked around a shiny red car. Off screen a voice said, "Yeah, that's my baby."

Nice," the kid by the car said. Then his head jerked up. What's that?"

"What? I don't hear anything."

"Shush, listen." A faint popping noise could be heard. "Is that gunfire?"

A window blew out of a house two houses down and across the street. The image wobbled. "Holy shit!"

The camera operator ran closer and took cover behind the car as two men with guns ran out the door of the house. More gunshots could be heard; it appeared that someone inside the house was firing at them. Then three more men appeared at the door. No—Laney squinted. Not just three men. Someone was caught in between the three.

Laney felt her jaw fall open when she saw the splash of white hair. *Victoria.* Two of the men turned and threw something inside the house, then they forced Victoria quickly away from the building. Seconds later, two explosions blew out every window in the house.

"Mom," Henry whispered.

The men hustled Victoria into a waiting van and tore off down the street, away from the camera. A few seconds passed with no movement. Then the video stopped.

The screen shifted back to the newscasters. "The men in the van have yet to be identified. If anyone has any—"

Jake stood up. "I'll see what I can find out." He walked away, already dialing someone on his phone.

Laney just sat staring at the now-muted screen. What had just happened?

"I've got it," Dom called.

Laney shook off her shock and walked over to Dom, who was leaning over a laptop. "Got what?"

"The cell phone recording. I've got it as clean as I can make it. It's actually not a bad picture for a cell phone. The quality has really been increasing ever since—"

"Dom," Henry said, his frustration evident.

Dom put up a hand. "Right, sorry, sorry."

Laney watched the gun battle play out again. "Close in on the woman with the white hair."

Dom did, and a second later, they had a close-up of Victoria.

Laney's breath hitched. Patrick grabbed her hand. "It'll be okay, honey."

Henry pointed to one of the men who had left the house before Victoria. "Dom, zoom in on this guy."

Dom shifted the focus of the shot, and Laney felt her world tilt. "What the hell?"

They had a perfect close-up of Gerard Thompson.

CHAPTER 24

LITTLE ROCK, ARKANSAS

Jorgen watched the last police van leave. The neighborhood was quiet. He nodded to the driver. "Time to go."

The driver pulled smoothly into the street. Jorgen looked at the destruction that had been caused to the little house. A giant gaping hole, burnt at the edges, dominated the first floor. Bullet holes dotted the rest of the home. The front door had been blow off.

Jorgen smiled.

His driver continued maneuvering through the streets until he pulled onto the 440. A few minutes later, they were at the private airfield not far from the Bill and Hillary Clinton National Airport.

Jorgen exited the car before his chauffeur had a chance to open the door. His head of security—a former military man with a barrel chest, white hair, and handlebar mustache—jogged over and came to an abrupt stop in front of him. Jorgen had hired legions of men for jobs over the years. But Sean Tidwell had managed to survive every purge—like the one at the house.

"Report?" Jorgen asked.

"All went as planned, sir. The Fallen captured Victoria and took her with them."

Jorgen smiled. "Excellent. The cleanup?"

"Complete, sir. Most of the men at the house were taken care of by the Fallen. There were three left alive, but they've been handled."

"Good. Let's move on to stage two."

Tidwell gave Jorgen a sharp nod and headed for the hangar. Jorgen dismissed the man from his thoughts. Tidwell was one of thousands of men he'd known throughout his life. Each was no different than the next.

Jorgen climbed the stairs to the plane. He nodded at the stewardess waiting for him. "A gin and tonic."

"Yes, sir." She scurried into the back to fill his drink order. Jorgen shrugged out of his overcoat and hung it over one of the leather chairs. He sat in another chair, noting that the file he'd requested had been placed on his desk.

The stewardess returned with his drink and placed it next to the folder. "Is there anything else you need, sir?"

"Nothing. I'll ring if I need you."

She nodded and disappeared once again to the back, taking his jacket with her.

Jorgen pulled the file over to him and flipped it open. He pulled out the four-by-six picture. Delaney McPhearson's red hair blew back past her shoulders. Her eyes were determined—focused on something in front of her.

He smiled. *She is magnificent*, he admitted grudgingly. He slid the photo back into the file and took a sip of his drink. *But if she gets in my way, she'll die just like all the rest.*

CHAPTER 25

BALTIMORE, MARYLAND

LANEY WALKED along the path from her cottage to the main building. They had spent all last night trying to get more details on the house in Arkansas. It was very late when she and Jake finally left Dom's bunker and crashed back at their cottage. But Laney's sleep had been plagued by nightmares.

When Laney had awoken, Jake had already gone to Henry's office to try and track down the Fallen's movements. Laney had lain in their bed, staring at the ceiling, questions looping through her mind, over and over again. Gerard Thompson had—what? "Rescued" Victoria from Jorgen? Why? Why would they take Victoria? What did they want from her? Was Victoria on the Fallen's side—or theirs?

Laney looked back toward Sharecropper Lane. She'd stopped in at Kati's last night, but Max was already asleep.

His mood the other day still bothered her. It was as if he had been trying to tell her something. They all knew he was psychic, and Max saying goodbye had made her nervous.

Maybe she was just reading too much into it.

The bushes near Laney rattled, and her heart raced. Her gaze whipped back to the trees as Cleo emerged.

Laney let out a breath and smiled. "There you are. I was beginning to wonder."

Cleo slunk closer, and Laney lowered her head to the big cat's.

Laney remembered the deferential treatment that Cleo had always demonstrated around Victoria. She pulled her head back and looked into Cleo's eyes. "You know who she is, don't you?"

Yes.

Laney went still. Her communication with Cleo was an offshoot of the ring. But sometimes the interpretation could be a little off. It wasn't really words that Laney heard—it was more of a feeling. Although in her own mind she translated the feelings into words.

"Who is she?" Laney whispered.

Mother.

Laney watched Cleo. "You mean *my* mother?"

Mother all.

Cleo gave Laney a lick, then walked back into the bush, her tail swishing behind her.

Laney stood still, staring after her. *Mother all?*

"Eve?" she whispered.

CHAPTER 26

LANEY SPENT the rest of the morning looking for something, anything that would link the Fallen to a physical location. She uncovered a few possibilities, but those had quickly been checked and crossed off the list.

So she was hopeful when Agent Matthew Clark of the SIA called. Matt had sent them his list of all known Fallen and their locations earlier. He'd even dispatched his own agents to check out every site they could manage.

"Any luck?" Laney asked.

Exasperation tinged Matt's words. "No. It's like they all decided to close up shop."

Laney closed her eyes and leaned back heavily in her chair. *Damn it.*

"But there is some other news," Matt said.

His tone was not uplifting. Laney opened her eyes, steeling herself. "Okay. Tell me."

"There's been an increase in Fallen incidents around the world."

"What do you mean?"

"Well, you know the SIA tracks and records any events that may involve the Fallen?"

"Yes." An offshoot of the Department of Defense, the SIA was the government agency in charge of monitoring the activities of the Fallen and nephilim around the world. Very few people knew of the agency's existence, however; and few of those that knew it existed knew what it actually did. "So what's changed?"

Matt's frustration came through loud and clear. "The frequency. There are more of them. We're running a little thin trying to investigate them all."

"What does that mean?"

"I don't know. But I'm willing to bet it bodes something ominous. And that's not the worst." He paused just long enough for Laney's stomach to drop a little. "Some circles in the government are beginning to take notice. And there's been talk."

Dread washed over Laney. The last thing they needed was the government getting involved in all this. "What kind of 'talk'?"

"Talk about concerns for the public at large."

Laney closed her eyes. "Oh, that can't be good."

All she could picture were the other times that governments had labeled groups of people as troublemakers—and those times had usually involved some type of internment camps. Throughout history, governmental methods of dealing with troublesome populations had not been morally uplifting.

In addition, government interest was liable to get them all get dragged into congressional hearings to discuss what they did. Besides the complete waste of time that would be, it would shove the world of the Fallen into the spotlight. And that was a horrible idea. Part of the reason that they had been able to keep this quiet was because the Fallen also seemed to want to keep their existence under the radar.

If that changes? She shivered. *All hell will literally break loose.*

"Is anyone making any moves to do something, or is it just talk?" Laney asked.

"Right now, it's just talk. But I'm monitoring it. I'll let you know if it gets more serious."

Laney slunk down lower in her seat. "Oh good, more to worry about."

The two fell into silence. Laney's mind was filled with worries for Victoria. It occurred to her that Victoria had probably seen ugly government reactions to troubled populations live and in person in at least one of her past lives.

"Matt," Laney began slowly, "do you know who Victoria is?"

Matt didn't respond right away. "No. We had already suspected that she may have lived many lives, but we've never been able to pin down a firm identity."

"But you have some theories."

Matt hesitated again, then sighed. "Laney, they're just guesses —probably no better than your own guesses."

"Our running favorite right now is that she's Eve."

"That's one of our guesses as well."

Laney closed her eyes. "Do you think she's part of the other triad?"

Laney, Jake, and Henry made up one triad, but they knew there was another one. They just weren't sure who exactly was in it, except for Samyaza.

Matt didn't speak for a moment. "You know, you could come down here and ask some of the ones we're holding where the Fallen might have taken Victoria."

Laney knew he was right. As the ring bearer, she had the ability to compel the Fallen to do her bidding. But she had been resistant to the idea. She didn't like the feeling of breaking someone's will. It didn't feel right. *But desperate circumstances…*

"If I don't learn anything new, I may have to."

Clark went silent for a moment. "I know you don't enjoy that particular ability. But it *could* help you find her."

"I know, I know." Laney paused. "Could you figure out who amongst your guests might have the most relevant information? If I'm coming down there, I don't want to waste any time."

"I'll have them ready. Just let me know."

"Will do."

"And let me know if you find anything. The SIA will help in any way possible."

"Thanks, Matt. Take care."

"You too, Laney."

Laney disconnected the call and placed her phone on the coffee table. She curled her feet under her and gazed out the windows. Who was Victoria? Was she part of the other triad? Laney knew Samyaza was one member, and it was a safe bet that Jorgen was another. That left only one other member. And if the other triad was consistent with her own, then that third member was a human.

But Victoria wasn't exactly a normal human. Did that discount her from the triad? Or just guarantee her membership?

Laney pulled her knees to her chest and rested her head on them. *She'll be okay. She's lived lifetime after lifetime. She can take care of herself.*

But her mind wouldn't shut down. Because if Victoria had lived lifetime after lifetime, going from young to old, there was only one thing they could be sure Victoria had done in each of those lifetimes.

She had died.

CHAPTER 27

LANEY STAYED in the office for another thirty minutes, after getting off the phone with Matt trying to figure out a new angle. But she couldn't seem to focus. She needed a break.

Maybe I'll go see if Patrick and Dom have discovered anything. She was heading for the doors when they opened.

Jake walked in, and for a moment, hope flared in Laney.

But he shook his head, and the hope died again. "Nothing. We're still looking."

Weariness fell over Laney and she dropped back onto the couch. "How can she have just disappeared without a trace? I mean, that's not possible, right?"

Jake ran his hands through his hair. "I don't know what to tell you. We've checked every form of transport out of the Little Rock area. Danny's grabbed every video and satellite feed, and we still can't find a trace."

Laney nodded. "If it's Samyaza behind this, she'll be good at hiding her footsteps."

"I know." He reached down to pull Laney up. "Come on. Let's get some fresh air. I think we both need it."

Laney let herself be led outside. They walked down the path

toward Sharecropper Lane, crossed it, and headed toward the outer fence. Cleo loped over and joined them.

Laney ran her hand over Cleo's back. "Hey, girl."

Together the three of them walked to the field that lay behind the cottages. Jake stopped. Laney knew why they were there. *Practice time.* She took the ring from the chain around her neck and put it on her finger.

"Ready?" Jake asked.

Laney nodded. "What will it be today?"

Jake rubbed his chin. "I think we should play with hail."

"Hail? Seriously?"

He nodded. "It could come in handy if you can make them large enough."

Laney let out a breath and turned to Cleo. "Stay out of the field."

Cleo took a step back and sat. Laney glanced at the sky. *Right. Hail.* She focused, feeling the energy fill her. Within moments, hail began to fall. It bounced along the entire length of the field.

Jake stepped up behind her, leaning down to whisper in her ear. "Concentrate. Make the focus smaller."

"Okay." Laney made the cloud above them shrink until it was only a few feet wide. Hail began to pile up on the ground directly underneath it.

"Now try to make the hailstones bigger," Jake urged.

Laney could do no more than nod—her concentration was entirely on the cloud. In her mind's eye, she pictured hail the size of softballs. Soon they were slamming into the ground and rolling along the grass.

Laney grinned and cut the storm off. She turned back to Jake.

He smiled at her. "Good. How do you feel?"

"Good. I'm not lightheaded. It's getting easier."

"I think it's probably like any other muscle. The more you use it, the stronger it becomes."

Laney and Jake had been focused on finding Victoria, but they had still made sure to practice twice a day ever since the incident at the airport. The last thing Laney wanted to worry about was that her powers would scare the people she was with.

"I think you're right," Laney said.

Cleo walked up and nudged Laney. Laney reached down to pet her. "What do you think?"

Good. Run.

Laney nodded. "All right." Cleo often liked to roam the estate by herself, but she enjoyed it more when Laney and Jake ran with her. Laney raised an eyebrow at Jake. "Race you to the north fence?"

"You got it," Jake said, and took off running.

"Cheater!" Laney called, running after him with a laugh. Cleo loped along beside her before sprinting ahead.

"Go get him, Cleo," Laney cheered, sprinting after them. And for just a small moment, she let herself focus on the here and now —and not on everything that was swirling around them.

CHAPTER 28

GERARD DROVE ALONG WINDING ROADS. It was pretty out here. He could see why Chandler had chosen this spot for his headquarters.

He pulled to the side of the road, then took out his phone and dialed, feeling a tingle of pride.

Elisabeta answered quickly. "Are you there?"

"Yes."

Gerard could hear the smile through the phone. "Excellent. You have done well, Gerard."

Gerard stilled. "Thank you."

"How long?" she asked.

Gerard glanced at his watch. "Ten minutes."

"Good. And she is safe?"

Gerard nodded. "I have four men on her. We'll meet up with them when we're finished here. And then I'll bring them both to you."

"Good."

The silence stretched out, and Gerard wasn't sure if he was supposed to hang up, say something, or just wait. He decided on the cautious route.

Finally, Elisabeta spoke. "Gerard, did we lose any men in Arkansas?"

"No. Not a one."

"Was Jorgen there?"

Doubt began to creep into Gerard's mind. Elisabeta rarely wanted the details of his missions. She just wanted to know that he had succeeded. "Um, no. He wasn't. We timed it perfectly."

"He left her alone?" Incredulity laced Elisabeta's words.

"Not alone. There were a dozen men there at least."

Elisabeta was silent.

"Is something wrong?"

"No. I'm just surprised. But maybe he's getting sloppy after all these years."

Gerard tried not to bristle at the insult.

"Well, call me when you're done."

"Yes, Elisabeta," Gerard said, but she had already disconnected the call.

He put his phone back in his pocket and leaned against the steering wheel. What had that been all about?

His phone beeped. A text.

We're in position.

Gerard put the car in drive and pulled back onto the street. Elisabeta's words were irrelevant. She just liked to keep them all uncertain—a rather annoying trait of hers. And an effective one.

That's all it is. She doesn't want me feeling too much pride in what I've accomplished. He nodded and straightened his back. *But after my next success, my accomplishment will be too great for her to deny.*

CHAPTER 29

LANEY SPRINTED along Sharecropper Lane behind Jake and Cleo, then burst out into the small field that led to the fence. Ahead of her, Cleo loped along easily next to Jake. Obviously the panther was just teasing him; she could outrun him any time she wanted.

And a dozen feet shy of the fence, she did just that. Cleo darted forward, stopped short of the fence, and then, just before Jake reached it, tapped it with her paw.

Laney laughed.

Jake grumbled good-naturedly. "No fair. You're running on four legs."

Cleo rubbed her head against his chest with a purr.

Jake scratched behind her ears. "Fine, fine. You win." He glanced up as Laney reached them. "Hey, did you stop for coffee?"

Laney whacked him on the shoulder. "You're a sore winner."

Jake draped his arm around her, and they headed back to Sharecropper Lane. "Well, you might be the ring bearer, but it's nice to know I can still beat you in a foot race."

Next to Laney, Cleo suddenly went still. Then she stepped behind Laney and began to push her forward, her fur standing on end.

Laney glanced back at her. "Cleo?"

Danger.

Laney grabbed Jake's hand. "Run!"

The three of them sprinted toward Sharecropper Lane. They were two hundred yards from the fence when it exploded.

CHAPTER 30

LANEY AND JAKE hit the ground and rolled. Laney lay still for a moment, taking stock to make sure everything was where it was supposed to be. Then with a groan, she sat up to a sitting position, her ears ringing.

Cleo walked over to Laney and nudged her back.

Laney patted her paw. *I'm okay.*

Jake stumbled to his knees and pulled out his phone.

Laney stared back at the fence. A twenty-foot-wide hole gaped right in the middle of it, and heavily armed men were now pouring through.

Pinpricks of electricity danced over her. *Fallen.* They must have held back so as not to warn her.

Laney reached for her waist and cursed. She glanced at Jake. He was unarmed as well. *Damn it.*

Bits of brick and metal bars from the fence were strewn around them, the result of the massive explosion. *Those will do.*

Cleo attempted to run for the intruders. "No! You stay with me!" Laney commanded, not willing to let Cleo get shot.

She called on the wind. Using its power, she lifted metal bars like javelins and tossed them at the men. The first three men to come through the hole in the fence were impaled. The rest quickly ducked back behind the fence. Laney rained chunks of brick and shards of metal on them from above.

From the corner of her eye she saw the first of the security details arrive. They took cover behind their Jeeps and opened fire on the intruders.

Laney continued her onslaught. But the men were no longer trying to enter the estate. They seemed content to just return gunfire. She narrowed her eyes. The Fallen could easily get through. What were they waiting for?

Laney went still; the rocks she had just pulled into the air slammed back into the ground.

Jake turned to head for the security Jeeps, but she grabbed his arm. "Wait."

"What?" He stared down at her.

"There are Fallen with them. But they're not coming into the estate. Why aren't they coming into the estate?"

Jake watched the exchange of gunfire with a frown. "That's not right."

"Why blow up the fence? Why not ram the front gate? Or better yet, just leap over it?"

"You're right. This is… too obvious," Jake said.

Flashes from the Book of Enoch rattled through Laney's mind. Samyaza, the leader of men, had gotten two hundred of his brethren to fall with him. He was the master of deceit and obfuscation. *So why this bold an attack?*

Jake grabbed his radio from his belt. "Jake for Kevin."

"Kevin here."

"Have there been any other breaches or inconsistencies in security in the last few days?"

Kevin didn't even question the odd request or the timing of it. "Just one—a section of the southeast corner kept giving out false readings. We actually shut it down. A repair crew is supposed to be out there in another half hour."

Laney met Jake's eyes. *The opposite side of the estate from the blast.*

Laney didn't wait for Jake. She ran for one of the security Jeeps that was just pulling up.

An officer stepped out. "Laney?"

"I need your Jeep."

He held open the door. "Yes ma'am. Keys are in it."

As Laney hopped in, she thought there was something to be said for hiring all former military. They didn't waste time on useless questions.

Jake hopped into the passenger seat, still on the phone. "Kevin, send whatever security details you can scrounge up to the east fence. *Now.*"

"Damn it." Laney slammed down on the accelerator. The back of the Jeep fishtailed as she left the paved road and hit the grass. Cleo loped along behind them.

Come on. Come on. Laney didn't have any idea what she would find on the other side of the estate. But she knew she needed to get there.

They burst out of the trees just in time to see a single figure leap over the fence. A tingle ran through Laney. "Fallen," she said through gritted teeth.

A smaller figure, on the near side of the fence, was walking across the field toward the Fallen.

Laney craned to see who it was.

"It can't be," Jake mumbled.

"Max?" Laney whispered.

Max glanced over his shoulder and saw the security car barreling toward him. He started to run toward the Fallen.

Laney couldn't believe what she was seeing. She slammed on the brakes and vaulted from the car. "Max!" She sprinted after him.

Max ran for the Fallen. The Fallen sprinted toward him in a blur, pausing only long enough to pick him up. But that pause was long enough for Laney to get a good look at the Fallen. *Gerard.*

And he was wearing headphones—noise-canceling, no doubt.

"Stop!" Laney yelled.

Gerard just smiled at her and then sprinted back for the fence. In less than two seconds, he was gone.

And so was Max.

Laney fell to her knees.

"What just happened?"

CHAPTER 31

LANEY KNELT IN THE GRASS, staring at the spot where Gerard had disappeared with Max. Vaguely she heard Jake calling for Kevin to pull up the cameras in the area and send patrols out after them. But Laney knew they wouldn't catch Gerard. This section of the fence was as far from the entrance as you could get.

Cleo walked up to Laney and sat down beside her.

Laney pictured Max running across the field—running away from her. She turned to Cleo. "Why did he do that?"

Cleo didn't have an answer for her.

Laney got to her feet and made her way back to Jake. Jake closed his phone and walked with her to the Jeep.

"He went with him willingly," Laney said. "You saw that, right?"

Jake opened the car door. "Yeah. I saw it."

Kevin's voice came over the radio. "Jake?"

"Go ahead."

"The intruders just took off. No one got in."

That's because the infiltration was much more subtle, Laney thought, tuning out the rest of the conversation. Gerard had taken Max. Which meant Samyaza had Max.

But why? Why did they want a five-year-old? And why had Max gone with them willingly? Maddox never would have—

Laney's back straightened. *Oh my God.* She sprinted around the car to the passenger door. "Jake, we need to get to Kati's. Maddox never would have let Max out on his own."

Jake jumped behind the wheel and hit the gas as soon as Laney had closed her door. Cleo bounded along behind them.

Laney held on to the dash, envisioning the worst. Ever since Max had been abducted two months ago, Maddox had been even more vigilant. He would never have let Max out alone, even on the estate. So how had Max gotten out?

Jake screeched to a halt in front of Kati's cottage. Laney was out the door before the car came to a complete stop. She vaulted up the steps and barreled through the front door. "Kati? Maddox?" she yelled.

No answer.

She ran into the den off the kitchen at the back of the house and slammed to a stop. Maddox and Kati sat together on the couch. Their heads were tilted back.

They weren't moving.

"Oh my God." On wobbly legs, Laney made her way over to them. She put her hands to Kati's neck. But her hands were shaking so hard she couldn't get a pulse.

Jake came up behind her, pulled her hand away, and put his own fingers on Kati's neck. "She's breathing."

Laney let out her own breath and sat down heavily on the coffee table as Cleo padded into the room and next to her.

Jake checked Maddox's pulse next. "He's breathing too."

The relief that flowed through Laney was so powerful, it made her almost dizzy.

Cleo leaned over to Kati and sniffed at her face. Jake shook Maddox. "Maddox. Wake up."

Maddox didn't show any sign of hearing him.

Laney shook Kati. "Kati, wake up."

No response either.

Without warning, Cleo let out a massive roar. Laney nearly hit the roof, but neither Kati nor Maddox moved.

Laney rubbed the ring on her finger and leaned down to Maddox. "Wake up, Maddox. *Wake up*," she ordered.

Maddox's head moved. A frown appeared on his lips.

"Come on, Maddox. Wake up," Laney said again.

Maddox's eyelids popped open, then closed. He opened them again and looked at Jake, then Laney.

"What's going on?" His words were slurred.

Jake looked around. Two mugs sat on the end tables next to the couch. "They've been drugged," he said.

Laney nodded. This was unreal.

"I'm going to look around," Jake said.

"Drugged?" Maddox blinked a few times. He turned to Kati, his eyes going wide. "Kati."

"She's been drugged too. But she's breathing," Laney said, struggling to think of how this could have happened.

Maddox grabbed Kati and held her close. A tremor ran through him, and his eyes were wild.

Laney took Maddox's hands in hers and looked into his eyes. "Maddox, I need you to focus. Has anyone besides you, Kati, and Max been in the house today?"

Maddox shook his head. His eyes were clearing, but his arms stayed wrapped protectively around Kati. "No. Why?" He looked around. "Where's Max?"

Laney swallowed. "He's gone. Gerard took him."

"What? How'd he get in?"

"He didn't. Max went to him."

Maddox's eyes narrowed. "What do you mean?"

Laney shrugged, her confusion and fear returning as she remembered Max reaching for Gerard. "I don't know how to explain it. Max left here deliberately to meet Gerard. He went with him willingly."

Jake returned, holding up a pill bottle. "This is why you guys didn't know."

"Those are Kati's sleeping pills," Maddox said.

Laney knew that Kati had been having trouble sleeping for the last few months—ever since the attack in Hershey, Pennsylvania.

Maddox picked the bottle up and shook it. It was empty. He paled. "She had this filled yesterday."

"Who had access to your drinks?" Jake asked.

"No one. Just me, Kati, and Max. Although I guess anyone could have laced them sometime when we were out."

Laney looked around the room. She knew Maddox kept the cottage locked up tight. "I suppose—but they couldn't know you were going to have tea at the right time."

Maddox went still. He spoke slowly. "The tea was Max's idea. He wanted us to have a tea party."

Shock pulled at Laney. None of this made any sense. Why would Max drug them and then go with Gerard?

Cleo nudged her. Laney wrapped her arm around the panther, happy for the cat's warmth, because all of a sudden she felt very cold.

"Has anything been different with Max?" Jake asked. "Anything off?"

Maddox still looked dazed, but he pulled himself together. "Not really. I mean, he sees things—you guys know that."

Laney nodded. "Anything else?"

Maddox paused, glancing between Jake and Laney before his gaze came to rest on Laney. "He's had the same nightmare for a few weeks now."

"What is it?" Laney asked.

"Someone attacks the estate. You and I die, along with a lot of other people. And then Max said he was taken anyway. Everyone dies, and it doesn't matter, because he gets taken anyway." Maddox shook his head. "But it was just a dream."

Laney leaned back. She was thinking about the explosion. "Are you sure about that?"

"I..." Maddox shook his head. "I don't know. But we need to find him."

"We will." Laney nodded to Kati. "Can you take her upstairs? I'll send the doc over to make sure she's all right."

Maddox nodded before gently lifting Kati into his arms.

Laney watched them go. Had Max foreseen the attack today? Had he given himself up in order to keep people from dying?

Jake walked over and put his arms around Laney.

She leaned back into him. "Victoria's gone, and now Max, too. What is going on, Jake?"

CHAPTER 32

LANEY WALKED along the perimeter of the fence with Cleo by her side. They'd already inspected the area where the explosion had occurred. Henry had brought a team in to repair it, and they would work all through the night. Now Laney was inspecting the area where the *real* assault had originated. Where Gerard had made off with Max.

Laney peered out through the fence. The afternoon sun had started its arc toward the horizon, although night was still a few hours off. She sighed, knowing it was stupid to think maybe she'd see something. They'd scanned all the cameras in the surrounding area for a hit on Gerard. Unsurprisingly, they'd come up with nothing. He was gone.

And so was Max.

Her heart clenched. *Damn it. Didn't we just go through this? Why is everyone so focused on a five-year-old boy?* It couldn't be just because he was important to Laney. He had to be important in his own right. But why?

Laney wanted to growl in frustration. She ran her hands through her hair. Kati was losing it, and Maddox was like a caged tiger. Laney had needed to get out of there. She'd needed to think.

Victoria and Max going missing at the same time wasn't a coincidence. She was sure of it. The Fallen had Victoria, and now they had Max as well. But why?

Victoria was born over and over again. They knew that. What precisely her role was they still didn't know, but there was no question that she was special.

But what was so special about Max? Was it because he talked to spirits? Because he could dream of the future? Did Gerard or Samyaza want to know something? Was that what was going on? But why would they think that Max would be able to help them? How would they even know about him?

Cleo picked up her head and sprinted across the grass. Danny and Moxy stepped out of the trees ahead of her. Moxy ran for Cleo, her tail wagging. She jumped around the giant cat, nipping playfully at her heels. Cleo turned around and around and then began to chase Moxy.

Laney watched them with a smile. Danny stopped next to her. "Hey."

Laney linked her arm in his. "Anything?"

Danny shook his head. "I have programs running through all the security footage. Now it's just a matter of waiting."

"And you needed to walk."

Danny nodded. Laney sighed. She knew how helpless he felt— because she felt the same way. Strange as it might sound, there was a comfort in knowing they were both sharing the same concerns. The two walked quietly together, just content to let their shared fear speak for them.

But Laney's mind couldn't help but play over everything she knew about Victoria and Cain.

Finally, she spoke. "Danny, is it possible for humans to be immortal?"

"Sure."

Laney waited for him to continue, then realized that this was his sum total of comment on the subject. "Care to explain for those of us without a genius IQ? I mean, because biologically speaking, the body breaks down. Most of the time when people speak about immortality, they're really talking about extending life a little bit or transferring consciousness to some type of technology. But is it possible to be biologically immortal?"

"Well," Danny said, "there are two promising lines of research. The first involves stretches of DNA known as telomeres. As we age, the telomeres shorten. When they disappear, the cell dies. Researchers theorize that if they're able to lengthen or stabilize the telomeres, immortality could be the result. Or, at a minimum, it would result in a significant increase in lifespan. The other line of research is, of course, the turritopsis dohrnii."

Again Laney waited for him to continue. He didn't.

Laney tried not to sigh. "And what exactly is a Turrito dorny?"

Danny smiled. "A turritopsis dohrnii—it's a jellyfish. It never dies."

"How is *that* possible?"

Danny opened his mouth and then closed it. Laney had the distinct impression he was trying to figure out a way to dumb down what he wanted to tell her. And she was happy he was doing so.

"You know the film, *Benjamin Button*?" Danny asked.

Laney nodded. *The Curious Case of Benjamin Button* told the story of a man who ages backward, so that at the very end of his life he's a baby.

"It's kind of like that," Danny said, "except the jellyfish ages normally—until it reverts back to a polyp and starts the process all over again."

"How long does that go on?" Laney asked.

Danny shrugged. "They're not sure. But they theorize it could be indefinite."

"An immortal jellyfish?"

Danny smiled. "Theoretically. Besides, immortality must be possible."

Laney paused, not sure what Danny was getting at. But then she understood. "Because Cain exists."

Danny nodded. "He *was* human once—and I suppose he

maybe still is. So if he can become immortal, there's no reason someone else can't also. They just need to figure out how."

Laney knew her mouth was hanging open. Immortality was possible. She let out a breath. *Okay. Shove that on the back burner for now.*

"I don't suppose you have any ideas about why Max would go with them?" she asked.

"No. I can't imagine it. I mean, he knows who they are. He knows what they've done. I just can't figure out why he'd go, unless somehow they convinced him they were the good guys. But how would they even reach him to convince him of that?"

"I'm coming up with blanks as well." She paused. "Maddox said Max has been having the same dream for a few weeks. Did you know about it?"

Danny nodded. His eyes looked bleak. "Yeah. He fell asleep when we were watching a movie once. He woke up screaming."

Laney closed her eyes, feeling Max's pain. *Damn it. No kid should have to deal with this.*

Danny's next words came out hesitantly, as if he was testing the waters. "I don't think it was just a dream."

Laney had been expecting that. "You think it was a premonition."

Danny nodded.

Laney sighed. "I think you're probably right. Maddox said that in the dream, both he and I die when the Fallen attack the estate."

"Like the attack yesterday."

Laney nodded. "But by running to Gerard, Max managed to prevent the rest of us from getting into a fight. He thought he was saving my life, and Maddox's. Maybe he was. Maybe he did."

They walked in silence for a bit, then Danny cleared his throat. "There's something else. I didn't say anything before because I wasn't sure what to make of it. It was just too weird."

Laney stopped and faced Danny. "*What* was too weird?"

Danny's gaze strayed over to where Cleo and Moxy were chasing each other. "The other day, Max fell asleep in my office.

Under his pillow was a book on chaos theory. When Max woke up, he knew the contents of the book."

Laney felt a tingling of recognition. "Chaos theory?" Laney wasn't sure *she* really understood chaos theory, and she'd read a few books on it. "Are you sure?"

Danny nodded. "I tested him."

"*Tested* him?"

Danny put up his hands. "I didn't hook him up to a lie detector or anything. I just asked him a bunch of questions related to the book over the next couple days."

"And?"

"And he passed. He knew all the answers. But I don't understand how. No one can learn that way. It's not possible."

Laney closed her eyes. "Oh, it's possible."

"What? You know someone who can do that?"

Laney felt numb. "Only one."

"Who?"

She pictured the man whose readings had begun all of this. Fear coated her nerves. "Edgar Cayce."

CHAPTER 33

LANEY FELT like she'd stepped into an alternate world—one where everything was upside down and inside out.

"Edgar Cayce could learn an entire book by *sleeping* on it?" Danny asked, his eyes huge.

"Allegedly. When Edgar Cayce was a child, he struggled in school. The story goes that one night his father made him stay at the table until he learned all of his spelling words. But he couldn't do it. He stayed there so long he fell asleep. Annoyed, his father woke him up and demanded he spell each and every word. And he did. And from then on, whenever he slept on a book, he learned it's contents."

"How?"

Laney shrugged and gestured to a bench nearby. They walked over and sat. She turned to Danny. "According to Cayce, he was able to access something called the 'Akashic record'—the written record of everything that had ever happened in this world or ever would. It's what allowed him to diagnose people's medical problems as well as foretell future events."

"Was he accurate?"

Laney looked away, knowing that Cayce was without a doubt one of the most successful psychics of all time. "He predicted the stock market crash of 1929, World War II, the beginning of the finding of Atlantis with the Bimini Road. He described the Essenes even before the Dead Sea Scrolls had been found. He predicted that blood would be used as a diagnostic tool in the future. He even somehow understood the link between changes in deep ocean currents and weather changes. There's no doubt that he knew things the rest of the world didn't."

Danny went silent, and Laney watched him, knowing the supernatural world was not his ballpark by any stretch of the imagination.

Danny looked up at Laney. "It's possible."

"What?" Laney couldn't have been more surprised if Danny had said he was going to clown college to fulfill his dream of joining a traveling circus. "You think Cayce was able to predict the future?"

Danny gave her a small grin. "I don't know if Cayce could, but theoretically, psychic abilities are possible."

Laney's mouth fell open. She shut it. "Do tell, professor."

Danny was quiet for a moment, and Laney let him have his thoughts. Danny was a facts and figures guy. Psychic ability was not something he would accept easily.

"Have you heard about the Chinese 'Super Psychics'?"

Laney nodded, her surprise growing. "I'm amazed you have."

Danny shrugged. "When I realized what Max could do, I did a little research."

"What do you think?" Laney was curious what someone with a brain like Danny's would make of the Super Psychics.

Danny bit his lower lip for a moment before speaking. "At first I wasn't sure. But then I started thinking about genetics. Most of our DNA is called 'junk DNA.' But the name is misleading. It's not useless. It's merely not being used. Research has learned that the junk DNA is the noncoding DNA."

"Right—DNA that has no stated function."

Danny nodded. "The ENCODE group found that junk DNA actually regulates genes and the evolution of genes. It's theorized that this junk DNA could actually create incredible abilities. Some have even suggested that within the junk DNA we contain the blueprints for different paranormal abilities."

"So it just needs to be turned on."

"And maybe in some of these kids, like Max, those abilities *have* been turned on."

Laney thought over what she'd read of Cayce. "You know, there were rumors that Atlanteans were incredibly powerful individuals, with psychic skills."

"I know."

"And Cayce, along with lots of other people, argued that humanity has gone through different stages of development."

"The root races," Danny said.

"Yes. According to Cayce, there have been four root races. But Cayce also had something extraordinary to say about the fifth root race. He said it would evolve with the children born after 1998. And that those children would be born with the skills of the long-ago Atlanteans."

"So you think—what? Atlantis is coming back?"

Laney looked away. "It just may be." She watched the trees blow in the wind, but her mind was sifting through the possibilities. Finally she shook her head and stood. "We should get going."

They headed back to the main house. Cleo and Moxy romped along the path in front of them, disappearing into the trees and then reappearing with giant grins on their faces.

"So what's the game plan?" Danny asked.

"You're running every camera and form of transport in the area, right?"

"Yep."

"I don't suppose you Lojacked Max again?"

Danny shook his head. "No. Sorry."

"We really should put a Lojack on each of us," Laney said, only half joking. "We all seem to be in need of help on a rather regular basis."

Danny raised an eyebrow. "You want me to do that?"

Laney opened her mouth to tell him she'd been joking, then closed it. She *had* been joking, but that didn't mean it was a horrible idea. "Maybe we should. Could you look into some piece of jewelry or something that someone could carry on them? Nothing too intrusive, just something—"

Laney's cell phone interrupted her. She glanced down at it. Jake.

She clicked it open, putting it on speaker for Danny to hear. "Did you find anything on Max?"

There was tension in Jake's voice. "No. It's something else. There's someone at the front gate who says he needs to speak with the triad."

Laney went still. "Who is it?"

"Ralph."

CHAPTER 34

LANEY RACED up the path to the main house. She'd ordered Cleo to stay with Danny and Moxy at the bunker. She wasn't sure what Ralph wanted or whose side he was on, and she wasn't about to take a chance with Danny's life.

Surprisingly, Danny hadn't fought her on it.

Laney's thoughts raced as her feet pounded down the path. Ralph. He was… something. She just didn't know what.

She heard steps running toward her and looked up in alarm. When Jake appeared ahead of her on the path, she let out a breath.

"I thought you'd want some company," he said.

She nodded, feeling grateful. This run was so different from their more carefree run a few hours ago.

"We'll meet them at the main house," Jake said.

Laney took her ring off its chain and slipped it onto her finger. Jake glanced down at her, one eyebrow raised.

She shrugged. "Just in case."

He patted the gun at his side. "Just in case."

When they reached the back of the house, they ducked in through one of the back entrances. The house was so large that it would be faster to cut through it than to try and go around it. They passed through the kitchen and made their way to the front entryway—the same entryway that had so entranced Laney when she'd first come to Chandler HQ. That was only two years ago. It felt like a lifetime.

Laney and Jake raced out the front door and down the marble steps. They could see the security Jeep approaching in the distance. Jake took Laney's hand as the Jeep neared, Henry at the wheel.

Questions ran through Laney's mind. Why was Ralph here? Where had he been since the attack at Victoria's house? And how the hell was he alive?

The Jeep was a hundred yards away when she felt a tingle of recognition drift through her—Henry. That sensation was followed a second later by a slice of electricity so fast and powerful all Laney could do was gasp as her knees nearly gave out. She grabbed on to Jake to keep from crashing to the ground.

"Laney," Jake exclaimed, holding her up.

Laney straightened but didn't look at Jake. She watched the man sitting next to Henry—the man who had guarded Victoria for thirty long years. Ralph was looking straight at Laney.

Laney held Ralph's gaze, but her words were for Jake. "He might not be a Fallen, but he sure as hell is something."

CHAPTER 35

HENRY PULLED the car to a stop in front of Laney and Jake. All the anger and annoyance Laney felt toward Ralph disappeared the moment she saw him up close. He looked like hell. Bags were under his eyes and he looked like he'd aged in just two days.

Laney stepped forward. "Ralph?"

He nodded wearily and stepped out of the Jeep. "Hi, Laney. Jake."

Henry came around the cart. "Why don't we head up to my office?"

"This way." Jake led Ralph up the stairs.

Laney fell in step with Henry a little farther back. She kept her voice low. "Did you feel anything when you saw him?"

Henry shook his head. "No. Why? Did you?"

Laney's eyes stayed on Ralph as he disappeared into the house. "It was a bolt so strong it nearly dropped me to my knees."

Henry's eyes grew large. "What?"

Laney nodded. "Let's go get some answers."

A few minutes later, they were ensconced in Henry's office.

Laney had ordered coffee for all of them and food for Ralph. Laney wanted answers first, but Ralph looked like he hadn't eaten since Victoria had been taken. What's more, he appeared about to drop from exhaustion. Part of Laney thought they should order the man to bed, but Henry wasn't willing to wait, and neither was she.

"Where have you been?" Henry asked Ralph.

"Looking for your mother."

"Have you found anything?" Jake asked.

Ralph shook his head. "I arrived at Little Rock just after Gerard and his men found her. I've checked out most of the Fallen locations I know, but there are others I haven't been able to check." He turned his gaze to Henry. "I was hoping you and your contacts would be able to help."

Jake stood. "Do you have a list?"

Ralph pulled a sheet of paper from his inside jacket pocket and handed it to Jake, who scanned it.

"We have operatives in most of these locations," Jake said. "A few are pretty remote. It'll take time to get someone there." He glanced between Laney and Henry. "I'll go get this started." He headed out.

Laney turned back to Ralph, who looked like he had fallen asleep. "Ralph?" She said quietly.

He jerked his eyes open. "Sorry. I'm here."

Henry sat with his arms across his chest. "Ralph, you need to tell us what's going on. Why did Jorgen Fuld take Mom? And why were there Fallen at the airport?"

"It was like they were having a tug-of-war over her," Laney said.

"In a way they are," Ralph said. "Your mother is a very important woman."

"*How* is she important? *Who* is she?" Henry asked.

A look of pain marred Ralph's features. "I can't tell you that."

"Why not?" Laney burst out, her annoyance, fear, and frustration coming to a head.

"Because it's my duty to keep her safe and to keep her identity under wraps."

"Your duty? Your duty to whom?" Henry asked.

"To everyone. To humanity," Ralph said.

Laney didn't know what to say to that, and she could tell Henry didn't either.

"Who are you, Ralph?" Laney asked quietly. She held up her ring. "I know you're not a normal human. That shock nearly dropped me to my knees."

Ralph looked at Laney for a moment, then turned to Henry. "It has been my honor to watch you grow. You have become every- thing your father and mother hoped you would be."

His eyes shifted back to Laney. "Both of you."

Laney and Henry stayed silent, waiting for answers. It felt like the air in the room crackled with energy.

Finally, Ralph spoke. "My given name is Uriel. I'm an archangel."

CHAPTER 36

LANEY STARED AT RALPH. "An archangel? They're real, too?"

A ghost of a smile crossed Ralph's lips. "Yes."

Henry pulled out a chair and sat down heavily. "And you've been tasked with what? Guarding Mom?"

Ralph nodded.

Laney's thoughts swirled. Enoch himself was said to have become one of the archangels: Metatron, the scribe of God, although he's never mentioned in the Bible, only in the Book of Enoch. She knew that the Book of Enoch mentioned seven archangels, but the Bible didn't recognize them. Instead, it focused on only three: Gabriel, Michael, and Raphael. And in the Bible tales, the archangels were only messengers. Laney couldn't remember ever seeing anything about an archangel taking up residence on Earth.

"Um, is that what archangels do?" she asked. "Protect people?"

Ralph shook his head. "Not necessarily. We are each tasked with a different mission."

"So you've been guarding our mother for thirty years?" Henry asked.

Ralph hesitated. "In this lifetime, yes."

Henry spoke slowly. "How many lifetimes have you guarded her?"

"Almost all of them."

Laney felt as if Ralph had somehow just morphed in front of her eyes. He was an archangel, one of the heavenly hosts. She had known Victoria was important, but now she had absolute confirmation. And even though Ralph had said he couldn't reveal Victoria's identity, Laney couldn't help but ask. "Is she Eve?"

Ralph's eyebrows went up, and Laney could tell he was weighing his next words carefully. Finally he shook his head. "No."

Laney sat back, not sure if she was more relieved or confused. Who *was* Victoria then? That question seemed to be perpetually burned into her brain. Even when she closed her eyes, it flashed at her from behind her eyelids like a neon sign.

Laney looked over at Henry; he looked as lost as she felt. She reached over and took his hand. "We'll find her, and then she'll answer all our questions."

Henry nodded, but Laney knew he was far from convinced. She just wasn't sure which part of her assertion gave him greater doubt: that they would find her, or that she would answer their questions when they did.

"Actually, that's why I'm here," Ralph said. He reached into the pocket of his jacket and pulled out a flash drive. "Your mother has something to tell you."

CHAPTER 37

CHICAGO, ILLINOIS

VICTORIA SAT in the dark in the basement of the old house. When the house was first built, this basement had been a root cellar. A water heater and boiler had since been moved in, but it did nothing to warm up the dirt floor and cold stone walls.

She pulled the blanket she'd been left around her shoulders. A cot had been placed in the corner for her, along with a bucket.

She curled her lip. All things considered, she preferred being held captive by Jorgen. He at least gave her a real bathroom.

The door at the top of the stairs opened, spilling light down the stairs. "Go," a voice ordered roughly, and then the door closed again.

Victoria heard breathing at the top of the stairs, then small creaks as someone made their way down. Victoria reached over and turned on the lantern she'd been left.

A small figure stepped into the light.

Victoria gasped. *Oh no.*

She stood up, her bones creaking. She stepped forward slowly, not wanting to spook him. Her voice was soft.

"Hello, Max. My name is Victoria."

Max wiped at the tears on his cheeks, his blue eyes rimmed in red. "I know. You're Laney's mom."

Victoria nodded, looking at him more intently, trying to figure out why they would have grabbed him. Was he just a means to an end? "I'm so sorry you're here."

Max looked down. "It was the only way…" His voice drifted off.

Victoria stared at him. *The only way?*

Max stepped farther into the light, and Victoria was startled by the serious expression on his face. It was so mature a look for—

The truth slammed into her. Her breath caught in her throat as she stared at this little boy whose shoulders were far too small for this burden.

"It was the only way for you to keep them safe," Victoria said.

He nodded.

"You didn't get kidnapped, did you?"

He shook his head.

Victoria's heart felt like it was going to break. She wanted to curse fate, destiny—all of it. She was used to this burden, and even for her, it was difficult. But how could anyone expect a small child to bear such a heavy load?

"You are a very brave boy, Max," she said, a catch in her voice.

She knelt down, holding her arms out. Max ran over to her and wrapped his arms around her neck in a hug.

Victoria closed her arms around him. She had intended to give him comfort. But somehow, with those little arms wrapped around her, it was she who felt comforted. She leaned her head on his shoulder and sighed.

They stayed like that, wrapped together, for a few moments. Victoria could feel the sobs the boy was trying hard not to let out. She rubbed his back. "It's okay to cry. I've got you."

Max's shoulders quaked and the sobs burst forth. Victoria lifted him up and sat on the bed with the boy curled in her lap. She kept her arms firmly wrapped around him and rocked back and forth.

Eventually he settled down. But Victoria kept him snuggled in her arms and continued to rock.

Finally, when she was convinced he was asleep, she stopped and looked down at him. Big eyes stared back at her.

She smiled. "I thought you had fallen asleep."

He shook his head. "Almost."

"Well, it's okay if you want to. I'll be right here."

The boy nodded. Victoria helped him stretch out on the cot. She pulled the blanket over him, cursing their captors for treating a little boy so cruelly. Then she sat on the cot next to him so she could provide him some of her warmth.

Victoria pushed Max's hair back, remembering when Henry was his size. It seemed like it was forever ago and yesterday at the same time. "I promise I'll protect you, Max. I hope you know you can trust me."

Max looked up at her with surprise on his face. "Of course I can trust you. I know who you are."

"You do?"

"You're the mother. The mother of all." Max closed his eyes and snuggled closer to her.

Victoria lay a hand on his back. She smiled. *The mother of all.* It had been a long time since someone had acknowledged her as such.

She rested her other hand on his head and murmured, "Yes, I am."

CHAPTER 38

RALPH HANDED the flash drive to Henry. "Victoria gave this to me when we were in Egypt." He looked over at Laney. "She knew you were the ring bearer. She knew things might move fast. And if the worst happened, she wanted you to understand."

Laney felt lightheaded. "The worst? She's dead?"

Ralph paused before shaking his head. "Her death would not be the worst. The worst would be if she fell into the hands of the Fallen."

Laney stared at him. "What?"

Jake stepped into the room and looked around. "What did I miss?"

Laney tore her eyes away from Ralph and quickly brought Jake up to speed. Jake turned to Ralph. "You're a soldier?"

Ralph nodded.

"What exactly is the difference between an archangel and a regular old angel?" Jake asked.

"Archangels are the first amongst angels—the highest order," Ralph explained. "God's most trusted."

"Like an elite guard," Jake said.

"Essentially."

"What are your mission parameters?" Jake asked.

"I protect Victoria from all threats to her mission."

Laney jolted. *Her mission?*

Laney opened her mouth to ask Ralph what he'd meant by that, but Henry spoke first. "Here we go," he said.

Jake took the seat next to Laney as the screen above the conference table came to life. Laney recognized the background—it was the home they had stayed in in Egypt. That incredible house.

The camera shifted, and Victoria came into view. She looked tired, but she smiled at the camera. "I am making this recording," she said, "with hopes that you never have to see it. But Laney has found the ring—and that means the world is coming to a difficult point."

Victoria took a breath. "Right now, Jake Rogan is resting comfortably in one of the guest rooms. He is alive. And it is that fact which leads me to the need for this tape. I brought Jake back to life with my blood. It mingled with his while we kept his heart pumping. That is how I was able to heal his wounds."

Laney's eyes flew to the small indent on Jake's forehead, the only indication that he had been shot.

"That act will undeniably become known to the Fallen," Victoria continued, "and when it does, they will come for me—as will another. If I fall into their hands, you must do everything in your power to get me away from them. Even if that means killing me."

Laney gasped. Henry's jaw dropped.

"She can't be serious," Jake said.

"Just listen," Ralph said quietly.

Victoria took a shaky breath. "My blood has the power to heal —you know that. But it also can do more. My blood can make someone immortal."

That's not possible, Laney thought. She felt Jake stir beside her. Her gaze flew to him. His eyes locked on hers and she knew they were thinking the same thing.

On screen, Victoria gave a small smile. "Jake, if you're listening, you're not immortal."

Beside her, Laney felt Jake let out a breath. And she felt the same relief.

"It takes much more blood than what you received from me. In fact, it takes *all* of it. If the Fallen learn this, I have no doubt they will take my blood and use it to make one of them immortal. And you can imagine what that would be like."

Jake sucked in a breath. Laney felt like her world was spinning. *An immortal Fallen.*

Fallen were already incredibly difficult to kill. And killing them was almost always the only way to stop them. They healed too quickly for other methods to be effective for long.

"There are actually two ways for the humans to become immortal," Victoria said. "My blood is one. It is also the way to destroy the other means." She took a trembling breath. "Henry, I have kept things from you. Not because I didn't trust you, but because I hoped you would never have to know. I didn't want this burden on your shoulders. And even when Laney returned to us, I still hoped you and she could be spared this."

Henry clenched his fists, the knuckles going white, but the expression on his face wasn't anger; it was grief. Laney knew he wished that Victoria hadn't felt like she'd had to shoulder this burden alone.

Laney's eyes shifted to Ralph, who stared at Victoria's image on the screen. His jaw was tight, but his eyes held fear. *But she wasn't entirely alone, was she?*

Victoria looked into the camera. Laney felt like she was looking right into Victoria's eyes.

"Laney, I have no doubt your mind is scrambling, trying to figure out how what I've said is possible." Victoria smiled. "The short answer is, I am a different kind of human. I am one of the first humans, and the only of my kind left. I die, but unlike everyone else, I remember my past lives. I am the keeper of humanity.

"My job is to help keep the balance from tipping in favor of the

Sons of Belial. And occasionally in my lives, that has required my death. That tipping point is here now, once again."

Victoria took another deep breath and stared into the camera. Her shoulders were level, her gaze straight, and her voice strong. "I will do what I can to keep the Fallen from learning the truth. Failing that, I will do what I can to keep them from getting my blood—by whatever means necessary. You must also do the same. My life doesn't matter. Humanity will never survive an immortal Fallen. I've seen it before; it is a world beyond cruel. And it is a world we must not allow to come again."

The screen went black.

CHAPTER 39

LANEY SAT BACK in her chair feeling stunned. Victoria's blood could make someone immortal. She pictured Azazyel and all the damage he had done. The only way they had been able to push him back was by injuring him. He had been afraid of being killed.

My God, what if he had been immortal? A chill ran through her. *He would have been unstoppable.*

"What did she mean that she's seen it before?" Jake asked.

Laney thought back to her conversation with Victoria about that very topic. "Victoria once told me that humans used to be immortal. That it was the Fallen who brought in death and destruction."

Ralph's head snapped up. He looked like he was about to say something but changed his mind.

"Why did she never tell me?" Henry asked quietly.

Laney's gaze flew to her brother. He looked devastated.

"She didn't want you to be concerned about something that might never come to pass," Ralph said. "And she also knew that you would lay down your life to protect hers. She couldn't let that happen."

"This has happened before?" Jake gestured to the screen. "Victoria having to sacrifice herself for the greater good?"

Ralph nodded, pain in his eyes. "Many times."

Laney looked away. The burden Victoria carried was unimaginable. Remembering humanity's history, having to stay apart from those she loved to keep them safe, and then having to sacrifice herself to save a humanity she had to keep at arm's length away.

"You should know," Ralph said, "that Victoria has helped where she could. She has managed to use her blood on rare occasions to bring about someone's recovery. But she always has to be very careful to make sure that everyone thinks it's a miraculous event and not due to her interference."

"Why, though?" Laney asked. "Why not just help?"

Ralph gave her a sad smile. "Because if people learned what her blood could do, they would clamor for it, and she only has so much. How would she decide who received it and who didn't? That's one reason. But worse, it would let the Fallen know. It wouldn't take them long to figure out that if a little blood could cure someone, a lot could make them immortal."

"And how come they don't know already?" Laney asked. "In the books, Victoria always looks the same. Wouldn't they simply recognize her?"

Ralph shook his head. "She's the only one with a perfect memory of her past lives. They only catch snippets of their own previous lives—and sometimes not even that. They have no memory of her. Or at least, they didn't."

"Now they do?" Henry asked.

"Yes. I think it was when Victoria saved Jake. A lot of people knew he was dead. And then he wasn't. And he's a member of the triad. That would be very interesting to the Fallen."

"Why did she save me?" Jake squeezed Laney's hand. "I appreciate it, but if it put her at risk..."

Ralph smiled, his gaze meeting Laney's. "Because she couldn't bear the thought of Laney going through that pain. It was a mother's instinct. Her daughter was in pain, and she had the key to alleviating it. There was no chance she wasn't going to help. Her children..." Ralph trailed off.

Henry finished the thought. "… are her greatest weakness."

"*And* her greatest strength," Ralph added gently. "Her children remind her why she has to do what needs to be done. There have been times when she didn't want this burden. When she wanted to push it aside and let humanity fend for themselves. But it was her children, and the memories of their love, that kept her going."

"Have there been others?" Laney asked. "Other children?"

"She's had five souls as children," Ralph said. "You and Henry are her two physical children this time. But the other three are around as well."

"Who are they?" Laney asked.

Ralph shook his head. "I can't tell you that. But they are in your life. They always are."

"Max," Henry said, looking up. "He's one. And Danny too."

Ralph looked surprised. "Yes. And there's one other."

Faces flew through Laney's mind. Jen, Lou, Rally, Kati, Maddox —an endless array of faces. When she'd met each of them, she'd felt a connection—immediate and familiar. It could be any of them. She had heard that that immediate connection was a sign that your soul recognized another soul. It was comforting to think that she'd known all these people lifetime after lifetime.

Ralph raised his hands. "I know you have more questions, but right now what we need is to focus on finding Victoria."

Laney looked at Henry; his eyes reflected her own fears. They both knew finding Victoria was the priority. But with what they had just learned, what did finding Victoria mean?

Laney swallowed. *When we find her, will it be to save her…*

… Or kill her?

CHAPTER 40

LANEY HEADED down to the kitchen in the main house with her iPad. She wasn't hungry, but she needed to speak with her uncle. He had returned from the Chandler School a few minutes ago, and she knew he'd stop in for a cup of tea.

She stepped into the kitchen. Sleek white cabinets, dark granite countertops, stainless steel appliances—it was a culinary chef's dream. In fact, Henry had a chef on staff for when he had guests.

Patrick was standing by the stove, pulling the kettle off the burner. He looked up and caught Laney's gaze. "I hear you've had a visitor."

Laney sank into one of the tall chairs at the island. "Yes. But first, how are the kids doing?"

Patrick sighed. "Not well. Max is kind of everybody's little brother. They all want to help."

Laney nodded. She hated that the kids at the school were getting yet another reminder of how dangerous the world they were now a part of was.

Patrick pulled a cup and saucer out of the cabinet, then placed a tea bag inside. "So, what does Ralph have to say?"

"Nothing much. He's been looking for Victoria—not having any luck. Oh, and he's an archangel."

Patrick paused for only a moment before continuing to pour water into his cup. "I see."

Laney placed her head on her hands and watched him. "Why do I feel like these revelations are never as shocking to you as they are to the rest of us?"

Patrick gave her a small smile. He added some milk and sugar to his tea, then picked up a plate of Irish soda bread and took a seat next to Laney. He pushed the plate toward her.

"It's not that I'm not shocked. It's more that I understand that we're not at the end of the revelations. I figure they're going to keep coming. So which archangel is he?"

"Uriel."

"Ah—the light of God."

"Light of God?"

"He's not mentioned in the Bible. But he is in the Book of Enoch. Enoch even suggests that Uriel outranks Michael."

"What was his job?"

"That's a matter of debate. But the most common belief was that he was responsible for keeping the meaning of existence secret."

Laney let out a laugh. "Well that fits." She placed her iPad on the counter. "And I'm glad you're expecting the unexpected, because I need you to watch something."

Patrick glanced at the screen. "What's this?"

"Victoria made us a recording."

Patrick raised an eyebrow but didn't say anything. He just took a sip of his tea and focused on the screen.

Laney queued up the recording and hit play. She nibbled on soda bread as she listened to Victoria, but this time she paid more attention to how Victoria looked. Her eyes were tired, her face drawn. Laney could see the cost of the burden on her.

When at last the tape ended, Patrick stared at the black screen for a moment, then leaned back in his chair, his hand on his chin.

While Laney waited for him to say something, she thought about the possibilities. Victoria had said she was one of the first

humans. And Laney knew that humanity's family tree was complicated. There were at least twenty different hominids that could be
classified as human, and probably more that were still literally
hidden in the sands of time. But Victoria didn't look like a throw-
back to an ancient human. She was too refined. Was she suggesting
she was the first homo sapiens? Or was she suggesting she was
something else altogether?

Patrick still sat in the same position, hand on his chin, staring
off into space. And despite his declaration earlier, Laney had the
distinct feeling that this particular revelation *had* thrown him.

She gently tapped his arm. "So? Thoughts? Ideas? What do you
think she means by 'the first humans'?"

Patrick gave her a small smile. "Well, I think I've learned
enough to know that I don't know enough."

Laney gave a little laugh. So much for thinking her uncle was
going to have some great insight. And she also had to acknowl-
edge the absolute truth of his statement. "So you really think
she's… what? An original human?"

"Weren't we just the other day suggesting she was Eve? Is this
really all that different? And tell me, honestly, do you really doubt
that she's telling the truth?"

Laney let out a breath and gazed out through the French doors
to the rolling hills that backed the main house. She remembered
when she first had seen this place. Azazyel was after her then,
because of Drew's paper. She had thought that that was the most
difficult thing she could imagine. Now it paled in comparison to
some of her other adventures.

She looked back at her uncle. "She's not, by the way."

"Not what?"

"Eve. Ralph told us that much, although he won't say exactly
who she is. And no, I don't doubt what she says. I just *wish* I did. It
would be nice if I could write off her words as the ramblings of a
crazy person. Because then…" Laney trailed off, not wanting to
say the words.

Patrick grasped her hand. "Because then none of this would be as dire as it feels."

Laney nodded, not trusting herself to speak. Her relationship with Victoria was complicated. But Laney wanted the time to *un*-complicate their relationship. She knew how much Victoria loved her and Henry. But right now she felt like there was a ticking clock counting down while she was just standing still.

"Doesn't *The Army of the Belial* book mention something about a sacrifice?" Patrick asked.

Laney nodded. "'*When the triads intersect, the time of judgment is at hand. The choice of sacrifice or death will be made.*'" She paused, her voice quiet. "I'm worried it might be her. I always thought it referred to me. That *I* was the one who was going to be sacrificed."

"But you *are* being asked to sacrifice," Patrick said quietly. "You will have to be willing to let her go."

Laney shook her head. "I just now found her. It doesn't seem fair that I have to let her go before I have a chance to even get to know her. And it doesn't seem fair that she has to keep doing this over and over again."

Patrick took her hand and kissed her forehead. "No. It's not fair. But life rarely is."

CHAPTER 41

HENRY SAT AT HIS DESK. He'd been sitting there ever since Ralph had shown them the video. Jake had gone off to get updates on Ralph's list. Ralph had gone to take a shower and get a change of clothes. And Laney had left to find Patrick.

But Henry had just sat there as the sun moved across the sky and time marched on. He couldn't seem to get beyond the idea of Ralph being an archangel. How had he not known? Ralph had been the father figure in his life. The one man he could always count on. How could his mother or Ralph not have told him?

An unending slide show of Ralph filled Henry's mind. Ralph teaching him to ride a two-wheeler when he was six. Ralph comforting him the day he came home crying because the kids at school had teased him about his height. Ralph sitting down with him and listening to every concern he had, every worry. And then telling him how proud he was of him—and how much he loved him.

Henry swallowed. He knew he wasn't being fair, but his mother and Ralph keeping Ralph's identity from him—it cut deep. He knew his mother's identity and her secrets were off-limits, but Ralph… he had always been an open book.

Or so I thought.

Henry leaned his head back. *How could I not have known this? How could they not tell me?*

He leaned his elbows on the desk, his head in his hands. And now what? He was supposed to let his mother die to save humanity from an immortal Fallen? How was that even possible?

And then there was Max. *Max, who can see….* Henry went still. *Max, who can see the future.*

Oh my God.

Henry walked quickly over to his office doors, glanced out into the hallway, then closed them. Back at his desk, he unlocked the drawer on the bottom right. He removed the unmarked envelope and pulled out the handwritten sheet of legal paper, trying to calm the tremor in his hands. *Why didn't I think of this sooner?*

He had provided Laney with a copy of the translation from *The Army of the Belial*. He had given her a translation of every single page—save one.

That page contained only three paragraphs. It was the last two that had kept him from showing anyone else the words. But now he worried that it was the first one he should have understood sooner:

When the triads arise, the seer will appear. In his hands, the outcomes will be known, but not fixed. The side that controls him, controls the final battle.

Max could see the future. *He* was the seer.

Guilt overcame Henry. If he had shared this translation with someone else… maybe they would have understood. Maybe they could have done something to save Max.

Henry gazed out the windows that lined the back of his office. No one had seen these words but him. In fact, he had never typed it into the file. He hadn't wanted to take the chance that Laney might find it. Or that Danny might uncover it.

But it wasn't the comments about the seer that had made him hold the translation back. It was the lines that followed them:

The ring bearer will be tested. The seer, an object of fire, will deter-

mine the fate of each side, and the ring bearer will fight alone. And then the war will begin.

If she is found worthy, the Children of the Light of One will have a chance to push back the tide. If she fails, the Belial will overrun the world.

He looked over the words again, feeling the fear. His mother was gone, and Max was the seer—he had to be. Which meant the Fallen now had the advantage.

He had never shown Laney this passage; he had hoped she wouldn't need to see it. For a moment, he realized he had done just what his mother had done. And he felt the hypocrisy of his anger. But showing Laney this passage would have only put more guilt on her shoulders, more worry. She would literally have the fate of the world in her hands. And he hadn't been able to lay that at her feet.

A knock sounded at the door. Henry flipped the paper over on his desk. "Come in."

Laney peeked her head in. "Hey."

"Hey."

"Are you okay?" She walked over and stood next to him, placing her hand on his shoulder.

He saw the worry on her face and felt comforted by it. He knew she would do anything to help him. But there was nothing to be done. There was no one who could take away the hole in his chest.

He gently placed his hand over hers. "I'm okay."

She squeezed his hand. "Liar," she said quietly before wrapping her arms around him. "We'll get through this. Together."

Henry held her close, leaning his head into hers. He had met Laney two years ago, but had automatically felt a connection to her—a need to protect her. Now he knew why. But he couldn't keep this translation from her any longer. There was too much at stake.

He pulled away and looked at her. "There's something I need to show you."

CHAPTER 42

LANEY STARED at the translation in disbelief. She'd read it twice now, but she still couldn't believe the words in front of her. *An object of fire*. The day Max was born, Laney had saved Max and Katie from a burning car. He was a child of fire. And he could see the future.

Everything fell into place. That's why the Fallen wanted Max. He could turn the tide in their favor. She had known he was part of all of this—but not how. And she had prayed that she was wrong. But now, she knew: he was a weapon.

"It never occurred to me that the seer could be Max. He's just so young," Henry said. Laney saw the grief on Henry's face. She knew he would never put Max in harm's way. It had honestly never occurred to him that Max was the seer.

She shook her head. "It's not your fault. He's so young. I wouldn't have thought it either." But even as the words left her mouth, she knew they were a lie. For over a month she had been trying to find the reason why someone would target Max—and if she had read this, she would have made the connection right away. But she shoved those thoughts aside.

"We need to get him back."

"We will, Laney. We will."

Laney stared down at the words again. *The ring bearer will fight alone.* She looked up into Henry's eyes. "How come you never showed me this?"

"You had enough going on. I didn't want you stressing about something that might not come to pass."

Laney let out a little laugh. "Apparently that's our family's motto."

Henry put his hand on Laney's shoulder. "But you won't be alone. Jake and I are with you."

Laney reached up and covered his hand with hers. She knew that when fate had a plan, no matter how hard you tried, you couldn't change it.

CHAPTER 43

A KNOCK at Henry's office door caused Laney and Henry to look over.

Ralph stood uncertainly in the doorway. "I'm sorry to interrupt. I can come back—"

"No. It's okay. Come in," Henry said, trying to tamp down his anger and hurt. He needed to keep it in check and focus on Max and his mother right now. The rest could wait.

Ralph walked over to the couch near Henry's desk. The shower seemed to have rejuvenated him. He didn't look as tired as before.

Laney squeezed Henry's shoulder before turning and walking around the desk. She stood leaning against it, her arms crossed. "I have some more questions."

Ralph took a quick glance at Henry. "I figured you would."

Henry studied Ralph. His face was wrinkled and his hair had grayed in the last thirty years. Ralph had aged normally. He looked like a man in his fifties should—albeit a man in great shape. There was nothing that indicated that he was anything but a normal person. Nothing screamed all-powerful angel.

"Was it your duty to protect both our mother and father?" Laney asked.

Ralph shook his head. "No—just your mother. Your father doesn't receive protection when he returns."

Henry pulled himself from his ruminations with a start. "What? But he's Metatron."

Ralph turned his eyes to Henry. "Yes. And he has abilities like you. But his role on Earth is not as important as your mother's."

Henry stared, dumbfounded and more than a little annoyed. What exactly was his mother's role?

"See, that's what I don't get," Laney said. "Who is she?"

"I'm sorry," Ralph said. "Like I said, I can't tell you that."

All the anger and resentment Henry was trying to keep a lid on boiled over. "How can you *not*? You *raised* me. You were the closest person I had to a father! How can you not tell me?"

Pain and regret flashed across Ralph's face. Henry steeled himself against it.

"I want to," Ralph said. "I want to tell you everything. But I am forbidden. I—I wish it were different."

Henry stood, clenching his fists. He turned his back to the room and looked out the window, trying to find his calm. For his whole life, secrets had been kept from him. Now they whirled through his mind, threatening to choke him. Laney was his sister. His father was an angel. He was a nephilim. And his mother was.... something. Someone important. Not just to him and Laney, but to the whole world.

When he looked back at Ralph, the anger burned away, leaving only sadness. Ralph had been a true friend all his life. "Why?"

"Henry, if I could, I would. Please believe that. You have been..." Ralph broke off and swallowed. "You have been one of the greatest pleasures of this life or any other. I have never had a son, but I love you like you were mine."

Henry looked into Ralph's eyes and knew that Ralph was telling him the truth.

Laney came to stand next to Henry, leaning into him and wrapping an arm around his waist. He wrapped his arm around her shoulders.

"Okay," Laney said, "if you can't tell us about Victoria, can you tell us why they would take Max now as well?"

Ralph's head whipped up and his eyes narrowed. "Max? Kati Simmons's son?"

Henry stared at Ralph. Ralph had never met Max—he was sure of that. And he couldn't remember ever having mentioned him to Ralph either, although it was possible. But Ralph's reaction... no, there was something else there. "How do you know Max?" he asked.

Ralph ignored the question. "When was he taken?"

Laney glanced at Henry before speaking. "Yesterday. But it wasn't so much that he was taken. He ran to join them."

"Max is psychic?" Ralph asked.

Laney started. "How did you know that?"

"He's the seer," Ralph said softly. His eyes were a world away.

"That's what we think," Laney said.

Henry looked between two of them. A chill came over him when he saw the expression on Ralph's face. "What do you know?" Henry asked.

Ralph appeared to be caught up in some inner thoughts. "The seer has the ability to read the future," he said. "Whichever side controls the seer can control the fate of the fight to come."

Henry felt a tremor run through Laney. He tightened his arm around her. "What will they do to him?"

Ralph seemed to snap back to the present. "He's a tool. They'll use him to get the information they want."

Henry felt sick. *A tool.* "What information? What are they looking for?"

"The other means of becoming immortal."

"What is the other way?" Henry asked, remembering what his mother had alluded to on the recording.

"A tree."

"A *tree*? All of this for a tree?" Laney asked.

Ralph met each of their eyes before his gaze came to rest on Henry. "Not just any tree. They're looking for the tree of life itself."

CHAPTER 44

LANEY STARED AT RALPH. "The tree of life? As in Genesis?"

Ralph nodded. Laney looked up at Henry, who stared back at her with what she was sure was the same incredulous look that was on her own face. "In the book of Genesis, Adam and Eve—"

Jake burst in the door. "We've found Victoria and Max."

All talk of the tree ceased.

"Where?" Henry asked.

"Outside Chicago." Jake strode over to the giant screen above the conference table. "I have a live feed."

Laney made her way to his side. "Chicago? Northgram's in Chicago."

"Yeah, but this isn't the Council," Jake said.

"Who's running the op?" Henry asked.

"Jordan. He's got Yoni and Jen with him."

Laney closed her eyes and said a small thank you. If she couldn't be there herself, those were the people she'd have chosen.

"They found the house. The Fallen must have been alerted, because they managed to get to their cars and head for the airport just as they arrived. Our people are right on their tail. They should be at the airport now if they were unable to stop them in transit."

On the screen, an airport scene came to life. A firefight was already in progress. Laney squinted as she tried to make out the players.

Her heart skipped a beat. "There's Max." She pointed to the top right. Max was being carried kicking and screaming into a plane.

"And Gerard," Henry muttered with disgust.

Laney recognized the man holding Max. "Where's Victoria?"

"There," Jake said. "Behind that van."

Laney held her breath as two men next to Victoria were shot and dropped. The plane behind her came to life.

"She can get away." *Run, Victoria, run*, Laney urged.

Victoria stood and did run—right to the plane. She climbed up the steps and disappeared inside. The door closed after her, and the plane headed for the runway. The shooting stopped. No one wanted to damage the plane as it took off.

Laney stared at the screen in disbelief. *First Max, now Victoria.* She stared at Henry, whose jaw was hanging open. *What is going on?*

CHAPTER 45

VICTORIA STRODE DOWN THE AISLE, stumbling a bit as the plane moved. Max screamed at Gerard, who held him.

Victoria's heart clenched at the sound. She grabbed Gerard's arm. "Let him go."

Gerard glared, then shoved Max into her. Stumbling under the boy's weight, Victoria leaned heavily against one of the seats but managed to stay upright.

Max clung to her, his shoulders shaking. Victoria moved past Gerard and fell into a seat as the plane picked up speed. She hugged Max to her, her heart breaking again at his terror. And her anger rose. *He's too young for this. He shouldn't be part of this.*

She ran her hand over Max's back, trying to calm him down. "It'll be all right, Max. It'll be all right." Victoria repeated the same words over and over until Max's shaking calmed.

After fifteen minutes, she saw with relief that he had fallen asleep. She shifted him so he lay curled in her lap, then pulled a blanket from the chair next to her and spread it over him. She placed a kiss on his forehead. "I wish you didn't need to be a part of this," she whispered.

She rested her head on the back of the seat and closed her own eyes. She was exhausted. The security feed from the airfield had no doubt already made it to Henry and Laney. And those were their own operatives that she'd run away from. She let out a shuddering breath. Would they have seen that she'd had a moment to escape and that she had chosen not to?

Her chest feeling heavy, she stared out the window at the clouds. *Please, God, help them understand why I've done the things I've done.*

"Not sleeping?" Elisabeta said, taking a seat across from her.

Victoria composed her face, wiping all trace of emotion from it. "What do you need?"

Elisabeta smiled, tracing a well-manicured finger over the armrest. "Why, nothing. I just wanted to compliment you on turning your back on your children. Not every mother would be able to do that."

Millennia of practice was the only thing that kept Victoria from launching herself at Elisabeta's smug face. Instead she pinned Elisabeta in place with her gaze.

Elisabeta blinked and narrowed her eyes. "Careful. You don't want to ruin my beneficence."

Victoria held her tongue and gripped the side of the chair, trying to keep her anger in check. Elisabeta had incredible power as well as incredible abilities and wealth. And yet it still wasn't enough. She wanted more. Even if that meant traumatizing a small child to get what she wanted.

Oblivious to Victoria's anger, Elisabeta leaned forward and pulled the blanket a little tighter around Max. "Such a beautiful child."

Victoria said nothing but gripped Max closer.

"You can let him sleep for now. I have a few things to arrange. But then I expect him to tell us where the tree is. And you would be advised to convince him to tell me. If not, one of my men will do the convincing."

Elisabeta's words left Victoria terrified. She had no doubt that Elisabeta would follow through on her threat.

Elisabeta stood. "Remember, it is only by my good graces that this little boy gets to live. My good graces and, of course, his coop-eration. You do what I say, and that little boy gets to live a long life. You disobey me, and as soon as I'm done with him... well, then I'm done with him." Elisabeta smiled and sauntered back to the bedroom at the back of the plane, closing the door behind her.

Victoria let out a trembling breath and held Max closer to her. "I won't let them hurt you, Max. I promise."

CHAPTER 46

BALTIMORE, MARYLAND

LANEY LOOKED at Ralph but pointed at the screen. "What was that?" she demanded. "Why didn't Victoria run? Why would she go with them?"

Ralph shook his head. "I don't know. But there must be a good reason."

"A good reason? What reason, Ralph? Who is she? Is she working with us or—"

Jake took Laney's hand. "She was protecting Max."

Laney stopped in mid-rant. "What?"

"Max," Jake said, his gaze capturing hers. "Think about it: would you have left Max in their hands to save your own skin?"

Relief washed over Laney. Relief and guilt. She'd been ready to blame Victoria based on one action—one misinterpreted action. She ran her hand through her hair. "Of course. I should have thought of that."

She looked over at Henry. "I'm sorry, Henry. I shouldn't have…"

"She makes it a little hard to trust her at times," Henry said.

"But she *is* a good person, Laney. I hope someday you can believe that."

Laney nodded, feeling horrible.

Jake pulled her to him. "Well, you can't think of everything."

She turned to Ralph. "Where's this tree that they're after?"

"Tree? What tree?" Jake asked.

"The tree of life," Laney answered.

"I don't know," Ralph said.

"Don't know, or won't say?" Henry asked.

Ralph shook his head. "Don't know. Only two archangels know the location of the tree."

"Okay, who are they?" Jake asked.

"The one who guards the tree and the one who guarded the tree before."

"Great. Well, let's just go chat with one of them," Jake said.

Ralph looked uneasy. "The only one we would be able to speak with is the prior guard. But he can be difficult."

Laney stood. "Well, we'll be sure to be very convincing."

Ralph looked at each of them. "I think it would be better if just Laney and I went."

"Why?" Jake demanded. "Is he scared of the triad?"

Ralph shook his head with a sigh. "No. He just has a thing for good-looking women."

CHAPTER 47

JORGEN NARROWED HIS EYES. "What do you mean there was gunfight involving Victoria?"

Sean stood at attention in front of Jorgen. "The Fallen have both Victoria and the child as planned. And Chandler did learn of their location."

"So they now have Victoria?"

"No, sir. They did not reacquire Ms. Chandler."

"You're telling me Henry Chandler, Jake Rogan, and Laney McPhearson failed?"

"No, sir. I'm telling you they were not at the airport."

They sent the B team. Jorgen shook his head. He supposed it was too much to hope they'd be able to reach her in time.

How much more of a trail can I leave for the idiots? "Victoria was not harmed?"

"No, sir."

"Good. Has our friend told us where Elisabeta is headed?"

"Yes, sir. To Pennsylvania to change jets, and then they're waiting for Max Simmons to give them a location."

Jorgen drummed his hands on the table. What a waste of fuel, trailing them all over the place. "And what about the Chandler group? Where are they?"

"Apparently one of the Chandler jets is being fueled up in Baltimore, although I don't have a destination."

Probably going to find an archangel. It's really their only chance.

"Very well. Let's head to Pennsylvania. Stay close enough that we can be in the air as soon as we receive word."

Sean gave Jorgen an abrupt nod. "Yes, sir."

CHAPTER 48

LANEY JOGGED the path from the main house to her cottage on Sharecropper Lane. She and Ralph would leave immediately for Vegas, where the archangel was located. It had taken Laney a moment to wrap her head around that idea. *An archangel in Vegas.*

Jake had wanted to come too, but Ralph had insisted that they would get further with just him and Laney. And even then he wasn't entirely optimistic that they would be successful.

So Henry and Jake had had to settle for following closely behind with supplies and men. It was a gamble. But Laney was hoping that the second archangel would be close to the first. Which meant, they'd get there quicker from Vegas.

But honestly, it was all just a big guess. By moving everyone across the country, they could be going in the completely wrong direction. So as a hedge, they were leaving Jordan and Jen in charge of the second group on the east coast.

Laney glanced at her watch. She had twenty minutes before they were leaving. She needed to grab her go-bag from her cottage, but she also really needed answers to her questions. Because she was really hoping they could forgo meeting with a difficult archangel and just head straight to the Garden of Eden.

Laney cut along the back of the cottages and pushed open the gate to her little yard. Normally the site of hydrangeas, roses, daisies, and another dozen flowers in the back of her yard filled her with joy. Today, she barely spared them a glance.

She looked up and said a quick thank-you that her uncle had gotten her message.

He stood up from the chair on the back porch. "Laney? What's going on?"

Laney hurried past him, opened the door, and made her way to the hall closet. Patrick followed. She pulled her bag from the top shelf and turned to him. "I need some information."

"About?"

"The tree of life."

His eyebrows shot up, and Laney quickly explained that they believed the Fallen were looking for the tree of life in order to achieve immortality.

Patrick sat down on one of the chairs at Laney's kitchen table, a thoughtful expression on his face.

Laney took a seat across from him. "Uncle Patrick, I know you probably want time to mull things over and come up with a cohesive argument. But I don't have time for that. I need to know what you know about the tree of life." She glanced at her watch. "And I need to know in the next ten minutes."

Patrick's gaze returned to Laney. "The tree of life. It was in the Garden of Eden."

"Right. In Genesis, it's the tree of life that Adam and Eve eat from that results in them being banished from Eden. "

"Actually, that's not entirely correct."

"What?"

"It was the other tree." Patrick smiled. "There wasn't one tree in the Garden. There were two."

CHAPTER 49

"Two trees? I don't remember that."

Patrick nodded. "Most people focus on the one Bible verse. *And the Lord God commanded the man, saying, 'Of every tree of the garden thou mayest freely eat. But of the tree of the knowledge of good and evil, thou shalt not eat of it, for in the day that thou eatest thereof thou shalt surely die.'"*

"That's right. I forgot. All those pictures of Adam and Eve—they include just one tree."

"And a serpent."

Laney nodded. "But it was the tree of life they were able to eat freely from. And that's what made them immortal."

"So it would seem. But they disobeyed and ate from the tree of knowledge. As a result of eating from that tree, their eyes were opened and they realized their sins."

Laney was intrigued by the idea of a tree of knowledge, but right now wasn't the time to go into that. "Okay. Let's focus on the tree of life. It was in the Garden of Eden, and I know there have been archaeological efforts aimed at uncovering it. Do you have any thoughts on where the Garden of Eden might be located?"

"Well, that's the problem. No one really knows. According to Genesis, it was located near four rivers: Pishon, Gihon, Tigris, and

Euphrates. But no one knows when it was alleged to exist. And topography has changed dramatically over thousands of years."

"Yeah, but the Tigris and Euphrates are still around."

"True, but that hasn't stopped people from throwing around all kinds of possible locations—Iran, Africa... even Jackson County, Missouri."

"Jackson County, Missouri? Seriously?"

"According to Mormon founder Joseph Smith, that's where it was."

"Why on earth would he think that?

Patrick shrugged. "I don't know. But most scholars agree the Garden was most likely originally located somewhere in the Persian Gulf. Although the river of Pishon was supposed to extend into the land of Cush, meaning Africa, which also makes that a possibility."

"If most agree it's in the Persian Gulf, would you say that's where we should start?"

"Well, some of those suggest that it's *in* the Persian Gulf, and others suggest that it's *under* it."

Laney closed her eyes and groaned. *Oh, come on.*

Patrick sat back, his hand on his chin. "And didn't Cayce suggest there was more than one Eden?"

Laney groaned again. "I'd forgotten about that."

Edgar Cayce had said that humanity had sprung up in five places at once. Although if she remembered correctly, he seemed to think the actual Biblical Garden of Eden was in Persia and the Carpathian Mountains.

She had hoped speaking with her uncle would help her zero in on a location, or at least a part of the world. That way she could send Henry and Jake ahead. But this conversation was just making her head hurt. She was beginning to feel like the whole situation was hopeless.

"Okay. Let's ignore Cayce for the moment, and all the other noise. Where do *you* think the most likely location for Eden is?"

Patrick sat back, and Laney could practically see the gears

shifting in his head. She tried not to glance at her watch, but she was very aware of time passing.

"Actually, some recent archaeological finds have suggested a new location that may be much more promising."

"Okay. Where?"

He gave her a small smile. "Gobekli Tepe."

CHAPTER 50

LANEY DIDN'T THINK she could have been more surprised if her uncle had said Jackson County, Mississippi. "Gobekli Tepe?"

The archaeological site of Gobekli Tepe was where all of this had begun. Her friend Drew had sent her a paper about his work on Gobekli Tepe. It was that paper which had led to Azazyel tracking her down—and so had kicked off the series of events that had brought her to her current life.

But even with all the negative events surrounding her experience with Gobekli Tepe, she understood people's fascination with the ancient site. There were so many aspects of Gobekli Tepe that simply boggled the mind. For instance, objects at the site had been carbon-dated to an astounding twelve thousand years BCE. And yet the artistry of those objects was simply unheard of for that time period.

Forty-five T-shaped obelisks had been unearthed at Gobekli Tepe, and it was believed that hundreds more were still waiting under the earth to see the light of day. The ones that had been uncovered depicted not only humans but ancient animals, many of which were not indigenous to the area. These pillars were arranged in concentric circles, like at Stonehenge, but the ones at

Gobekli Tepe covered an astounding eighteen thousand square miles.

Some scholars even suggested that the location was a stone version of Noah's ark. But Laney had never heard of it being linked to the Garden of Eden.

Patrick nodded. "Some have argued that the location is actually a temple to the Garden of Eden."

"Why would they suggest that?"

"The images on the obelisks reveal the fall of man—from living in paradise to toiling in the soil. And they even go so far as to show the physical changes in man. We were depicted as more robust initially, and eventually we were skinnier, with less muscle."

Laney knew that that was an accurate portrayal of how humans would have changed as they shifted from a more nomadic lifestyle to a more settled lifestyle. With civilization came the difficulties of providing enough protein to maintain muscle mass.

"I can't be certain, but I believe the Garden of Eden was nearby," Patrick said. "The Persian Gulf is simply the most reasonable location for it."

Laney stood. "So you think Gobekli Tepe is close to the original garden of Eden?"

Patrick nodded. "Yes."

"Good. I'm going to have Henry and Jake prep and head there."

An electrical shock rolled through Laney and she gripped the island. Gritting her teeth, she looked over at the doorway.

"Unfortunately, it's not going to be that easy," Ralph said, entering.

Frustration washed over Laney. "Why not?"

"Because when humans were expelled from the Garden, the tree was moved."

"The tree was moved? Are you kidding me?" Laney asked.

"I'm afraid not," Ralph said. He nodded at Patrick. "And it's time to go."

Laney looked back at Patrick. "Is he right?"

Patrick shrugged. "The last mention of the Garden is after humans are expelled. An archangel is said to have been put in place to guard the entry to it."

"That's correct," Ralph said. "But from time to time, humans have gotten close. So the Garden and its contents had to be moved."

"Moved where?"

"Only two archangels have that information."

"Which means your friend in Vegas," Laney said.

"Yes. He is the only one who knows where it is."

"Do you think he'll tell us?" Laney asked.

Ralph looked at Patrick before his gaze met Laney's. "No."

CHAPTER 51

Victoria rubbed Max's back as he slept next to her. He whimpered a little in his sleep, and the sounds tore at Victoria's heart.

The landing gear was deployed and the jet gave a shudder. Max's eyes sprang wide open.

"Shh, shh, it's okay. We're just landing, that's all," Victoria said.

Max scooted into a sitting position and tucked himself into Victoria's side. "You stayed."

She smiled. "I wouldn't leave you behind."

"I couldn't see if you would or not."

Victoria sighed, pulling him into her side. "It's got to be difficult seeing what's going to happen."

Max shrugged but said nothing.

"Are you hungry?"

Max nodded.

Victoria pulled over the bag of chips she had been offered while Max slept. She'd known he'd need something, and this was apparently as good as it got right now. She opened the bag and Max dug in. Victoria opened a water for him and handed it over. He took a long swallow before handing it back to her.

"Better?" Victoria asked.

"Yes, thank you." Max looked around. "Where is she?"

Victoria nodded toward the back of the plane. "Back there. She probably won't be out until we land." Victoria hesitated. "She wants you to tell her where the tree is."

"We can't go there yet. It's not time."

Victoria glanced around to make sure no one else could hear them. "Max, if you know where it is, you need to tell them. I don't want you to get hurt."

"I know. But there's somewhere we need to go first."

"Where?"

He looked up at her with his little boy face, but his words were from a much older soul. "Back to where it all began."

CHAPTER 52

LANEY STRETCHED her back as she stood in the doorway of the Chandler jet at McCarran airport. She had slept a little on the plane. Vegas was three hours behind Baltimore, so it was actually early evening.

A town car pulled up only a little away from the stairs, and Ralph headed down toward it. To her right, Laney could see the Strip in the distance. *Back in Vegas.* Before this all began, she'd never been to Vegas. Now she'd been here more times than she liked to think about.

She peered in the distance to the north. The sister site to Gobekli Tepe was somewhere out there, in Montana. *Gobekli Tepe.* Everything began with Gobekli Tepe, and now it seemed as though she was coming full circle.

A chill ran through her. *Almost like everything's ending.* She shoved the morbid thought aside. No. This was just one more situation they needed to overcome. That was all. But the sense of doom still lingered in the back of her mind, just as it had ever since her uncle had mentioned the ancient site.

Patrick stepped up beside her. They had decided it might be helpful to have Patrick nearby if they needed any more archaeological or religious help. He hugged her tight. "Be careful."

"I will." She headed down the stairs. She stopped at the bottom and looked back up. "If you see any trace of the Fallen…"

"I will make sure we take off as fast as humanly possible."

Humanly possible. She winced at his choice of words. She hoped humanly fast would be fast enough.

"Go, Laney. You can't protect everyone at the same time. There are things you need to do."

She nodded, knowing he was right and wishing he wasn't. She slid into the back seat of the car next to Ralph and closed the door.

"So, where exactly are we going?"

"To the Illustra," Ralph said, naming one of the newer hotels on the Strip.

"Your friend's there?"

Ralph grimaced. "I wouldn't exactly call him a 'friend,' but yes —he's there."

Laney watched as the Strip loomed closer. Even from here she could see the ads for a handful of shows. Entertainers' pictures were plastered across buildings, ten stories high.

One of the posters was of David Copperfield; Laney remembered his TV specials she'd seen as a kid. In one he'd made the Statute of Liberty disappear. She looked up at his face. Either they had airbrushed the heck out of the poster, or the man hadn't changed in years.

They took one of the roads that paralleled the Strip to avoid the bumper-to-bumper traffic. Laney looked out her window and shook her head.

"What is it?" Ralph asked. "You don't approve?"

"No, it's not that. It's just, I've been here for almost every Fallen-related situation I've been involved in. I can't figure out why."

Ralph was quiet for a moment. "There are different places in the world that have an aura, a feeling to them that draws people in. Some are incredibly beautiful spots, like the Grand Canyon and the national parks near here. They draw people in just to be mesmerized and filled with peace. Others sites attract a baser nature."

Laney thought about what they had learned about Mount Hermon a few months ago. Alleged to hide the gates to hell, it had attracted humans interested less in the wellbeing of their fellow man and more in the satisfaction of their own individual interests.

Laney surveyed the overly developed buildings that made up Las Vegas's superhotels. The city itself had begun as a place where couples could get quickie divorces in the early 1900s. Casinos followed, and then Las Vegas was born.

Laney looked toward the west. Back in 1945, you would have even been able to have seen the test of the first atomic bomb.

Was Ralph right? Did this place draw evil in? Or was it simply a tourist destination where people could relax for a little while?

Of course, either way the hedonism would appeal to the Fallen.

A vision of Lou wafted through Laney's brain. But what about the *good* Fallen? It wasn't black and white. Just as with humans, there were bad Fallen and there were good Fallen, and everything in between.

"So what's the plan when we hit the hotel?" Laney asked.

"I though we'd take in a show."

Laney's gaze flew to Ralph. "What?"

CHAPTER 53

THIRTY MINUTES LATER, Laney walked into the Illustra Theatre tugging at the skirt of her dress. Her go-bag did not include an outfit for a night on the town—it ran more to T-shirts, jeans, and Kevlar—so Ralph had picked her up a dress while she'd found shoes at the mall attached to the Illustra.

"I can't believe I let you talk me into wearing this," she grumbled.

"Sorry, that's all they had in your size."

Yeah, not sure this is my size, Laney thought. The dress probably should have been put in the toddler section. She sighed. *Well, too late now.*

Laney took her seat in the balcony next to Ralph. The theatre was packed. Laney wasn't sure how Ralph had managed to get them tickets.

The stage was lit with two bright spotlights, which focused on the enormous, fifty-foot-tall pictures of the show's star—Drake Diablo—that flanked the sides of the stage. His legs were encased in tight-fitting leather pants. His black shirt had only one button buttoned, showing off a muscular chest and six-pack abs. Laney had heard of him, but had never been all that interested in seeing his show. He was a little too showy and impressed with himself for her taste.

He'd been Vegas's entertainer of the year for the last fifteen years. And somehow, like almost every other Vegas entertainer, he had not aged a bit. Laney squinted. He must be at least nearing fifty, but he looked like he was in his late twenties—early thirties at the most.

The lights dimmed, and Laney glanced over at Ralph. He sat with his arms crossed, a frown on his face. Ralph had chosen the show, but he really didn't look like a fan. She'd tried to pressure him into going directly to see the archangel, but Ralph had explained that the archangel wouldn't be available until later.

Trying to tamp down the urgency that was welling up inside of her, Laney counted to ten. Sitting here was a waste of time. Of course, not doing anything until they met the archangel would probably drive her even more nuts.

The lights dimmed and went black. Music with a heavy bass began to play, drowning out any chance for conversation. Shaking her head at the missed opportunity, Laney turned her attention to the stage as Drake stepped out. He was as good-looking as his posters; light brown hair framed a well-tanned, perfectly symmetrical face with piercing blue eyes. With a sigh, Laney did her best to enjoy the show.

Over an hour later, Laney was leaning forward, holding her breath. The show had been incredible. Even with all the loud music and flash, it was hard not to be enthralled.

Laney glanced over at Ralph.

He sat with his arms crossed, a frown on his face. "Time for the big finale."

"You've seen this before?"

Ralph nodded, and Laney stared at him in shock. Ralph had taken in a Vegas show before? When?

Drake's assistants pushed a giant tank of water onto the stage. Drake smiled as he climbed the ladder next to it, wrapped in chains. With a grin at the audience, he jumped into the tank. The chains dragged him to the bottom. He turned from side to side, trying to undo them.

The giant clock next to the tank counted down.

Laney watched as Drake struggled in the tank. The assistants began to look nervous. Laney leaned forward with a frown. Was this part of the show?

A glance at the clock showed that a minute had passed.

In the tank, Drake went still—his eyes wide. One of the assistants screamed. People in the audience stood up.

"Get him out!" someone shouted.

A man from the wings ran out with a sledgehammer. He took a swing, but the glass didn't break. Another two swings and the glass began to fracture.

Laney looked back and forth between the clock and Drake's body, which floated, unmoving. Her hand covered her mouth. "Oh my God."

Paramedics rushed the stage as the stagehand swung again. At last the glass broke, and water gushed out, along with Drake's body.

The audience collectively gasped. A few people screamed.

The paramedics rolled the body onto its back and pushed against his stomach.

And then the body disappeared.

Everyone in the room went still.

Laney looked over at Ralph, who looked completely unimpressed.

"Looking for me?" a voice called out.

Sitting on a swing suspended thirty feet from the stage, Drake grinned down at the audience.

The crowd erupted in cheers.

"Holy cow." Laney felt a little faint. "How did he do that?"

Drake stood on the swing and performed a deep bow before diving from the swing, tucking and rolling as he hit the stage. He leapt to his feet, his arms outstretched. Applause thundered back at him.

Ralph grunted. Laney looked at him in disbelief. "How could you not like that?"

"Laney, put on your ring."

She looked at him curiously, then removed the chain from around her neck. As she slid the ring on her finger, she tensed in anticipation of the jolt from Ralph's presence.

The jolt ripped through her, but she was all right with that. She had prepared for it. It was the *second* jolt she hadn't been prepared for.

She gasped, staring at Ralph. "*He's* the archangel?"

CHAPTER 54

L ANEY FOLLOWED Ralph backstage after the show. She still couldn't believe that Drake Diablo was an archangel. She wasn't sure what she had expected an archangel to look like, but it certainly wasn't Liberace's not-so-distant cousin.

Noise assaulted them as they pushed through the stage doors. Drake had a line of groupies waiting outside his dressing room—women of all ages and ethnicities. All in short dresses, all focused on getting in to see Drake.

A group of groupies, she mused. *Or is it a gaggle of groupies?*

Laney started to settle against a wall down the hall from them, but Ralph took her by the arm and led her forward.

"Hey," a few of the women called out as Ralph cut in front of them. Ralph ignored them and knocked on the door. He waited only a second before opening it.

Drake sat at his dressing table—one of those old-fashioned ones with dozens of light bulbs ringing it. He had two young women in very tight dresses pressed up against him.

Drake caught sight of Ralph in the reflection and raised an eyebrow. "So you've finally decided to take a vacation?"

Ralph grunted. "Hardly. We need to talk."

Drake nuzzled the neck of one of the women. "Well, as you can see, I'm a little busy right now. Why don't you try me in a few hours?"

One of the women pouted.

Drake smiled. "Actually, tomorrow would probably be better."

The women giggled, and Laney struggled not to gag.

Drake craned his neck and met Laney's eyes. "My, my, my, have you brought me a present? That is very considerate of you. And who might you be, my dear?"

"I'm the one about to throw up all over your dressing room if you keep talking that way."

Drake paused—then his eyes locked onto Laney's ring. The smile dropped from his face. "Oh, shit. You're the ring bearer."

CHAPTER 55

DRAKE USHERED the two women from his dressing room with the promise of meeting up with them later—a promise sealed with a kiss. Laney looked at Ralph, who rolled his eyes. Drake kept his bedroom expression on his face until the door closed behind the two groupies.

Then all pretense dropped. "I'd say I'm happy to meet you, but I'm not." He turned to Ralph. "Why is *she* here?"

"*She* can speak for herself," Laney said.

Drake ignored her, his attention on Ralph. "Why?"

"The Fallen are making a play for the tree."

"Which one?"

Laney started. *Which one?*

"Life."

Drake let out a dramatic sigh and flopped onto the couch in the back of the room. "What a pain in the ass."

Laney waited for more, but apparently that was the sum total of Drake's thoughts on the subject. She turned to Ralph. "*This* is our great hope? He seems kind of useless."

Drake laughed. "I'm trying to be."

Again Ralph rolled his eyes. "We need to know where the tree is."

Drake let out a lusty sigh. "Why? Why not just let them have it? Aren't you sick of always running around on these errands? There's more to life than duty."

Laney gestured around the room. "This is your grand life? A Vegas show?"

"It's hedonism at its best—and why not? I've done my time." He looked pointedly at Ralph. "More than others."

Laney looked at Ralph as well. "What does he mean?"

Drake crossed his legs on the coffee table in front of him. "Archangels who guard the tree are supposed to spend their lives in solitude, focused on their task. It's not a lot of fun."

Laney eyed Drake doubtfully. "*You* spent time in solitude?"

He flashed a grin at her. "And now I'm making up for it."

Ralph simply stared at Drake without a word.

Laney couldn't figure out the dynamic here. What were these two? Friends? Enemies? Frenemies? "So there's no contact with others?" she asked.

"Not while on duty," Drake said.

Laney looked around the dressing room. A red lace bra hung from a dresser along the back wall. "And now you're… what? On vacation?"

Drake and Ralph exchanged a look before Drake spoke. "I suppose you could say that. The previous guardian of the tree is given a sabbatical of sorts on Earth after their time is up. A way to recharge after their tour of duty."

"For how long?"

"A thousand years," Drake said.

Laney's eyes went wide. "That's a lot of recharging."

Drake waved his hand and scoffed. "Hardly."

"That's the length of time an angel guards the tree," Ralph said. "But it's more than a vacation. They're also the backup should anything go wrong with the next guardian."

Laney tried to imagine what could go wrong. They were super-charged beings in a hidden location. She came up blank. "Go wrong? Like what?"

"Sometimes the angels get a little bored," Ralph said.

"Or a little crazy," Drake muttered.

"Crazy?" Laney asked.

Ralph shrugged. "It's happened. An archangel ventures out. Occasionally a human or two catches sight of one of us. And then the stories grow."

"Stories?" She struggled to come up with something that would fit the idea of an archangel hanging out among humans.

"The last one was known as Karasu Tengu," Drake said.

Laney looked between the two of them. "I have absolutely no idea who that is."

Ralph smiled. "He's a Japanese legend. He is said to have lived deep in the forests around Mount Fuji. He could appear and disappear in a moment. He was believed to be half-man, half-bird."

"Mainly because of his big nose." Drake extended his hand from his own nose. "That thing was huge."

Ralph ignored him. "Occasionally Karasu would help find a lost child or even make someone he thought deserved it get lost—"

"Or go a little mad," Drake said not so quietly under his breath.

Ralph nodded. "True. He did not do too well at the isolation. And he only started playing little tricks at around year seven hundred. It's understandable."

"So he was recalled?" Laney asked.

Drake nodded. "Yup. And I took his place. So I got part of his term and then all of mine. Fun, fun, fun."

Laney tried to imagine Drake spending centuries on his own. She just couldn't do it. "So how do you go from archangel to Vegas headliner?

Drake leaned back in his chair, placing his feet on top of the dressing table. "Trust me, if you spent centuries on your own, you'd be looking for a lot of human interaction too. And what better place than Vegas? The place never sleeps, there's always new people winging through, and the weather's a hell of a lot better than New York."

"How long have you been here?" Laney asked.

Drake shrugged. "I don't know—about twenty, thirty years."

Laney's jaw fell open. "And no one's noticed you haven't aged?"

Drake flashed her another smile. "It's Vegas, baby. Nobody ages."

Ralph grunted. Laney looked between the two of them. Ralph and Drake couldn't be more different, and yet they were both archangels. How on earth was that possible?

She turned to Ralph. "But *you* age."

Ralph nodded. "I've chosen to. I could easily choose not to."

Drake got to his feet. "A much *better* choice, in my not even slightly humble opinion. Anybody want a drink?"

Laney and Ralph both shook their heads.

Drake walked to the refrigerator in the corner and pulled out a beer. Flipping off the cap, he took a deep drink before speaking again. "No one notices anything in Vegas. Besides, with all the plastic in the entertainers around here, no one needs a flotation device when swimming. So let's just say that when it comes to denying the hands of time, I'm in good company. I just don't have to pay a surgeon."

Laney pictured the Copperfield poster she'd seen on the way in. Drake wasn't wrong.

"Well, we need to know where the tree of life is," Laney said.

Drake gave her a killer smile that she was sure had set legions of girls swooning. He walked over to her and traced his finger along her chin, waiting until she met his eyes.

"Absolutely not."

CHAPTER 56

MOUNT HERMON, LEBANON

BACK TO WHERE *it all began.* Further questioning of Max had at last resulted in a location: Mount Hermon. Victoria had relayed the information to Elisabeta, who had only raised her eyebrows in response. A short time later, they had switched planes and headed across the ocean.

Mount Hermon—the place where the Fallen angels had originally touched down. It was located between three warring countries: Israel, Lebanon, and Syria. Elisabeta had flown them into Lebanon. From there, they'd taken two helicopters to the base of Mount Hermon.

Victoria looked out as the helicopter touched down. She had kept Max's hand firmly grasped in hers the whole trip. She knew the tree of life wasn't here. It couldn't be. So why had Max led them here?

Victoria helped Max out of the chopper. Three jeeps were waiting outside. Gerard walked over to Victoria and Max. "You two are with me."

They followed behind him. As they walked toward the Jeep,

Victoria met Max's eyes. He nodded toward Gerard meaningfully. Victoria stumbled for a moment, realizing what Max wanted her to do.

They climbed into the back seat of the Jeep, and Gerard and another Fallen—a man of Spanish descent named Hakeem—took the front seats. Victoria knew the drive would only be about twenty minutes.

Ten minutes into the journey, once she was convinced that neither Fallen was paying attention to them, she leaned down to Max and whispered. "Are you sure it's him?"

"Yes. He can help us."

Victoria studied the tall blond Fallen. She'd seen no inkling of kindness in him—only deference to Samyaza. But when she peered into Max's eyes, she saw the conviction there. She nodded. "Okay."

A few minutes later they pulled to a stop. Elisabeta's group had arrived ahead of them and had already started down the short mountainous path to the remains of the temple. Victoria climbed out of the Jeep, feeling sore. She was not made for these trips anymore.

She took Max's hand and tried to give him a reassuring smile. "You're sure?" she asked one last time.

"Trust me."

As Victoria peered down at him, she realized that she did.

Gerard came around the car. "Let's go. We need to catch up." He gestured for them to walk ahead of him.

Victoria did, falling in step behind Hakeem. She walked silently for a few minutes with Max beside her, debating when to make her move. Up ahead, she heard Elisabeta speaking. Her stomach clenched. There was no more time.

She slowed and fell back to Gerard's side, then stopped.

He stopped too, and frowned. "What are you doing? Keep walking."

She reached for his face, keeping his gaze locked on hers.

He reared back.

"Don't," Victoria said softly, and Gerard stopped moving.

"What are you doing?" he repeated.

She placed her hand on his cheek, feeling the energy stir inside her. "Helping you remember."

CHAPTER 57

GERARD FELT as if all the air had been sucked from his lungs. He dropped to his knees, gasping for breath. Then he inhaled, and the scenery around him began to swirl and disappear. His breath rushed back to him as the world around him came to a dizzying stop.

He looked around in wonder, holding his head. It was the same… but different. Why? What had changed?

Victoria was gone. Max was gone. Samyaza was—

He paused and squinted. There was a group on the summit, a large group—perhaps two hundred men. He rose to his feet and walked toward them.

His shoulders tensed as one of the men turned around and looked at him. Or rather, at the space he occupied. The man's eyes glided right past him with not a flicker of acknowledgment. *They can't see me.*

As Gerard walked forward, he felt a sudden jolt of recognition. He *knew* these men. Kakabel, Aaron, Baraquel, Gadreel, Ramuel, Turel. Their names flowed through his mind in an unending stream as his eyes darted from face to face. He knew them all as well as he knew himself.

He stopped when he saw the tall Fallen who stood between

Tamiel and Penume. He knew the man well. His name was Batraal. *He is me.*

Gerard studied this earlier version of himself; he was confident, his back straight, his eyes focused. He was darker in this first incarnation, both in eyes and hair. But his face was much the same.

Then all the men turned, and Gerard saw one man standing higher than the others. He walked quickly forward to get a better view, realizing he could walk right through the men without them sensing him. When he reached the center of the group, he came to a dead stop.

Samyaza stood atop a rock. The jolt of recognition nearly dropped Gerard. He was so used to seeing Samyaza as Elisabeta that he had forgotten how powerful he had once been. His shoulders were broad. His long blond hair was twisted into a braid that ran halfway down his back. His eyes scanned the crowd, looking for deception, danger. This was the Samyaza who had convinced them all to fall.

And while Samyaza was their leader, the man to his right was without a doubt his primary weapon. *Azazyel.* Even though Samyaza stood on a rock, the man next to him was almost his height. He towered above the others, giving the impression of strength and violence. Where the rest of the men wore loose-fitting tunics, Azazyel wore metal and held a large spear in his hands. And even though he was surrounded by his brothers, his eyes constantly scanned for threats. His blond hair and bright blue eyes did nothing to soften his expression.

Gerard examined the two men. He had forgotten how alike in appearance they had been.

Samyaza began to speak. "We have been loyal soldiers. Always following orders, never demanding anything for ourselves." He cast his hand down the mountain. "But look at these humans. They love, hate, cry, laugh. They choose for themselves what to do with their lives. They are not controlled. They have wives and children."

His brothers gazed around uneasily, but more than one nodded his head in agreement. Gerard remembered how enamored he himself had been of the humans. Their lives were filled with ups and downs, and they pushed through all of it. But the most shocking part of their lives had been their joy. They found joy in the most simple of things. The laugh of a child. The first flower of spring. He remembered wondering how on earth that was possible.

Samyaza looked intently around the group, trying, it seemed, to pin down each of the two hundred with his gaze. "It is *our* turn for that freedom. It is our turn to enjoy the spoils of this planet. It is our turn to have children and family. We are owed this."

Gerard knew what came next: the pledge. He leaned forward, eager to hear the exchange again. But the vision disappeared.

No! Gerard screamed, but he knew that no sound left his lips. He felt like he was falling, the gray sky around him swirling in anger. Once again, he crashed to the ground, but this time a jolt shuddered through his knees at the impact.

As he closed his eyes against the pain, he felt sun on his face. He opened his eyes again in confusion. He was in a field covered in tall grasses. The sun was high in the sky, and it was warm. Birds flew overhead and he could hear a river somewhere nearby.

Getting to his feet, he looked around at the empty hillside. Soon his eyes picked up matted grass, indicating a well-worn path. He followed it, not sure where he was heading. But somewhere in the back of his mind he knew he'd been to this place before. That it had once meant something to him.

A child's laugh cut through the air, and Gerard went still. Another child's giggle answered it. Fear pierced Gerard, but he didn't know why. Frantic, he scrambled to the top of the hill. Spread out on the other side lay a small village. There looked to be about a dozen tents, with livestock penned close to a quiet river. Without looking, he knew the pens held goats and pigs.

At the base of the hill, two children played—a girl and a boy, six years old.

Twins, he knew in his heart.

The girl, Arya, caught the boy in a hug. "Got you!"

Peter turned to her with a pout. "I let you catch me." Soon, though, the pout disappeared with a smile. Peter pointed to the sky. "Look, a falcon!"

The two children looked up, offering Gerard the first glimpse of their faces.

For the third time, Gerard stumbled to his knees. He knew these children. Grief threatened to overwhelm him.

They are mine.

CHAPTER 58

LAS VEGAS, NEVADA

Laney stared at Drake. He wouldn't tell them where the tree of life was located. "What? Why not?"

Drake resumed his seat. "I can't just hand over that information willy-nilly. There's a reason we protect the tree."

Ralph stepped forward. "It's in danger. If the Fallen reach it, they'll use it to become immortal."

Drake shrugged. "Not seeing how that's my problem."

"Think of the destruction they'll rain down," Laney said. "They'll enslave everyone!"

"Not me," Drake said. "Besides, I never really understood why their punishment was so harsh. So they wanted to diddle a couple of humans. Who doesn't? An eternity of damnation seems a bit harsh."

"But it wasn't just that they wanted to sleep with women. It was the evil they brought into the world. The violence, the death," Laney said.

Drake raised an eyebrow. "Oh, they brought death into the world, did they?"

Laney paused and looked at Ralph, whose jaw was tight. "Why do I think I'm missing something?"

"Because you are, my dear. Because you are." Drake stood up. "Well, I'm famished. How about we go get a bite to eat?"

Laney stared at him, incredulous. The Fallen were after immortality, and Drake wanted to grab a burger? She stepped forward.

Ralph grabbed her arm and shook his head. "I could stand a bite to eat as well."

Laney threw up her hands. "Great. Let's eat."

Laney and Ralph rode with Drake in his Maybach. Laney had tried to take the back seat, but Drake had insisted she ride up front with him. Laney was pretty sure it was so he could check out her legs—which only made her more aware of them. She struggled not to move them.

Which she was pretty sure Drake was also aware of.

Outside the Illustra, the Strip was lit up like a Christmas tree. They drove slowly by Harrods, Paris, little kiosks, vendors selling half-price shows, and a never-slowing tide of tourists.

Laney expected Drake to pull into one of the high-end hotels; she figured he'd be the type to go top drawer. But in a few minutes they had left the Strip behind and were heading into the Las Vegas that not many tourists ever bothered visiting.

"Where are we going?" Laney asked.

"My favorite place," Drake answered.

Ralph sighed loudly from the back.

Buildings appeared farther and farther apart as they drove, eventually giving way to open desert. They drove along in silence for another few minutes before lights appeared on the horizon. A couple of loud Harleys came up on them from behind, then sped past toward the first building Laney had seen for miles.

Laney closed her eyes as dread filled her. *Please tell me he's kidding.*

Drake pulled to a stop about twenty feet from the building. It wasn't really a parking lot so much as dirt that people parked on.

Laney stared at the ramshackle building with its long porch, faded cedar shingles, and, most notably, over three dozen motorcycles parked around it. At least a dozen bikers of various shapes, sizes, and ages stood along the porch. They all turned when Drake parked.

Laney turned to Drake. "*This* is your favorite place?"

Drake grinned. "Sure is. Of course, I've been banned for fifteen years. But hopefully they've forgotten by now."

Laney shook her head and closed her eyes. *Oh, crap.*

Drake got out of the car, and Laney did the same, taking a moment to pull down her dress, which had crept up in the car. Ralph stood protectively behind her.

Without a word, Laney and Ralph followed Drake.

Laney would have liked to have said that Drake walked up the stairs, but the truth was that it was a more of a sashay, his hips swinging from side to side. It was made even worse by his leather pants and his unbuttoned black shirt.

Laney rolled her eyes. "Is he trying to get us killed?" she muttered to Ralph.

"Probably," Ralph said with a frown.

The bikers on the porch stared daggers at Drake. Drake gave them all a jaunty wave and pulled open the door. He held it open, bowing low. "Ladies first."

Laney grimaced and stepped through the door. The moment she did, she felt every eye in the place on her. It was so abrupt she wouldn't have been surprised if the music had screeched to a halt like in some bad movie.

Drake stepped up next to her. She gritted her teeth and looked over at him. "I hate you."

He grasped her arm, leading her forward. "That is unfortunate, because you're really beginning to grow on me."

He led them over to a vacant table with two chairs, squeezed between four other tables packed with very large occupants. Drake wiped off a chair and held it out for Laney. "My lady."

Laney shook her head and took the seat. Ralph took the other one. Laney leaned over to him. "Why didn't he just cartwheel in and then jump on the tables? It would have been less obvious."

"Oh, it'll get worse," Ralph warned. "Just be ready."

Drake made his way across the room. "May I borrow this chair?" he asked a man at another table.

A biker with a leather vest and black hair in two long braids glared at him.

"I'll take that as a yes." Drake picked up the chair and carried it above his head across the space. With a flourish, he dropped it in place and took a seat. "So, what's everyone hungry for?"

Laney noted the sticky floor, the scarred tables, and the bartender with the long gray beard and bandana. "Um, somehow I don't seem to have much of an appetite."

The bartender stared at the three of them for a moment, then stiffened and reached under the bar. He pulled out a baseball bat, then walked around the bar and headed for their table.

"Um, Drake, I think we should go," Laney said.

Drake waved her off. "Nonsense. We just got here."

A group of six guys fell in line behind the bartender as he made his way over. Laney quietly slipped her heels off under the table. "Drake, I think the bartender remembers you."

Drake looked over and then stood, a giant grin on his face. "Mouse. It's great to see you. How's your sister?"

Mouse swung the bat at Drake's head.

CHAPTER 59

GERARD STARED down the hill at his son and daughter; the memories of that long-ago life crashed into him. He gulped in air, feeling weak.

He jerked his head up as a woman called out to the children.

He stared at her—her long brown hair, her tanned complexion. And even though he could not see them from here, he could picture her pale blue eyes.

Kyra.

The image disappeared, and the swirling gray reappeared. A longing coursed through him, so deep it felt like it incorporated the depth of the world. *How could I have forgotten them?*

But then the gray that had enveloped him quickly disappeared. It was night, in the same village. But now the village was ablaze. People screamed in terror. Gerard got to his feet on trembling legs even though he knew that no one could see him and he would be unable to help.

He flew down the hill toward the river. Bodies burned in their tents; others were strewn across the pathways. He dodged them, feeling sick. He had known these people. He had cared about these people. He ran to the river's edge.

A group of six warriors stood there; in front of them a man was on his knees, cradling two small, unmoving bodies to his chest. Gerard's heart constricted at the sight of Peter and Arya. He glanced at his own face and felt the pain course through him again.

"Why?" Batraal yelled at the warrior towering over him.

Samyaza shook his head with disgust. "They made you weak. They made you vulnerable. Now you have no weakness."

"You had no right! They were mine! They were..." His voice broke off.

"We did not come here for this." Samyaza nodded to two of his men, who moved toward Batraal.

Batraal laid the bodies of his dead children on the ground, seized his staff from beside him, and leapt up, his anger barely leashed. "You will not *touch them!*"

In a blur of movement he had impaled both men through the heart.

Samyaza watched impassively. "This is how it is? You would turn on your own brothers?"

"You killed my family!"

Samyaza scoffed. "We did not come here to play house. We came here to be *gods*. God commanded humans to be fruitful, to replenish the earth, to subdue it, and to have dominion over every living thing."

Batraal's voice rang with anger and disgust. "That was never his command. That was yours. Animals, humans... they lived in peace before we arrived. We destroyed them. We destroyed this world."

Samyaza narrowed his eyes. "You would deny the Father's command?"

"We *all* denied his command! And no, I do not deny his commands now. I deny yours!"

Samyaza narrowed his eyes. "You dare to speak this way to me?"

"I dare it and more." Rage coursed through Batraal. "We came here for exactly this! You have forgotten why we fell. We came to have families, to live our lives as we chose. I chose *them.*"

THE BELIAL ORIGINS   195

Samyaza adjusted his grip on his sword. "You chose wrong."

Batraal stepped over his children's bodies, and for once Samyaza did not intimidate him. All he felt was pure undiluted rage.

He lunged, his fist ramming through Samyaza's chest. "No. You did."

CHAPTER 60

LAS VEGAS, NEVADA

DRAKE DUCKED out of way of the bat and Laney shoved her chair back as well to avoid getting hit. Unfortunately, she knocked into the man at the table behind her, who was just taking a drink from his beer. It sloshed all over him and one of the other occupants at the table.

"Hey!" he yelled, getting to his feet.

"Uh, sorry," Laney said. But her words were lost as the men behind Mouse rushed Drake and Ralph.

"Ralph!" Laney yelled. She kicked the back of the legs of the first man she could reach, then yanked him back by the hair. He slammed to the ground, crashing on top of another man. The second man threw him off, but not without first punching him in the face.

And that was it. The whole place erupted.

A man grabbed Laney's left arm. She reached over with her right hand and twisted the man's hand at a ninety-degree angle. Then she shoved the man face-first into another table.

She caught a glimpse of her reflection in the mirror and saw a man preparing to throw a hook at the back of her head. She dodged out of the way, twirled under his arm, and landed a punch to his stomach and an open palm to his face. Then she dodged back under his arm, pushed his head away from her, and slammed the heel of her foot into the side of his knee. She slammed her palm underneath his chin, forcing his head back, and he crumpled to the ground.

Another man rushed her, and she unleashed a sidekick that sent him sprawling. Turning, she barely managed to avoid a fist aimed at her face. She stumbled over a bottle on the floor and landed on her butt. A man reached down for her, so she fell onto her back and kicked him in the face with both feet. He flew backward.

Laney rolled to her stomach and got to her feet. Someone grabbed her by the hair, yanking her up. She stepped to the side and slammed her closed fist into his groin. He let out a grunt and loosened his grip. She elbowed him in the stomach. Then she turned and threw another elbow into his jaw.

He released her with a yell and her front kick sent him flying.

Another man ran at her. Laney brought up her fists.

Then a shotgun blast cut through the bar, and everyone went still.

CHAPTER 61

EVERYONE WENT STILL.

A woman with long gray hair stood on top of the bar. She bore a close enough resemblance to Mouse that Laney was pretty sure she was his sister.

"Enough." Mouse's sister swept the barrel of the gun across the crowd. She stared out at the room. Her eyes came to rest on Laney. She grinned. "Nice."

Laney nodded, accepting the compliment.

Mouse's sister's smile dropped as she stared daggers at the rest of the room. "Now, you are all done fighting. If not, me and the General here"—the woman nodded to her gun—"are going to join you. Any questions?"

No one said anything.

"Good. Now clean up." The woman turned her back on the group and climbed down from the bar.

Laney looked around tensely in case anyone wasn't quite done yet. But everyone seemed to be over it. A few men laughed and slapped each other on the back. The man who'd tried to tackle Laney from behind walked over to her. "Hey, sorry about that— heat of the moment."

Laney nodded. "No harm, no foul."

He grinned, and a gold tooth blinked back at her. "You have some pretty good moves for a little thing. Where'd you learn to fight like that?"

"I was raised by a Marine." The man grinned and pointed to a tattoo on his left bicep—the American flag with "Semper Fi" underneath it. "Me too. How about I buy you a drink?"

Laney looked over to where Ralph and Drake were speaking with some of the other bikers. Neither looked too bad, although their clothes were a little ripped and stained. Laney was pretty sure her dress wasn't faring any better.

She turned back to the man in front of her and shrugged. "Sure. Why not?"

For the next two hours, Laney chatted with her new friend and another six that joined them. By the end of that time, they were each trying to outdo one another with their stories.

"No, I'm serious," said Chief, the man who'd bought Laney her first beer. "There were five of 'em. I barely made it out."

"Yeah, five midgets maybe," one of the other men muttered with a grin.

Chief whacked him on the back of the head. "They were all normal sized."

"Sorry to break this up." Drake stood behind Laney; she hadn't heard him approach. "But I'm afraid it's past Laney's bedtime."

"Aw, come on, one more round," someone said.

Drake placed his hands on Laney's shoulders. "Sorry. It's a school night."

Laney stood up. "Thank you for a wonderful evening. And some much-needed exercise."

Chief stood up and gave her a hug. "Stop in the next time you're in Vegas."

"Will do," Laney said. She waved at the rest of the group. "Take care."

Drake offered Laney his arm, and she accepted.

"Admit it," he said. "You had fun."

She tried to not smile, but the truth was, it *had* been fun—even the bar fight. It hadn't been life and death, after all—just bruises and bones at risk—which was a refreshing change from her usual fights.

Then the smile dropped from her face and she groaned. "Oh, God, I'm now the type of woman who views a bar fight as good, wholesome fun."

Drake reached over and squeezed her hand. "It just means you're living a little. Nothing wrong with having a little fun now and then."

Laney glanced back at the group of men she'd been chatting with. "They're a good group of guys." She turned back to Drake and raised an eyebrow. "How about you? I saw you speaking with Mouse's sister."

Drake grinned. "Just remembering old times."

They stepped outside, and a few men nodded at them as they made their way to the car. Ralph was already there, waiting for them. He opened Laney's door with one eyebrow raised. "You all right?"

Laney glanced back at the bar and waved at Chief, who'd come outside to see them off. He waved back with a grin. Laney sank into the passenger seat with a sigh. "Actually, it was fun."

Ralph closed the door after her and got in the back. Drake started the car and headed back to Vegas.

Laney looked over at Drake. "So, what was that all about?"

Drake gave her an innocent expression. "What do you mean?"

Laney gestured back to the bar. "That whole thing. You knew what was going to happen."

Drake grinned. "Let's say I just wanted to see the ring bearer in action."

"So we've never met before?" Laney asked.

Drake stared at her in surprise. "That's right. Of course, you don't remember from lifetime to lifetime. But no, we've never met."

"So? Thoughts?" she prodded.

"You live up to your reputation."

"Is that a good thing or a bad one?"

"Oh, it's good. But I needed to be sure. I needed to know you'd be able to handle the fight to come. Otherwise you could easily get Remiel or Ralph hurt."

"Remiel?"

"The current guardian," Ralph said.

Laney looked back at Ralph, who was staring out the window. "You're protecting them."

Drake looked surprised. "Of course I am. They're my brothers." Apparently Drake wasn't as cold-hearted or frivolous as he appeared.

"So does this mean you'll tell us where the tree is?"

Drake stayed silent. The miles passed, and Laney assumed he wasn't going to answer. She closed her eyes, feeling the weariness settle over her.

"What will you sacrifice to keep it safe?" Drake asked softly.

Laney's eyes opened. For the first time, Drake looked like an archangel. There was no flippancy in his tone or face. He was deadly serious.

Laney opened her mouth to answer, then shut it. What was she willing to do? If the Fallen were made immortal, the world would change. And none of those changes would be good for mankind. She remembered what Victoria had said about humanity and its cruelty and apathy. She pictured the children she had helped save only a month ago. She pictured Max. What kind of world was that for a child to grow up in?

Visions of people with absolute power floated through her mind. Hitler, Stalin, Pol Pot. And they had been mere humans. The destruction a Fallen could wreak with an unrestrained lifeline would surpass the wreckage of all history's monsters combined. And then she remembered the phrase from *The Army of the Belial*: *When the triads intersect, the time of judgment is at hand. The choice of sacrifice or death will be made.*

What was she willing to sacrifice? Her life? The lives of those she cared about? What if it came to a choice between Max and the tree? Would she be able to give him up?

A year ago, she would have said no. But now? She wasn't sure. All she did know was that she was willing to die trying to protect both Max and the tree.

"I'll do whatever is necessary," she said at last.

Drake nodded and settled back into his seat. "That's what I wanted to hear."

They settled into a comfortable silence, and before Laney knew it, they were crossing the Las Vegas Strip and pulling up to Drake's private entrance at the Illustra.

Laney reached for her door handle, but Ralph was already outside her door, pulling it open. His eyes studied her from head to toe. "Are you sure you're okay?"

She nodded. "I'm fine. Really."

Drake handed the valet the keys and then joined Laney and Ralph on the sidewalk. The three of them watched the car drive out of view.

Drake turned and kissed Laney on the cheek. "Thank you for the wonderful evening. I haven't had such fun in a while."

Ralph studied the two of them. "So, did you come to any resolution?"

Laney looked at Drake. "Did we?"

Drake paused before he nodded. "We did. And when the time is right, I will tell you where the tree is."

Laney started. "Wait a minute. The Fallen are going for it now."

"Yes, they are. But they haven't found it yet. They aren't even close."

"And when will they be close?"

"When they find the book."

Laney looked between Ralph and Drake. "Book?"

Ralph shook his head and shrugged.

"Don't look at Ralph. He doesn't know about it," Drake said. "Only the archangels charged with guarding the tree are aware of the book. It's a written record of the archangels and their assignments. But for obvious reasons, its location is protected. And until they find the book, there's no reason for you to worry—and no reason for me to reveal the tree's location. Now, if you'll excuse me, it's been lovely meeting you. Once you have this all wrapped up, stop back and we'll have some real fun." Drake placed another kiss on Laney's cheek and headed for the hotel entrance.

Laney pictured Max. "The Fallen—they have the seer," she called out.

Drake froze, his shoulders tensing. He turned, and his gaze pinned Laney in place. "What did you say?"

"The seer—his name is Max. He's only a boy. They have him."

"And Victoria too," Ralph said quietly.

Drake let out a breath and closed his eyes. "Well damn." He walked back over to Laney and Ralph. "I still won't tell you where the tree is. But the book is in India."

"India?" Laney wasn't familiar with the ins and outs of the country. What she did know was that it had over a billion people and covered over a million square miles. "Could you be a little more specific?"

"You'll find it in Thiruvananthapuram."

Laney raised her eyebrows.

"On the western coast of India in the Sree Padmanabhaswamy Temple." Drake took Laney's hand, his face serious. "You need to get the book before they do."

"Will you help us?"

Drake shook his head. "No. This is not my fight."

Laney stared at him. "But we're talking about the Fallen being made immortal."

"I have done my time. I've spent a thousand years protecting humanity. You've spent, what, two years? Call me in another nine hundred ninety-eight."

"How—"

Ralph's hand on her arm stopped her. "Laney, don't."

She looked up at him. She wanted to push Drake more to help them. Two archangels on their side would be a huge boon. But one look at Ralph's face and she changed her mind. She turned back to Drake. "Why is there even a book? It seems like a pretty huge security risk."

Drake smiled. "Well, every bureaucracy has its redundancies. Even ours."

Laney pictured a group of powerful archangels sitting in cubicles, answering phones.

Drake tapped her shoulder. "Now, you run along and keep the book from getting into their grubby little paws. Do that, and you won't have any problems."

"But can't the seer just tell us or them where the tree is?" Laney asked.

"That knowledge is kept even from him," Drake said.

Exasperation ran through her. "Why? If he can see where the book is, why can't he see where the tree is?"

It was Ralph who answered. "To give humanity a chance to stop what's about to come."

Drake shook his head. "No. Not humanity." He took Laney's hand. "You. *You* must stop what's about to come. Now get to work."

CHAPTER 62

WHEN THE WORLD STOPPED SWIRLING, Gerard still felt the anger and grief that had enveloped him as he'd sat on the riverbank holding the bodies of his children. He relived killing Samyaza, the feel of Samyaza's blood running through his hands. But even that did not dull the ache caused by the loss of Kyra, Arya, and Peter.

He was back in the present time. Ahead of him, Elisabeta turned to look at Max.

"Where are we going?" Elisabeta demanded.

"To Qasr Antar. It's just up here," Max said, pointing forward.

Qasr Antar—the temple found at the highest elevation of the ancient world, Gerard thought.

Then he looked around in confusion. No one had even looked his way. Why was no one asking him what had happened?

"They do not realize you have seen anything," Victoria said softly.

Gerard's grief was still fresh. "What… what *was* that?"

Victoria looked at him quietly for a moment. "You know what that was. It was *you*. It was what your leader did to you when you made your own choice rather than follow him blindly."

Gerard shook his head but said nothing. Was this some kind of trick? It didn't feel like a trick. It was as if a door had been opened in him—a door that now refused to close.

He walked forward to where Elisabeta stood.

Max walked away from them, heading to the northwest corner of what had once been the temple. He pointed to an array of rocks. "It's under there."

Two men started forward to move them, but Gerard waved them away, stepping forward himself. Emotions churned through him and he needed the physical activity. He grabbed the first boulder and tossed it away like a Tinkertoy. Several more boulders quickly followed. Underneath was a small cavern only a few feet deep.

Gerard squinted. "There's something in here." He reached down and pulled out a stone tablet. And the moment he touched the tablet, a memory appeared, intact, in his mind: he saw himself chiseling it out and placing it here after he had buried his wife, his children, and the rest of the village. He hadn't buried Samyaza and his troops. He'd left them to rot.

Gerard knew that in 1869, Sir Charles Warren had split this tablet in two, taking half to the British Museum. On that half, an ancient message had been inscribed: *According to the command of the greatest and Holy God, those who take an oath proceed from here.*

Gerard's hand gripped the edge of the stone and crumbled it.

"Careful!" Elisabeta barked.

An image of Samyaza covered in his family's blood entered Gerard's mind. He swallowed down the anger and schooled his features.

Then he stood and handed the stone tablet to Elisabeta. It was written in Greek. It said, *Go forth and live the lives we were promised. Fulfill the roles we were meant to play.* In his grief, Gerard had written it to remind his brothers of why they had come.

Gerard remembered this, but he knew that in this life he could not read Greek. So he looked at Elisabeta. "What does it say?"

"That we are the chosen ones," she said. "That this world belongs to us. That we should have dominion over all." She nodded at Max, narrowing her eyes. "A good reminder, but also a stall. Where is the book?"

Max ducked behind Victoria. Elisabeta reached for him.

"No." Victoria clutched Max to her, but another guard grabbed her and pulled her away.

Max looked at Gerard, his eyes huge. But Gerard saw another child's eyes. Without thinking, he rushed to Max and pulled him into his arms.

Elisabeta stepped back, her eyes narrowing. "What are you doing?"

"The boy is already scared. It will be easier to get the information out of him if we do not scare him further."

Elisabeta studied Gerard curiously for a moment, then glanced back at the tablet. "And that is the *only* reason you are protecting him?"

Gerard forced a scowl to his face and scoffed. "Protecting him? Hardly. We need answers, that is all."

Elisabeta paused. Gerard held his breath. Finally, she waved her hand. "Very well. Get what we need and bring him down when you're done."

Gerard nodded as Elisabeta gestured for the guard to take Victoria with them. Gerard watched them go before he turned to Max. Blue eyes watched him seriously. "I need you to tell me where we go next," Gerard said.

"India," Max replied without hesitation.

"That's where the tree is?"

Max shook his head. "No. That's where the book is. It will tell you where the tree is."

Gerard looked out over the valley. He remembered when he and his brothers had first arrived here. He remembered the heady rush of freedom. He remembered Kyra. He closed his eyes and took a trembling breath. Opening them, he spoke, not looking at Max. "Why was I shown that?"

Max leaned his head on Gerard's shoulder. "Your path is not

set. You can't choose a side without knowing both sides of your history."

Gerard looked down at this strange little boy. "But I *have* chosen. I have chosen my brothers. I have chosen Samyaza."

Max's large eyes studied him. "Have you really?"

Gerard turned away. He'd chosen long ago. But his family's faces pulled at him. He remembered the love, the contentment. And he knew he had not felt that way before—or since. In this life, Elisabeta had found him when he was a teenager, just come into his powers. And he'd chosen to stay with her. After all, she had shown him what he was capable of.

Gerard hefted Max up higher and began the long walk down the mountain. "I have made my choice," he repeated.

But even in his mind, the little's boy's words haunted him. *Have you really?*

CHAPTER 63

WHEN LANEY and Ralph reached McCarran Airport, Jake and Henry were already there, waiting for them, and the Chandler jet was ready to go. Laney and Ralph boarded, and they were on their way.

Once settled on the plane, Laney called Clark and found that, by some miracle, they had a safe house in that part of India, although it currently wasn't staffed. It did have an up-to-date medical suite though. Laney swallowed, hoping they wouldn't have to avail themselves of that particular service.

Clark also had agents based in Europe, Asia, and Africa, and he'd sent them on their way to the site as well. Hopefully they could get to the temple before the Fallen. So far there hadn't been any reports of any problems in the temple.

But the Fallen had now had Max for over twenty-four hours. If he told them right away where the book was, they'd have a huge head start. Laney prayed that somehow Max and Victoria had been able to stall.

Jake closed his phone and Laney looked over. "Jordan and Jen are getting the second group together. They'll be a few hours behind us," he said.

Laney sighed. She wished they were closer, but it couldn't be helped. "Okay."

Jake took her hand. "So what's the archangel like?"

Laney pictured Drake in his leather pants. "Not what you'd expect." She told Jake about Drake, starting with his show and ending with their goodbyes back at the Illustra.

"So you got into a fight at a biker bar?"

Laney grinned. "With a surprisingly friendly group of guys. Well, *after* the fight, at least."

But then her smile dropped as the conversation with Drake at the Illustra floated through her mind. "He wouldn't help us, Jake. The world is spiraling out of control. We could be dealing with an immortal Fallen, and he wouldn't help. I don't get it."

Jake remained silent.

Laney looked over at him. "You agree with him."

Jake sighed. "He's a soldier. He's following orders."

"But that's not right. He should—"

"Laney, the military works because soldiers don't question orders. They do what they're told because they know they don't have all the information—and because they trust that the role they play in things is important. I'm guessing it's the same for the angels." Laney tried to interrupt, but Jake continued. "I mean, let's play this out. Drake jumps in to help us. It becomes a slippery slope. Let's say we succeed and protect the tree. What happens if the archangels start disobeying orders and one day one of them stops guarding the tree? Think of the danger to the world! The battle would be never-ending."

A part of Laney knew Jake was right. But she still couldn't help but think that having two archangels on their side could tip things in their favor. "I don't know. I still wish he was helping us."

"I know. But we'll play the cards we've been dealt."

Laney sighed. *What other choice do we have?*

Jake went back to reviewing the information on the Sree Padmanabhaswamy Temple that the SIA had forwarded them. But Laney was too keyed up to focus on that right now. The flight time from Las Vegas to India was supposed to be close to twenty hours, although the pilot had said he might be able to shave a few hours off if they were lucky. Laney hoped the time would pass quickly.

She turned in her seat and looked back at the rest of their group. Ralph sat quietly, staring out the window. He looked calm, but his hands were curled into fists in his lap. Henry sat near him, but the air between the two was still strained. Farther back, Laney's uncle was sitting with Kati and Maddox. Kati's presence had been a surprise when Laney had met up with the group at the Las Vegas airport. But Kati had refused to be left behind—and Laney couldn't blame her.

Her uncle and Kati sat with their heads bowed, their hands clasped together. Kati was saying something quietly, and even though Laney couldn't hear the words, she knew the prayer. *Hail Mary Full of Grace, the Lord is with thee.*

Turning away, Laney closed her own eyes, offering her own informal prayer. *God, please take care of Max. He's just a little boy.*

She opened her eyes and looked out the window, unsure if her plea had had any effect. She knew she didn't *feel* any more assured of a positive outcome. You would think that with everything that was happening— all the Biblical tales that were being substantiated—her faith in the existence of God would have increased. But she had a hard time believing He was around when all these horrible things kept happening.

A hand on her shoulder pulled her from her thoughts. Her uncle sat down across from her and Jake. "Are you all right?"

Laney sighed. "Not really. How's Kati?"

"She's…" Patrick paused, searching for the right word. "She's dealing. She knows everyone here will do everything in their power to get Max back. And she's trying to hold it together. But it's difficult."

It's difficult. What a simple statement. It had been the motto for Laney's life since all of this had begun. Laney nodded but didn't say anything. After all, what was there to say?

Next to her, Jake had pulled up a schematic of the Sree

Padmanabhaswamy Temple on his cell. Laney glanced over, looking for a distraction.

Jake nodded toward his phone. "So what's so special about this temple?"

"Actually, a lot," Laney said. "In fact, recently it's received a lot of media attention. Hold on a sec." She pulled out her own phone and quickly brought up an aerial picture of the temple. It was seven stories high and rimmed in lights. Laney flipped to another view, and the human figures painstakingly carved into each story of the temple became clear.

"Have either of you ever been inside?" Jake asked.

Laney shook her head.

"No. Only Hindus are allowed inside," Patrick said.

Jake glanced between the two of them. "You two would love to get a glimpse, wouldn't you?"

"Absolutely," Laney said, looking at the amazing designs that rimmed the building. "For the architecture alone." The temple was considered an incredible example of Dravidian architecture—pyramid-shaped temples made of sandstone, soapstone, or granite that were popular in southern India. It was reported that the temple had incredible murals and a gallery of deities, and that one corridor was supposed to hold 365 intricately carved granite columns.

Laney might not have ever been inside it, but she had read up. The temple was dedicated to the god Vishnu—the Protector, one of the three main deities of Hinduism. Vishnu was often depicted as having blue skin and four arms, and was usually shown holding a lotus flower. Laney couldn't help but note the commonality with the statue that was alleged to have been in the cave in the Grand Canyon. It, too, had been holding a lotus flower.

Laney pointed at the schematic on Jake's phone. "Beyond the thick walls surrounding the temple lie, among other things, an eighteen-foot statue of Lord Padmanabhaswamy reclining. For centuries, the devout have left offerings to Vishnu there. They've been collected in vaults on the temple grounds."

"Who built it?" Jake asked.

Patrick answered. "It was allegedly built by a sage who received a visit from Vishnu in the guise of a troublemaking child. The child defiled a statue, and the sage ran him off. Later, the sage searched for the boy. When he found him, the boy changed into an Indian butter tree. The tree was immense and fell down. It was allegedly eight miles long."

Laney remembered when she'd first read of the temple and its origin. "The sage begged for Lord Padmanabhaswamy to shrink the tree—which was an image of the reclining Vishnu—so that he could see him better. A temple was later built on that spot, and within the temple walls is that statue of the reclining Vishnu."

"Do you believe that's true?" Jake asked Patrick.

Patrick smiled. "Well, the last two years have taught me to have a healthy respect for ancient stories. It is true that the origins of the temple itself are unknown. As to when the encounter between Vishnu and the sage occurred, no one is sure. Some scholars argue that the Sree Padmanabhaswamy Temple was the Golden Temple referred to in Tamil literature, which would date its origin to possibly as early as five hundred BCE. But others argue that it's closer to five thousand years old."

Jake turned to Laney. "You mentioned it was in the press recently."

Laney nodded. "The temple has been under the stewardship of the Travancore family for centuries. In 1750 the family offered themselves to the deity as servants who would take care of the temple."

Patrick smiled. "But there have been some concerns raised by different groups that the Travancores have been failing in their duty. As a result, some people called for an audit of the temple and all its wealth. And they found much more than they expected."

"Had some of the wealth gone missing?" Jake asked.

Laney shook her head, and Patrick waved her on. "Actually, the opposite. They found over twenty-two billion dollars' worth of treasure in two vaults in the basement of the temple."

Jake's mouth fell open. "Twenty two *billion*? How's that even possible?"

"In the Hindu religion, people offer wealth to the deities when they petition them for help. The Travancores have been storing all of Vishnu's wealth in the vaults. Not to mention the wealth received from neighboring kingdoms," Patrick said.

"And it's all been just sitting there?" Jake asked.

Patrick nodded.

"But that wasn't even the most interesting find," Laney said. "There was a third unknown vault in the basement." Laney paused, realizing that it was this third vault that they probably needed to get to. She pictured the vault and the mystery surrounding it. *I wonder if…*

"The third vault?" Jake prodded.

"Right, sorry. They've been unable to open it so far."

"And some people say they *shouldn't* open it," Patrick added.

"Why not?" Jake asked.

"The vault door allegedly has no handles, no noticeable locks. It's simply a heavy door that no one seems to know how to open," Patrick said.

"Can't they just drill it?" Jake asked.

"I'm sure they could," Patrick said. "But even then there are concerns. You see, two entwined snakes are carved into the door."

"A warning."

"Yes. And people are taking that warning seriously. Even the man who originally sued to have the temple audited died before the door could be opened."

Laney chimed in. "Of course, he was in his seventies, so that might be completely unrelated."

"People are drawing parallels with the legends of the curses on ancient Egyptian tombs," Patrick said.

"So what will happen if the vault is opened?" Jake asked.

Laney and Patrick exchanged a look. "I'm not sure," Laney said slowly. "But it's probably a good idea if we don't let that happen."

CHAPTER 64

GERARD SAT ON THE PLANE, sipping a glass of scotch, ignoring the show playing on the screen in front of him. He might physically be sitting in the twenty-first century, but his mind was reliving his life in Greece.

He had met Kyra when he was out patrolling one day. She had been tending to a herd of sheep. He had never in his life seen anyone or anything more beautiful. He watched her for days, trying to find a way to speak with her. Finally, he gathered what wealth he had and presented himself to her father.

They were married a week later. And he knew a happiness he had never even dreamed of.

Gerard thought back to when Arya and Peter came along. Even now, the joy at their birth was overwhelming. These two little creatures that were part him and part Kyra had not only taken over his heart, they had made it grow.

And it was then that he had come to understand why humans fought so hard to protect their families. And so he had lain down his own sword. He could not bring that pain to another family.

For seven years, he had lived in peace.

Until Samyaza returned and slaughtered them all.

Gerard gripped the armrests. He took deep breaths, trying to control the storm raging inside him. It felt as if that day had just happened.

His eyes scanned the cabin, coming to rest on Victoria. The witch had brought back all this pain. He narrowed his eyes. He should kill her for it. But something held him back.

And he looked at that something curled up next to her: Max. The boy's words echoed through his mind. *Your path is not set.*

I have a side, Gerard thought stubbornly, but even in his mind his words sounded hollow.

"And what are you looking so pensive about?" Elisabeta said, taking the seat next to him.

Gerard forced a smile. "Nothing. Just trying to think of everything that could go wrong. Foresee any problems."

"You have always been a good soldier, Gerard. Looking for the problems before they appear."

He inclined his head toward her. "Well, I have learned from the best."

She leaned toward him. "Yes, you have." Without blinking, she plunged a syringe into his arm and then leaped out of his range.

Gerard stared at her. "What are you doing?" His words came out slurred.

She gestured for two men to restrain him. "I'm doing exactly what I taught you to do: taking care of problems before they *become* problems."

CHAPTER 65

LANEY STARED out the window at the landscape below. She'd never been to India. All she knew of it was what she'd seen in movies, where it was depicted as a colorful country with great joy for life despite an inordinate amount of poverty.

As she stared at the skyline, however, it was hard to reconcile that movie image with what she was seeing below. To be honest, from this altitude, it looked like any other city that she had flown into.

They would be landing at Trivandrum International Airport, which was only a few miles from the temple. *At least we have that in our favor.* With a country the size of India, she had worried they'd be in for a long drive.

Jake leaned over and placed a hand on Laney's shaking leg. "We're good, Laney. They'll be okay."

She shook her head. "We don't know that. They could have come and gone from the temple already."

"Then we'll deal with it."

Laney took his hand, but she didn't share his optimism—not this time.

Her cell rang and she snatched it up, glancing at the number before answering it. "Matt?"

The SIA agent's voice was rushed. "Laney, I'm still about an hour away, but I managed to get some of my operatives into the area. They're already at the temple site."

Laney closed her eyes and let out a breath. "Good. That's good. Any sign of Victoria and Max?"

"Not yet. I've also set up the safe house. I'm sending you the coordinates now."

Laney's phone buzzed as a text came through. "Okay, good. We'll be landing in a few minutes. I'm going to send my uncle and Kati ahead to the safe house."

"I'll let the agents there know to expect them." He paused, and Laney could hear voices in the background. "Hold on a sec."

Laney opened her mouth to say okay, but Matt was already gone.

Jake looked at her, an eyebrow raised. She shook her head, feeling the beginnings of fear.

Matt came back on the line. "The Fallen have been spotted. They just landed and disembarked."

"You're sure?"

"We have visual confirmation of Max, Victoria, and Elisabeta Roccori."

Laney started. "Elisabeta? She's here?"

"Yes."

"Where are they now?"

"Getting into a car."

Laney did the math. "It'll take us at least twenty minutes to get there. We won't make it in time."

"My men are at the temple site and ready. What do you want us to do?"

Laney stared into Jake's eyes. He gave her a nod; he was leaving it up to her.

Laney knew that Matt's men were well trained, but still, she couldn't trust them with Victoria's and Max's lives. They would prioritize making sure Elisabeta and her cohorts didn't escape. Laney couldn't risk it.

"Tell them to do nothing. Just observe. We'll get there as fast as we can."

CHAPTER 66

ELISABETA STRODE down the aisle toward the open door of the cabin. Hakeem walked over and gestured impatiently. "Get up."

Victoria stood, then helped Max to his feet.

Hakeem had been put in charge of them after Gerard had been incapacitated. Gerard was now bound and gagged in the back of the plane, his arm attached to a drip. *Some sort of sedative, no doubt.*

Elisabeta must have found out, or realized, that Gerard remembered. Victoria had hoped, if push came to shove, Gerard might be pulled in their direction. She looked down at Max. *Or at least Max's.*

But as she was hustled out of the plane and to a waiting Mercedes SUV, that hope died. She climbed into the back with Max; Hakeem entered from the other side, careful not to touch her. Victoria wrapped an arm protectively around Max.

She fingered the sari she had been instructed to put on while on the plane. It was a deep green that sparkled when the light hit it. It was truly beautiful. In fact, all the members of this horrific ensemble were now wearing native Indian dress, even Max. Although with Max being so young, he had been given a pair of plain linen pants and a simple shirt, not the traditional dhoti that men usually wore.

The wardrobe change gave Victoria a little hope. The clothes were clearly intended to help them blend in—which meant, perhaps, that Elisabeta intended to reach the vault with subterfuge rather than force. And more innocent people wouldn't have to lose their lives.

Max had told them that the book they needed was in the unopened vault in the subbasement of the main temple. Victoria had never been there, but she knew that the vault was locked in such a way that no one had yet been able to figure it out.

She squeezed Max's shoulders. Elisabeta would expect the boy to be able to open it. Victoria hoped he was up to the task.

And she was terrified of what would happen if he wasn't.

Victoria ran through dozens of possible scenarios to at least get Max away from the Fallen. Their best chance would be causing a scene at the temple entrance. Victoria knew it was well guarded, but she also knew Elisabeta would think nothing of taking out innocent bystanders. And none of the forces at the temple were prepared to take on the Fallen.

Victoria looked out the window. She had been sure Henry and Laney would be waiting for them. She glanced back over her shoulder, hoping to see a car trailing them. She couldn't spot one. Doubt began to creep over her. What if they didn't know where they were? What if they didn't reach them in time?

Max squeezed her hand. She looked down into his solemn blue eyes. "They'll find us," he said quietly.

"What was that?" Hakeem demanded. Like all of Elisabeta's men, he was muscular and no-nonsense. But also like the others, he had a fear that Victoria could sense—fear of Victoria and Max. It tended to make the men even gruffer with their two prisoners.

"Nothing," Victoria said. "He just needs to go to the bathroom."

"He should have gone on the plane."

"He'll be fine," Victoria said.

Hakeem scowled and stared out the window.

Victoria could feel Max shaking. She pulled her arm tighter

around him, and he leaned into her. Victoria put her chin on top of his head. She wasn't sure how she was going to get out of this. But on her life, she was going to get Max out.

The city of Thiruvananthapuram flashed by as they sped along the highway. Motorcycles and mopeds dipped in and out between the cars. Hyundais and Kias made up a large portion of the cars driving by; most were older models, but occasionally a new car zipped through and disappeared in a flash of shiny color.

It's all so different, she thought, recalling the last time she was here.

With a shock, she realized that it had been almost two hundred years—back before cars, skyscrapers, and planes. She looked around. She didn't think India had benefited from the modern age. Truth be told, she didn't care for big cities. Too many people crammed into too few buildings. Humans were not meant to live like this.

Before long, Victoria could see the temple in the distance, looming over the skyline. As they approached, the crowds and traffic grew thicker, and stall vendors lined the sides of the roads. The car slowed, and she could smell curry-flavored dishes even through the closed windows.

Victoria said a silent thank-you for the delay. The more time it took them to get there, the better chances they had of Elisabeta's plan failing.

A police car pulled in front of them, its lights blaring. Victoria's hopes rose. Maybe Henry and Laney had been in contact with the police, or the SIA.

But then Victoria realized with dismay that the police car was carving a path for them through the crowd. Elisabeta must have paid off the cops. Too soon, they were at their destination.

Following the discovery in the vaults, the government had taken over security at the temple. Everything within one hundred feet of the temple was designated as a security zone and was surrounded by a police barricade. The five to ten thousand pilgrims who visited daily had to go through metal detectors and submit to patdowns, and armed commandos in camouflage ringed the site.

"Get out," the driver of their car ordered.

"It's okay, Max," Victoria said as she opened the door and pulled him out with her. She held his hand carefully within hers as she stared up at the temple. It was an incredible work of art. Each floor had figures carved into the eastern facade. Up close she could see the giant entryway that loomed above the crowds. In front of it was a flagpole covered in gold-plated copper.

Just ahead of them were a few of the armed guards that encircled the temple. Victoria had hoped perhaps they had been warned, but none of them paid much attention to Victoria and her group. And more worrisome, none of the Fallen seemed concerned.

Elisabeta headed to the left through the crowd, her Fallen following behind her.

Hakeem shoved Victoria forward. "Move."

Victoria swallowed down her anger, clasped Max's hand, and headed after Elisabeta. Her eyes darted around, looking for any sign of Laney, Henry, or Jake. But there was none.

Ahead, Elisabeta walked the length of the temple and turned. By the time Victoria had turned the corner, a Fallen was shaking hands with one of the guards. *No doubt a few crisp bills are hidden in that handshake.* The guard opened a side door with a key and waved them through.

Victoria looked around. Where was the rest of the security?

Max clutched her hand and pointed to a dumpster along the side of the temple. Two pairs of boots could be seen sticking out of the top.

There was a tremor in Max's voice. "Victoria?"

She patted his hand, careful to keep her voice calm even as her heart began to beat faster. "Let's go."

She shepherded Max forward and stepped through the door, feeling the violation. None of them should be here. The temple was forbidden to people outside the Hindu faith. Victoria closed her eyes. *I'm sorry.* She wasn't sure who she was apologizing to, but it seemed the right thing to do.

She and Max made their way down a dimly lit hallway, Hakeem and two other of Elisabeta's men right behind them. Victoria glanced through a room and the window at the far side gave a view of the reclining Vishnu. Along the walls were incredible paintings and murals, most of them depicting Hindu scenes, such as Vishnu disguised as a child meeting the sage, or Vishnu in his more common depiction with blue skin and four arms.

The group walked out of the side hallway into a busy, stone courtyard. The reclining Vishnu in his golden splendor was to their right at the far end. Pilgrims milled around, some with their heads bowed. Others spoke quietly. But all were respectful in their movements.

Elisabeta, though, rushed them through quickly. Victoria held her breath, expecting someone to yell at them to stop, but no one paid them any extra attention. With their saris and dhotis, they looked no different than any of the other devotees.

Ahead, a man with a gray beard and a well-used dhoti stood, shifting from foot to foot, apparently waiting for them. When Elisabeta approached, he nodded and began to walk quickly down the main temple hall. He paused for only a moment before turning and heading down a side staircase.

"Hold on to the rail," Victoria said as she and Max followed.

The cooler air rose up to greet them as they descended the stone steps. Max stumbled on the second-to-last step, nearly pulling Victoria and him over.

Victoria steadied him. "Are you all right?"

Max nodded, but even in the dim light Victoria could see that he was paler, and she didn't think it was the stairs that had caused him to stumble. She struggled for something to say to reassure him, but she knew there was no point: he knew almost better than she did how dire the stakes were. So instead she just took his hand with a gentle squeeze and continued down the hall.

A line of goose bumps broke out over Victoria's skin, and she felt a shiver run through Max as well.

They followed the man who had met them quickly down the tiled hall, cold stone walls lining the way. Two large vault rooms were hewn out of the rock, their solid double doors guarding their contents. These vaults held the bulk of the temple's wealth. Inside, Victoria knew, was a treasure hunter's dream: coins, gems, ancient art, relics. Victoria glanced around, wondering where the guards were. But perhaps guards weren't allowed in the temple itself.

But Elisabeta wasn't interested in that kind of wealth.

The man made his way down the hall and turned another corner. Ahead stood an unremarkable bamboo door.

The man stood to the side. Once everyone had arrived at the door, he left without a word, hurrying back down the hall the way they had come.

A smile crept across Elisabeta's face. "Finally."

She stepped forward and pulled back the bamboo door. Behind it was another door—the vault door. Two cobras were inscribed there with their mouths open, their fangs large. Without looking, Victoria knew that the door would have no noticeable nuts, bolts, or locks. This door was sealed in a way that had eluded modern man's ability to understand it.

And now Elisabeta was depending upon a five-year-old boy to open it.

Victoria took Max's hand and knelt down in front of him. "Max, just do what they want. It's okay."

"But you…"

Victoria wiped a stray lock of hair from his forehead, and for a moment, it was Henry in front of her, not Max. Her heart felt tight. She blinked the image away and focused on the actual boy in front of her. "It will be all right. I know what's going to happen as well as you. And it is meant to be. It's my destiny. You know that."

Tears crested in his eyes. "But—"

Victoria shook her head. "What you see is not carved in stone. Laney, Henry, and Jake will be here. They'll help."

Max leaned forward and wrapped his arms around her, his words muffled in her shoulder. "But it won't spare you the pain."

She held him to her, feeling a tremor run though him. She spoke quietly into his ear. "That fate was determined a long time ago."

"I'm sorry for all you've been through," Max said. "I wish I could help you avoid this."

Victoria closed her eyes, surprisingly comforted once again by the feel of those little arms around her. And reminded why what was to come was meant to be.

"Max, it's time," Elisabeta said, her voice uncharacteristically gentle.

Max pulled back and looked into Victoria's eyes. Her heart broke at the innocence there. She kissed him on the forehead. "It's all right. Go on."

Max looked at her for a long moment before turning away. And Victoria could have sworn she saw a little of his innocence give way to duty.

As Max walked up to the giant door, everyone in the room fell silent. And for a moment, he just stared at the door, unmoving. Victoria held her breath; she worried he wasn't up to the task. *What will they do to him if he can't open it?*

Then Max took a deep breath and began to speak softly. No, not speak. Chant.

Relief flowed through Victoria. Of course. There were no locks, no keyholes. The key was sound. The vibrations in the notes Max was using would affect the lock.

Over and over again he repeated a phrase she hadn't heard in thousands of years. His voice rose and fell in a language humanity had no record of. Even Victoria had forgotten of its existence until Max's sweet voice rang out.

Max's voice became louder with each note. In her mind she remembered the last time she'd heard those notes; it had been a different temple, a different lock.

Her eyes flicked to Max. *But the same soul.*

The hairs on the back of her neck began to rise. It felt like an electric pulse was sliding over her skin, and she broke out in fresh goose bumps. Elisabeta looked uneasy—as did the guards with her.

An energy began to fill the room. Victoria could feel it building. Up until this moment, a small part of her had doubted that Max was truly the seer—perhaps he was just gifted. But now all doubt was banished. No one else would know these words, this sound.

Laney had been dragged into all of this because of the Belial Stone, an ancient acoustical weapon. Now another acoustical tool would lead to the next weapon.

Max's voice grew louder. The ancient tumblers groaned, and then a screech of metal signaled their release. The door shuddered; then shuddered again. Finally, the ancient door moved forward a few inches.

Max went silent and stepped back.

Elisabeta looked at the boy with a predatory smile. She ran her hand through Max's hair, and her voice held a note of sincere awe. "Well done. Well done indeed."

She gestured for two of her men to step forward. Victoria reached over and pulled Max to her and out of the way, but like everyone else, she kept her eyes glued to the door. The sense of foreboding weighed on her like a heavy blanket, and she couldn't help but think of Pandora's box. She stared at the door, knowing that what Elisabeta did today was just as dangerous for the world as the legendary opening of Pandora's box so long ago.

Elisabeta's men pulled the door open.

A dark chasm lurked beyond.

Elisabeta barked at the men. "Flashlights." The men hurriedly pulled flashlights from their pockets and shined them into the dark space.

Max looked up at Victoria. "Some doors should never be opened."

"You're right, Max. You're right."

CHAPTER 67

LANEY, Jake, Henry, Ralph, and Maddox had ditched the car. The streets were simply too congested. Of course, the sidewalks weren't much better. But the sight of Maddox and Henry barreling down the paths seemed to encourage people to move out of the way.

Quickly.

They'd made good time from the airport. Jake had been behind the wheel and had stopped for nothing. Halfway through the ride, Laney had just closed her eyes and prayed they didn't wreck.

Up ahead, the Sree Padmanabhaswamy Temple loomed. In its presence, it was odd to see the street vendors, the small cafes, the people on the way home, bags of food over their shoulders, or standing around chatting amiably—ordinary, everyday activity that contrasted sharply with the incredibly ornate temple in the distance. *Modern life versus ancient life.*

Even with Henry and Maddox leading the way, it took them some time to wind their way through the crowds. But at last they reached the edge of the temple grounds.

"Hold up," Jake said. They stopped just before the security perimeter. Laney's eyes searched the crowd and the guards, but nothing seemed to be out of the ordinary. Everything was calm.

"Are they even here?" she asked. "Is there anyway we could have beaten them here?"

Jake frowned. "I don't see how."

Laney watched the hundreds of tourist that milled about in front. For the entire history of the temple's existence, no one had been allowed to enter it except for Hindus who were paying homage to the deity. For Laney and her friends to go in there didn't feel right. But Laney knew there was probably no avoiding that. And of course, Elisabeta and her minions would have had no such concerns.

She eyed the four commandos by the metal detector with concern. A few years ago, there had been no such security. It was said that the temple had been guarded by nothing more than a few men armed with wooden batons.

Laney shook her head. Billions of dollars in gems and minerals, and it had been protected by seventeenth century weaponry. *Although right now, it would make things a lot easier if the security was still using those rudimentary weapons.*

She looked up at the facade of the temple. "There's what? Seven floors?"

Ralph nodded. "The vaults are in the bowels, one flight down."

Laney's phone chimed; she glanced down before answering. "Clark?"

"Some of my men are inside. And one is embedded with the guards."

Laney let out a breath. Thank God. Info. "What do you know?"

"One of my agents is coming over to brief you. He should be right there."

Laney looked around, trying to figure out who in the swirling mass of humanity was the SIA agent. Her gaze flitted from face to face—and then it flew back to a face she recognized.

"Mustafa?"

The Egyptian SIA agent walked over and gave her a little bow. His hair was just as dark as the last time she saw him, and his complexion was a little darker. *He must have been spending some time outdoors.*

"Dr. McPhearson. It is a pleasure to see you again. When Clark contacted me, I dropped everything and headed here."

Laney quickly made introductions to Jake, Henry, Ralph, and Maddox. Laney noted that Mustafa's gaze lingered on Jake a little longer than the others. She couldn't blame him. The last time she had seen Mustafa, Laney had been overcome with grief at Jake's death. Now Jake stood in front of him, alive and well.

Mustafa turned back to Laney. "I have three men inside. I regret to inform you that Elisabeta is already in the vault."

Laney let out a breath. *Damn.* "Is there a child and an older woman with them?"

Mustafa nodded. "Yes—as well as a half dozen men. They had two men stationed outside as well. We have taken care of them."

"Were they Fallen?"

Mustafa nodded.

"How did you 'take care of them'?" Jake asked.

Mustafa tilted his head to a rooftop across the street. "I also brought some friends."

Laney followed his gaze and spotted the sniper perched on the edge of the roof. She looked around and saw at least another four snipers.

"What did you do with them?" Jake asked.

Mustafa smiled. "They're in a van under heavy sedation. They will not be joining the party."

"What about the men inside?" Henry asked.

"They went into the subbasement thirty minutes ago," Mustafa said.

Laney's gaze shifted to the building. "They're in the vault with Elisabeta."

Mustafa's face was grim. "I'm afraid so."

CHAPTER 68

SEAN LOWERED HIS BINOCULARS. "Mr. Fuld? I believe the party you've been waiting for has arrived."

Jorgen placed his tea on the table and used a white linen napkin to wipe at the corners of his mouth. He stood and crossed to the balcony, then grimaced at the mass of people whirling below. He hated India. Too many people. Too much filth. He'd be glad when they moved on.

Taking the binoculars, he scanned the crowd in front of the temple. "Where are they?"

"They're at the front, by the barricade. Look for McPhearson's red hair."

Jorgen did, and a few seconds later he found the group. Sean was right: her hair did stand out in the sea of dark-haired individuals. "Any reports from inside?"

"They've reached the vault."

"Were they able to open it?"

"Yes."

Jorgen frowned. *You are disappointing me, Ms. McPhearson.* "And what of their captives? They are all right?"

"Yes, sir. So far. What would you have us do?"

Jorgen watched the Chandler group through the lenses for another few moments. He focused on Laney. *Do not disappoint me again.*

He lowered the binoculars. "Nothing for now. Keep an eye on the situation and let me know when things get exciting."

CHAPTER 69

JAKE NOTICED that the guards were paying them a little too much attention—probably due to the fact that Henry and Maddox towered over the rest of the people in the crowd. He moved them farther away from the entrance.

"We have to assume they've gotten into the vault," he said.

Laney pictured the layout of the temple in her mind. "How many civilians are in there?"

Mustafa shrugged. "We do not have an exact count. But it should be at least four hundred, probably more."

"With our size of force, we can't chance trying to take them inside," Maddox said. "We won't be able to cover everything, and innocents will undeniably be hurt."

Laney knew which innocent was foremost in his mind.

Laney stared at the temple, willing another option to appear—but apparently her wishes weren't being granted today. "We'll have to wait until they come out. Maddox and Henry, you two need to stay back." She looked over at Ralph. "Is there any chance Elisabeta can sense you?"

"It's possible."

"Then you stay back too."

Ralph nodded, but Maddox crossed his arms over his head. "I am *not* staying back."

Laney felt his frustration, but they had to be smart. "They'll sense you, Maddox. You'll let them know we're here. We can't chance that."

Laney saw the war of logic and emotion rage through Maddox. She knew he wanted to rush in right now and protect Max. But she also knew Maddox was smart enough to realize that doing so would only put Max in more danger.

Finally he gave her a terse nod, his jaw set.

Laney put a hand on his arm. "Max is our priority. *Everyone's* priority."

Maddox tilted his head toward Mustafa, his eyes hard. "Even theirs?"

"Even theirs," Laney said, her eyes on Mustafa.

Mustafa nodded quickly. "Dr. McPhearson is in charge. If she says the woman and child are the priority, then that is how it will be. I will convey this to my men." He stepped back and pulled out a radio.

Laney turned away from him and studied the commandos. Each wore a bulletproof vest and was heavily armed. She saw an AK-47, a few old Kalashnikovs, some Colt M4s, and a few other weapons she couldn't identify. They all also had handguns in holsters at their waist. And then there were the police who wandered through the crowd as well.

Jake leaned down to her. "It would be easier if the commandos were on our side."

Laney sighed. "I know."

They had debated back and forth whether to contact the security at the temple. But they didn't know whom to trust—Elisabeta seemed to have a deep reach—and they couldn't take the chance of the commandos giving something away.

Still, the last thing they needed was a shootout with Max and Victoria caught in the middle.

"Are your agents in place with the temple security?" Laney asked Mustafa when he rejoined them.

He nodded. "Yes. My man is with the commander. He will speak with him as soon as you give the notice."

"Do you know where the Fallen will come out?" Henry asked.

"Southeast corner entrance is the most likely. It's where they went in and where they had their men stationed."

"Are the temple security working with them?"

Mustafa grimaced. "Not all of them. Two bodies were left in a dumpster near where they entered."

Laney's heart clenched, and worry for Max and Victoria flowed through her. She shoved it aside. She could freak out later. Right now, she needed to focus.

"Well, let's get this show on the road," Jake said.

Laney gave a nod, but inside she was shaking. This situation was untenable. They had scores of civilians wandering around, an armed force who didn't know they were there, the Fallen, and Max and Victoria right in the middle.

She glanced up with dread at the towering temple. The carved figures there seemed to be mocking them. She tried to swallow down her fear, but a little piece escaped and echoed in her mind. *You'll never be able to protect them all.*

CHAPTER 70

THE FLASHLIGHTS PIERCED the darkness of the vault. Victoria pulled Max behind her as she peered forward. From up ahead they heard hisses, followed by the sound of something slithering through the dark.

Elisabeta nodded at Hakeem and one of the other men. "Cobras. Take care of them."

The men stepped into the darkness, flashlights lined up along the barrels of their weapons. A part of Victoria hoped the men got bitten. But even that hope was chased away by reality: even if they were bitten, the venom wouldn't kill them.

A few puffs of air sounded inside the vault, followed by a curse, then weapons fire. Victoria counted at least a dozen shots.

Hakeem stepped back out. "We've cleared most of them out, but there are a lot of hiding spots. We'll need to be careful."

Elisabeta grimaced. "Fine. Let's go. Bring the boy."

Max ducked behind Victoria. Hakeem reached for him.

Victoria pushed his hand away. "Don't touch him."

Hakeem glared down at Victoria.

She stared back defiantly. "Just try it," she warned.

Hakeem growled low in his throat before looking at Elisabeta.

She sighed. "Oh, enough. Victoria, would you please escort Max into the vault?"

Victoria continued to glare at Hakeem until he slowly backed away. Only then did Victoria turn to face Max. "It's okay, Max. We'll go together."

Max took her hand.

Steeling herself, Victoria walked through the door.

She hadn't been sure what to expect, yet she was surprised to find that the vault was actually quite small: only about twelve feet by fourteen. Shelves lined the walls, filled with papyrus rolls, leather scrolls, and some leather-bound journals; a few chests were arranged neatly in one corner.

Elisabeta stepped inside and immediately strode to the center. She turned in a full circle, inspecting each corner of the room. When she was done, she looked at Max.

"Which one is it?"

Max's mouth fell open. He shook his head. "I don't know."

Elisabeta's eyes narrowed. "Listen here, you little—"

"Stop." Victoria stepped between Max and Elisabeta.

Elisabeta stepped forward until she was practically toe-to-toe with Victoria. "Get out of the way."

Victoria raised her eyebrows. "You really want to do this?"

Elisabeta narrowed her eyes.

"Besides, Max is not the one you should be asking," Victoria said.

Surprise flashed across Elisabeta's face. She stepped back, spreading her arms wide. "Really? Well, then. By all means."

Victoria squeezed Max's hand, stepped away from him, and began to carefully survey the room.

She disregarded the scrolls immediately. She glanced briefly at the books, but none was quite right. Besides, even hidden in the bowels of a temple, and behind two nearly unopenable doors, the book would not be left in plain sight.

She turned to Elisabeta. "I need a flashlight."

Elisabeta faced the man nearest Victoria. "Give her yours."

Victoria took the man's flashlight and shone it along the walls, conscious of everyone's eyes on her. The truth was, she didn't know what she was looking for. Her words to Elisabeta had been a bit of a bluff. But now she needed to come through.

She squinted at a discoloration on one shelf and stepped over to it, then wiped her hand over the wood. *Just age damage.*

She methodically moved the flashlight across the shelves, going side to side from top to bottom. On the lowest shelf, she spotted something. She knelt down and ran her hands over it. Something had been carved there.

She wiped away the dust.

Elisabeta leaned over her shoulder. "What is it?"

Victoria ignored her, tracing the symbol—the star of David, and Enoch's symbol. *Hello, my love.*

Victoria ran her hand along the edge of the shelf. Sure enough, there was a groove there. She squeezed her finger in and felt a latch. She pushed to the left, but nothing happened. She pushed to the right, and it gave.

A drawer popped out along the base of the shelving.

Victoria's shoulders slumped in a combination of relief and disappointment. She hadn't wanted Max hurt, but she also didn't want them to get this book.

When she started to reach in to grab the book, Elisabeta waved her back. "We'll take it from here."

Victoria hesitated but knew there was nothing she could do. Her knees protesting, she stood with some difficulty, and Elisabeta took her place. Victoria crossed back over to Max with a quick glance at the open door.

The Fallen moved toward Elisabeta, trying to get a peek at the book; none of them were paying any attention to their two prisoners. Victoria grabbed Max's hand and took a step backward toward the door, pulling Max with her. When he glanced up at her, she put her finger to her mouth and took another few steps back. She glanced out into the hall—still empty.

Elisabeta pulled a leather-bound book from the drawer.

Victoria tugged on Max's hand. He glanced up at her, his eyes wide.

Run, she mouthed.

And she pushed him out the vault.

Max needed no further urging. He sprinted down the hall and disappeared from view. Victoria felt relief wash over her and tears spring to her eyes. She edged toward the door herself, knowing she wouldn't slip out as easily, but hopeful that she could at least—

"Where's the boy?" Elisabeta barked.

Victoria's gaze locked on Elisabeta's. And then she threw her body at the door, knowing that if she got it closed none of them would be able to escape.

"No!" Elisabeta yelled, sprinting across the room.

The door was only inches away from sealing them all in forever when Hakeem's hand slipped into the crack between the door and the frame, stopping it. He shoved Victoria out of the way. She stumbled back, crashing into a shelf.

Elisabeta stood over her, her hands clenched into fists. "Your usefulness is over."

Victoria slowly got to her feet and nodded at the book. "Are you sure?"

Elisabeta's eyes narrowed. But Victoria knew Samyaza had not reached her position by making rash decisions. Her lips in a tight line, Elisabeta waved at two of her men. "Get the boy. And bring her."

Hakeem grabbed Victoria roughly by the arm as Elisabeta pulled open the door. Two men sprinted down the hall, disappearing in a blur.

Victoria could focus on only one thought. *Run, Max, run.*

CHAPTER 71

As LANEY JOGGED NEXT to Mustafa, she watched the SIA agent from the corner of her eye. He was glancing around constantly, checking for signs of danger. Laney had seen him in action in Egypt, and she knew she could trust him in a fight. But could she trust him with Max and Victoria?

Ahead, Jake stopped at the corner of the building. When Mustafa and Laney caught up to him, Laney peeked around it. "What do we know?"

"The entrance is only a few meters down," Mustafa said. "There were two guards stationed there."

"Were?" Laney asked.

"The Fallen took care of them," Mustafa said, his mouth grim.

The security perimeter had been extended to this point—sawhorses blocked the way. The SIA had moved two vans to block the alley leading to the side of the temple. Two SIA agents were shooing away any tourists who happened to wander over. Not great, but better than she had expected.

Laney turned back to Mustafa. "Make sure your men know the priority is getting Max and Victoria out."

Mustafa opened his mouth, and Laney knew he was going to argue with her. She cut him off with a shake of her head, and when she spoke, she left no uncertainty in her tone. "No. They *are* the priority. They come before anything,"

Mustafa hesitated, then nodded with a bow. "Very well."

To Maddox, Laney said, "You get Max and get out. That is your *only* priority. We'll meet you back at the safe house. For now, you and Henry need to stay out of their range. We can't take the chance of them sensing you."

Maddox nodded, his jaw taut.

Laney looked at Henry, Ralph, and Jake. "We're in charge of Victoria. Okay?"

Mustafa's radio burst to life. "We have Max. He's alone. We're coming out with him."

"Go," Laney yelled at Maddox, but he was already sprinting for the door. The Fallen would know they were there, but Max had to come before that. And she knew without a doubt that Victoria would agree.

Seconds later, Maddox was on his way back. He came to a halt in front of them, Max clutched tightly in his arms.

Laney reached up and hugged him. "Max."

He hugged her back. "Victoria's still in there."

"We'll get her," Laney promised, nodding at Maddox. "Go."

Maddox needed no further urging. He disappeared in a blur.

Laney turned to Jake, who gave her a grin. "One down…"

"One to go," Laney said.

"They're coming out. Two in front," the voice called through Mustafa's radio. "I think they're looking for Max."

"Hold until they're outside," Laney ordered, and she and Jake ran for an old produce truck that SIA agents had maneuvered into the alley earlier. They leaned on the hood of the truck, taking aim at the entrance. Mustafa was right behind them, speaking quietly into the radio.

"Remember, " Jake said, "center mass."

Laney nodded, not taking her eyes from the entrance. Electric tingles ran over her as she lined up the door in her sight. Two men stepped out.

Laney pulled the trigger over and over again. The two men collapsed. The SIA agents hidden on either side of the door pulled the men away from the doorway, put their weapons to the men's chests, and emptied them. Then they shoved the men against the temple wall.

Jake winked at Laney. "Nice shooting."

She smiled. "I had a good teacher."

"The rest are coming out. Victoria is with them," Mustafa said.

Laney took position again, and they waited.

Soon, more electric tingles ran over Laney. "Here they come. Everyone hold until Victoria is out the door."

Yelling from the right drew Laney's attention. The commandos from the temple security were rounding the corner. *Damn it.* "Mustafa, what's going on?"

"My man spoke with the commander. But he won't play ball, especially after finding out two of his men were down. He notified security and ordered us to stand down."

"Like hell. Make sure Victoria is protected. Just try not to kill any of the security guards," Laney said, her heart racing into overdrive.

Mustafa relayed the instructions into the radio just as the first Fallen stepped out of the entrance.

At the same moment, the commandos barreled down the alley toward them, shouting something Laney couldn't understand.

"No, no, no," Laney whispered, picturing the bloodbath that was about to occur.

More Fallen appeared at the entrance; they immediately opened fire on the commandos. Laney, Jake, and the SIA opened fire on the Fallen, just as the last of the Fallen stepped out—along with Samyaza and Victoria.

A blur appeared to Laney's side. From the sharp pain that jolted through her, she knew it was Ralph. He sprinted past the Fallen and pushed Victoria to the ground, then shielded her with his body.

"Take them now!" Mustafa yelled over the radio.

Laney wasted no time. She lined up Elisabeta and got her in the shoulder. Elisabeta flew back with the force of the hit.

Two of the Fallen grabbed Elisabeta and took off at a run. The third Fallen fell in line behind them.

"Don't let them escape!" Laney yelled.

But it was too late. The Fallen blurred and disappeared.

Two of the commandos lay on the ground, blood pooling around them. Two more were storming toward Laney, Jake, and Mustafa, their guns raised. "Hands up! Get your hands up!" one of the men yelled, his face contorted with anger.

Jake cursed and dropped his weapon on the hood of the car.

Laney did the same, then put her hands in the air. Her eyes were focused on where Ralph lay.

Slowly Ralph stood up. He reached down and helped Victoria to her feet. She dusted herself off and then gave Ralph a grateful smile.

A call came over the commandos' radios, and the looks on their faces went from angry to disbelieving to seriously ticked off.

One of them glared at Laney and Jake. "You can put down your hands. And we're…" He growled, obviously reluctant to say the next words. "We're sorry for any problems we may have caused."

Laney raised an eyebrow. "No problem." She quickly walked around the truck.

Ahead of her, Henry reached Victoria and pulled her into a hug. Laney felt a tremor run through her. *She's all right.*

Laney reached the two of them and Henry stepped back. Laney looked into Victoria's face. She was pale, and a little dirt smudged her cheeks, but her eyes were bright.

"You're okay?" Laney asked, surprised at how shaky her voice was.

Victoria pulled Laney into a hug. "I am now."

CHAPTER 72

JAKE SPOKE with temple security and quickly got permission to leave the scene. One of the SIA agents would stay behind to answer any questions.

Henry and Ralph took up position on either side of Victoria as they made their way to the cars. Laney and Jake followed behind. Mustafa's people had cleared out the exit route.

Sitting in an alley a few blocks away were two late-model Renault Dusters. Henry headed for one. One of the SIA agents moved to the driver's door.

"No," Jake said. "We'll follow you."

The agent gave a short bow and headed to the other car. Laney piled into the back with Victoria and Henry. Ralph took the passenger seat up front. Less than a minute later, they pulled out behind Mustafa.

The car ride was tense. No one said much of anything as they raced through the tight streets. They were pretty sure the Fallen had fled, but no one was taking any chances.

A few times, crowds and traffic jams stalled them, but Mustafa's driver always seemed to know how to get around them. Twenty minutes later, they were away from the city, and Laney felt her shoulders relax a little.

Mustafa's voice came over the radio. "I just had a call. The Fallen have taken off on their plane."

"Did your people get a chance to put a tracker on it?" Jake asked.

Laney glanced at him in surprise. She hadn't even thought of that.

"Yes. But the Fallen must have found it. My agent saw the plane take off, but the tracker showed it was still on the ground. All we know is that they're heading north. We'll let you know when we have a better indication of their destination."

Laney reached up and touched Jake's shoulder. "Jake?"

He gave her a nod and slowed down a little. "We're clear for now."

Laney sat back against the seat and looked out the window. A bull was being led down the side of the road by a kid no more than thirteen. She shook her head. It always amazed her how life could be normal only a few miles from the craziness that was her own life.

Victoria took both Laney's hand and Henry's. "I knew you would come."

Laney felt relief that Victoria was back. But she also felt the same old confusion about what this was really all about. And she knew she couldn't put off the conversation any longer.

She squeezed Victoria's hand but spoke to Jake. "How long until we get to the safe house?"

"About thirty minutes," he said, his eyes meeting hers in the rearview mirror.

Taking a breath, Laney turned to Victoria. "I think it's time we talked."

CHAPTER 73

LANEY WOULD HAVE LIKED to have had this conversation while sitting in a nice parlor, maybe with a steaming cup of coffee and some pastries. She hadn't pictured finding out her mother's identity while on the run and squished in the back of an old Renault. But as with so many things in her life lately, she wasn't given a lot of options.

Victoria nodded. "Yes. It is past time." Then she fell silent.

Henry shifted so he was facing Victoria. "We know Ralph is an archangel."

Victoria looked between Henry and Laney. "I thought you would know by now. You felt the charge, didn't you?"

Laney nodded. "Yes."

Victoria sighed and looked past Laney out the window. "First, you need to understand why I have kept my identity from you. It's not because I didn't trust you. It's because I didn't want to burden you with it."

"How can an identity be a burden?" Jake asked.

Victoria gave a mirthless laugh. "Oh, you'd be surprised. How did you find Max and me, by the way?"

Laney knew Victoria was stalling, but honestly, Laney needed a moment to prepare herself for what she was going to hear. "The last archangel who guarded the tree told us."

Victoria's eyebrows rose. "You went to see Drake?"

"You *know* Drake?" Laney asked. It was hard for her to envision her mother spending time with the over-the-top Drake.

"Ralph and I have seen his show a few times."

Laney's jaw dropped open. Her mother? In Vegas? Sightseeing? She glanced at Ralph, who was busy scanning both ahead of them and behind for any threat.

"I guess what happens in Vegas really does stay in Vegas," Jake muttered.

Laney shoved the unwanted image of her mother playing roulette at a casino with Drake and Ralph cheering her on out of her mind.

"Mom," Henry said, "we need to know."

Victoria's eyes roamed from Henry to Jake to Ralph, who looked back and gave her a subtle nod. Then, taking a breath, she turned to Laney. "I've imagined telling you, all of you, for so long... and now that the moment is here, I'm not sure how to begin."

"Well, how about we start with something easy," Henry said. "Like your name."

Victoria smiled. "You'd think that would be easy. But I've had more names than I can remember."

"And more lifetimes?" Laney asked quickly.

Victoria hesitated a moment. "Yes."

Laney could feel her hands grow damp and her heart rate quicken. "Okay, well how about we start with the first name you can remember."

Victoria looked out the window. "This is a beautiful country. I've always loved the flowers here—the nilofar, the water lilies. Did you know the water lilies here come in an array of colors?"

No one answered Victoria's question, and Laney knew she hadn't expected one. As much as Henry, Laney, and Jake had to prepare themselves for this conversation, Laney knew that Victoria did as well. It was as if everyone in the car was collectively holding their breath.

Victoria's voice was soft. "No matter where I was born, or in what country, I have always found a way to have a garden."

Laney swallowed, staying silent.

Finally, Victoria turned back to them. She took a shuddering breath. "I am the first woman. Two of us were created—a man and a woman."

Jake's eyes flicked to Ralph, his tone hardening. "You said she wasn't Eve."

Victoria gave a small smile. "I'm not Eve."

Laney watched her for a moment, her disbelief growing. Her mother, who seemed to know everything about the past. Her mother, who knew even before Laney was born that she would face an important destiny. Her mother, whom Cleo had called the mother of all.

Laney felt lightheaded when the truth crashed down on her. *Why didn't I see it sooner?*

Victoria's striking purple eyes held Laney's gaze, and she gave her a nod. "Yes," she said softly.

Henry looked between the two of them. "Who is she?" he asked.

Wonder filled Laney's voice—and just a trace of fear. "She's Lilith."

CHAPTER 74

LANEY WATCHED VICTORIA'S FACE—NO, Lilith's—and saw nothing. No fear, no smugness. Just Victoria. But Lilith was supposed to be this evil being who lurks at the edges of tales about mankind's beginning. How could that woman be Victoria's true identity?

"Lilith? *The* Lilith? Adam and Eve's Lilith?" Henry asked.

Victoria nodded.

Lilith. She's Lilith. Laney's mind couldn't seem to move beyond those few words.

"Who the hell is Lilith?" Jake demanded.

Laney tore her gaze from her mother. She took in Henry's dazed expression before turning to Jake. "She was the first wife of Adam."

"Um, I know I'm not the religious scholar like the rest of you," Jake said, "but I'm pretty sure the first two humans, according to the Bible, were Adam and Eve."

"Not exactly," Laney said, her eyes retuning to Victoria. "Eve was the second wife of Adam."

Laney's mind raced through everything she could recall about the wives of Adam. According to the Midrashic literature, Eve was the second wife of Adam. The first wife was named Lilith, and she was put aside because she demanded to be equal to Adam, not subservient.

"But the Bible doesn't mention anything about that," Jake said.

"Actually, it kind of does," Laney replied, keeping her gaze on Victoria. "In Genesis, there are two creation stories. It's the second story that most people are familiar with. God creates the world, then plants, animals, and finally man. And woman is created out of man's rib.

"But in the first tale of Creation, male and female were created together—as equals. It's only in the later tale that woman is created from man, and hence subservient to him." Laney looked at Victoria. "The story everyone knows—that was Eve's tale. The first story was yours."

Victoria nodded. "Yes."

Laney sat back, feeling overwhelmed. Her mother was the first woman ever created.

Henry looked back at his mom, his eyebrows drawn. "But how are you related to all the rest of this? Why are you so important? How come you live over and over again?"

"Does Adam?" Laney asked.

"No. He died a very long time ago," Victoria said.

The confusion was clear on Henry's face. "Then why are you still here? Why do you have an archangel protecting you?"

"I suppose you've heard what the tales say about Lilith," Victoria said.

Laney struggled for a diplomatic choice of words. "Yes, she was said to be… independent."

Victoria tilted her head to the side, and a small smile crossed her face. "I believe the early writings had a bit more to say about her than that."

Laney nodded. "Yes." But she didn't say any more.

Victoria did. "According to tradition, I am one of the first monsters. Even my name translates unkindly: night monster, night hag. Not to mention the idea that I am a hairy beast who lives in caves, preying on the weak and defenseless."

Laney was familiar with the references and was surprised that she hadn't thought of Lilith when trying to figure out who Victoria was. But Lilith had always been portrayed as evil—and as much as Laney sometimes doubted Victoria, she'd never thought of her as evil.

"I am the monster that parents once used to scare their children into behaving," Victoria said.

"That's in the Bible?" Jake asked.

"Not exactly," Laney said. "Most of the references to Lilith come from Judaism, not Christianity. The Judaic writings were an attempt to explain the contradictions found in the Bible."

"Such as the two creation stories," Henry added.

Laney nodded. "Yes. In fact, the only mention of Lilith by name in the Bible is as part of a list of unclean animals."

"The Bible as it is known has many passages and books that have been lost to time. My true story was one of those left out," Victoria said.

"So in the Judaic tradition, you're the boogey monster?" Jake asked.

"Yes. As well as the beast that takes the lives of innocent babies. They put amulets up to keep me at bay."

"But that's not true," Henry said.

Victoria was quiet for a moment. Laney's breath caught. *No, she couldn't—*

"Actually," Victoria said, "there is some truth there."

CHAPTER 75

"You killed babies?" Laney asked, horrified.

Victoria shook her head. "Not exactly. But I created a way for them to die."

Laney was both shocked and confused. "I don't understand. Why would you do that?"

Victoria sighed. "Do you remember when we spoke about the immortality of man?"

Laney remembered the conversation on the cliff at Victoria's home in Maine. "You said that humans lived for thousands of years."

"Yes. That was true. The ancient texts that tell of people living for long periods of time are not wrong. Originally, when mankind was created, we were practically immortal."

"Practically?" Henry asked.

"People lived for incredible lengths of time—thousands of years. They could die from an accident, but it was rare."

Laney felt the same jolt of disbelief that she'd felt when Victoria had first told her this. "So why aren't we 'practically immortal' anymore?"

Victoria took a deep breath before speaking. "I made a deal with God that allowed humanity to become mortal."

Laney stared at her mother in horror. Victoria had created a way for humans to die.

Henry's eyes were large. "Why would you do that?"

Laney wondered the same thing. "Immortality is a gift. Imagine all we could learn and create."

Victoria nodded. "Yes, originally it was a gift. And the advances we made were incredible. But like all good things that go on for too long, humanity became corrupted. There was no accountability, no responsibility for actions. People became lazy, complacent, and cruel. At first, it was only a few. But when the Fallen arrived, they exploited this weakness in humanity, and it began to spread like a virus. After all, why be good when you live every day in paradise? People would put things off because there was always a tomorrow. People became selfish, only concerned with themselves."

"Surely there was another way to change people without killing them," Jake said.

Victoria sighed, and Laney could feel her weariness. "No. I struggled for centuries to find another way. I begged God for help. But none came. The strange irony is that, without death, no one truly lives either. The true test of life is to live each moment with fulfillment. It can't be done without death, without an end. *Mortality* is the gift—not immortality. Knowing that your life has an end… it forces you to make each day count."

"How did you do it?" Henry asked. "How did you make us mortal?"

Victoria was quiet for a moment. When she spoke, the sadness in her voice was undeniable. "It was a trade. Humanity's mortality… for my chance at heaven."

Her chance at heaven. Laney was stunned. She remembered the tale.

Lilith ran from Adam. Three angels were sent to retrieve her. She refused to return. She was warned that one hundred of her children would die every day if she did not. Still she refused to return. And her refusal that day was the moment death entered the world.

Drake's face flashed through her mind, along with his words: *Oh, they brought death into the world, did they?*

Drake had known it was Victoria who had chosen this fate for humanity.

Laney glanced at Ralph. He knew as well.

And yet the archangels were tasked with protecting Victoria. Did that make her choice the right one? But why would they *still* be protecting her? She'd made the choice long ago.

A chill crept over Laney. *Unless there's still a way for her to choose differently.*

"Why does that matter? The chance at heaven?" Jake asked.

"Each human is born with a soul," Victoria explained. "That soul is struggling in each lifetime to become its truest self. That is why souls became human to begin with. And when they reach that point, they return to the Father. Those that don't are reborn—with another chance."

"Why not just let us enter heaven?" Henry asked.

"Souls are delicate entities," Victoria said. "They need to be nurtured, cared for. If a person were to enter heaven without first nurturing their soul, they would spend their eternity in torment. All the doubts, insecurities, and negativities of their life would hound them forever. There would be no peace for them. It is only by being reborn that they can hope to find that peace."

Silence settled over the car before Henry spoke, his words full of pain. "But what about you? Will you never get peace?"

Victoria smiled. "One day. When humanity understands the importance of the soul, I will be released from my deal."

Laney thought of all the headlines she had seen recently: kidnappings, murders, terrorism spreading across the globe. Every day seemed to bring a new and unreal horror to the world stage. "I have a feeling that might not be for a while."

Victoria grasped Laney's hand. "Probably. But there *is* great kindness and courage in the world. It gets greater by the day. And now that the fifth root race has appeared, well, let's just say there is a great deal of hope."

"So it's true," Henry said quietly. "Max and Danny are part of the root race."

Victoria nodded. "People are regaining some old abilities that humanity has forgotten we ever had."

Laney went silent, not really ready to go down that path. "If we've all had these past lives, how come we don't remember them?" she asked.

Victoria patted Laney's hand. "It's a blessing to not remember them, although some fears slip through. Sometimes people are born with a fear they can't explain; those fears come from their past lives. And when people are young, they often remember a little of their former lives. But soon, those memories disappear."

"So we live and die, unaware of what we've done before," Jake said.

"It's true—everyone lives and dies, even me," Victoria said. "But I remember each life. I remember each person I have loved and lost. I remember each person I couldn't save. That is the cost for my choice: the memories."

Shock flashed through Laney. "That seems cruel."

Victoria shook her head. "No, not cruel. And I don't remember until I turn thirteen. I always have a childhood before duty calls."

Laney tried to imagine Victoria as a carefree child. One who would one day wake up and her whole life would be different. She squeezed Victoria's hand. "I'm so sorry."

Victoria gave her a gentle smile and covered Laney's hand with her own. "Don't be sorry. It is difficult, but each lifetime I have love. And that is more than many people can say." She glanced at Ralph. "And I have friends."

Laney felt tears threaten at the back of her eyes. What a hard road Victoria had. Each life, duty came before anything else. She looked at her mother with new eyes. This was a woman who put the world in front of her own desires. Laney felt guilt for ever having doubted her, but at the same time, she didn't understand why Victoria hadn't told them sooner.

Victoria cut into her thoughts. "There is much that needs to be done. The danger is not over. We need to get to the tree before they do."

Laney started. *The tree.* With everything that Victoria had just told them, she had forgotten that the Fallen were making a play for the tree of life. "How do you fit into all of this, Victoria? Jake, Henry, and I are part of one triad. And I'm guessing Cain and Elisabeta are part of the other."

"As well as Gerard."

Laney's eyes widened. "*He's* the other member?"

Victoria nodded. "He is now."

Laney didn't understand that remark, but it could wait for another day. There were more pressing concerns right now.

"So if you're not a member of either triangle," Jake asked, "where do you fit in?"

Victoria looked at them each in turn. "I am the place where the triangles intersect."

CHAPTER 76

THE PLACE where the triangles intersect?

"What does that even mean?" Laney asked.

"I took everyone's immortality away, including the Fallen's," Victoria said. "I can also give it back. Or make it impossible for them to become immortal."

"How?" Henry asked.

"When I reach the tree of life, I have the ability to destroy it," Victoria said.

Laney watched her mother, her eyes narrowing. Something was off. "*How* do you destroy it?"

"That's not important. What is important is that we get to the tree. The Fallen cannot be allowed to reach it. If they do, humanity will not survive. Not even with the three of you to defend it. Getting to the tree is the priority."

Henry nodded. "We'll get to it. We'll make sure it gets destroyed."

"I need each of you to promise that you will do whatever is necessary to make sure the Fallen do *not* get the tree. The stakes for humanity have never been higher."

Laney studied her mother as Henry and Jake gave her their promises. Something was definitely off.

"Laney?" Victoria turned to her.

Laney noticed that Victoria's hands were clutched together in her lap. *What am I missing?*

"I promise I will protect mankind," Laney said slowly.

Victoria raised an eyebrow.

Laney shook her head. "That's the best you'll get out of me right now. Where is the tree?"

Victoria looked surprised. "I have no idea."

CHAPTER 77

LANEY PUT down her cell phone. They would be at the safe house in ten minutes. Jen and the rest of their crew would be arriving in about an hour, and then they'd beat a hasty retreat out of India.

Ralph had called Drake but had been unable to reach him. He would keep trying; right now, the flamboyant archangel was their only hope of finding the tree. Hopefully he would be willing to help. If not, Laney had no idea how they were going to track the tree down.

Laney watched the landscape fly by outside. Henry was talking quietly on the phone and Jake was focused on driving. She glanced over at Victoria, whose head was leaning on Henry's shoulder, her hand clasped in his.

They were so close, those two. Even with all Victoria's secrets and her big revelation, the bond between the two of them was unbreakable. Laney couldn't help feel a little jealous. She had just gotten to know her mother. She wanted that kind of bond with her.

Victoria opened her eyes and reached for Laney's hand. "Are you all right?"

Laney nodded. "Just taking it all in."

Victoria squeezed her hand. "I know it's a lot."

Victoria closed her eyes again, but kept hold of Laney's hand. Laney smiled, feeling the warmth seep from her mother into her. It was hard to reconcile this caring woman with the demoness Lilith —the hairy demon who killed children in their sleep.

Laney knew that women had long been maligned in the Roman Catholic Church. Some argued that it was due to the growing influence of Mary Magdalene, who was allegedly Jesus's wife. In 591 AD, Pope Gregory the Great had associated Magdalene with a prostitute, even though there was no evidence to indicate that Magdalene had actually been the woman described in the well-known passage—and a great deal of evidence to suggest that she was incredibly important to Jesus.

Had a similar smear campaign been aimed at Lilith? A memory flickered through Laney's mind and she tried to catch it. Something about Edgar Cayce and Lilith. But she couldn't chase it down. She pulled out her phone and entered the words "Edgar Cayce Lilith" into a search engine. Thousands of results popped up.

But she didn't need to read them. The first headline was enough to recall the prophet's ideas to the forefront of her mind. Lilith, one of the Atlantean goddesses. The first wife and companion of Amilius, another name for Adam. In Cayce's view, there was nothing evil in Lilith—only equality with her companion. And she and Amilius were the first incarnation of humans in physical form—or what Cayce called the "third root race."

"Heads up!" Jake yelled.

Laney jerked and looked forward; in front of them, Mustafa's car had slammed to a stop. Two large trees blocked the road.

"Jake…" Henry said, a warning in his tone.

"On it." Jake threw the car into reverse—they both knew this roadblock was no coincidence.

Sure enough, two SUVs raced out from the thick trees that bordered one side of the road, blocking the road behind them. Along the other side of the road ran a river, swollen from recent heavy rains, further boxing them in.

Armed men poured out from both the trees and the SUVs. Laney's head swung from side to side, trying to find an escape route. She caught Jake's eyes in the rearview mirror, and he gave her a subtle shake of his head.

They were trapped.

CHAPTER 78

MUSTAFA'S VOICE came over the car radio. "What do you want us to do?"

More men had appeared from behind the downed trees. By Laney's count, there were at least twelve in total. One man from the group in front of them stepped forward and motioned for them to get out.

"Laney?" Jake asked.

She ran her finger over the ring. "They're human."

Jake's jaw was taut. He grabbed the radio. "Right now, we do as he says. Everybody out."

Slowly, they all climbed out of the car, keeping their hands in the air. Mustafa and the three agents in his car did the same.

The gunmen waved Mustafa and his men back to join the group from the second car. Laney felt better having them next to her. Not for protection, but because she was already planning how to take the gunmen down and she needed them out of the way.

"What do you want?" Jake said.

The lead gunman smiled. "We're not who wants to talk to you."

The men parted a little.

Jorgen stormed forward, pointing a finger at Laney. "You're supposed to protect her! How can you take her to the tree?"

Laney stared at him in disbelief. *How did he—*

Henry stepped forward, his anger barely concealed. "What do you want, Cain?"

Jorgen reared back, surprise on his face. But it disappeared in a flash. He pulled off his glasses. Black eyes stared them down. "Well, I guess the time for hiding is over."

Jake and Henry started at his eyes. Laney didn't.

Jorgen looked over the group, his gaze pinning Laney in her place. "You are leading her to her death."

Laney looked to Victoria. "What is he talking about?"

But Jorgen didn't give her a chance to explain. He stormed forward, his intent clear.

Laney pushed Victoria toward Ralph. "Get her out of here."

Ralph grabbed her, but before he could take a step, three men behind them raised their weapons.

Laney whirled toward Jorgen. "What are you doing? If you're worried about her safety, why would you point a gun at her?"

Jorgen smiled. "The guns aren't pointed at her."

CHAPTER 79

ELISABETA SETTLED back in her chair, her anger still burning. They had rushed to the airport and taken off. She had instructed the pilot to head toward Europe, although she wasn't sure if that was where they would land. For now she just needed to put some distance between herself and Victoria's little bastards.

She glanced down at the hole in her shirt and curled her lip. That had been too close.

She drummed her hands on the table in front of her, staring at the leather journal. They'd lost Victoria and Max, but she supposed it didn't matter. They had the book—that was the important thing.

Elisabeta pulled the journal over to her and ran her hand over it. There was nothing written on the cover; to all outside appearances, it was just an ordinary worn leather journal. She cracked it open carefully. Dust rose from it.

She read the first line and frowned. What was this—Aramaic? She quickly scanned through the book and identified at least seven other languages. *Damn it.* She hadn't expected this, but she should have. She slammed the book shut.

"Hakeem."

Hakeem quickly made his way over. "Yes, Samyaza?"

Elisabeta held out the book. "Have this scanned and sent to my people in London. Tell them I need it translated immediately."

Hakeem bowed and took the journal.

Two hours later, Elisabeta finally had the translation sitting in front of her. And as she read it, she grew more and more annoyed. What the hell was this? Ramblings about birds? Phases of the moon? Where was the information on the tree?

With an angry swipe, she turned another page. *This is ridiculous.* She pictured Victoria's face and imagined smashing her fist through it.

She glared down at the words and then went still. She narrowed her eyes. What was this? *The first humans emerged both male and female, equal in their spirit and minds.*

It was followed by a description of the beginning of mankind and the fall of Adam and Eve—although this accounting was an accurate one. It included the tale of Lilith, the first woman, who had fought humans' baser nature and had led the Children of the Law of One.

Elisabeta smiled at the mention of herself—the leader of the Sons of Belial. But when she reached the part of the story where she died—her first death, killed by one of her own—she glowered. That death still stung most of all—because of the surprise. She had had no idea they had been made mortal.

And now it's time to change that.

Elisabeta's eyes flitted through the tale of the first time the tree was moved. She smiled when she saw the list that followed—all the previous locations of the tree. Elisabeta's eyes scanned down it: Nineveh, Sanggyeong, Atlantis, Paris, Aguateca, Copan, and another dozen or so. The last location on the list was in Japan. Mount Fuji.

Elisabeta flipped the page, her heart beginning to race. As she read the entry there, a smile crept across her face. *Finally.* She was about to call for the pilot when she noticed the writing on the opposite page.

Curious, she continued reading. And with each word, her anger and surprise grew.

"That bitch," she muttered.

Elisabeta's hands clutched the translation angrily and yanked—ripping it in two. Her Fallen looked up, but no one dared say a word.

Elisabeta tossed the pieces onto the table; scraps of paper scattered across the cabin. The answer had been in front of her the whole time. She grabbed the armrests, trying to calm down and think clearly.

Victoria and her brats would no doubt be heading for the tree. Elisabeta's eyes darted to the journal. *Which could be an advantage.*

She pictured Victoria—then pictured draining her of all her blood. *If I can't get the book, I can become immortal another way. After all, only I really need to be immortal.* She flicked her eyes to her men, and then to Gerard, who was still sedated. *None of them deserve that honor. Besides, they might try to take a run at my role, and that will never do.*

She smiled. This was actually a blessing. Now instead of one chance to achieve immortality, she had two.

Elisabeta waved Hakeem over. "Tell the pilot we need to change course."

"Where to, my liege?"

Elisabeta smiled. "China."

CHAPTER 80

TIME SEEMED to be moving by in slow motion. Laney struggled to figure out a way out of the stalemate. They could take out the shooters, but someone would undoubtedly get hurt. And worst of all, no one could harm Jorgen without receiving the same damage sevenfold.

On the other side of the car she noticed Henry and Jake nod subtly at one another. Jake looked over at her, then flicked his eyes toward the shooters in front of them.

Laney's gut clenched. She kept her eyes on the men, but her mind was focused on the sky. She gave Jake the subtlest of nods when she was ready.

Jake turned and opened fire on the gunmen in front.

Laney blasted the remaining gunmen with wind, throwing them into the river that ran along the road. Mustafa and his men took care of the gunmen behind them.

From the corner of her eye, Laney saw a blur as Henry raced for Jorgen. Laney's heart all but stopped when he plowed into him and the two of them collapsed to the ground.

Henry's scream was loud, but it still didn't drown out the sound of his bones breaking.

"No!" Laney yelled as Jorgen crawled from underneath Henry, cradling his arm.

Laney ran over to Henry and kneeled at his side. Her eyes went wide. His arms and legs were broken at crazy angles, and there was no telling what other bones had shattered. He appeared to be unconscious, no doubt a result of the pain. *Just please don't let it be a head injury.*

Laney looked up as a shadow fell over her.

Jorgen stood a few feet away, at the edge of the riverbank. He pulled a gun from his jacket and pointed it at Laney. "You should have let me take her."

Laney covered Henry's body with her own without taking her eyes off Jorgen. She heard Jake shout something, and then Jorgen's body jerked backward as two bullets slammed into him. He stared at Laney for a moment, his face incredulous, and then toppled over the side of the bank. The raging river dragged his body under.

Jake. Laney turned in time to see him fall to his knees. For a moment, time stopped, and her heart went still. Then blood burst from wounds in Jake's shoulder, his arms, his legs. Without counting, Laney knew there were fourteen bullet wounds.

"Jake!" Laney scrambled over to him. She tugged off her jacket and pushed it against the wounds in his chest. Victoria and Ralph appeared beside her, and they also helped put pressure on Jake's wounds.

Laney looked up into her mother's eyes. "Help him. Please."

Victoria shook her head. "I'm sorry. My blood won't work this time. Not against injuries from Cain."

Laney looked back at Henry's broken body, then again at Jake, his blood running through her fingers. She was shaking so hard, her teeth were chattering. Jake and Henry were both down. How was that possible?

The ring bearer will fight alone. The words from the book appeared unbidden in her mind. She stared in disbelief at the proof that those words were true.

Through a fog she heard Mustafa calling for the medical unit.

Two of the SIA agents squatted down next to her with a med kit, gently pushing her aside.

Laney moved to Jake's head and cradled it on her lap. She stared numbly at the blood soaking into the dry earth.

This can't be happening. Not again.

CHAPTER 81

LANEY SAT in the back of the van with Jake laid out on the stretcher next to her. Luckily the SIA had had a full mobile surgical unit at standby at the safe house; they had rushed over when Mustafa called. Laney was more than grateful for the SIA's foresight.

Henry was in a separate van, accompanied by Ralph and Victoria, although his wounds, thankfully, weren't life-threatening.

Laney reached out a shaky hand and ran it along Jake's face. "Hold on, Jake. Just a little longer."

Ahead of them, the gates to a walled village were pulled open and the vans were waved through. Although as Laney looked around, she thought that "village" might be a little too strong a term. There were only about a dozen buildings here.

There were also very few people. And the ones she saw did not look Indian.

Laney leaned forward to Mustafa. "Where are we?"

"This village was abandoned about ten years ago. We've borrowed it for the time being. We'll be leaving here as soon as the reinforcements arrive, assuming Mr. Rogan and Mr. Chandler can travel."

"Shouldn't we take Jake to a hospital?" Laney asked.

Mustafa shook his head. "In this part of the country, you do not want to visit the hospital. Trust me, what we have here is much better for Mr. Rogan."

Laney looked into the kind Egyptian's eyes and nodded. She'd have to trust Mustafa's judgment.

They pulled up in front of what was the largest house in the community by far. It was two stories; white columns held up the second story and more columns lined the balcony on the second floor. The rest of the buildings in the village were simple, with stucco walls and thatched roofs.

The door to the van opened before they had completely stopped. SIA agents in surgical gear slid the stretcher out and were carrying Jake into the building before Laney was even out of the van.

She stepped out slowly, then watched another group grab Henry's stretcher from the other van, followed by Ralph and Maddox. Mustafa made his way quickly over and escorted Victoria inside.

Laney watched them all go, feeling numb.

"Laney?"

She turned to find her uncle's knowing eyes and opened arms.

In two quick steps, she wrapped her arms around him and buried her head in his chest. He held her while she let the tears fall, but she cut them off quickly. There were things to be done.

She wiped at her eyes and started to step away. "I need to go see—"

Patrick gently took her arm and held her in place. "Laney, the first thing you need to do is go speak with Kati."

Laney turned back to him. Fear for Max crowded in next to her fears for Henry and Jake. "Kati? Is Max okay?"

Patrick patted her arm. "He's fine."

Laney let out a breath. "Then it will have to wait. I need to check on—"

"They're leaving."

Laney nodded. "That's good. The sooner they get back to the States—"

"No, Laney." Patrick took both her arms in his hands, forcing her to give him her undivided attention. "They're not going back to the States. They're leaving us."

CHAPTER 82

L<small>ANEY STARED AT HER UNCLE.</small> "What? Why?"

But even as she said the words, she knew why. Max had been in mortal danger for the last year. They had barely let him out of their sight the entire time. And even so, he had been grabbed, not once but twice.

She closed her eyes. Exhaustion, terror, fear, and sadness crashed down on her. It was too much. She forced her eyes open. She was going to have to face it regardless. "Where is she?"

Patrick tilted his chin toward the building just as Kati stepped out. "Right there. I'll go stay with Jake." Patrick walked toward the building, stopping to give Kati a hug and a whisper in her ear before disappearing through the door.

Kati came over to Laney and pulled her into a hug. "I'm so sorry about Henry and Jake."

Laney wrapped her arms around Kati and, for a moment, let herself grieve. She pulled back after just a few seconds though, because she knew if she gave into the emotions running through her, she'd be no good to anyone.

Laney studied Kati's face, but Kati was keeping all her emotions in check. "Is Max okay?" she asked.

Kati nodded, and her eyes searched Laney's face just as Laney had searched hers a moment ago. "He's fine. He's with Maddox. Are *you* all right?"

Laney opened her mouth to say yes—then shut it. She didn't have the energy to lie. She shrugged instead. "I don't know."

An uncomfortable silence stretched between them.

Laney looked at Kati, this woman with whom she had lived for five years. They were sisters in every real sense of the word. Their house had always been full of laughter and conversation. But right now she couldn't seem to think of anything to say.

With a jolt, she realized she hadn't actually lived in their house in two years. And Kati and Max hadn't lived there for the last six months. Time was marching on, things were changing, and Laney hadn't even been seeing it.

Her uncle's words replayed through her mind. *They're not going back to the States. They're leaving us.* Jake and Henry were hurt, and now she was losing Max and Kati, too.

Laney's heart began to pound.

Kati looked away. "Let's sit around back. There's a deck."

Laney nodded mutely then followed behind Kati as she led the way. Kati skirted the house and stepped onto an old deck with a tree springing out from its center. She walked to the edge and sat in the shade created by the house, her feet dangling over the side.

Laney sat next to her. "What's going on, Kati?"

Kati let out a shaky breath and grasped Laney's hand. "Laney, you have been my best friend for the last five years. More than that, you've been my *family*. Max's, too. We wouldn't even be alive without you." Kati looked over at Laney, tears in her eyes. "But now, Max and I need to leave."

Emotion welled up in Laney, choking off her words. Kati couldn't be saying this right now. This wasn't happening. Laney's words burst out of her. "We'll get you on the first plane back to the States. I'll arrange for twenty-four-hour protection."

Kati smiled sadly. "No. We need to leave all of this. We need to leave you."

Laney felt like she'd been slapped. "Kati, I never meant…"

Kati took both of Laney's hands in her own. When she spoke, Laney could feel her pain, and her love, in every word. "I know. I know you would do anything to protect us. You've proved that time and again. But I don't want you to have to anymore."

A tear rolled down Laney's cheek.

Kati wiped it away for her. "None of this is your fault. All of our fates were assigned long before we met, long before we were even born. And I thank God every day that you were brought into our lives. But I want Max to have as normal a life as possible." Her words drifted off and she bit her lip.

Laney knew what Kati meant. "I want that too."

"I know you do." Tears glistened in Kati's eyes. "Maddox and I are taking Max away. Maddox will look out for us. We're going to start a new life with new identities. And the only way for us to stay safe…" Kati looked away as a tear finally tracked down her own cheek.

Laney felt hollow. "Is to cut off all ties with us."

Kati nodded.

Laney stared out at the water. It was green and polluted; a few dead fish floated on top. But here and there she saw air bubbles. Something survived in that filth. She closed her eyes, picturing Max growing up constantly under guard, without any chance at a real life. She didn't want that for him.

"You'll need money. IDs."

"Maddox has already taken care of it."

"You've been thinking about this for a while."

Kati nodded.

"When are you leaving?"

"Now."

Laney gasped and stared, but then nodded her head. "That's probably best." A little of the tidal wave of emotion she was holding back slipped through. "I'm going to miss you two so much."

Kati hugged Laney, her shoulders shaking. "You are my sister. And you always will be."

Laney nodded into her shoulder.

They stayed clasped together like that for a few minutes. When Kati finally extricated herself, she all but fled inside. Laney watched her go, tears streaming down her face.

Maddox, Kati, and Max were leaving. Henry was out of commission. Jake was on the edge of death—again. Everything was falling apart. And there was nothing Laney could do about any of it.

Except watch it fall.

CHAPTER 83

LANEY STAYED at the edge of the dock for a while longer, composing herself. She needed to speak with Victoria. She needed to say goodbye to Max. She needed to check on Jake and Henry. *Need, need, need. My life is all about need.*

But she couldn't seem to make herself move. She heard footsteps behind her and turned, expecting to see her uncle. She was wrong.

"Hi, Laney," Max said.

"Hey, Max." Laney opened up her arms and Max flew across the short distance into them.

Laney hugged him tight. "Are you all right?"

He nodded against her chest. Laney closed her eyes, trying to savor the moment. She rocked with him in her lap. *He'll be too big to be held like this soon.*

With a start, she realized that the next time she saw him—if she saw him again—he might not even want her to hug him. He might not feel the bond the way she did; he might not even remember her. The thought made her hold him even tighter.

They stayed locked together like that for a few moments, and Laney let herself focus only on the moment, knowing it would end too soon.

Finally, Max scooted off her lap and sat next to her. His little legs swung back and forth under the dock.

Laney wrapped one arm around him. "I'm so glad you're safe."

His expression made him look much older than he should. "I'm not safe—not yet."

Laney studied him. His blue eyes looked so serious, so mature. He should be a little boy, not someone who literally had to worry about the fate of the world. "Once you leave, will you be safe?" Laney asked.

Max nodded. "Yes."

Laney's heart pained to see him go, but she was overjoyed to know that he would, finally, have a chance at a normal life. She just wished she could be a part of it.

She hugged him tight. "I'm going to miss you so much."

Max curled into her chest. "Not as much as I'm going to miss you."

Laney took in a shuddering breath. She hated that it had come to this—that she had to let two people she loved so much go away in order to keep them safe.

And right then she hated the Fallen. She hated her damn destiny. And she hated Victoria and all her secrets.

Max wrapped his hand in Laney's. "She protected me."

Laney looked down at him. "Who?"

"Victoria. Samyaza would have hurt me if Victoria hadn't stayed. That's why she walked away from you. To protect me."

Laney looked toward the house, trying to tamp down her anger at Victoria, knowing it wasn't fair. Victoria had no more choice in all this than Laney did.

"She is good, isn't she?" Laney asked softly.

Max looked up at Laney, and waited until she looked back at him. "She's the best. She loves you. She loves all of us. You need to trust her, Laney. And you need to find the tree."

Laney had to ask Max one more question. But she was afraid to hear the answer.

"Can I stop all of this?" she asked quietly.

"Yes. But it's going to cost you."

As Laney looked into Max's bright blue eyes, she didn't see the little boy she had helped raise. She saw the old soul who inhabited him.

Tears sprang to her eyes. "It already has."

CHAPTER 84

LANEY WALKED BACK to the front of the building with Max's hand clasped in hers. Tears threatened to overwhelm her, but she held them back. There'd be time for tears later. Right now, they each had jobs to do, and those jobs came before anything.

Maddox and Kati stood waiting by an old white Suzuki, a little rusted at the tire wells and bumper, and with more than a few dents. It was no different than dozens of cars Laney had seen on their drive here. It would blend right in.

Patrick stood waiting with his arm around Kati. He gave Laney a small smile, but she could see the moisture gathering in his eyes. He was putting on a brave face. Laney tried to keep her face blank, which was as close to brave as she could manage right now. Her emotions were too raw for anything else.

A few feet from the car, Laney knelt down. She turned Max to face her and held his arms. "Remember, wherever you are, I am somewhere thinking about you and loving you. And if you ever need me, I will come running."

"I know." He put his hand on her cheek. "Be careful, Laney."

"You too." She wrapped her arms around him and hugged him tight. Then she took a steadying breath and let him go, fearing that if she didn't do it right this second, she'd never be able to.

Patrick scooped him away and into his own hug while Laney stood and turned to Maddox. "Take care of them."

"With my very life."

Laney blinked back her tears. "Well, let's hope it doesn't come to that." She looked at her uncle hugging Kati before she looked back at Maddox. "Just help them be happy, okay?"

"I will."

Laney wrapped her arms around him. "And let yourself be happy, too."

"I owe you my life, Laney."

Laney stepped back. "No. You don't owe me a thing. Have a good life, Maddox. And if you need us—"

"I'll call."

She nodded. "Take care of them." Maddox hugged her quickly one more time. Then he turned, got into the driver's seat of the car, and started it up.

Laney walked slowly around the car. This all felt so unreal. She was saying goodbye to Kati and Max. How was it possible that it had come to this?

Kati waited by the open passenger door.

"You ready?" Laney asked.

Kati nodded, her chin trembling. "I think so."

Laney looked away. "Don't you dare cry. Because if you cry, I'll cry, and then you'll never get out of here."

"Okay," Kati said, but there was still a tremor in her voice.

Laney pulled her into a hug. "We'll see each other again. I promise."

Kati nodded into her shoulder.

Laney pulled away.

"Tell Jen—" Kati shook her head and gave Laney a watery smile. "I don't know. Make up something good and tell her I said it."

Laney choked out a laugh. "You got it."

Kati climbed into the passenger seat and closed the door. Laney stepped back. Max waved at her from the back seat and

Kati from the front. Laney gave them both a smile and blew Max a kiss.

Maddox pulled away, and a car of SIA agents pulled out after them. The agents would escort them to an airfield where Maddox had arranged for a friend to meet them.

And that would be it. From there, no one but Maddox would know where they were going.

Laney watched the car until it was out of sight.

Patrick came and stood next to her. "You all right?"

She leaned in to him. "Not by a long shot."

He went to wrap his arms around her, but Laney stepped away. "No. If you do that, then I'll start to cry, and there's no time for that now." She took a deep breath. "How are Jake and Henry?"

"The doctor was still sewing up Jake when I last checked. But she's very optimistic. Henry's all right. Well, all right in the sense that he has seven broken bones and another seven fractures scattered throughout his body."

Laney winced. "He's healing though?"

"Yes, but not fast. Victoria said Henry's abilities are immune to injuries from Cain. He'll heal, but only at the rate of a normal human."

Laney closed her eyes. Henry, hurt. It wasn't something she was used to.

"Okay," she said. "Let's go check on Jake."

CHAPTER 85

LANEY WALKED into the building with her uncle. A parlor was on the right and a living room on the left. Straight ahead was the kitchen, which had been converted into a makeshift hospital suite. Laney swallowed as she caught sight of blood on the floor. Her uncle walked ahead of her, coming to a stop at the entrance of the kitchen before turning down the hall toward Henry's room.

Mustafa walked to the doorway to meet them. Laney's breath held as her gaze met his. He smiled. "Jake will be all right. By some miracle, none of the wounds were to anything critical. It will take him some time to recover his strength, but he *will* recover it."

Laney sagged and reached for the wall. "Thank God. When will he be able to be moved?"

"Barring gunfights, he should be ready to move within the hour."

"Can I see him?"

"They're still cleaning him up. Besides, he won't be conscious for a while. When they're done, they'll move him down the hall to the room next to Henry."

"How is Henry?" Laney asked.

"In pain. But he too will be all right. His mother is with him." Mustafa held out his hand. "I have something for you."

Laney held out her own hand and Mustafa dropped a small rectangular object in it. Laney inspected it. "What is this?"

"I took the liberty of scanning Victoria and Max when we returned. I found that sewn into the hem of Victoria's jacket. I believe it's how Jorgen found us on the road. It's wired for audio. Whatever you were saying in the car, he heard it."

Laney closed her fingers over the bug. "Damn it. I should have thought of that."

Mustafa placed a hand on her shoulder. "No. It was highly unexpected." He stepped back. "Your friends should be arriving soon. I will go make sure the guards are aware of who they are."

Laney nodded as Mustafa walked past her. "Mustafa?" she called over her shoulder.

He looked back at her.

"Thank you for everything."

Mustafa's eyes twinkled and he gave her a small bow. "It is *you* who *I* should be thanking."

He walked out and Laney shook her head. She'd only met Mustafa once before, but she felt like he was a friend and that they had known each other for a long time. *I suppose I probably have*, she thought, remembering what Victoria had said.

Taking a breath, Laney skirted the kitchen and walked down the long hall. Ralph stood outside a doorway on the right.

Laney stopped next to him. "Have you heard from Drake?"

Ralph shook his head. "No. I left messages at the box office and the hotel as well as on his cell. He *will* call as soon as he gets the message."

Laney looked into the room. Victoria sat next to Henry's bed— well, *beds*. They'd had to add a second bed to the bottom of the first to accommodate his height. Victoria had both of her hands wrapped around one of Henry's. And for the first time, Laney thought that mother and son looked fragile.

"Victoria?" Laney called softly.

Victoria turned, wiping her eyes. "Hi. I didn't realize you were there."

Laney stepped into the room. "How is he?"

"No change. The doctor says he should be all right, but it will take him time to recover."

"Why is that? Why didn't he heal automatically?"

"Part of Cain's curse. It supersedes any supernatural ability."

Laney walked over to the bed and pushed a lock of hair away from Henry's forehead. He didn't stir, but Laney hadn't expected him to. They had him on some pretty heavy-duty painkillers. He would sleep well into tomorrow.

"I've always viewed him as indestructible," Laney said quietly.

"That's how little sisters are supposed to view their big brothers."

Laney took a shaky breath and looked over at Victoria. "I think we need to chat a little more."

Victoria nodded with a resigned sigh. "Yes."

CHAPTER 86

LANEY AND VICTORIA walked out to the same dock where Laney and Kati had sat less than an hour earlier. Laney didn't want to be too far away from Henry or Jake, but she had a feeling she would want a little space for this conversation. And before they left the house, Patrick had said he'd come find her if there were any changes in Jake's status.

As Laney stepped onto the dock, she realized she hadn't told Patrick who Victoria was. With everything that was going on, there just hadn't been an opportunity.

Laney sat in the middle of the dock, her back leaning against the tree in its center. Victoria took a seat in an old rattan chair after checking to make sure it would hold her weight.

A million questions floated through Laney's mind. But first she needed a minute. She needed the peace. She watched two dragon-flies chase each other across the fetid water. Soon a third joined in the game. Eventually, though, the dragonflies disappeared into the vegetation, and Laney knew she had to get to business. Time was slipping away.

Still, she wanted to ease into her real questions. "There's something about the creation stories that have bothered me," she said.

"What?"

"In Genesis, allegedly God said man should have dominion over everything—the land, the animals." She paused. "But then he takes it to the next step and says that humans should *subjugate* animals, and the world, to our will."

Victoria nodded. "Yes. That's what it says."

"See, that's the problem. The subjugation part. Why? I mean, Cayce's argument is the exact opposite. That we're supposed to be working in communion with nature and animals. Not as overlords. So why would God give that order?"

Victoria's eyes looked even more violet in the sunlight. "You tell me."

Laney went silent. She wasn't sure she wanted to say what she was thinking. But the thought remained firmly stuck in her mind, and she had to let it out. "I don't think He did. It wasn't God who commanded it. It was the Fallen. Animals, vegetation… all of that was here before us. And it thrived. Why would anyone tell us to subjugate it? Where is the justice in that? The fairness?"

Victoria nodded. "The Fallen knew how to play on our doubts, our insecurities. We had been so far from the spirit for so long, many couldn't remember what it was like. All they could remember was the physical world—and that became all they cared about."

"So before the Fallen, humanity was at peace?"

"Before the Fallen, we were at peace. Then they showed up and everything was turned upside down."

"They claimed they were speaking for God."

"Yes. Subjugation of living things is right from their playbook. It benefits them. It justifies violence. It justifies their acts."

Laney shook her head. From the beginning the Fallen had been plotting, scheming, doing everything in their power to gain more power. It was overwhelming. But it also needed to be faced. She took a breath and let it out slowly. "What can you tell me about the tree?"

Victoria placed her hands in her lap and took a moment to compose her thoughts before speaking. "When humanity first arrived, we ate from the tree. It is what made us immortal. But then the tree was hidden."

"Drake said there were two trees."

Victoria smiled. "Actually, there were many. But most people focus on the two trees: the tree of life and the tree of knowledge.

"Where is the tree of knowledge?"

Victoria gave a wry smile. "You sure you want to go down that road right now?"

Laney paused and then shook her head. "No. You're right. One's enough. But when this is all over, we'll sit down and chat about that other tree."

Victoria nodded, her gaze on the water. And Laney realized she looked paler than Laney could ever remember her being. Although all things considered, Victoria was holding up incredibly well after all she'd been through—two abductions, numerous gun battles, keeping Max safe, then sitting by her son's bed while he recovered from wounds received from Cain.

That last thought brought Laney to her real question.

"Why did Cain grab you? If he had left you alone, we wouldn't have known about any of this."

"You've answered your own question. He grabbed me so you would know about all this." Victoria looked out over the water and sighed. "Cain is a complicated man."

Laney's jaw fell open. "What? He *wanted* us to know? Why on earth would he do that?"

"Whoever controls the tree controls immortality."

"But why does Cain care? He's already immortal."

Victoria watched the water for a moment before speaking. "Cain has been the sole immortal in this world for tens of thousands of years. And he doesn't want to share his immortality with anyone. He needed you to know about the tree, and that the Fallen were making a play for it… so you would stop them."

"Why doesn't *he* just stop them?"

"Believe it or not, Cain's not a fighter. He's never had to be. He doesn't want to face off against the Fallen. He wants you to do that for him."

Laney stared at Victoria in shock. "We're Cain's proxy fighters?"

Victoria shrugged.

Laney shook her head. Crazy as it was, they were actually on Cain's side in this fight. But imagining a world with immortal Fallen, Laney suspected that Cain's interest went deeper than merely being the only immortal.

"Cain would also be the *weakest* immortal, wouldn't he?" she said. "And I suppose there's no guarantee his sevenfold injury thing would still work against them." As she thought it through, she had another question about Cain. "But why is Cain immortal in the first place? If everyone else became mortal, how did he escape that fate?"

Victoria sighed. "When Cain was punished, he was banished from God's sight."

Laney frowned. "But he was punished for killing Abel. And that must have occurred *after* humans became mortal, or he wouldn't have been able to kill his brother."

Victoria nodded. "I had just made the deal when Cain struck Abel. If he had done it the day before, Abel would have survived. But on that day, Cain became the world's first murderer. His punishment was his immortality—to walk the world forever."

"Is that really a punishment though? I mean, people throughout time have been driven to incredible lengths to achieve immortality. Isn't that a gift?"

Victoria shook her head. "Think about it. Everyone you ever care about will leave you. They will age, and you will stay the same—over and over again it will happen. And not only that, but Cain is marked—people will always be startled by him, frightened by him. To make any real connection with a human he will first have to overcome their revulsion. Oh, his punishment is very real."

Laney realized Victoria wasn't just speaking about Cain. She was also speaking about herself. "Because God didn't want to see him."

"And his mark made it even worse."

Laney sat back, imagining what that would do to a person. "A mark that guarantees that everybody gives you a wide berth. Even if people don't want to do you harm, they will still stay away from you. That must twist someone's mind—the isolation."

"I think it has driven him a little bit mad over the years."

"But he's still powerful. He could do damage if he intended to."

"True. Cain is cursed, but he's also the most powerful human in the world, if he chooses to be."

Laney pictured Cain falling into the swollen river. "He's not dead, is he?"

Victoria shook her head. "I highly doubt it."

CHAPTER 87

LANEY SAT by Jake's bed. He'd been brought in about fifteen minutes ago but still hadn't regained consciousness. Somewhere in the house a cell phone rang and someone spoke quietly.

She reached out and took Jake's hand. "I'm right here, Jake. You're going to be fine," she whispered. It was going to be a long recovery, but Jake would make it through.

Laney glanced out into the hallway. She could see Ralph standing outside Henry's door. She knew she needed to get moving. Once the Fallen deciphered the book, they'd go after the tree. She had probably already wasted too much time. She could feel the seconds ticking away.

Elisabeta would need to translate the book but still that would only provide them with a few hours at best. Laney looked back down at Jake. There was no way either Jake or Henry was going to be able to help. There would be no rapid recovery for either one, not this time.

Laney swallowed. *Which means it's up to me.*

But she couldn't get herself to leave. Not until Jen and the reinforcements arrived. The Chandler plane had run into some bad weather, which had slowed them down. *Of course, even if I left right now, it wouldn't really help. We still have no idea where the tree is.*

Patrick stepped into the room. "Do you need anything?" he asked.

Laney shook her head. "No. I'm good."

Patrick pulled up a chair next to her. "The doctor said he'll make a full recovery."

"I know." Laney's eyes flicked to the heart monitor, needing the reassurance that Jake was still with her. Her uncle sat next to her silently.

Laney finally turned to him. "Victoria is Lilith."

Patrick nodded, his gaze not meeting hers.

Laney stared at him in disbelief. "Yet again you know something before the rest of us."

"I didn't know. I suspected."

"How?"

"When we spoke about Eve, I knew there was another possibility. And when you told me that Ralph said she wasn't Eve… well, Lilith was the most reasonable choice."

"You always know these things. How is that?"

Patrick took her hand. "Let's just say that, since all of this happened, I've tried to keep an open mind."

Laney studied her uncle; he seemed oddly at peace. "How are you okay with all of this? I mean, as a priest this must throw a lot of what you believe into question."

"It does." Patrick paused. "But it doesn't change what the church stands for—following Jesus's example. It just broadens the picture a little more."

"You are *way* too well-adjusted."

Patrick gave a small laugh. "It has been hard-won, let me tell you."

They both fell silent, but it wasn't uncomfortable. In fact it was the opposite. It was the comfort of being with someone who knew you inside and out and loved you in spite of it.

Laney's gaze drifted out to the hallway. She knew Victoria was sitting with Henry next door, and she could see Ralph standing guard at the door. "Do you think she's... good?" Laney asked quietly.

Patrick considered. "I do. But what I think doesn't really matter, does it? It's what *you* think that counts. So what do you think?"

"Max said she's good. That I should trust her."

"Do you?"

"I think I do. I think my hesitation has nothing to do with her secrets or her being Lilith or her knowing just about everything."

"It's because you just found out she's your mother."

Laney nodded. "Yeah," she said softly.

A soft rap on the doorframe drew her attention.

Ralph stood there, his cell phone extended toward her. "It's for you."

"Go ahead," Patrick said. He nodded at Jake. "I'll stay with him."

Laney brushed a quick kiss on Jake's forehead, then took the phone and headed into the hall. "Hello?"

"Ah, ring bearer. It's lovely to hear your melodic voice again."

Laney sank against a wall. "Hi, Drake."

"What? Is that how you greet your most ardent fan?"

"It's been a rough day."

Drake's tone turned gentle. "So I've heard. They have the book?"

"Yeah."

"You were supposed to prevent that from happening."

"Well, you know, Drake, the ring doesn't make me omnipotent."

"True enough. Well, you need to get moving if you're going to protect the tree."

"Happy to—except for the small fact that the Fallen have the book which has the tree's location, and you've already made clear that you won't tell me. I don't suppose there's any chance you've changed your mind?"

"I told you I wouldn't tell you before because the tree wasn't in immediate danger. But times have changed, haven't they?"

Laney closed her eyes. *Thank God.* "Where is it?"

"Ah, right to business. I like the focus. The tree is located in Tianmen Shan, in the northwestern Hunan province of China."

Tianmen Shan. Laney knew that name. She looked down the hall to Jake's doorway as the recollection dawned. "Heaven's Gate."

Laney could hear the smile in Drake's voice. "Happy hunting."

CHAPTER 88

LANEY ONLY STARED at the disconnected phone for a moment before she strode down the hall to talk to Victoria and Henry. An agent called to her from the front door. "Dr. McPhearson?"

She turned around. "Yes?"

"Your guests are arriving."

Laney smiled and changed directions, feeling a little lighter. *Reinforcements.*

A tingle ran over her skin as she stepped outside. She nodded at the two SIA agents who guarded the door. The agents had been busy. Electronic surveillance had been strung all over the area, and guards were now hidden in multiple locations for a half mile in each direction.

It was those guards who had contacted the agent in the house to let her know the car was coming. Laney watched the old Range Rover bump across the ground toward her.

The SUV came to a halt ten feet away. Laney coughed at the dust it kicked up, waving her hand in front of her face. When the passenger door opened, a tall, dark-haired woman with Asian features got out. She made her way over to Laney and enveloped her in a hug. "I'm so sorry, Laney."

Laney hugged Jen Witt back. "And I am so glad you're here."

Jen was one of Laney's best friends, and one of the only people she trusted to protect Henry and Jake—in part because Jen was also nephilim, but also in part because Laney knew how much Henry meant to her. Jen wouldn't let anyone get to him.

Two tall blond men also got out of the Range Rover. Laney detangled herself from Jen and hugged each of them. "Thanks for coming, guys."

Mike Witt, Jen's adopted brother, nodded. "You know we'd do anything for Jake and Henry."

Jordan, Mike's twin, nodded his agreement. The brothers had both served with Jake and were the closest thing Jake had to family. They had all saved one another's lives at one point or another. Mike worked for the FBI, and Jordan worked for the Chandler Group—and they both would do whatever they had to in order to protect Jake.

Laney felt a lump in her throat, and for what felt like the thousandth time, she said a silent thank-you that the Witts were part of their lives.

Jordan nodded toward the door. "How are they doing?"

"They'll make it. But it's going to be a long recovery."

Jordan looked around, taking in their location. "Tell me about the security in place."

Laney quickly ran it down.

When she was done, Jordan nodded. "Okay. That's good. The rest of the group is a few minutes behind. Is all right if we go in?"

Laney gestured to the door. "Of course. Go ahead."

Jordan and Mike nodded at the two SIA agents standing guard as they headed inside. When they had disappeared from view, Jen linked her arm through Laney's. "Now tell me how you're *really* doing."

Laney leaned her head into Jen's shoulder. "I'm terrified. Stressed. Sad. Scared. And really, *really* angry."

"I'm sorry, Laney. I really am."

"How's Danny handling all this?" Laney asked. Laney had

spoken with Danny on the phone earlier, and he had said he was doing fine. But she could tell he was putting on a brave facade.

Jen shook her head. "Not good. He's scared. Henry being hurt —it's new to him."

"It's new to all of us," Laney agreed.

"But we no longer have to worry about Cain, right? He's dead?"

The image of Cain plunging into the river appeared in Laney's mind. She shrugged. "I don't know. He got pulled away in the water. I hope so."

"Okay. So what's the plan?"

"Step one, make sure Henry and Jake are safe." Laney paused, seeing another few Range Rovers heading toward them.

"Step two?" Jen asked.

Laney saw a mental picture of she and Jen. She smiled. "I'll explain it after I say hello."

Jen grimaced. "Okay, and maybe *you* can shake her out of her mood. She's been a little cranky ever since your phone call. I'll go say hi to Jake and Henry." She disappeared into the house after her brothers.

The Range Rovers parked in a line next to Jen's. Some of the Chandler operatives Laney knew climbed out. She nodded at them, but headed for the third SUV without stopping. A roar sounded from inside it.

Scared.

I know, girl, Laney thought back at Cleo. She nodded to the operative who was standing next to the SUV. "It's okay. I've got her."

He gave her a nervous smile and walked away. Laney shook her head. She knew Cleo wouldn't hurt any of them, but people who weren't familiar with the big cat weren't nearly as convinced of that fact.

Laney opened the back door and opened the cage. She stepped back quickly as Cleo leaped from her cell. Cleo walked around, stretching, then came up to Laney and leaned her head against her chest.

Laney rubbed the big cat's head and ears. "I'm glad to see you too, girl."

SIA had used their connections to get Cleo into the country. Normally it would have taken months of quarantine and paperwork.

"I need you to take care of them for me. Keep them safe," Laney whispered into Cleo's ear.

Cleo lifted her head and gave Laney a look that was almost human. *You?*

"I'll be okay. I'm going to get the people who did this."

Dangerous.

Laney thought about lying, but what was the point? "Yes. It will be. But I'll be better able to focus if I know Henry and Jake are safe."

Cleo leaned her head down to Laney's, their foreheads resting against one another. *Scared.*

Laney wrapped her hands around the back of Cleo's neck. "Me too, girl. Me too."

CHAPTER 89

LANEY WALKED into the house with Cleo at her side. She poked her head into Henry's room—Victoria sat on one side of Henry's bed, Jen on the other. Jen had her arms crossed, a frown on her face, and one eye on Victoria at all times. Apparently Jen wasn't quite ready to jump on the Victoria bandwagon just yet.

Laney bit back a smile. "Victoria?"

Victoria looked up.

"We need to talk."

Laney turned to find Ralph right behind her.

"You have a location?" he asked.

Laney nodded and looked past him to Jake's room, where Jordan and Mike sat. An iPad was propped on the table in front of Jake. Dom's face was on the screen. "The duality of transformational…" Dom droned on.

Laney stifled a laugh. "What's going on in there?"

A smile twitched at Ralph's mouth. "Um, Dom apparently convinced the brothers that if he read to Jake it would help Jake recover."

The brothers probably figured that ten minutes of Dom reading to Jake would spur Jake into consciousness—if only to tell Dom to shut up.

Shaking her head, Laney motioned for Ralph and Victoria to follow her down the hall. With Cleo still at her side, they entered what had once been a formal living room. Victoria took a seat on the couch and Cleo walked over to say hello.

Victoria petted her gently. "Hello, Cleo dear."

Content with her greeting, Cleo then took up position at the open doorway, her back to the room. Ralph stood only a few feet from her, also on guard.

Laney stood over by the windows, too keyed up to sit. She quickly relayed what Drake had told her.

"It must be Heaven's Gate," Ralph said.

Laney nodded. "That's what I figured. When we get there, will you be able to sense it?"

Ralph nodded. "Yes. And so will you."

Laney hadn't expected that. "O… kay. Well, we'll leave in thirty minutes." Laney turned to Victoria. "When we reach the tree, we'll contact you, and you can tell us how to destroy it."

Victoria shook her head. "That won't work. I'm the only one who can destroy it. I have to be there."

"You both have to go," Ralph said. "As the ring bearer, only you can open the doorway. And Victoria is the only one who can destroy it."

"Yeah, you never did mention how that happens," Laney said.

Victoria and Ralph exchanged a quick glance. "You'll understand when we get there," she said.

Still with the secrets, Laney thought. "What else do you know about the hiding spot?"

"Weapons are not allowed. No one can enter if they are armed," Ralph said.

Laney's hope rose. "Does that mean the Fallen can't enter?"

Ralph shook his head. "No, but they can only enter if they are unarmed."

"Right, as unarmed as a super-powered being can be," Laney muttered.

"Now we need to figure out who's accompanying us," Ralph said.

"Actually, I already decided that." Laney had been thinking about the trip to find the tree ever since they left the temple. And Henry and Jake getting hurt had just reinforced her view.

"And?" Victoria asked.

She looked at each of them and then at Cleo, who stared back at her. *I'm sorry,* Laney thought to her friend, before looking back at Victoria and Ralph. "It's only going to be the three of us."

CHAPTER 90

JEN LEANED back against the Range Rover. "You have got to be kidding me."

Laney sighed. She had just explained to Jen her plan to go after the tree of life with only Ralph and Victoria. And Jen wasn't exactly taking it well.

"Jen, this is the only way."

"No, actually, it's not. The other way would be to take the rest of us with you. Better yet, let Clark prove his worth and get a nice big military force to accompany you."

Laney closed her eyes. She should have known Jen would react this way. "Jen, this is how it has to happen. If we're lucky, we'll get in, destroy the tree, and get out without anyone being the wiser."

"And when the hell have we been lucky?" Jen stood up straight, towering over Laney. "We are *perpetually* unlucky. And you know Elisabeta is going to throw everything she can at getting that tree. You need more help."

Laney looked back at the house. She pictured Henry and Jake. She would like to have them with her—the intact trio. The three of them had done incredible things. But she was already down two members of the triad in this little adventure. She wasn't willing to chance anyone else.

"No. This is how it's going to happen. I need you to stay here and keep Henry and Jake safe. Because if I don't succeed, they're going to have to figure out a way to defeat Elisabeta when she has the tree."

"All the more reason to throw everything we have at her now! We take her out and then no problem."

"Like you said, it's never that simple. This is Samyaza, the strategist. The one who started all of it. We can't just run up at her with brute force. We need to hold something in reserve. If I don't succeed, I need to know there's someone who can at least give her a run for her money."

"But—"

"Jen, do you really think Samyaza has left us alone? She knows Henry and Jake are both my strength *and* my weakness. She's going to come after them—probably right when I'm in the middle of things. Because she knows if something happens to them, I'll be devastated. And I will fail."

Laney took a deep breath. "I need them *safe*. And I know you, your brothers, Cleo, the Chandler operatives, the SIA agents—*you* are my guarantee that they will be safe. You're the reason I'll be able to focus on what needs to be done."

Jen looked away, her fists clenched. "I hate this. First Kati, Maddox, and Max, and now you going off on your own. It's like everything is splitting apart."

Laney swallowed hard. She wrapped an arm around Jen. "I hate it just as much. But we're at the time of hard choices. And this is what needs to be done. I need to know they're safe. And I know whatever Samyaza throws at you, you'll be able to keep them that way."

Jen looked down at Laney. "I *will* keep them safe. Now promise me that you'll keep *yourself* safe."

Laney sighed and looked out over at the hills, but she didn't say anything. Because that was one promise she wasn't sure she was going to be able to keep.

CHAPTER 91

LANEY TOOK A STEELING BREATH. *Just one more conversation.* And she had a feeling this one was going to be the hardest.

She walked down the road to the little house next door. She'd left Cleo with Jake and Henry. She would need a little privacy for this conversation.

As she opened the door, she could hear her uncle arranging for Jake's and Henry's medical treatment back home. Laney leaned against the wall to wait, and a few seconds later Patrick disconnected the call. He turned around, surprise flashing across his face.

"I didn't hear you come in."

"Yeah, you were on the phone." She hesitated. "Listen, I have to go away for a little while."

"What? Where?"

She let out a breath. "I'm going after the tree."

He looked at her for long moment, then sighed and nodded. "Who's going with you?"

"Ralph and Victoria."

His eyes narrowed. "And who else?"

"That's it."

Patrick stared at her, his mouth agape, before he shut it. "You can't be serious. Take Jen, the Witts, all of Clark's men."

Laney moved closer to him. "Uncle Patrick, it can't be that way, and you know it."

"No, I don't know that." He stared at her. Laney just watched him, not saying a word.

"This is because of that stupid book, isn't it?"

She tried to put a little levity in her tone. "Stupid book? That's sacrilege coming from you."

"Don't joke, Laney."

She sighed. "I'm not. And it's not just because of the book. Henry and Jake are out of this fight for now. And I need them safe."

"They can be safe without you putting yourself at risk."

"I need to do this without them—without all of you."

Patrick looked into her eyes, and Laney could see the anger overtake him. "Don't you dare put our safety ahead of yours," he said. "You know Henry and Jake would never let you do this if they were awake."

"But they're not awake," Laney said quietly. "I'm the last one standing, and it's my call. And if Samyaza is smart, which she is, she'll come after you to keep me away. I can't take that chance. I need to get to the tree, but I need to know you're safe. This is the only way."

"It's not. The tree will wait. We'll—"

Laney covered her uncle's hand with her own. "It can't wait. You know that."

Patrick stared into her eyes, and she saw all the love and fear he had for her. "You don't have to do this alone."

"I'm not alone. I take all of you with me." And right then, Laney understood how Victoria had continued on. She was right. She was never alone. All the people she loved walked with her.

"I can't talk you out of this, can I?"

Laney shook her head.

Patrick's voice shook when he spoke. "You bring yourself back, you hear me? No matter what you have to do, you bring yourself back. I don't give a damn about what any book says."

Laney leaned forward and hugged him, giving him a kiss on the cheek. But she stayed silent.

She turned to walked away, knowing if she stayed a second longer she wouldn't be able to leave.

His voice stopped her at the door. "I love you, Delaney. You are my daughter in every way that counts."

"I know. And I love you too." Laney stepped out of the room and straightened her shoulders, wiping at the tears on her cheeks. And she didn't look back.

CHAPTER 92

LANEY AND JEN stood next to the Range Rovers; Jordan and Mike, as well as the rest of the Chandler operatives and SIA agents, had created a perimeter around the SUVs. Laney did not feel reassured. She felt exposed.

"Are you ready?" Mustafa asked as he walked up.

Laney gave him an abrupt nod. "You're sure this is the best way?"

"It's safer if we all leave together—safer for them, safer for you."

Laney watched Matt and Ralph carry the stretcher with Henry over to the van. Jake's stretcher had already been loaded up. Victoria stood perched in the doorway behind, Patrick at her side.

"You know they'll be watching us as we head to the airport," Laney said. "It's our most vulnerable time."

"We know. We have prepared for that."

"Mustafa?" she said.

He looked over at her.

"These people are the most important people in the world to me. Promise me you will keep them safe."

Mustafa's face was solemn. "On my life, I will let nothing happen to them."

She nodded and looked away.

Cleo slunk from around the back of the house and made her way over to Laney. "You ready, girl?"

Cleo licked the side of her face.

Laney laughed. "I'll take that as a yes."

Jen nudged Laney's shoulder. "We need to get going."

Laney let out a breath. The fate of the world hinged on them being able to get out of the country without getting killed. And that all hinged on this one car ride.

"Okay. Let's head out."

CHAPTER 93

ELISABETA DRUMMED her hands on the table in the plane cabin. She had taken them in the wrong direction when they'd left India. It had been a miscalculation, but they would make up the time on the way back.

Her spies had told her about the gunfight with Cain before Laney's group had reached the safe house. She knew that Henry and Jake were out of this fight for now. She smiled. *Thank you, dear Jorgen, for your assistance.*

The smile dimmed a little when she thought about the reports of the seer going missing. But no matter—she no longer needed him. And if she ever did need him at some point in the future, why, she'd just run him to ground.

Now I just have the little ring bearer to deal with. And Laney was probably so traumatized by her losses that she was immobile.

Elisabeta rubbed her hands as she watched the live feed from the airport. She had debated whether or not to finish the ring bearer as she and her friends left their little safe enclosure. But she had decided against it. She wanted to wait until they reached the airport. She wanted them to feel that taste of hope that they had made it—and then snatch it away.

She smiled. *So stupid. So trusting.* It was like fighting with babies.

They should be at the airfield any minute now. Elisabeta had left behind Kendrick—one of her nephilim—and a few mercenaries she had hired for just this occasion. It wasn't a large group, but it didn't need to be. They had only one goal: take out McPhearson.

Elisabeta picked up her phone and dialed. She spoke quickly. "No one moves in until the target has been located. Do you understand me?"

"Yes, ma'am. I've made sure the men are aware," Kendrick said.

Elisabeta put the phone on speaker, then settled back in her seat, a glass of wine in her hand, ready for the show. They were a hundred miles outside of India, but she wasn't worried. Once the ring bearer and her group were taken care of, they could take their time tracking down the tree. And Samyaza planned on enjoying herself. This was going to be a momentous occasion. She wanted to savor it.

"The caravan has entered the airport," Kendrick reported.

Elisabeta leaned forward, staring at the screen. *Any minute now.*

Four Range Rovers pulled up near the Chandler plane. Some SIA agents hopped out and took up positions around the plane. Elisabeta's smile grew larger. *Oh, God, this is fun.*

"Do you have eyes on the target?" she asked.

"Not yet."

Two stretchers were offloaded from the SUVs. A giant panther slunk from the back of one, stopped, and looked straight at the camera. Elisabeta stared back at the animal. *What an unusual beast. Maybe I should have my people catch her.*

Disregarding the animal, she focused on the people exiting the cars. *Where is she?*

Kendrick's voice came over the phone. "Samyaza. She's not here."

Wine sloshed over the edge of Elisabeta's glass as she lowered it to the table. *"What?"*

"There are four missing from the Range Rovers. When they started the trip, there were twenty-two passengers. Now there are only eighteen."

"How is that possible? Did they stop somewhere?"

"No, ma'am. They came directly here. We were behind them the whole time."

Elisabeta glared at the screen. *How did they elude us?*

"Ma'am? The rest of the group is entering the plane. Do you want us to—"

Kendrick's voice cut out.

"Kendrick? Report, Kendrick." There was no reply. Elisabeta checked her phone. The call was still connected. So why—

"Hello, Samyaza," a voice called pleasantly over the phone.

"Who is this?" Elisabeta demanded.

"Agent Matthew Clark of the SIA. We've taken out a few of your men. I know there are still more out there. The next move is up to you."

Elisabeta stared at the screen in disbelief. She'd been outmaneuvered. With a yell, she punched through the screen.

That bitch had outsmarted her. Elisabeta paced the short length of the cabin; her followers studiously avoided making eye contact. She took a deep breath, then another, and with each one, she imagined another way she could kill the ring bearer.

Finally Elisabeta smiled. When she caught up with McPhearson, she was going to extend her death. In fact, she was first going to make the ring bearer watch while she killed everyone she knew. And then…

She pictured the ring bearer's tortured face as she squeezed the breath out of her.

CHAPTER 94

I CAN'T BELIEVE that worked, Laney thought, staring out the window at the clouds. Originally, she had wanted Victoria, Ralph, and herself to slip off by themselves, but Clark had suggested they slip away in transit.

So Laney had created a dust storm a few minutes into the ride. Clark had wrapped Laney in his arms and rolled from the car, then regained his feet quickly and sprinted away from the caravan. Ralph had done the same for Victoria.

And no one had been the wiser.

Laney, Ralph, and Victoria had taken the car that was waiting for them and driven to a private plane, which they took to the Bodhgaya Airport where Victoria's private jet was waiting. Clark had been met by an SIA helicopter and flown to the airfield. There he and his team had located Samyaza's men and kept them under observation until they moved in.

Laney glanced down at her phone and the text Jen had sent.

We're all good. In the air.

She smiled. Jen had sent the text over an hour ago, but Laney liked to glance at it—to reassure herself. And also because it was the last message she would receive from them until this was all over. Laney had gotten Jen to promise not to call even if there was a problem. There was nothing Laney could do to help them now, and she needed to get to the tree. That came first.

Laney stared out the plane window, but there was nothing to see. It was still dark. It would take them at least eight hours to reach the Changsha Huanghua International Airport, and then another few hours from there to Heaven's Gate.

Laney knew she should sleep, but it eluded her. She had picked up her phone half a dozen times, but there was no one to call. She needed everyone focused on their own jobs. And those jobs were to protect Jake and Henry.

She glanced at her watch. The others should be well on their way back to the States by now.

"Not tired?" Victoria asked softly from next to her.

Laney looked over with a start. She had thought Victoria had fallen asleep. She gave her a small smile. "Oh, I'm tired. I just can't seem to sleep."

Victoria took her hand. "Do you want to talk about it?"

Laney gave a rueful laugh. "I don't know where to start. There's so much going on."

"Well, is there anything you'd like to ask me?"

Laney examined her mother. She was Lilith—the first woman. She had been around since the very beginning of time. She had sacrificed her chance at eternity to give the rest of humanity that chance. Laney was bowled over by that act of compassion. And by the fact that Victoria now had to suffer through each life and be born again with all that knowledge.

Ignorance really was bliss.

"How do you do it?" Laney asked quietly.

"Do what?"

"Start over. Start again."

Victoria smiled softly. "It's not a choice. It has to be done."

"But don't you ever despair? Don't you ever just want to check out, find an island, live your days in peace?"

Victoria smiled. "Well, not every lifetime is as exciting as this one. And there are moments of peace. But I suppose in many ways my life is no different than anyone else's: there's joy, sadness, laughter, love, grief."

Laney looked at Victoria's face, and what she saw there was peace and acceptance. "You're really not angry, are you?"

"Oh, I have been angry—many times. I have wanted to rail against the injustice of it all. But eventually those feelings pass. And I know what I'm doing is what needs to be done."

"But the loss…" Laney bit her lip as images of Kati, Max, Maddox, Henry, and Jake swam through her mind.

"The loss is always hard. But no one ever truly goes away. We see them again and again. In this life or the next."

"But what if you don't recognize them?"

Victoria's voice held no uncertainty. "You will."

Laney wanted to believe that was true. That the people she cared about would never be truly gone from her life. That she would see them again. That Drew, Rocky, her parents—they would all still be part of her existence in some way.

"Haven't you ever met someone and felt like you knew them even though you had just met?" Victoria asked.

Laney nodded. "Yes."

"That's because you *have* known them before, in a different life. They come into your life when you need them, and you come into theirs when they need you."

Laney thought of how she'd come into Kati and Max's life. How Henry and Jake had shown up in hers. It was true that the people she needed and the people who needed her had arrived when they were needed—even Mustafa and Matt.

"Take your Uncle Patrick," Victoria said.

Laney looked at her in surprise. "Uncle Patrick?"

"He is always in your life. And in much the same role."

A memory of the vision she'd had when she'd found the ring in Saqqara slipped though her mind. "In ancient Egypt, when the former ring bearer—I mean I—hid the ring. I was accompanied by a man named Gaius. Was he…?"

"Yes. That was your uncle as well."

Laney was quiet for a moment, her mind drifting through all the twists and turns her life had taken lately, all the revelations that seemed to rock her world. And she realized that this one didn't shock her nearly as much as most. In fact, it comforted her.

But one thought didn't. "I've lived a few lives too, right?"

"Yes."

"Do I have the same deal as you, except without the memories?"

"Oh, no, sweetheart, no. It's true that you have lived many lives. But you are not reborn every lifetime like me. You are born only when you are needed."

"And when I'm not needed?"

"You are at peace."

Laney felt relief, but also a little guilt. Victoria lived life after life with no reprieve in sight. She made all these decisions and faced all these challenges, not for her own good, but for everyone else's. "I'm sorry."

Surprise flashed across Victoria's face. "For what?"

"I've been so mad at you. I couldn't understand why you gave me up. Why you turned your back on me but kept Henry."

"Oh, I never turned my back on you, Laney. And giving you up was the hardest thing I ever had to do. Kind of like you letting Kati and Max go."

"I get that now. You needed to give me a chance to be safe. Just like I need to give them a chance to be safe." Laney looked over at her. "Thank you."

Victoria's breath hitched. She reached up and cupped Laney's cheek. "You are so important to me. I would do anything to keep you safe."

"I love you, Mom." The words came quietly from Laney's lips, and she was surprised to hear herself say them. But she also knew how right they felt. And if there was anything she had learned from all of this, it was that life is short, and you need to make sure the important people in your life know how much you care about them before it's too late.

"I love you too, daughter."

They sat together in silence. Laney felt a true connection to her mother for the first time. But soon, the thoughts of what they were up against intruded. Images from the ancient stories of Lilith ran through Laney's mind. Every so often, she would glance over at Victoria. She sat there with her eyes closed, looking at peace. How did she do it?

"What is it, Laney?" Victoria asked, her eyes still closed.

Laney cringed—apparently she hadn't been as stealthy in her observation as she had thought. "Um, just thinking."

Victoria opened an eye. "About me?"

Laney nodded.

With a sigh, Victoria pushed her seat back up. "Fire away."

All the questions she had flew through her mind, but the one she was most curious about brought a blush to her cheeks. She swallowed her discomfort and asked it anyway. "According to the legend, Lilith ran away from Adam because she wouldn't have sex with him."

Victoria laughed out loud. "Oh, please. The men who wrote those tales never thought of women as anything but sexual objects. So of course in their minds, if I refused Adam, it could only have been because of sex."

"So why was it really?"

Victoria smiled. "Adam and I had been together for thousands of years. Most marriages these days make it a few years and people call it a success. I'd say we surpassed those by quite a margin. Even so, we had reached a point where we wanted different things."

"What did he want?"

Victoria sighed. "He had begun to be intrigued by the Fallen, by the power they wielded. By the wealth they had acquired. I was not so enamored."

Laney frowned. "But in the story, you refused to lie with him. And fled. The angels found you, and that's when you made the deal."

Victoria stayed silent.

Laney's mind churned. "But that doesn't make any sense, because when you made the deal, Cain was already grown; he killed Abel the very next day. So Adam was already with Eve by then—and had been for a while."

"That's right. Adam and I were no longer together. He was with Eve at that point."

"So what was the fight between you and Adam about?"

"The fight was about equality, but not only between men and women. It was about the weak versus the strong, the rich versus the poor. Society had reached a point where those who were strongest, those who had the most, were controlling those without. And it was not between me and Adam. As I was the first woman, the Fallen wanted me to stand with them and agree that's the way it should be—that the strong should have power over the weak. I refused."

"What happened?"

"I escaped. It wasn't easy. But there were people who believed the same way I did."

"The Children of the Law of One."

"Yes. And I had to make a choice—either allow humanity to continue on its destructive path, or give us all a chance at redemption. I chose the latter."

Laney was silent for a moment. What an incredible woman. Victoria had not just stood up to the Fallen, but really to all of humanity. And she was still fighting the same fight.

And now there was a threat that might reverse all that Victoria had done, all she had sacrificed.

"Is this the first time someone has made a play for the tree?"

"No. There have been other attempts."

Laney thought of the tales of different emperors and kings who throughout time had tried and failed to find the secret to eternal life. The most famous person attached to a search for the Fountain of Youth was probably Ponce de Leon. But Laney recalled a Smithsonian article that suggested he never had in fact been searching for immortality, and that he wasn't even associated with a quest for eternal youth until fourteen years after his death.

Chinese emperors, however, were a different story. China's first emperor, Qin Shi Huang, became obsessed with obtaining immortality. And the Chinese emperors following Qin Shi Huang were similarly driven to find the cure for mortality. They encouraged monks to explore chemical combinations that could stave off death. Ironically, it was through those experiments that they actually ended up creating gunpowder.

"Has anyone ever gotten close?" Laney asked.

Victoria nodded. "One searcher actually succeeded."

"Who?"

"Gilgamesh."

Laney sat back in surprise. She thought of the tale of Gilgamesh, looking at it with fresh eyes in light of what she now knew. Gilgamesh was most famous for the tale of the flood. But there was another aspect of his story that had drawn many researchers to it: Gilgamesh's quest for immortality.

Gilgamesh was born into royalty, and due to his innate abilities and his privileged birth, he was given everything he wanted. Which made him spoiled and obnoxious, but also very lonely. As a result, the gods created a friend for Gilgamesh, his other half: Enkidu.

Enkidu was reported to have been as powerfully built as Gilgamesh, but he was described as a wild man. Together the two wreaked quite a bit of havoc, and eventually, their exploits caught up with them. Enkidu was punished for their transgression. The punishment was death.

Enkidu's death was Gilgamesh's first exposure to loss. He was beside himself with grief. So he searched out an immortal human named Utnapishtim. Utnapishtim told Gilgamesh that there was a plant at the bottom of the sea that would make him immortal. Gilgamesh managed to get the plant—but then when he was drunk, a snake stole the plant and carried it away.

Laney looked back out the window. *The bottom of the sea. The place where some scholars place the original Garden of Eden.* She wondered for a moment about the snake and how it was alleged to have gotten the plant back from Gilgamesh. Snakes seemed to dominate the stories she'd been hearing lately: the snake in the Garden, the snakes on the door of the vault in the temple, the snake stealing the plant from Gilgamesh.

"That was the first Garden of Eden," Laney said.

Victoria nodded. "And the first time it was moved."

Laney's eyes went wide when the second realization hit her. She turned back to Victoria. "*You* were the snake. You got the plant back from Gilgamesh."

Victoria winced. "It's one of my least favorite descriptions of myself, but one which, sadly, has stuck. But yes, Gilgamesh wasn't a dangerous man, but he was a man caught in the throes of guilt. He was not ready for immortality, and neither was the world. So yes, I retrieved the fruit of the tree from him, with a little more difficulty than the poem suggests, but also without bloodshed."

Laney looked at Victoria in amazement. She had done so much, and no one even knew who she was. In fact, she was demonized by society. It was so unfair. "Do you think we'll be able to achieve this retrieval without blood shed this time?"

Victoria paused for a moment. "I sincerely doubt it."

CHAPTER 95

THIRUVANANTHAPURAM, KERALA, INDIA

MATT CLARK STARED out the window of the helicopter at the river below. The current was powerful, devastating, and it had been hours since Jorgen had gone in. It would be a huge stroke of luck if they found any evidence of him.

"Sir, we haven't found anything three miles out. Do you want us to keep looking?"

Ever since they'd gotten everyone safely in the air, he'd had two choppers, as well as agents on foot, looking for a sign of Jorgen. But what little hope he'd had at the beginning of this search was dwindling into nothingness as the hours dragged on.

Matt spoke into the microphone attached to his headset. "Yes. Let me know if you find anything."

"Orders?" the pilot asked.

"Make another sweep. Farther downriver this time."

"Yes, sir."

The chopper headed north. Matt stared out the window. *Come on, where are you?* He had wanted to start the search earlier, but the priority had been getting Henry and Jake safely out of the country.

He owed Laney that much. But that time may have cost them their chance at finding Cain.

Mustafa spoke from the back of the chopper. "We'll need to refuel soon."

Matt nodded but stayed silent. Even if Cain were dead, Matt knew there was a good chance the body would never be recovered. But it was also possible that Cain had simply washed up on shore, healed, and walked away.

Damn it. Matt curled his fists. They needed to know, one way or the other.

They rode in silence. The pilot hugged the riverbank as much as he could. Fifteen minutes later, Matt was acknowledging the futility of this search. The river would only give up its prize when —and if—it wanted to.

Then Matt saw something black standing out against the brown bank below. He squinted. *What is that?*

He looked back at Mustafa and pointed. "Do you see that?"

"Yeah. We should check it out," Mustafa said.

Matt smiled, his hopes rising. Maybe this hadn't been so futile after all.

CHAPTER 96

HUNAN PROVINCE, CHINA

LANEY SAT in the back of the car as Ralph expertly handled the windy road leading along the edge of cliffs up to Heaven's Gate. They had arrived in Zhangjiajie Hehua Airport a few hours ago and then driven to Tianmen Mountain.

Now they were on the final leg of their journey. And she'd had no sense of the Fallen.

Laney stared out the window. *Heaven's Gate.* She'd never been there, but it had been on her bucket list. The official name of the location was "the Heaven's Gate Mountain," but when people used the term "Heaven's Gate" they were usually referring to a particular aspect of the mountain: the giant hole that punched completely through it.

It was a natural phenomenon, and incredible—or at least Laney had always thought so from the pictures she'd seen. It had originally been a cave, but the back end of the cave had collapsed in 263 C.E., leaving only the entrance still intact. The name was then switched from Songliang Mountain to Tianmen—the "sky-hole mountain." Millions of visitors came to this part of China to experience the natural wonder every year.

Ralph took another turn, and Laney swallowed nervously as she looked out at the cliff's edge—way too close to the car door for comfort. The road was almost seven miles of hairpin turns—ninety-nine of them to be precise. Called Tongtian Avenue, it symbolized the nine heavens.

Laney imagined that the ride was frightening enough during the day. Right now it was pitch black out, and it was mind-numbingly terrifying.

Laney clutched the side of the car as she felt one of the wheels come off the road. *Apparently I was worrying about the wrong thing. I'm going to die in a car crash instead of in a showdown with the Fallen.*

Twenty tense minutes later, they were still only halfway down the road. Ralph turned a corner and Laney was pretty sure another one of the wheels went airborne. She sucked in a breath.

Victoria glanced back at Laney from the front seat. "Okay?"

"Oh, sure. Just a leisurely drive."

Victoria gave a small laugh.

Laney smiled at her. "See? And you were worried we never got to do any mother-daughter activities. Here we are taking in the tourist traps."

Victoria smiled. "Well, let's enjoy it then."

As they headed up the mountain, the sides of road grew higher, making it more difficult to see over the side—which was fine with Laney, because the view was a little too heart-attack-inducing for her taste.

The wind picked up, and the car was pushed a little across the road.

Laney focused on taking calming breaths, but her pounding heart made it clear that meditation was not her thing. Instead, she managed to keep replaying a vision of the brakes giving out and them careening off the side of the road and plummeting to their deaths.

Finally, Ralph made it around the last turn and pulled into an empty parking lot.

Laney let out a breath and took a moment to steady her breathing. She grabbed her backpack and opened the door. Ralph was already helping Victoria out. Laney stood and stretched. Her legs felt like jelly.

Victoria looked over at her. "Are you ready?"

Laney gave a laugh, feeling her nerves stretch her smile tight. "Honestly? Probably not."

Victoria kissed her cheek. "You're ready. Trust me."

Laney looked at Victoria and realized that she did trust her. She trusted her implicitly. "Okay. Let's go."

They stepped onto the path together; Ralph followed behind. The moon shone brightly through the center of the arch. It truly did look supernatural—like a gateway to some incredible place. It looked impossible.

But then Laney's gaze fell on the stairs leading up to it, and she sighed. *And that's not the only thing that looks impossible.*

She was about to say something to Victoria, but then she felt a tug from somewhere up ahead, up the stairs. *What was that?*

"We'll have to take the stairs," Ralph said. "The chair will put us in the wrong spot."

Laney knew there was a chair that took tourists up to the summit, if they couldn't handle the steps.

She struggled to keep in the groan. "All nine hundred ninety-nine steps?"

"We won't be going all the way to the top." Ralph offered Victoria his arm. "Victoria?"

Victoria wrapped her arm around his. "Let's go."

Ralph gestured for Laney to take the lead. She did, and with each step the pull got stronger.

They walked in silence with only the crickets to keep them company. A chill fell over Laney, and she was pretty sure it wasn't from the evening air. They were heading for the Garden of Eden and the tree of life. How was that possible? The enormity of this undertaking wasn't lost on her.

Laney forced herself to take note of her surroundings. Every year millions of tourists visited this mountain, but she knew not many got to see it like this. She could see why it had been named Heaven's Gate.

She glanced up at the huge hole. *Tonight, it should probably be called Hell's Gate.* If the Fallen reached the tree before them, the impact on the world would be devastating. But so far, there was no sign of the Fallen. There was no sign of anyone. *Maybe we will do this without a fight. Wow—that would be a nice change of pace.*

About two thirds of the way up the stairs, Laney felt a tug from her left. She stopped. "It's this way."

She led them off the stairs and into the woods that bordered the sides. Trees and shadow kept her from being able to see much, but it didn't take long for them to reach the mountain face. Laney still felt the pull urging her forward, but there was nowhere to go.

She looked around. "Um, are we climbing?"

Ralph released Victoria and stepped toward the rock. "Nope. We'll use the door."

Even with the shadows, it was obvious there was no door. There wasn't even a cave.

But Ralph placed his hands against the rock face and smiled. "It's here." He nodded to Laney. "Go ahead. Like this."

"Um, okay." Laney placed her hands on the rock face as well. Immediately she felt a heat rise through her and into the rock. The rock seemed to shimmer for a moment, and then it disappeared, leaving a roughly doorway-sized hole.

Laney's jaw dropped. "Wow."

"Nice job," Victoria said.

Laney peered inside. It was pitch black. She slung off her pack and knelt down to unzip it. Pulling out three flashlights, she handed one each to Ralph and Victoria.

Ralph stepped through the doorway, turning on his flashlight as he did so. Victoria followed him. Laney took a deep breath and stepped forward last. She slammed into an invisible wall.

She stepped back, rubbing her nose. "Ouch."

Ralph turned back, an eyebrow raised. "Are you carrying weapons?"

Feeling sheepish, Laney pulled her knife and sheath from her belt.

Ralph shook his head. "Didn't I say no weapons?"

"Yes. But I tend not to like going against Fallen without a little something."

"You'll have to leave it out there. You won't be allowed in with it."

Laney held out the hand with the ring of Solomon on it. "What about this?"

"That's allowed," Ralph said.

Swallowing a curse, Laney dropped her knife beside the opening. She hated the idea of walking into this unarmed. But apparently, she had no choice: no one would be able to get inside with weapons—even the Fallen. That last thought didn't bring her much comfort though—she knew what the Fallen could do even without weapons.

Eyeing the opening, Laney reached out her hand. It passed through without any problems. Holding her breath, she stepped forward and crossed over.

She let out her breath. "Okay. That's better."

Ralph shook his head at her.

"Yeah, yeah, I know." Laney looked around. "How was this place created?"

Victoria shrugged. "It just was."

Laney looked back at the door. "Shouldn't we close that?"

"No," Ralph said. "Once opened, it cannot be closed. The seal has been broken. The Guardian will now make a decision whether to re-seal it or move the tree."

"So that means if the Fallen are right behind us, they'll be able to get in," Laney said.

Ralph nodded.

"Okay," Laney said. "So let's get a move on."

Ralph pointed down with his flashlight to their right. An opening could be seen in the rock. "The entry to the cave is through there. But we cannot enter unless you are prepared to be tested."

Laney stopped short. "Tested? How?"

"To see the heart of the ring bearer," Victoria said. "If you are going to be the ring bearer you must pass the test."

Laney looked between the two of them. "What do you mean *if* I'm going to be the ring bearer? Aren't I already the ring bearer?"

Victoria eyes were full of both compassion and sadness. "You have been the ring bearer for a long time. But you were not always the ring bearer. There were others."

"And what happened to them?"

"They were not worthy," Ralph said.

"So the ring was taken from them," Victoria said.

Ralph nodded. "As well as their life."

CHAPTER 97

Laney gaped, her gaze shifting from Ralph to Victoria and back again. "So if I fail this test, I die?"

Victoria nodded.

"You couldn't have mentioned this sooner?"

"We thought it would be best this way," Victoria said.

"Right, because God forbid I have time to focus on my potential death."

"You can always say no, Laney. We can stop here, find out a way to close up the entrance, go home, and hope the Fallen don't reach the tree," Victoria said.

Laney shook her head. Of course she couldn't do that.

"The ring bearer is called upon time and time again to sacrifice," Ralph said. "Even if you do not lose your life today, you may be asked to risk it again. And again. By stepping into that doorway, you accept that life of sacrifice."

Way to sell it, Ralph. Laney looked at her mother and thought of all she had already sacrificed. Images of all those important in her life flashed through her mind on a continuous reel. And the last images were of her Uncle Patrick, Henry, and Jake. She pictured the three of them at dinner over at Henry's last week. Her chest felt tight. The three men that she loved would be safe only if she succeeded.

But she knew what her choice would be. She had known ever since she had read those words in *The Army of the Belial*. Even if the people she loved weren't in danger, how could she put the rest of the world at risk? Mothers, fathers, children, friends, family—the world was full of love, even with all the anger and strife that seemed to dominate the headlines.

And if the Fallen succeeded, that love would be twisted, abused, tested, and destroyed. Laney couldn't let that happen.

Drake's words drifted through her mind. *What will you sacrifice to keep it safe?*

At the time, she had thought she had the answer. But now she really did. She would sacrifice *herself*. Without hesitation. Because her life was unimportant when stacked against all of those whom the Fallen would destroy.

Laney looked up, shocked to realize that tears had rolled down her cheeks. But she didn't wipe them away. Tears weren't weakness. They demonstrated how much you cared. And caring was strength.

"You have an answer?" Ralph asked.

Laney nodded. "I'll take the test."

CHAPTER 98

LANEY STOOD at the entrance of a cave. The flickering of light farther in told her that the cave was long and narrow. She glanced over at her mother and gave her a smile. "I'll be right back."

Victoria held onto Ralph's arm tightly, but she kept her voice light. "I know you will."

"Laney," Ralph called out.

She turned.

"Whatever you do, you must reach the end of the path. Do not let anything deter you."

Laney gave him an abrupt nod. Then she stepped inside.

The path was wide, but it narrowed as she moved along. Soon she could touch both sides of the cave simultaneously. A fog seemed to settle over her as she went, but when the path ended at a large cavern, the fog disappeared.

Laney paused at the entrance of the cavern. Giant stalactites reached down from the ceiling forty feet above her. Stalagmites rose from the ground. *Okay, you can do this.*

Heart hammering, Laney stepped into the large space.

Nothing happened.

She stepped farther in, her eyes darting about, but still nothing moved. Confused, Laney stared up at the ceiling. What was the test? It couldn't be—

Movement on the ceiling drew her attention. A dark shape shifted. Squinting, she realized it wasn't a shape, but *shapes*. Laney's pulse raced. Hundreds of bats lined the ceiling of the cave. As if realizing they'd been seen, they swooped as one down toward Laney.

Laney sprinted for the other side of the cavern, the bats diving at her from all sides. She tripped and slid onto her stomach. The bats swarmed, nipping at her back and pulling on her hair. Panicked, she flailed her arms and legs, trying to shove them off, but to no avail.

Stop, she commanded herself. Focusing all her attention on the ring, she called up a wind and slammed the bats into the wall. The attack lessened, but a few still dove at her. Without a thought, Laney called up rain next. It came down in sheets, drenching both the bats and herself.

The bats flew off, and she jumped to her feet. She ran for other side of the cavern. There were three openings in the far wall.

Oh, come on. She chose the one on the right and sprinted through. Torches sprang to life in the distance.

Twenty feet in, Laney glanced behind her, but none of the bats were giving chase. It was as if they couldn't move beyond the boundary of the cavern. She stopped. Letting out a breath, she shook out her arms and wrung out both her hair and her shirt. *Okay, apparently this is going to be a test of skill.*

Shaking off the panic the bats had caused, Laney continued forward. She had lost her flashlight in the mad dash, but a torch flickered down the tunnel around a bend, providing faint light.

Laney again looked behind her. The bats were now swarming around the entrance of the tunnel, clearly unable to enter. *It's either go through the bats again or face the unknown around the corner.* For a hysterical moment she felt like she was in some horrible game show.

Ralph's words came back to her. *You must reach the end of the path.*

Squaring her shoulders, Laney headed toward the light. Something glinted on the floor. She knelt down and pushed away the dirt. A dagger. Laney picked it up. It was serrated, with a wooden handle.

What are you doing here? I thought weapons weren't allowed.

Pausing for only a second, Laney tucked it into her belt. Weapons might not be allowed to come in, but if one was *already* in here, it seemed stupid to not take advantage of it.

She took another step forward, and immediately a jolt of electricity shot through her. She grabbed onto the wall and gritted her teeth as she waited for the weakness in her legs to pass. *Damned archangels.* But at least now she knew what was around the corner.

As she rounded the bend, a muscular man with dark skin stood waiting twenty feet ahead. Behind him was a rope bridge with a wooden base, not all that different from the ones the Shuar had used.

"Ring bearer," he said, "I am Gabriel."

Laney started. Gabriel, the messenger of God.

He stepped away from the bridge and gestured toward it. "You may continue on your journey. The end of the path is just over the bridge."

Laney studied him. *This is too easy. What am I missing?* She looked to both sides of the bridge. It was too dark to see anything. She stepped forward and heard a sound to her right—a muffled squeak.

Laney stopped. "What's over there?"

"It's nothing, ring bearer. Your time is limited. You must cross the bridge to complete your mission."

Laney stared hard at the spot where she'd heard the noise. Something was swaying there. "I want to see what's there."

"Very well." Gabriel waved his hand, and torches ringing the cavern flared to life.

Laney gasped. A cage was suspended over the empty space

next to the bridge. Within were two bound and gagged figures: a woman of Asian descent with dark hair and eyes, and a small girl who was undeniably her daughter.

Laney whirled toward Gabriel. "What is the meaning of this?"

Gabriel's eyes narrowed, and his tone was harsh. "Nothing, ring bearer. They are not your concern."

The little girl's eyes stared back at Laney, pleading for help.

Laney turned to Gabriel. "Are they being punished for something?"

"No."

Anger built inside Laney. "Release them."

"No. And your time is running short."

Laney glared at Gabriel before turning her attention back to the cage. One of the torches was lit near where the rope was tied to the wall. Smoke drifted from the spot. *Oh my God.*

"They'll be killed."

Gabriel's voice was hard. "Remember your mission, ring bearer. They are not your concern. Stay on the path."

Laney stared helplessly at the mother and child. Everything that was resting on her shoulders ran through her mind. If she crossed the bridge and ignored their suffering, she would pass the test. The world could be saved. If she didn't, she would be killed, and it would fall to her friends to beat back the Fallen.

The mother's gaze locked on Laney's. The fear and desperation the woman felt for her daughter was palpable.

No. If the ring bearer is supposed to let people die, then they've got the wrong girl. Laney ran to the edge of the landing and called on the wind. But nothing came. She stared down at her ring and then at Gabriel. He looked back at her, his face blank.

She tried again, but still nothing. *So, no powers.*

The smoke near the rope had grown thicker. It wouldn't last much longer.

"Do not be distracted, ring bearer. You know what needs to be done."

Laney glared at the angel, reading only coldness in his face, no compassion. Then she turned back to the mother and child. *Yes. I do know what needs to be done.*

Laney ran back from the edge of the cliff, paused only long enough to take a breath, then sprinted for the edge. She leapt at the last possible second. She flew through the air, her fingers barely catching the edge of the cage.

Heart pounding, forearms straining, she pulled herself up, and threw her right foot around one of the bars. From there she pulled herself to a standing position on the outside of the cage.

The girl and her mother stared at her, tears streaming down both their faces.

"It's going to be okay," Laney panted. She climbed around the cage to the door, which was held tight by a thickly knotted rope. Using her dagger, Laney sliced through the rope and climbed inside. She removed the mother's binds and then the child's, all the while stealing glances at the smoking rope that held them all aloft.

Laney gestured at the cage bars. "You need to hold on."

The mother grabbed hold of her daughter, then wrapped her arms around the bars, keeping her daughter in front of her.

Laney climbed back out, positioning herself at the side farthest from the bridge. Using her legs and arms for power, she shoved at the cage, treating it as if it were a giant swing. Slowly, little by little, the cage began to sway. She pushed harder and harder, her gaze shifting between the rope and the bridge.

Gabriel had disappeared. Laney struggled not to think about what that meant.

Come on. Come on.

The cage swung over the bridge. Laney reached out to grab one of the bridge's anchor ropes, but missed. She swung harder, and she managed to snag one on their next swing. But the cage was too heavy, and her hand slipped.

Pushing harder, she came back around for another swing. This time she wrapped her feet around the bars and reached out to the anchor rope with both hands. She grabbed it and held; but she knew she wouldn't be able to hold it for long. Already her hands were beginning to slip.

"Get out. Get out!" Laney yelled.

The woman hauled her child toward the doorway. At the edge, she pushed the girl toward the bridge. For one heartbreaking moment, Laney thought the girl would miss. But she grabbed on to the bridge and with her mother's help from above, she scrambled onto it.

Laney's fingers began to slip. *No, no.*

It was the mother's turn. She leapt for the bridge. She made it.

Thank God. But Laney's fingers had reached the breaking point; she lost her hold. The cage swung backward, Laney hanging on by her feet.

And then the rope snapped.

In horror, Laney watched the darkness rush up to meet her. She closed her eyes, picturing Jake and Henry. *I'm sorry. I failed.*

CHAPTER 99

BALTIMORE, MARYLAND

PATRICK GAZED out the window in the hospital room at Johns Hopkins. Below him, cars zipped by and people walked along the sidewalks chatting on phones, occasionally alone. Patrick examined each of them, trying to pick out the SIA agents and Chandler operatives. He knew they were out in full force, both outside the hospital and within.

Finally he sighed and turned away from the window. The activity hadn't been as distracting as he had hoped.

Henry was in the room next door. Jen and Danny were with him. Henry was doing as well as could be expected, but it would still be weeks, if not months, before he was back to normal.

Patrick looked at Jake, asleep in the bed next to him. Jake's recovery would be no quicker.

All the Chandler resources were out in force to keep Henry and Jake safe. And Laney was out there with only Ralph and Victoria against an army of Fallen. Patrick rolled his hands into fists.

Keep her safe. He'd prayed those same words he didn't know how many times since this had all begun. But right now, his fear was stronger than he could remember. The closest it had come was when Laney was grabbed by Azazyel and he felt like she was alone. And now with Henry and Jake down, he felt that again.

"Laney?" Jake's voice was weak.

Patrick hurried to the side of the bed.

Jake blinked up at Patrick. "Patrick?"

Patrick forced a smile to his face as he patted Jake's shoulder. "Hey, Jake. You're all right. You're in the hospital in Baltimore."

Jake struggled to sit up. "Where's Laney? Is she all right?"

Patrick pressed Jake's shoulder gently back down. "She's fine. She wasn't hurt. It's you and Henry we're all worried about."

"Henry?"

Patrick quickly explained about Henry's injuries and why he was healing slowly.

Jake leaned back heavily, closing his eyes. "What about Jorgen?"

"No one's sure. He was pulled away by the river."

"So where's Laney? With Henry?"

Patrick looked at the man whom Laney loved with all her heart. He knew Jake loved her back just as fiercely. And he hated to have to tell him the truth. He thought for a moment about lying—at least until Jake was better—but he knew how angry Jake would be if the truth was kept from him.

"She went after the tree."

Jake's jaw tightened. "I'd like to say I'm surprised, but I'm not. How many people did she take with her?"

"Two."

Jake's eyes flew open. "What? But the Fallen will be there. Tons of them."

Patrick nodded, a cold ball of fear expanding in his stomach. "I know. And so did she."

Jake met Patrick's eyes and didn't look away. "She'll make it back to us. She will."

Patrick nodded, but tears clogged his throat. And the fear that had been running around his brain in an unending loop sprang to his lips. "But if it comes to a question of saving her life and everyone else's, what do you think she'll choose?"

Jake's gaze shifted away from Patrick's, his jaw tightening. "She'll come back."

But this time Jake's words sounded less like a statement and more like a hope.

CHAPTER 100

TIANMEN MOUNTAIN, CHINA

"LANEY, LANEY." A voice called to her in the darkness. Laney shied away from the voice, happy where she was. It was warm. It was safe.

But the voice was insistent. "Laney, wake up. I need you to wake up."

I know that voice.

"Wake up."

Victoria. Laney's memories rushed back, and her eyes flew open with a gasp. She sat upright, and the world swam for a moment.

"Easy." Ralph crouched next to her, helping to keep her steady. Laney blinked and tried to focus. Her mother knelt in front of her, her hands wrapped around Laney's.

An image of the cave flashed through Laney's mind. "The woman, the child. Are they all right?"

A smile lit Victoria's face. "They're fine."

Laney felt the disappointment crash down on her. "Don't smile. I failed. I couldn't finish the test."

Victoria ran her hand along Laney's hair. "No, my love. You passed."

Laney stared, not understanding. "But I didn't. I got off the path. I stopped. There was a mother and child in danger. I stopped to help them and I fell. I fell, I—"

Laney looked down at herself. There were no rips in her clothes from the bats, no bruises. She stretched her legs and arms. She had no injuries. *How…?* She stared at Victoria. "None of that actually happened, did it?"

Both Ralph and Victoria shook their heads.

Laney wiped at her eyes, wishing she could do the same to her mind, which seemed to be working slower than usual. "The fog— it was a hallucinogen."

"Yes." Victoria stood, and Ralph took Laney by the shoulders and helped her to her feet.

"But I still failed," Laney said. "I left the path."

"Which is why you passed," Ralph said. "You didn't stick to your mission because you stopped to save a life. Lives. You did the right thing. That was the test. Not how well you could use your abilities. You wouldn't be here if that's all it was."

Victoria smiled. "It was a test of your character, Laney. And you passed with flying colors."

Laney looked between the two of them. Understanding dawned, along with happiness. "I passed?"

Victoria nodded. "Now we just need to get to the tree."

Ralph beckoned them forward. Laney followed him on wobbly legs, but she couldn't contain her joy. She had passed. It was going to be all right.

But as Laney looked at Ralph and Victoria, her joy began to wane. They didn't look happy. The darkness at the edge of her mind returned. *The time of sacrifice or death will be at hand.* The truth hit her with the force of a train.

It's not over. The sacrifice is still to come.

Torches came to life along the path as if on cue.

"He knows we're here," Ralph murmured.

"That's a good thing, right?" Laney asked.

Ralph didn't answer. He just moved forward toward an

opening in the rock. As Laney stepped in behind him, she saw rock steps winding upward. She remembered a nightmare she'd once had—she'd been chased down a set of stairs just like this one. She hoped she wasn't going to experience the same fate on this set of stairs.

Ralph climbed the stairs first, and Laney followed. He had pocketed the flashlight and pulled one of the torches from the wall to light the way. Shadows danced as they went.

Laney glanced back at Victoria. "Are you all right?"

Victoria waved her on. "Don't worry about me."

But Laney *was* worried. Victoria was hiding something. She knew that.

When they reached the top of the stairs, Ralph stopped. Laney stepped up next to him. "Where to now?"

Ralph pointed. "There."

It was dark up ahead, and Laney squinted to see. Then suddenly torches flamed to life, illuminating an ancient rock bridge sitting over a deep chasm. She could just make out the ledge on the other side. It ran along the edge of the chasm before disappearing into the darkness beyond.

"I guess we're going over that?" Laney asked, hoping they would say she was mistaken.

"He's lighting the way," Victoria said.

"I can't feel him."

"You will soon," Ralph replied.

Laney looked ahead. "You never answered me before: the archangel knowing we're coming is a good thing, right?"

Again, neither Ralph nor Victoria answered. They just started forward.

Laney swallowed. *Right. Across the creepy bridge in the creepy cave to meet the all-powerful archangel. It must be Tuesday.*

CHAPTER 101

LANEY HELPED VICTORIA across the bridge. It wasn't shaky, like the Shuar bridges down in Ecuador, but it was awfully narrow and had no walls or railings at the sides. Laney glanced down only once—and that once had been more than enough. The light only pierced through the darkness a short way, but Laney had the feeling it went awfully far down.

And she couldn't shake the memory of her falling through a space like that after rescuing the woman and child. It may have been only a hallucination, but it had been a very realistic one.

When they reached the other side of the bridge and stepped onto solid ground again, Laney felt thankful.

Victoria gave her a wobbly smile. "Well, that was exciting."

Laney let out a nervous laugh. "Let's not do that again any time soon."

Ralph called out to them from ahead. "We're almost there."

Taking Victoria's arm, Laney followed but kept one hand along the rock wall to her left. Ralph waited at the end of the narrow path.

Laney felt a piercing jolt of electricity shoot through her. She gasped and dropped to her knees.

"Laney!" Victoria knelt down next to her. "What is it?"

Laney took a moment to get her breath back. She patted Victoria's hand. "I'm okay. But we're getting close."

Laney got to her feet, her legs a little shaky yet again. Whoever this archangel was, he was more powerful than either Ralph or Drake. Even more powerful than Gabriel had been.

This time it was Victoria who helped Laney along.

Soon Laney felt fine again, but a fine tingle of electricity continued to dance over her skin. She knew the archangel was not far ahead.

When she and Victoria joined Ralph, Laney realized the path did not end, it curved around the wall of rock. She stepped out. A long shelf stood out from the rock wall, at least a hundred yards long and maybe thirty wide, bordered on the other side by the chasm the bridge had been built over. The chasm ran beside the ledge like a river, twisting and turning. And fifty yards ahead of them stood a powerfully built man with olive skin, his arms crossed over his chest, gold bands wrapped around his biceps. Another towering rock wall loomed above him.

Laney could feel even from a distance how dangerous the man was. And that was before he pulled a sword from the scabbard at his waist. A sword that glowed with fire.

His words echoed through the cavern, sounding as if they had been rolled in gravel. "You have made a mistake coming here, ring bearer."

CHAPTER 102

LANEY STARED in disbelief at the vision of violence that stalked toward them. They had come all this way and were now about to be dispatched by the very angel they sought? *Seriously?*

Victoria stepped up next to Laney. "Halt." The command in her voice rang out through the cave.

The archangel stopped, pausing for only a second to re-sheath his sword before dropping to one knee. "Mother Earth, I did not realize you were here."

Victoria moved forward. "Rise, Remiel. The tree is in danger. It must be moved."

He stood and eyed her. "You know the sacrifice required to make that happen?"

Victoria nodded. "I do. And I am willing."

"Wait, "Laney interrupted. "What sacrifice?" She looked at Victoria, but it was Remiel who answered. "The only way to move the tree is through the lifeblood of the mother."

"You mean a couple of drops, right?" Laney asked, keeping her eyes on her mother.

Victoria pursed her lips and gave a small shake of her head.

"How much blood?" Laney demanded, although she dreaded the answer.

"Someone's coming!" Remiel shouted, pulling his sword once more.

Laney stared at Victoria for a moment longer before turning to face the new threat. *My mother's blood.* Laney's mind reviled the thought.

But she didn't have time to focus on that, as her early warning system was letting her know that Fallen were nearby.

And there were a lot of them.

Laney nodded at the flaming sword in Remiel's hand. "I don't suppose you have an extra one of those?"

Remiel grasped his sword with two hands and ripped it apart. He now held two flaming swords, one in each hand. He tossed one to Laney and she caught it at the hilt.

Fire danced across the blade—orange along the base, turning blue as it spread out. The sword itself was surprisingly light, and she couldn't feel any heat coming off of it. But she didn't doubt that it would do damage. After all, what was the likelihood an archangel would arm himself with a useless weapon?

Laney twirled it a few times, getting a feel for it. *Yeah, this will work.*

"You are not welcome here." Remiel's voice rang through the cave.

Laney's head whipped back toward the path.

Elisabeta stepped into view. She was accompanied by a group of twenty Fallen, another dozen nephilim, and another twenty or so humans.

Laney swallowed. *I don't like these odds.* "Victoria, get behind Remiel and Ralph."

Victoria hesitated, but did as she was told. Laney positioned herself between the two archangels. Victoria was behind them, standing against the wall.

Elisabeta stepped forward. Her eyes were narrowed, her tone confident and condescending. "You are outnumbered. Step out of the way."

"It is you who will meet your death, traitor," Remiel growled. "This is your last chance to leave."

"We're not going anywhere except through you," Elisabeta said.

"As you wish." Remiel leapt forward. Three Fallen blurred toward him. Remiel cut them down with two swipes of his sword.

"Take them!" Elisabeta yelled.

Ralph moved forward, taking on a group of nephilim and dispatching them quickly. Laney held back, not wanting to leave Victoria unguarded. Elisabeta glared at her from across the cavern. She sent a group of humans for her.

Laney narrowed her eyes. *My turn.*

A man ran at her, trying to tackle her. She sidestepped and brought her sword down on his arm. At the first touch of the blade, his whole body was engulfed in flames—and within seconds, he had turned to ash. Momentarily stunned, Laney stepped back, staring at the sword in her hand. Apparently Fallen were injured by it, but humans were reduced to ash. *Well, all right then.*

Two more men started for her but Laney was ready. She cut one across the stomach and twirled out of the way, cutting the other at an angle starting at the shoulder. Both men burst into flame and turned to ash. Laney became a swirl of movement. She didn't so much lunge as dance from human to human, her sword never stopping its arcs.

In only a few seconds, she had defeated all the humans. But the Fallen were coming closer—like a tide heaving toward shore. Ralph and Remiel were fighting them off, but they were grossly outnumbered. And now more humans and Fallen poured in from behind Elisabeta. There were too many. They would be overrun.

We can't fight them one by one. We need another way. Laney stared at the stalactites above, focusing all her energy on them. With a burst of wind, she tore them from their perch and hurled them at the advancing Fallen. One group of Fallen was knocked off the ledge and into the abyss. Their screams echoed through the cave as they fell.

Laney caught one of the stalactites with another gust of wind and flung it at Elisabeta. Elisabeta barely dove out of way in time. The next few stalactites bottlenecked the path, keeping any new reinforcements from entering the arena.

Behind Laney, Victoria screamed. Laney whirled around. A Fallen had grabbed Victoria by the arm. Laney pulled her arm back and let her sword fly. It impaled itself into the chest of the Fallen. Laney caught a blur in the corner of her eye as a Fallen ran for her.

"Throw yourself from the cliff," Laney ordered.

The Fallen sprinted for the edge and leapt.

Laney scrambled over the bodies of Fallen already littering the ground to get to Victoria and pull her to her feet. A cut ran along the side of Victoria's chest.

"Oh my God," Laney said.

Victoria shook her head. "It's nothing. We need to worry about *them*." She gestured back to entranceway. The Fallen had pushed the stalactites out of the way and were clambering through yet again.

The numbers were overwhelming. *We can never defeat this many.*

Remiel sliced through a group of men and pitched them over the side. "Uriel, take them to the tree. I will cover you."

Ralph dispatched two nephilim running for him, then sprinted to Laney and Victoria. "Laney—watch my back."

Two humans ran for Laney and Victoria. The first aimed a front kick at Laney's chest. She sidestepped, caught the leg, and pushed down on the man's hip while forcing his leg up. The man slammed onto his back. Laney kicked her foot into his groin.

The second man aimed a punch at Laney's head. She dropped the first man's leg and leapt out of the way. He punched again. She let the punch pass in front of her, slid her hand down his arm, and pulled it at the elbow. Then she latched both hands onto his wrist and swung him over her. She felt his shoulder pop out of place. He screamed as he landed, hard.

Another two Fallen ran for her. "Jump over the cliff," she ordered.

They grinned and kept coming.

Laney grimaced. *Stupid earplugs.*

Laney yanked her sword out of the chest of the Fallen she'd flung it at. It circled above her head. She took out one Fallen with an elegant swipe and whirled around, slicing the other across the stomach. The second Fallen grabbed onto the sword as it fell back, stumbling into the chasm. Laney had to release the sword to avoid being pulled in as well.

From the corner of her eye, Laney saw Ralph placing his hands on the wall behind Victoria. The wall shimmered for a moment and then disappeared, leaving a seven-foot doorway.

"They've opened the door!" Elisabeta yelled.

Ralph grabbed Victoria and pushed her through the doorway. "Laney, bring down the roof!"

"But Remiel—"

"Do it!" Ralph yelled.

Laney hesitated for only a second. Ralph stepped in front of her, fighting off the Fallen who tried to charge. Remiel joined him, holding them at bay.

Laney stared at the ceiling. She pulled all the power she could manage from the ring, all her emotion coursing through her and to the ceiling. A thunderous crack sounded; then another. Huge, boulder-sized chunks of rock broke off from the ceiling and came crashing down onto the Fallen. Soon some of them were running back for the path, trying to reach the bridge before the ceiling collapsed.

"Go, Uriel! Get them out of here!" Remiel yelled.

Ralph grabbed Laney around the waist and dove through the doorway he'd made in the rock wall. As they tumbled to the ground, a massive shard of rock crashed down behind them, sealing off the doorway. Thunderous thumps and screams came from the other side of the rock.

Laney scrambled to her feet. "But Remiel—"

"Has already gone from this place," Ralph said quietly.

Laney stared up at him, her shoulders slumping, sadness washing over her.

"Are you all right?" Victoria asked, rushing over to her.

Laney hugged her tight. "I'm okay. Are you?"

"Yes." She took Laney's hand and led her through a narrow tunnel. There were no torches here, but somewhere up ahead, light glistened. As they moved closer to it, Laney heard chirping. *Birds?*

She stepped out of the tunnel with Victoria and stopped in awe. They stood in the largest cavern Laney had ever seen. The ceiling was hundreds—a thousand?—feet above them, and in the center of it was a hole through which sunlight shone. But what grabbed Laney's attention was the giant tree, at least three hundred feet tall, standing right in the center of the cavern. Birds flew between its limbs with their draped leaves.

It looks like the willow tree in front of Victoria's house.

"It's beautiful," Laney said.

Victoria smiled. "Yes, it is."

Laney stared up at the hole in the ceiling allowing the sunlight in and frowned. It wasn't even dawn yet. "How is there sun in here?" she asked. "And couldn't we just have rappelled in rather than walking through the creepy cave?"

"This is not a normal cave," Ralph replied simply.

Laney wanted to ask more questions, but honestly, it didn't really matter right now. *Magical cave, magical tree. Got it.*

Behind the tree she could make out the entrance and another tunnel. Her heart lifted. *A way out.*

Victoria walked up to the tree and pulled on a branch that hung nearly to the ground. Laney noticed for the first time the fruit that grew all across the tree. It was shaped like a very small pineapple but was deep purple in color.

Victoria plucked one of the fruits and handed it to Laney. "You need to see that this gets to Drake."

Laney stared down at the fruit in her hand. "I don't understand. We just need to plant the fruit and a new tree sprouts up? It's that simple?"

Victoria nodded. "That's all there is to it."

"And immortality… does it come from eating the fruit?"

"Yes. The fruit sustains a human's life indefinitely."

Laney wondered if the fruit lengthened or stabilized the telomeres Danny had spoken of. But she supposed at the same time that it didn't really matter. Humanity had a lot to figure out before they were ready for that.

"Drake will get it to the next archangel," Ralph said.

Laney looked up at the tree. "Okay, then. Let's just torch this thing, and we'll be good."

Ralph and Victoria exchanged a look.

Laney felt cold, remembering Remiel's words about Victoria's sacrifice. "What?"

Victoria turned to Ralph. "Could you give us a minute?"

Ralph nodded, his face expressionless, his jaw tight. A sense of dread built up in Laney's chest as she watched the look that passed between Ralph and Victoria. *When the triads intersect, the time of judgment is at hand. The choice of sacrifice or death will be made.*

Laney spoke slowly. "Victoria, in *The Army of the Belial*, it says that at the time of judgment there will be a choice of sacrifice or death. What is the sacrifice?"

Victoria's purple eyes met Laney's directly. "It's me."

CHAPTER 103

THIRUVANANTHAPURAM, KERALA, INDIA

CLARK STARED at the object on the bank of the river. The longer he looked, the more sure he was it was a man.

He turned to the pilot. "We need to get down there."

The pilot quickly found a spot to land. Matt jumped down from the chopper. Mustafa was out just a few seconds after him. The other two agents followed, one of them bringing the silver medical case.

Matt headed to the spot where they'd seen the man. He stopped at the bank and searched up and down, trying to pinpoint the spot he'd seen from the air.

"There!" Mustafa called. He pointed to a dark jumble down the bank to their left. Matt ran over, but slowed as he got closer. He held up his hand for silence and walked up to the man. He didn't touch him, just walked around him. Shoulder-length dark hair, olive complexion.

Matt looked back at his men. "It's him."

The agent carrying the med kit knelt on the ground. He reached over and gently felt the man's neck. "I have a pulse. It's getting stronger. We need to move fast."

One of the other agents had already opened the med kit. He pulled out two syringes and some alcohol swabs. Mustafa knelt down and gently pushed up the sleeve of Cain's shirt. He held out his hand for a swab, and an agent placed one in his hand. Mustafa swabbed Cain's upper arm.

Mustafa looked up at Matt. "We're ready."

Matt nodded. "Proceed."

Mustafa picked up both of the syringes. He handed one to Matt. "Be quick."

Matt nodded. The two other agents positioned themselves behind Mustafa. Matt took off the cap and squeezed out a bit of air. He looked at Mustafa. "Ready."

Blowing out a breath, Mustafa plunged the needle into Cain's arm and jammed down on the plunger. He fell back with a scream as blood bloomed across his own arm from a deep slash. The two agents behind Mustafa caught him quickly, laying him down.

"Move!" Matt yelled, dropping to Mustafa's side. The agents scampered back.

Matt plunged the syringe of adrenaline into Mustafa's chest. The other agents put pressure on the wound on his arm.

"Come on, come on," Matt urged as he placed his hand on Mustafa's neck. His pulse was weak, but getting stronger.

After a moment, Matt breathed a sigh of relief. He nodded at the other two agents. "He'll be all right. Call in the extraction unit."

One of the agents stepped away to make the call. Matt moved next to Cain and felt his pulse. It was barely there. *Perfect.*

A few minutes later, both Mustafa and Cain were strapped to stretchers and loaded into the second helicopter. Matt rode with them. He hated that one of his men had been injured, but there had been no other way to get this particular target into their custody safely.

When they landed at the airport, they transferred both men to a larger plane. The whole transfer took less than five minutes and then they were taxiing down the runway. Matt felt like he was taking his first breath since they had seen Cain on the riverbank. *I can't believe that worked.*

He walked to the back of the plane, where a medic was checking Cain's vitals. "How is he?"

"Good. The sedation should last for at least another six hours."

Matt knew that there was a good chance someone would have to inject Cain again. But they had prepared for that possibility.

Matt moved back to the front of the plane and sat next to the stretcher that held Mustafa. Mustafa's eyes were closed and his complexion was paler than Matt would have liked. He patted Mustafa on the shoulder and leaned over to whisper in his ear. "You did well, old friend."

Then Matt leaned back and closed his eyes.

Thirty minutes later, he was roused by a rustle from the stretcher next to him. Mustafa's eyelids fluttered.

Matt leaned forward. "Hey, Mustafa. You're going to be fine."

Mustafa's voice was weak. "Did we get him?"

Matt nodded, feeling the smile spread across his face.

Mustafa squinted; Matt knew that was the closest he could manage to a smile at this moment. "Great. But next time, *you* get to sedate him."

"Hey, I'm the director. I can't be incapacitated."

"Just think of the example you'll set for us underlings. Taking one for the team."

Matt gave a laugh, but they both knew that Matt had volunteered to give Cain the shot. Mustafa had overruled him based on the very reason Matt had just provided.

"Are we on schedule?" Mustafa asked.

Clark glanced at his watch. "Yup. In another ten hours, Cain will be incarcerated in our West Virginia facility."

Mustafa closed his eyes. "Are you going to tell Delaney?"

Matt looked at the dark immortal strapped to the stretcher only a few feet away. "Not yet."

Mustafa's eyes flew open and he winced, sucking in a breath. "Why not? She should know."

R.D. BRADY

"Yes, but she's…" Matt struggled to find the right word. Finally he laughed. "She's good, Mustafa. We need to learn everything we can about him before we tell her we have him."

Mustafa watched him intently. "Because she won't approve of your methods?"

Matt looked away from Mustafa's probing gaze. He knew Mustafa didn't approve of his methods either. But Mustafa at least seemed to recognize that the immoral was sometimes acceptable, and perhaps even necessary, in the fight against evil.

Matt did not think Laney shared that mindset.

"You will tell her at some point that you have him," Mustafa said.

It wasn't a question, but Matt treated it like it was. "When the time is right."

CHAPTER 104

Laney crossed her arms over her chest. "No. You are *not* allowed to sacrifice yourself."

Victoria looked at her daughter and felt such incredible pride. She had known Laney would not agree to this course of action. It was why they hadn't told her until now. No matter the odds, Laney always thought there was a way she could save someone.

But in this case there wasn't.

"Some things must happen in a certain way," Victoria said softly, her heart breaking as her daughter struggled to accept what could not be changed.

Tears crested in Laney's eyes, and Victoria felt the pressure at the back of her own eyes as well. After all they had been through, the two of them had finally come to a place where they could trust one another, where they could be in one another's lives. And now, they had to say goodbye.

Laney angrily swiped away the tears on her cheeks. "No. There has to be another way. There is *always* another way."

Victoria felt her heart lurch, but she knew she had to stay strong. "There isn't. Not this time."

Laney's eyes were hard despite the tears glistening in them. "I don't believe that."

Victoria admired her daughter's spirit. Laney never accepted things as unchangeable. And look at all she had accomplished because of that. But this was not one of those occasions where sheer will could change things. Some things were, in fact, immutable.

"I am the one who fated humanity to live time and time again —to give them a chance to find everlasting peace. So I am the one who must pay this price. It is my penance."

Laney shook her head. There was anger in her voice. "No. You've paid your penance. Time and time again. What kind of God would require you to do this?"

"A kind one. An optimistic one who believes in the goodness in us all. Each lifetime, we have a chance to find our eternal reward. And I am here to make sure we retain our chance to do that."

"No. You don't get to do this. I won't let you."

Victoria shook her head. "The only way to destroy the tree is with my blood. *All* of my blood. There is no substitute for that. Believe me, I've tried. Besides, the Fallen now know that I can grant them immortality. They will stop at nothing to attain that. Whatever life I have left, I would spend it running."

Laney's voice shook, but Victoria didn't doubt the conviction in her words. "Then we'll run. I'll run with you."

"And you'll leave all the students at the school behind? Patrick? Henry? Jake? All those that need the ring bearer to protect them?"

Laney looked away. "This can't be how it ends."

"Nothing ever truly ends." Victoria took Laney's face in her trembling hands. "Each time we meet, I am amazed by your strength and your desire to fight the good fight, no matter the odds. Your heart is your strongest weapon. Never forget that."

Tears ran down Laney's cheeks. "Please don't do this," she pleaded. "Please. I feel like we just found each other."

Victoria placed a shaky kiss on Laney's forehead. "Every time, I think I can't love you more. And then I do."

Sobs tore through Laney, and each one pierced Victoria's heart.

Struggling to hold back her own tears, Victoria ran her finger from Laney's forehead to the bridge of her nose. "Sleep, my beautiful daughter."

And with that, Laney collapsed into Victoria's arms. Victoria clutched her daughter to her, wishing more than anything that she could stay. That she could be a part of her daughter's life. That she would have a chance to see Laney and Jake marry. To hold their children in her arms. But that was not to be.

Not this time.

A tear slipped past her lashes and dropped onto Laney's hair—hair the same color Victoria's had once been.

Ralph appeared beside Victoria, his voice gentle. "I'll take her."

Victoria just nodded, not capable of speaking.

Ralph lifted Laney and carried her away from the tree, over by the tunnel that led out.

Victoria took a shuddering breath as she watched them go. But instead of leaving, Ralph placed Laney gently on the ground. Then he turned and walked back to Victoria.

Victoria held out her hand. Ralph handed her the knife he had taken from the base of the tree—the knife that was as much a part of the tree as its roots and leaves. The knife Victoria had used a handful of times before. Victoria reached out to take it.

Ralph held it back. "Are you sure there's no other way?"

"You know there isn't."

"You should go. You don't need to be here for this."

Ralph tipped Victoria's chin up and looked into her eyes. "Yes, I do."

Ralph took a shaky breath and Victoria nearly lost her control at that small sound.

"Let me do it," Ralph said.

Victoria shook her head, closing her hand over his. "No, my friend. That decision is mine, as always."

Gently, she pried the knife from his hand. She hesitated for a moment. "You'll make sure Laney is safe?"

Ralph nodded. A single tear tracked its way down his cheek.

Victoria wiped it away. "Thank you for being my friend."

Before he could speak, she swiped at her wrists with a practiced move. Then she gasped as pain and blood bloomed at the same time.

The knife slipped from her hand. She fell back, but Ralph caught her before she could fall to the ground. Keeping her nestled in his arms, he carried her to the base of the tree. Her blood dripped into its roots. Above her she could already see the leaves begin to curl.

Victoria leaned back into Ralph's embrace. She wanted the comfort, but she also wanted to spare him this moment. "You don't have to stay for this."

Ralph's lips gently brushed the top of her head. He leaned down, his lips against her ear. "Yes I do," he whispered. He held her tighter. "It never gets easier."

Victoria closed her eyes, death pulling at her. "It's not supposed to."

CHAPTER 105

"BE HAPPY, LANEY. YOU DESERVE IT." Laney hugged Victoria to her, enjoying the embrace. *Mom.*

But then Victoria disappeared, and Laney could hear birds calling to her. Birds?

Laney's eyelids fluttered open. And she saw trees, the mountain with the hole punched through, and a pale pink sky above her. *Pretty,* she thought, closing her eyes again.

Then her eyes snapped open and she sat upright, the world swimming for a moment. Grief pierced her heart. *Victoria.*

She looked around frantically. She was at the top of the stairs at Heaven's Gate. Thoughts of Victoria pushed through the molasses in her mind. She pictured Victoria's body alone inside the mountain.

Her hand flew to her mouth as her own body began to shake. She shut her eyes, but that only served to bring the image into more vivid clarity. Opening her eyes, she looked over her shoulder. A splash of blue caught her attention. A body lay twenty feet away.

Laney scrambled over on shaking hands and knees. *Ralph.* She touched his chest. No movement. She looked at his face. A smile lay on his lips.

But his eyes saw nothing.

The loss crashed over her. Ralph and Victoria—both gone.

Laney stared back at the mountain. She knew she'd never be able to find the entrance again. Besides, even if she did, there was nothing she could do. She'd collapsed the cavern. She'd never get through.

So she just sat next to Ralph, her knees to her chest, rocking back and forth. She allowed the tears to stream down her face. Ralph was gone. Victoria was gone. Laney pulled the fruit from her pocket. But the tree was safe.

She just wasn't sure the trade was worth it.

The rising sun pulled her from her grief. The park would open soon, and she really didn't want to deal with the Chinese police. Shoving the fruit back in her pocket, she got to her feet. In some part of her mind, she wondered how exactly she was going to get home.

But the larger part of her was too numb to care.

She looked down at Ralph. What was she supposed to do about him? She couldn't leave him here. And there was no way she was going to be able to carry him down the nine hundred and ninety-nine steps to the parking lot.

Sunlight touched Ralph's face. *He looks peaceful,* Laney thought.

And then, slowly, as the sunlight covered him, Ralph began to disappear.

Laney watched in shock. Ralph simply faded away. No ash, no sign, nothing. He was gone, and all that was left was the grass that had been underneath him. It looked completely undisturbed.

Wiping the tears from her cheeks, Laney turned. Her backpack lay next to the path. Somehow, Ralph had managed to grab that as well.

Unzipping it, she pulled out the sat phone. She should probably call someone. People were no doubt worried about her.

But she just stared at the phone like it was a foreign object. Then she put it back in her pack. She zipped up the bag and slung it over her shoulder. *Not yet.*

Laney started down the steps, counting them as she went. The counting kept her mind focused on the here and now, which was what she wanted. She wasn't ready to deal with all that had happened, and she was nowhere near ready to think about what came next.

The sun was fully up in the sky by the time Laney reached the bottom. She swatted at the tears on her cheeks, not sure when she had started crying. Or maybe she had never stopped.

She walked back toward the car, feeling so incredibly tired. An electric shock burned through her, and she jerked her head up. A familiar figure leaned against a car only twenty feet away.

"Drake?"

He stepped away from the car. "Ring bearer."

Laney stared at him for a moment. *Drake? In China?* "Um, what are you doing here?"

"I thought you might need some help getting out of the country."

It was Victoria and Ralph's contacts that had gotten them in the country in the first place, and Laney had no passport, no papers of any kind. She couldn't imagine the Chinese government was going to be too thrilled with her. She felt weary at the very idea of it. She really wasn't up for dealing with bureaucratic red tape.

Drake rested his hand on her shoulder. "I have some fans in the Chinese government. One of them lets me borrow his plane when I ask. It's waiting at the airport. We can avoid official channels."

"Thank you."

"Is the tree destroyed?" Drake asked.

Laney nodded, not looking at him. "Yes." She pulled the fruit from her pocket and handed it over.

Drake's face fell as he took it in. Then he clasped it to him with a nod and led her over to his car. There were only two cars parked there. Laney forced herself not to look at the one Ralph had driven them here in.

Laney slipped into the passenger seat and Drake closed the door after her. He walked around and got into the driver's seat.

But he didn't start the car right away. Laney looked over. "Will the tree be safe now?"

"Yes," he said. "It will be."

She looked over the incredible landscape, trying to keep her mind blank. Mountains rose in the distance, clouds circling their peaks. "I don't suppose there's another book, or parchment, or cave drawing out there somewhere, telling us its new location?"

"No. The location will be hidden again. It won't appear for another few hundred years—not until humanity has forgotten about it again." Drake hesitated. "And… Ralph?"

Laney pictured Ralph's smile—and his body as it disappeared. She let out a shaky breath. "He went home."

Drake's jaw tightened; grief flashed for a moment across his face. He glanced back at the Gate. "Godspeed, brother," he whispered softly. He turned back to Laney. "I'm sorry about Victoria. She is a good woman. Do you want to talk about it?"

Grief welled up in Laney and threatened to choke her. She turned her head, taking some deep breaths, and shook her head.

Drake turned the key in the ignition and put the car into drive. "Fair enough."

Laney watched the trees fly by, not really caring where Drake was heading. She should call Henry and Jake. Her uncle. But she wasn't ready for that. As soon as she spoke with them, it would be real.

And the minute she heard any of their voices, she was going to lose it. She couldn't do that. Not yet. She wanted to be home with them when she told them.

Laney pictured Victoria's face.

Tears rolled down her cheeks as she stared at the spectacular sunrise. A reluctant smile crossed her face. *I love you too, Mom.*

CHAPTER 106

CLAIRE AND BRUCE CHAPMAN stared up at Heaven's Gate. It was beautiful. They had planned this trip for two years. They had both grown up in the Midwest, and together they had raised two beautiful girls who were now out of the house and on their own.

Now it was Claire and Bruce's turn. China was the third stop on their trip. They'd already been to Japan and Australia.

Claire's eyes closed as she felt the early morning sun on her face. She sighed, feeling her spirit lift just being here. A rock crashed somewhere to her left, but she ignored it, focusing on the peace of the moment.

More rocks crashed. Annoyed, Claire opened her eyes. "What *is* that?"

Bruce stared open-mouthed as a group of people emerged from a hole in the side of the mountain. Blood was splattered on their tattered clothes.

Claire gasped. "Oh my God. There must have been a cave-in."

Her husband stood up. "I'll go see if I can help."

But before he could take a step, two police officers took note of the ruckus. They ran over, blowing their whistles, and waved everyone back, shouting something in Mandarin.

One of the tattered people, a dark-haired man, started to walk right past one of the officers. The officer grabbed his arm. The man turned, and even from a short distance, Claire could see the anger on his face.

The man wrapped his hands around the officer's head and twisted. The officer went still and then dropped. The other officer pulled his weapon, but a woman appeared behind him and punched right through his chest.

Screaming tourists scattered. Bruce turned around and grabbed Claire, yanking her off the steps and behind a tree.

Claire's heart pounded. She peered out and saw the angry man and the punching woman making their way down the steps, the rest of their party following behind.

Claire couldn't make out much of what they were saying, but what she did hear didn't make any sense.

"We're done hiding. It's time for the world to know what we can do."

EPILOGUE

NINE MONTHS LATER

PERTH, AUSTRALIA

Iᴀɪɴ Sᴏᴍᴇʀꜰɪᴇʟᴅ ꜱᴛʀᴏᴅᴇ through the hospital doors. Iain worked for the Holocene Impact Working Group—a group that examined evidence that giant meteorites had crashed on the Earth within the last ten thousand years. Their main focus was a 4,800-year-old crater in the Indian Ocean that was believed to have created tsunamis thirteen times the size of the one that had devastated Indonesia in 2004.

He'd been with the group for the last year. He'd spent the five years before that in the military, but when his wife Fiona had become pregnant, he'd immediately resigned from the Special Operations Engineer Regiment of the Australian Defense Force and signed up with the Impact project. He hadn't wanted to miss a minute with his new family.

This morning, he'd been speaking with a group of investors in the conference room. He ground his teeth. And he'd left his cell phone in his office. He hadn't even wanted to go to work this morning, but Fiona had insisted. She'd said the baby was nowhere near ready to arrive. He'd believed her.

He hurried to the reception desk.

A woman with gray hair and kind eyes spoke before he had a chance to. "Maternity ward?"

"How—?"

She gestured toward the teddy bear clutched in his hand and the balloons that floated above his head with a smile. "Just a guess. ID?"

Iain handed her the teddy bear while he fished out his license. He drummed his fingers on the counter while she quickly typed his information into the computer and handed him an ID sticker.

"Take the gold elevator to the fourth floor. It'll be on your right."

He nodded and started to head down the hall.

"Mr. Somerfield?" He turned back, and she waved the teddy bear at him.

"Oh, right." He walked back and took the bear. "Thank you."

"You're welcome. And congratulations, Daddy."

He smiled as he turned for the elevators. *Daddy. I'm a daddy.* He picked up his pace. The gold elevator bank was on the left and he pushed the button for the elevators and tapped his foot impatiently.

Finally the doors popped open. A quick trip up and he was stepping out onto the fourth floor. "Maternity Ward" was emblazoned above the double doors ahead of him, and a menagerie of cartoon animals lined the walls.

Excitement coursed through him. He pushed through the doors and looked for the room numbers. 118, 130, 122. *Who organized these?*

A nurse stopped him. "Can I help you?"

"Um, Fiona Somerfield?"

The nurse pointed to the last room on the right. "Just down there."

"Thanks," he said over his shoulder as he hustled down the

hallway. He reached the doorway the nurse had pointed to and stopped.

Fiona lay inside with her eyes closed. Her red hair looked even brighter against the stark white hospital sheets. Red hair was the one thing they both agreed their daughter would have. After all, with two redheaded parents, what other choice would she have?

Iain smiled as he looked at his lovely wife. The love he felt for this incredible woman was all but bursting out of his chest. *How did I get so lucky?*

She opened her eyes. "Hey, you."

"Hey." He walked to the side of the bed and attached the balloons to one of the rails. He leaned over and kissed his wife gently on the lips. "I'm so sorry I wasn't here."

Fiona smiled, her blue eyes shining up at him. "It's okay. Your daughter was very impatient to be born. We barely made it to the hospital."

Iain looked at the bassinet on the other side of the bed. "Is she all right?"

"Go look for yourself."

Iain clutched the teddy bear and walked slowly around Fiona's bed. He was so nervous. He stopped beside the bassinet. The baby lay there with her eyes closed, wrapped tightly in a blanket, a pink cap on her head.

Iain felt like he'd been punched in the gut. The love and protectiveness he felt for this little girl rushed through him. And he pledged then and there to do everything in his power to keep her safe and make her happy.

"You can pick her up," Fiona said.

"I don't want to wake her."

Fiona gave a soft laugh. "I think she'll be okay with being woken by her daddy. Go ahead. You won't break her."

Iain wasn't so sure about that. She looked so fragile. He placed the teddy on the end of the bed and stared down at his daughter, nervousness flitting through him. He reached down. His hands looked like giant mitts as they gently picked her up and snuggled her into his chest.

"She's so tiny," he whispered.

"So says the person who didn't have to push her out," Fiona grumbled.

He laughed. "True."

His laugh jostled Isabel. A frown crossed her face. Iain held his breath.

Her eyes opened.

Iain stared into his daughter's eyes—and he knew everything that he had ever done had all been leading up to this exact moment in time. "Hello, Isabel. I'm your daddy."

Father and daughter stared at one another. Iain would have been happy to stay there for hours. He turned toward the window, and sunlight fell across Isabel's face.

He gasped.

"What is it?" Fiona asked, concern in her voice.

He looked back at his wife in wonder. "Her eyes. They're the most amazing color."

"What color?"

He looked down again to make sure it wasn't a trick of the light. No. It was no trick. He turned back at Fiona.

"They're purple."

————

Delaney McPhearson's adventure continues in The Belial Search. Now available on Amazon.

A NOTE FROM THE AUTHOR

I have known who Victoria would be since book one in the series. And it broke my heart to write the scene between her and Laney at the tree. That poor woman has been through so much—which is why, of course, I had to write the epilogue in the hospital.

This is not the end of the story for Laney, Henry, and Jake. There are still a few more adventures for them to go on. The next book in the Belial series is entitled *The Belial Search,* and it will be out in November 2015.

There are currently a number of books outside the series that I am also working on. Two of those will be published before the next Belial installment. They are *Runs Deep* in June and *Hominid* in August. If you'd like to be notified about upcoming books, receive my monthly newsletter, and have access to exclusive content, please sign up for my mailing list. And as always, thank you for joining me on my journey and thank you to all the readers who were kind enough to get in touch. It makes my day to hear from you!

Thank you again and I hope to see you next time. And whatever you read next, I hope you get lost in it! :)

Until next time,
   R.D.

FACT OR FICTION?

Whenever I start one of the Belial books, I have the basic plot in mind. For this one, I knew it was going to be all about Victoria. But because of who Victoria is, the story needed to be bigger than just some ancient artifact. It had to be one of THE ancient artifacts. And there were really only a few that fit the bill. Once I decided on this story being a quest for the tree of life, I needed to fill in the details. Some facts below I knew before I began, but quite a few I learned as I went along. In fact, I'm always amazed how I seem to uncover a fact just as I need it.

Interestingly, at least for me, the research for this book, and for *The Belial Children,* has lent itself to a story idea for another book outside this series, which I've tentatively titled *Hominid.* But more on that once I get that book in better shape. For now, I have included a list of some of the references found for *The Belial Origins.* As always, they are in no particular order.

Immortality. Danny's discussion about immortality is taken from real life. Scientists do believe that telomeres may be the key to extending human life dramatically. And yes, there is an immortal jellyfish called the Turritopsis dohrnii. As explained in the text, once the jellyfish reaches its oldest age it reverts back to its polyp form. Scientists are not sure how long this pattern continues, but some suggest it could be indefinite.

Ponce De Leon—who I, and millions of other school children, learned was searching for the Fountain of Youth—may not have actually been searching for any such thing. According to a Smithsonian article, de Leon was not associated with the quest until years after his death, in an effort to discredit him. In reality, he was ousted from his position in Puerto Rico and given an expedition to the island of Bimini as a consolation prize, but it is unlikely he ever went searching for the Fountain of Youth.

Unlike de Leon, the Chinese emperors were indeed focused on finding the key to immortality. And in their searches they did unintentionally create gunpowder.

Karasu Tengu. There is an old Japanese legend about a being known as Karasu Tengu. He lived high in the mountains and, as depicted in this book, would appear at times to help a lost individual, occasionally driving a deserving individual mad. Most of the time he is depicted as half-bird, half-man.

Sree Padmanabhaswamy Temple. The Sree Padmanabhaswamy Temple is real. All depictions in *The Belial Origins* are taken from photos and from descriptions by individuals who have been inside.

The origin story of the temple is, as depicted here, cloaked in mystery, although the story of the sage chasing off the troublemaking child who was later revealed to be Krishna is the explanation usually provided for why the temple was created. The date for the temple's creation is equally unclear—according to scholars it was built either in 500 BCE or closer to 3000 BCE.

More importantly, at least for this story, there really was a treasure valued at $22 billion found in vaults underneath the temple. And one vault, with two entwined cobras carved into the door, has yet to be opened. Why? Because they can't figure out how to open it. And some say they shouldn't.

Archangels. Archangels are said to be the highest order of angels. In the Bible, only three archangels are mentioned. In the Book of Enoch, there were many more discussed.

Lilith. Ah, who is Lilith? The Midrashic literature does discuss Lilith as the first wife of Adam, and the tale was created to address inconsistencies in the book of Genesis—specifically, the two creation stories. Quotes from each creation story are found at the beginning of *The Belial Origins*. In the first creation story, man and woman were created equal. It is in the second story where Eve was created from Adam's rib.

In the Bible, the only specific mention of Lilith is as an unclean animal. But there is a wealth of legends and tales surrounding her existence. In most she is depicted as an evil creature of the night, but within other circles, she is viewed as a wronged woman, the example of a male-interpreted history. Personally, I've been fascinated by her ever since hearing the idea that she was the first woman, pushed aside by history in favor of Eve.

Was she real? Well, Edgar Cayce thought so.

And yes, Lilith is often portrayed as a snake, particularly the snake in the Garden of Eden.

Edgar Cayce. As always, Edgar Cayce starts everything off. In Edgar Cayce's description of the creation of man, men and woman were created equal. In Cayce's telling, the woman was named Lilith and the man was Amilius. Honestly, the more I read his writings, the more fascinating it all becomes. If you are interested in learning more about Edgar Cayce, check out his foundation: Edgar Cayce's A.R.E. (Association for Research and Enlightenment).

Heaven's Gate. The Heaven's Gate Mountain is a real location in the Hunan Province of China. When you see the mountain, it does look as if someone has punched through it. And, as mentioned in *The Belial Origins*, the hole was created by a cave collapse in the third century AD. There are ninety-nine heart-attack-inducing turns on the road to the mountain, as well as nine hundred ninety-nine steps. To my knowledge, there is no secret cave containing a new Garden of Eden or the Tree of Life within the mountain.

Garden of Eden. There have been many archaeological endeavors undertaken to find the original location of the Garden of Eden. In the Bible, and as depicted in *The Belial Origins*, the Garden of Eden is said to fall between four rivers: the Tigris, Euphrates, Cush, and Pishon. While the Tigris and Euphrates exist, the exact location of the other two rivers has been lost to the sands of time. And as mentioned, the locations of the Tigris and Euphrates have changed over time. But if the Garden of Eden *did* originally exist near those four rivers, scholars believe it is now most likely under the sea.

Is there an archangel guarding the Garden? According to the Bible, when humans were expelled from the Garden, an archangel was placed at its entrance to protect it.

Trees in the Garden of Eden. There were numerous trees in the Garden, but the two most famous are the tree of life and the tree of knowledge. Originally humans were allowed to eat freely from the tree of life; it was only the tree of knowledge they were forbidden from eating from. The tree of knowledge was supposed to open people's eyes to the truth of their existence. Interestingly, there are rumors of the existence of fruit that accomplishes that same goal.

Drake Diablo. Drake is of course a fictional creation. But I was in Las Vegas not too long ago, and Drake was inspired by some of the shows there and the posters that lined the sides of many of the hotels.

Gilgamesh. In the tale of Gilgamesh, Gilgamesh did indeed have a great friend known as Enkidu. And when Enkidu died, Gilgamesh went in search of immortality. He allegedly was instructed by Utnapishtim to retrieve a plant from the bottom of the sea that would allow him to live forever. According to the tale, Gilgamesh did retrieve the plant, and it was taken from him by a snake.

The Mark of Cain. According to the Bible, Cain was given a mark that would make everyone pause before thinking of harming him. I struggled to figure out what that mark would be, because it is not described anywhere. I thought completely black eyes would be suitable. As I explain in the novel, other marks run the risk of being culturally misinterpreted. But even your most hardened soldier would pause at the sight of black eyes. At least, I think they would.

Cain. I thought I knew the story of Cain when I began my research for *The Belial Origins*. But I did not realize that there were so many cultural differences in the story of Cain. Everyone does agree that Cain kills Abel, making him the first murderer. However, there is disagreement as to the motivation underlying the act. According to the Bible, it was jealousy over God's preference for Abel. Cain is depicted as a jealous, spiteful individual from an early age. In other legends of the doomed brothers, however, the reason for Abel's death was attributed to anger over Adam and Eve's decision to give Abel Cain's twin as a wife and to give Cain Abel's twin as a wife. Cain felt his twin was more beautiful, and therefore he should be the one that married her.

According to the Bible, Cain was banished from God's sight and continues to walk the earth. In fact, some argue that Cain's descendants became the inhabitants of the cities of Sodom and Gomorrah and/or Canaan.

Mount Hermon tablet. In 1869, a tablet was discovered in a temple at Mount Hermon by Sir Charles Warren. Warren broke the tablet in two and took one half home with him to the British Museum. The inscription used in *The Belial Origins* is the actual Greek inscription found on the tablets: "According to the command of the greatest and holy God, those who take an oath, proceed from here." It is not known who inscribed the tablets. The second half of the tablet was left on the mount and to my knowledge has not been recovered. Therefore, the second half of the tablet and the inscription upon it are works of fiction.

Junk DNA. The research into junk DNA that is presented by Danny is accurate: researchers now know that junk DNA is not in fact "junk." Junk DNA is non-coding DNA, or DNA that currently does not have a purpose but theoretically could. It is just waiting for someone to turn it on.

Chinese Super Psychics. Allegedly China has indeed been nurturing a group of children with psychic abilities. Of course, due to the closed nature of China's society, verifying these children is a bit tricky. But there is a book out that discusses the program, and there are a number of videos discussing the children. The choice is yours whether to believe it or not.

The Fifth Root Race. Edgar Cayce did say that the fifth root race would begin in 1998, and that the children born after that date would demonstrate the skills of the people of Atlantis.

Thank you for reading *The Belial Origins*. I hope you enjoyed it and that the Victoria reveal was worth the wait. If you get a chance, please consider leaving a review. And don't forget to sign up for my mailing list.

THE
BELIAL
SEARCH

BOOK 7

AMAZON BEST-SELLING AUTHOR
R.D. BRADY

Keep reading for a peek
at *The Belial Search*

THE BELIAL SEARCH

SHOREHAM, LONG ISLAND

1902

James Franklin II looked out the window as his driver pulled to a stop. It had taken hours to get here from Manhattan. Thank God he'd been able to borrow Mr. Morgan's Curved Dash Oldsmobile and driver. But his bum was still sore from the bumpy ride.

Irritated, he pulled out his handkerchief and wiped his face. This was lunacy to begin with. He couldn't understand why a man of Mr. Morgan's intellect would have bought into it. Thank goodness he'd finally seen the light.

Smoothing down his coat, James picked up his bowler hat from the seat next to him as the driver hustled to open the door.

He stepped out, looking around with distaste at WardneClyffe Tower—a metal skeleton that rose 186 feet in the air before ending in a metal dome. To Franklin, it looked like a giant mushroom. *Wireless electricity for the east coast. Ridiculous notion.*

Some people claimed Nikola Tesla was a genius who was in tune with a knowledge greater than that of mere mortals. Even his birth was something out of a story: a ferocious lightning storm was said to have hit the night Tesla was born. The midwife had thought it was an omen and claimed he would be a child of darkness. His mother had retorted, "No. He will be a child of light."

James had also heard that the man had a peculiar fondness for pigeons and a complete fear of germs. The man was insane.

"You, boy," he called to a dark-skinned figure kneeling on the ground and banging something. The boy turned, and James realized he was much older than James had assumed, closer to James's own age of fifty. Not that he apologized.

The man got to his feet, removed his cap, and held it in front of him. "Yes, sir?"

"Where is Mr. Tesla?"

The man pointed to the building. "He's in his lab. Do you know the way?"

"Yes, yes of course." James paused, glancing at the building warily. "Is he conducting an experiment?"

James had seen more than enough of Tesla's demonstrations. Tesla could stand in the middle of balls of electricity—have them shooting out of his hands, in fact. James wasn't sure how he did it without killing himself, or someone else.

The man smiled. "No. Just writing something."

"Very well." With a determined stride, James headed across the barren lawn to the building. He rapped sharply on the door before pulling it open. "Mr. Tesla?"

Inside, two men stopped their conversation to stare at him. Nikola Tesla, with his dark hair and mustache, pierced him with his blue eyes. He had this uncanny ability to look as if he was staring right through a person. The man next to him had bushy white hair and wore a white suit with pinstripes.

James's eyes grew large. "Mr. Clemens, I'm sorry I didn't realize you were here."

Samuel Clemens turned to Tesla. "Who's this, Nikola?"

"The money," Nikola said dryly.

"Ah, well, that's my exit cue then. Next week in Manhattan?"

Nikola nodded. "I'll be there."

Samuel nodded at James as he departed.

James watched him go. He'd heard that the two were on friendly terms, but he had no idea the great writer would be here today.

"Could you shut the door? You're letting the flies in," Nikola said from behind him.

"Right." James hastily reached for the handle and shut the door. He turned. "Mr. Tesla—" Tesla was nowhere to be seen. "Mr. Tesla?" But the man did not appear.

James stalked forward. "Mr. Tesla?" He wandered through the rows of tables and piles of metal, making his way toward the office in the back. A light was on, and Tesla sat behind his desk.

James shook his head as he stormed up. "Mr. Tesla, I need to speak with you."

Tesla did not look up. "Then speak."

James ground his teeth. "Right, fine. Well, Mr. Morgan has decided to cut extraneous expenses due to the downturn of the market."

Tesla continued making notes on the schematic in front of him.

"He won't be able to continue funding your project," James said.

Tesla's pencil stilled, and James gave a satisfied smile. Finally, the man was paying attention.

Tesla looked up, his eyes narrowed. "What did you say?"

James swallowed and took an involuntary step back. "Mr. Morgan has been a generous supporter of your work. But now—"

"Do you have any idea what I am doing here? I could control the weather. Reduce the impact of storms. I will make it possible for people to have electricity without having any wires. Do you get what that could mean for mankind? What this could lead to?"

"Yes, well, Mr. Morgan is not convinced the project will be successful. Nothing like this has even been done before."

Tesla stood up and stalked around the desk. "Yes it has. But you people are too blind to see it. *I* have seen it. I *know* it will work."

James was rethinking not having his driver come in with him. He knew Tesla was viewed by some as being only a hair's breadth from crazy. The man claimed that he could envision entire machines, mold and change them in his mind.

But James knew that was not how inventions happened. They didn't magically appear. And nowhere in human history had mankind been able to control the weather, for goodness' sakes.

"Nevertheless, Mr. Morgan will not be funding the project any further," James said.

"Then Morgan is a fool."

"Good day, Mr. Tesla." James backed out of the office, keeping an eye on Tesla. But Tesla was staring off into space, caught up in something in his own mind. James quickly made his way back through the lab and toward the door. The man was crazy.

A few minutes later, James was being driven quickly away. He stared out the window at the metal skeleton Tesla had erected, and scoffed.

Control the weather. What hubris. That is God's work, not man's.

Check out The Belial Search on Amazon today!

ABOUT THE AUTHOR

Author, Criminologist, Terrorism Expert, Jeet Kune Do Black Sash, Runner, Dog Lover.

Amazon best-selling author R.D. Brady writes supernatural and science fiction thrillers. Her thrillers include ancient mysteries, unusual facts, non-stop action, and fierce women with heart.

Prior to beginning her writing career, RD Brady was a criminologist who specialized in life-course criminology and international terrorism. She's lectured and written numerous academic articles on the genetic influence on criminal behavior, factors that influence terrorist ideology, and delinquent behavior formation.

After visiting counter-terrorism units in Israel, RD returned home with a sabbatical in front of her and decided to write that book she'd been thinking about. Four years later she left academia with the publication of her first book, *The Belial Stone*, and hasn't looked back.

To learn about her upcoming publications, sign up for her newsletter here or on her website (rdbradybooks.com).

f

ACKNOWLEDGMENTS

The Belial Origins was a labor of love. So first off, I have to thank all the readers who encouraged, pushed, and occasionally kicked me toward the finish line. I know you love these characters as much as I do. Thank you for staying with me on this journey.

Thank you to my family who is usually understanding when I close the office door and hide myself away. I'm grateful to you not only for your understanding, but also for dragging me back into the world and not letting me always disappear into my books. I love writing, but I love you all more.

Thank you to my parents for encouraging me to read and to learn. I started early with the why questions and have never really stopped asking them. Thank you for encouraging them.

Thank you to David Gatewood for all your incredible help. I am very lucky to have found you.

Thank you to Damonza for the incredible cover work. We went through a lot of revisions getting the cover right this time, and I thank you for all your patience.

And the to staff at my hamburger joint, thank you for letting me sit for hours in my little booth and not giving me evil looks. Instead you give me smiles and constantly refill my drink. You keep me on point even when I would much rather give myself the day off.

I'd also like to thank my group of beta readers, who helped make this version of *The Belial Origins* a much better copy. Thank you for reading. And thank you for all your work.

Thank you for reading and making a dream I didn't know I

had come true. When I was younger, I never considered being a writer—not once. Oh, I would constantly make up stories in my head, but I grew up in a house where you knew that when you grew up you needed a real job—one that paid you regularly and on time. Writing never figured into that equation. But then, one day a few years back, I started writing some of those stories in my head—and now I can't seem to stop! I love this job, and I thank you for allowing me to do it. I cannot imagine doing anything else. So thank you, thank you!

BOOKS BY R.D. BRADY

Hominid

The Belial Series (in order)
The Belial Stone
The Belial Library
The Belial Ring
Recruit: A Belial Series Novella
The Belial Children
The Belial Origins
The Belial Search
The Belial Guard
The Belial Warrior
The Belial Plan
The Belial Witches
The Belial War
The Belial Fall
The Belial Sacrifice

The Belial Rebirth Series
The Belial Rebirth
The Belial Spear

The Belial Restored
The Belial Blood
The Belial Angel
The Belial Templar

The A.L.I.V.E. Series
B.E.G.I.N.
A.L.I.V.E.
D.E.A.D.
R.I.S.E.
S.A.V.E.

The H.A.L.T. Series
Into the Cage
Into the Dark

The Steve Kane Series
Runs Deep
Runs Deeper

The Unwelcome Series
Protect
Seek
Proxy

The Nola James Series
Surrender the Fear
Escape the Fear
Tackle the Fear
Return the Fear

The Gates of Artemis Series
The Key of Apollo
The Curse of Hecate
The Return of the Gods

R.D. BRADY WRITING AS SADIE HOBBES

The Demon Cursed Series
Demon Cursed
Demon Revealed
Demon Heir

The Four Kingdoms
Order of the Goddess

Be sure to sign up for R.D.'s mailing list to be the first to hear when she has a new release!

Made in United States
North Haven, CT
02 February 2024

48237404R00238